POWER OF WILL

TARREN GUY

ISBN: 978-0-6489721-0-5

Dedication

To Dad for your birthday, 60 years strong.
You have been an influential, supportive, loving and dedicated
figure in my life. Love you

Acknowledgments

First of all I would like to thank my editor, Sapodia Lindley, for the many hours of work put into making some sense of my ramblings. She has been instrumental in getting the book to where it is today and without her this would still be on a shelf somewhere.

The 200 Rogues, a group of well rounded, compassionate, and helpful friends. I am grateful for all the support over the years.

My Beta Readers, you have shown me all my flaws and helped me to become a better writer. Thank you Marissa Gramoll, Raissa Karlsen, Sarah Howlett, Rosie Mansfield.

To my cover artist, Cheri at authorsassembler.com, Thank you for giving my book a face. I enjoyed the process and love what you have done.

A special thanks to Blueline. I know I should have been working in the half hour leading up to lunch but I was too excited to write The End on my first draft. Thank you

"Magic is but an illusion, a deception created by those who seek to play on the minds and gullible nature of the human race. No, the true power of this world is Will. It lies dormant within all of us waiting to be manipulated and brought into existence. It is raw, wild and infinite in its possibilities."

Prologue

Hidden at the top of the home, a room full of adventure awaited. The attic was dark and musty with a single beam of light filtering in through a clouded window. Dust motes danced across the light only to fade back into an insubstantial existence. Evidence of a leak in the roof gave the room a damp, mouldy smell. Creaks and groans shuddered across the ceiling as the sun danced around the clouds radiating heat down on the tin.

As the two boys allowed their eyes to adjust they peered into the obscure attic. Junk, both forgotten and useless, littered the room. Items were stacked atop one another in gravity defying towers. Boxes with rat chewed corners were placed randomly throughout. Some were marked. Others just closed and left to the imagination. The boys started to make their way across the room looking here and there for anything of interest. Lately, all the fun they have had has been listening to their Grandpa tell boring stories of the old days without technology or watching an old TV that didn't even have a remote. There weren't even any children their own age in the area as they were on a farm miles from nowhere.

"How far in are we going?" The younger of the two asked. Allen had clearly not progressed as far as the older boy, Gregory, had. There was an unsure look on his freckled face. His brow was furrowed below locks of brown hair and his blue eyes glanced from side to side as if he was about to be ambushed.

"Why?" Gregory asked, a smirk crossing his face. "You scared, Allen?"

"No," Allen replied quickly. He stood up defiantly. "I... I just don't think Grandpa would want us snooping through his stuff, Gregory."

Gregory watched his younger brother's stance slowly change from defiant to troubled. Allen even glanced back at the hole in the floor leading to the relative safety of the main house. His bare feet were fidgeting, kicking dust into the air. Extending the silence, Gregory finally answered. He was actually a lot like Allen when he was twelve. Not only did they look similar with brown hair and blue eyes, but Gregory also had the same imagination. An imagination that gave life to all kinds of monsters in every shadow. At sixteen, it took almost four years to get over these fantasies and push himself into the unfamiliar or uncomfortable.

"I'm sure Grandpa won't mind," Gregory replied. "What else are you going to do?"

"I... I'm... I," Allen stammered, looking for words. Gregory laughed aloud.

"It's okay, Allen. You go do what you need to and I'll keep searching up here," Gregory said, giving him an out. "If I find anything I'll let you know straight away. If I don't, then it was only one of us that wasted their time. How does that sound?"

"Yeah, sounds good," Allen said. He was already making his way back to the opening. After a moment he had disappeared down the hole. Now alone, Gregory started his exploration again. He climbed over boxes and skimmed the edges of unsteady towers. He looked at everything as he went by, not wanting to miss anything that may brighten his stay at their Grandpa's house. The deeper he got, the denser the dust covering the floor became. Gregory wondered just how long it had been since anyone had stood where he was standing. Years? Decades maybe?

As Gregory passed another box barricade something against the wall caught his eye. Investigating, he found a gold trimmed chest made from deep mahogany wood. Around the lock two dragons fought, interlocking talons, bodies twisting together. However, this uncommon chest was not what caught Gregory's attention. Upon the lid, and around the floor in the immediate vicinity, no dust had settled. Gregory could not get his mind around this one observation. There were no fresh tracks to the box so it was not new to the room.

Approaching the chest, Gregory moved his hand across the mahogany lid though could not feel the grain of the wood. Reaching for the edges of the lid, he took hold of the corners and applied an upward force hoping the chest was unlocked. Gregory's hopes were dashed as he couldn't budge the lid even a little. To his amazement, after he stepped back, the dragons uncoiled and shrunk away from the lock. Taken aback, he stood and stared for a moment before collecting himself. He drew in close to the lock, looking for traces of the mechanism that allowed the dragons to move, but found none. Trying the lid again, Gregory smiled as it opened easily.

Peering inside, Gregory was instantly disappointed with the contents. They were beautifully crafted everyday items but no matter how extravagant they were, a jade comb was still a comb, an ivory china set with intricately painted settings was still a teapot and cups, and a silver, jewel encrusted mirror was still a mirror. Tucked in the back, Gregory could see the top of a picture frame. He pulled it from the chest to find a black and white photo. In front of an old castle made of stone and mortar, complete with creeping vines and a drawbridge, five people were posing for the photo. The picture was simply titled "Eckhart Castle'. On closer inspection, Gregory recognised one of the people to be his Grandpa. This was something his Grandpa hadn't told him about, so he made a mental note to get the story. Placing the photo back, he then reached for the cold handle of the mirror and peered at himself. He looked deep into his own eyes, never quite happy with the colour he saw. Tingles ran down his arm to his hand and, seemingly affecting the mirror, the glass started to glow white. Soft at first, the glare became so strong that Gregory had to close his eyes. He dropped the mirror and retreated from the room, tripping and stumbling through his relative blindness. Making it down the ladder and closing the latch he fell to his knees breathing heavily. He pretended, and tried to convince himself, that he must have caught the only light coming into the room. A light angled towards the opposite wall.

Deep within his left eye, outside what was possible to see, a pixel or two had changed to a rich yellow... a third transitioned in his right.

Chapter 1

An old, red pickup truck bounced along the broken road. Each pothole brought a new groan from the suspension. Every hill was a struggle between gravity and machine, the engine not always faring well. The vehicle sported a single cab with a bench seat, making any trip for three uncomfortable to whoever was unlucky enough to be in the middle. Today this fell to Gregory, who had been grumbling to himself for over an hour. His little brother, Allen, was leaning over towards the window looking with amazement at everything that was passing by. Farms and animals, lakes and mountains, nothing was too insubstantial for this young mind.

Turning the other way, Gregory looked at his Grandpa. The man bounced to the rhythm of the road, completely in tune with the pickup truck. His hair was grey and thinning on top, the beard he sported also grew less each year. For his age, his skin showed little sign of wrinkles and he had no health problems. The man looked at him and smiled, showing his teeth. They were all still intact, though stained yellow from tobacco smoke. The pickup dipped into a substantial pothole, forcing Gregory into the protruding gear stick, knocking it out of gear. The vehicle revved wildly as his Grandpa wrestled it back into place.

"Why do I have to be the one stuck in this seat for such a long trip?" Gregory whined. "I'm too big for it and as the oldest, I should get first pick."

"As the elder, you should give first pick, Gregory," his Grandpa said back. "Look at the joy on Allen's face. You should seek to give that to everyone you meet."

"Why must I give up my happiness for other people?"

"It's not about giving up your happiness, or your freedom, or any other silly notion that is imparted into young minds. It's about being selfless without asking for anything in return. It's about doing something which may brighten someone's day and for a moment allows them to forget that life can be just as cruel."

"I still don't understand."

"That's okay. You're still young, Gregory. You have so much ahead of you to experience. Good, bad, joyous, painful. Take nothing for granted," he said smiling again. "Enough about that, you'll be happy to know that over this rise and into the valley we'll see Mandaloo, our destination. Half an hour from now you will be stretching those legs of yours and this trip will be behind you. For Allen, he will remember it far longer."

Gregory had travelled this road before, therefore, the impact of the scene that unfolded was drastically reduced. Rolling over the top of the rise, a large crater hundreds of meters deep and miles across, that was previously hidden from view, opened up to them. A meteorite would have made this many millennia before people took advantage of the natural outcome. There was a forest of oak to the north. Birds chased each other above the canopy and dipped below the surface, swerving through branches. Three streams on the plains above, all ended as great waterfalls on the western side. The spray casting a constant rainbow in the morning sun. In the valley, the streams all converged into a shimmering lake that emptied below the rock face in the east.

The south side of the crater held the city of Mandaloo. It was one of the largest cities in the region with over one hundred thousand residents. There were skyscrapers and shopping complexes in the city centre, zoning for industries, parks and residential housing, and even a small amusement park. The roads out of Mandaloo wound their way up the side of the crater so tightly that Gregory cringed every time his Grandpa had to pull hard on the steering wheel. The pickup had no power steering and he could see the effort put into turning the car. Gregory knew that he would not be coming back from a fall so high up. Thankfully though, they made it to the flats safely and started to head towards the city.

Out of nowhere traffic started to increase. The pickup was soon weaving in and out of traffic. They took side streets to avoid tolls and on occasion would get lost and have to double back. Finally, they made it into the city centre. Allen was continually looking up at the tops of buildings trying to keep track of the sky. He could not understand how things so tall and slim could stay standing.

They pulled into a rather large, half filled, car park with an old building at the end. The building was five stories high and had different wings off each side. Gargoyles and spires along the roof suggested gothic architecture which was very old and appeared to house a museum

"This is the adventure that you wanted to bring us on, Grandpa?" Gregory asked a little sulky. "I don't think that this day is going to be very entertaining."

"Reserve your judgment until the end, Gregory," his Grandpa said a little hurt. He guided the pickup into an empty park. "You still don't know what's inside."

"I have a pretty good idea. But you're right, I'll reserve my judgement until I'm inside."

Allen jumped out of the car and was enthusiastic about exploring the place. As Gregory hopped out his leg started to cramp. Limping around in circles, he tried to get the circulation running again. He told his Grandpa that he would meet up with him and Allen inside.

Gregory watched them move to the front door and saw them pause to talk to the doorman. Grandpa probably knows him by name, Gregory thought. Finally able to walk properly, he too made his way to the door. But instead of going straight in, Gregory had to wait behind a bunch of students about his age who had gotten off a bus close to the entrance. He saw each of the students place different coloured coins into a small box beside the doorman. They ranged from light purples to bright reds. One student placed a red coin in the box that was so deep and pure the colour almost looked alive. Finally, it was Gregory's turn.

"Your coin," the doorman said gesturing to the box. Gregory shook his head.

"I'm not with the school. I didn't bring any coins... or any money for that matter."

"You won't be able to enter without payment,"

"My Grandpa and younger brother went in moments before the school came along. Surely they covered my fair."

"No, they didn't. Each person pays their own way in. No

6

exceptions. Check your pockets. You must have something of worth."

"I'm telling you I don't have anything," Gregory said reaching into his pockets. "Grandpa told me I wouldn't need..." his voice trailed off as his hand hit something round and solid. That definitely wasn't in his pocket on the car ride as it would have annoyed his cramped position even more than he had been. He pulled it out and uncurled his fingers to examine the object. The doorman's eyes narrowed then his composure returned to normal. Unlike the other students, this coin had no colour. It was clearer than glass to the point of almost being invisible. 'will this do?" He asked the doorman.

"Yes, that is perfect. Please place it in the box and enjoy your stay," Gregory felt there was more to that comment than just a day trip to a museum, but he dismissed it and entered.

"So Lord Baras is taking on an Empty," the doorman said to himself. "The castle is going to be entertaining this year."

Gregory entered the building not quite knowing how it would look inside. He was blown away. The entrance hall was a large open area that reached from the dark marble floor to what Gregory thought was the roof of the building. The area ran to the back of the building making a thirty-metre wide corridor. Doorways even opened at intervals to the different exhibits in the museum. White marble columns spaced evenly apart held up balconies on each level. People were leaning against the railings talking to friends or taking in the room from above. Gregory then noticed that the dark marble floor had a pattern through it, creating a mural which could be fully appreciated from the upper levels. Mirrored to this the roof was richly painted in vibrant colours creating scenes of war, love, worship, royalty and death. Gregory was appreciating the building more than he thought he would. A tug at his sleeve drew his attention to someone next to him. There stood Allen, alone and looking unsure.

"Where's Grandpa, Allen?" Gregory asked.

"He left me to wait for you. He's going to be busy for a while and said we can explore as much as we like," Allen replied.

This made Gregory annoyed. Not just at the fact that his

Grandpa had left Allen alone, but also because Gregory had planned to sneak off on his own for a while. He wasn't able to do that now that he was taking care of Allen.

"That's inconvenient. I thought Grandpa wanted to spend time with us," Gregory feigned. "I guess it's just us now. Where would you like to go first, Allen?"

"How about... That door there," Allen pointed to a door part way down the hall. In Allen's mind, the choice was like a game. Some doors leading to victory, while others lead to failure. He hoped that he chose correctly.

"Okay, let's go," Gregory said jogging ahead. Allen yelped and gave chase, calling for Gregory to slow down. Gregory waited at the door for Allen and the two brothers entered together. As Gregory expected, these rooms were not as extravagant as the entrance hall. Plain cream walls encompassed a number of glass cabinets. The only constant was the dark marble floors that flowed in from outside. Gregory and Allen looked into a glass cabinet and were confused by what they saw. The items inside weren't anything that Gregory recognised, either from a historical view or from a cultural view. Shapes, colours, adornments, nothing seemed like they should fit together.

"What are they, Gregory?" Allen asked.

Gregory quickly looked for an information plate to look smart in front of his little brother. Gold plates with writing made up solely of symbols were placed in front of each item, but this didn't help Gregory at all.

"I really don't know, Allen," Gregory finally admitted.

"You serious," a voice scoffed. "How could you not know about the aligning fragments or the celestial orphans? They are basic equipment." The boys turned to face the intruding voice. He was a teen about Gregory's age. He was of Asian descent with dark hair and eyes, Gregory guessed Japanese. He wore a uniform consisting of grey pants, a white shirt with a shield emblem, and a navy tie. Must be one of those school kids, Gregory thought to himself.

"Never heard of them," he told the boy. "What're they used for?"

8

"Why don't you go buy a Transcribe from the vending machines? Looking through those will allow you to translate the information in front of each item. I don't have time to be your personal guide."

"I'll be right. I didn't bring any money anyway," Gregory said.

The boy just looked at him like he was stupid. "Use your coin," he said.

"I already used it to get in."

"Okay, you really are stupid."

"Excuse me?" Gregory was taken aback by his rudeness.

"The coins they... Argh, whatever. Whatever... I don't need to deal with people like you," he said. "If you really want to learn something, go find a teacher of one of the many schools here or the museum tour guides. They are more than happy to talk dribble. Better yet, follow me to one of the testing rooms and see for yourself what this is all about."

"Who are you?"

"My name is my own," with that he turned and walked off. The boy believed that names held power over the one it belonged to. He did not want to tell this stupid boy, who he had never met before, that his name was Kinsami Otoma. Heir to the Otoma Empire.

"I'm Gregory Williams," he called out, chasing after Kinsami with Allen in tow.

"I don't care," Kinsami said with a wave over his shoulder. "I only started talking to you because I couldn't believe that the level of stupidity you possess existed."

Gregory didn't say any more, rather, he glared at Kinsami's back, imagining some unique torture techniques.

The boys followed Kinsami through a number of similar rooms. The only thing that changed was the items on display. Sometimes even skeletons were in the display cases. Gregory knew that these were fake as they depicted beasts he knew didn't exist. He was starting to get the impression that this wasn't a museum at all, but some sort of game house. That they were going to a testing room solidified this idea in his mind. The items in the cabinets reflected items in the game, and the skeletons were those of the enemies they would face. He was starting to get wise to what was going on. He even thought Kinsami may be trying to show this newbie up. With the large number of games that Gregory played back at his parent's home, he felt he had a chance at least.

"We are here," Kinsami said. "Join the line and we can enter through the painting."

Gregory saw a bunch of kids dressed in school uniforms lined up in front of a ceiling high painting of a castle. Gregory recognised it immediately from the picture in his Grandpa's attic.

"That's Eckhart isn't it?" Gregory exclaimed

"Well at least you aren't a total loss," Kinsami clapped sarcastically. "Only the great and the strongest like me will get to go there though."

"We'll see who gets to go," Gregory said looking Kinsami in the eyes, challenge written all over his face.

"Whoa, boy. You have no chance if you don't even know how to use your coin properly." Gregory faced forward and waited his turn, watching as students slowly stepped through the painting. It would shimmer and settle back again. Must be a hologram, he thought.

"Your turn," a guide at the edge of the painting said to Gregory.

"Coming Allen?" Gregory asked his little brother.

"No! One at a time," the guide scolded. Allen gripped onto Gregory's arm.

"You're scaring him," Gregory replied. "It's not going to affect anything if he comes in with me." With that, Gregory stepped forward with Allen towards the portal.

"You are going to be denied and hit a wall," the guide replied, reaching out to stop them. He just missed them as the two boys disappeared into the painting. The guide stood amazed at what had happened. He looked at Kinsami and the eyes he saw echoed the same astonishment at the significance of the event. As the painting settled Kinsami followed.

"See. Not the end of the world like he thought," Gregory said to him as his focus came back. Kinsami looked at this idiot and wondered who he was.

Gregory looked at the room they had entered. It was dark with only dim globes on the side walls, casting any light. The room had a stand against the longer wall with a steep gradient sporting four rows of seats. Students had already started to fill the seats and Gregory took Allen to the highest row, sitting close to a side wall. Kinsami followed them to the top row. They looked at a blank wall, the only exception to this was a single, plain door in the middle of it. Above the area were strips of metal suspended from the ceiling forming a crisscross patterned canopy. At each cross section sat a large cream candle. They weren't lit and Gregory saw no reason for them to be there.

As the last of the students started to filter in, Gregory noticed a girl with long red hair sit down on the floor near the corner of the room. She was sitting cross legged and had her head bowed. Guess she wasn't too interested, Gregory thought. At that moment the single door opened and two robed figures stepped out. One was a small slim female with short, blonde hair robed in green. She walked almost like she was in a trance, floating across the floor. The other was a tall, bald man robed in purple. He was the complete opposite to the first. He was strong and had a spark in his step that spoke of both speed and skill. Stopping in the middle of the room each suddenly looked at the crowd of adolescents.

"Begin," they both said at once. Their voices echoing throughout the small room. Suddenly a boy towards the front stood and gave a low growl. Both Allen and Gregory ducked low as the candles came alive with flames reaching towards the ceiling. As the flames died again the brothers sat back up. The boy at the front sat down again looking content.

Next, a girl stood up in the middle row. She too made a noise though it was closer to a squeal. Again flames burst into life. This time though, they were fiercer but died off quickly. Each person randomly started to get up and make some sort of gesture towards the candles above. Gregory started to see what was happening. The candles must have a sensor that read the noise each person made and reflect it in flames. He didn't

11

know the key yet but he believed that if he went big he would produce something of merit. At least that boy won't think he was stupid.

Allen was growing very nervous with the flames going off above his head. He had always been timid but this was starting to get to him. He reached over and clung onto his brother's arm. Gregory smiled and looked at his little brother.

"It's okay Allen," Gregory assured him. "The flames are reacting to the voices of everyone. Depending on what a person does, it creates different flames. Watch, I'll go next and you'll see flames rise as I shout."

The current person sat down and Gregory now stood. He raised his arms to the candles trying to imagine the type of flame that may be produced but could not picture any. With a loud roar, he shouted upwards... Nothing.

Another roar started to sound across the room though this time it was the laughter of everyone seated in the stands. None of them noticed however that the girl seated on the floor was now lying face down. Blood was slowly flowing out of her nose. The woman robed in green walked across and knelt beside her speaking softly. Gregory sat down completely embarrassed.

"Come on, Kinsami. Show us how it's done," someone shouted. Others took up the plea and soon they were all chanting for Kinsami. Kinsami stood up and the group went quiet. He raised a hand towards the roof and simply clicked his fingers. Small wisps of flame encircled his fingers at the gesture.

Again, nothing. This time, there was no laughter, no jeers, and no mockery. Hushed whispers ran through the group about what may be going on. The look on Kinsami's face showed he was both mortified and annoyed at what had happened.

"Oh well," Gregory shrugged his shoulders. "Looks like we're equals."

"You're not my equal," Kinsami sneered. He was leaning more towards annoyance now and was looking for someone to take his feelings out on, Gregory was in his sights. "What did you do to the candles? You can't just start yelling at the roof hoping something will happen. You need to control your Will. You're such an idiot!" As the others listened to the exchange they started mirroring his words and even throwing in some of their own.

"Idiot!"

"Bastard!"

"Stupid head," this was from a younger girl at the front.

"Silence!" The room became instantly mute. Unnoticed at the front of the room another robed figure had stepped in. His robe was a blue of the deepest oceans. With his hood pulled far over his face, no one could make out his features. He looked over to where the green robed woman was caring for the girl who passed out. The girl was now sitting back against the wall. The woman had a hand on her shoulder and was talking to her softly. She was very pale. The man in the blue robe turned back to the room.

"The apparatus has failed. All those who've not had their turn make your way to Kirkwall castle," he ordered. "The rest move into the next room for assessment. Kinsami, Lavi and Gregory. You three stay."

The room slowly filtered out into the required directions. Lavi was helped as she walked into the middle of the room in front of the robed figures. Kinsami, Gregory and Allen also made their way to that point. The bald man robed in purple squatted in front of Allen.

"You don't need to be here little one," he said. "Did you want me to take you to Kirkwall Castle?"

"He is staying with me," Gregory said placing his arm around his brother's shoulder.

"For this, he will need to step out," the man said.

"It's okay, Adaman," the blue robed man said pulling back his hood. Gregory and Allen immediately recognised him.

"Grandpa!" they both exclaimed. The other four all looked at the brothers with surprise. Kinsami looked like he would reach out and kill Gregory at any moment.

"What is this, Baras?" Kinsami started at the brother's grandpa. "That boy has acted like he knew nothing about Will. He has played me this whole time, and before I even had a chance to show myself to you, he destroys the testing apparatus."

"Lord Baras," Baras replied.

"What?"

"You will address me as Lord Baras."

"Fine. *Lord* Baras," Kinsami said emphasising the Lord very sarcastically. "What are you going to do to fix this?"

"I'm not going to be fixing anything," Baras replied. "I have already assessed the three of you and all of you have gained access to the castle."

"But I haven't even done anything! And all the girl has done is faint," Kinsami raged. "I understand that your kin gets automatic access."

Baras ignored him. "Lavi," he said turning to the young girl who fainted during the test. "If it was just me assessing the group I would have completely missed what you'd done. You are not of my elements. Celes, though," he gestured to the woman in green. "Noticed your skill straight away. Imbuing the air around the candles with your Will to measure the power of others was dangerous as you have found. But it is also extremely hard to hold as long as you did. We can see the practice and commitment you have put in."

"Thank you," Lavi said. A little colour coming back to her cheeks as she blushed.

"Kinsami," Baras now looked at the young hot head. "The red element in you, gives you both pride and power. This can be a dangerous combination to your personality but that is not part of the tests. You have shown amazing ability today."

"How?" Kinsami demanded. He could not help feeling that he was being cheated.

"Gregory has made the candles impossible to use for a regular student. You, though, have impressed even me with what you have achieved. I'll start with the flames you produce around your hand. Does it hurt or burn?

"No," Kinsami answered. "Once I used to feel the warmth of the flames but this has disappeared over time. I use it on special occasions to add a spectacle to what I can do. It isn't that big a deal."

14

"How many others of the red have you seen produce flame anywhere around their body?" Adaman asked him.

"It is rare but one or two of my kin do this."

"It is very rare and even more that there is no warmth from the flames. If you work on it you will eventually be able to wrap yourself in flaming armour. The flames will burn with a ferocity that can eat anything that comes into contact with it, and protect you at the same time. Just don't experiment in leaps and bounds. This is something that you will need to take on slowly. You run the risk of self-imploding otherwise." Kinsami's eyes widened a little and he just nodded.

"The second testament to your ability," Baras took over. "Was the fact you created a flame upon the candles."

"There were no flames, *Lord*," Kinsami said again exaggerating the Lord.

"You are wrong, Kinsami. You produced a flame for 1/100th of a second. No one with mediocre ability could achieve this. Gregory produced a flame atop the candles. The flames burnt with such intensity that they were invisible to the naked eye. They still burn this very second," the three adolescents looked up trying to find signs of the invisible flames. "To produce flame within what Gregory has crafted is amazing, to say the least."

"I don't believe you old man," Kinsami said dropping all titles of respect. "No one is that powerful. Not even you."

"Address me as such again and I'll be writing back to your parents with my deepest sympathies at the loss of their son. Adaman can you produce the coin Gregory used to enter this room."

Adaman stretched his arm out before him, palm up. He focused for a moment and a pale blue coin appeared upon his hand.

"With such a pale colour I doubt he could produce any flame at all," Kinsami said seeing the coin.

"With a coin as pale as this I would believe you Kinsami," Baras replied with a smile. "But this is not his coin alone. You have forgotten he entered with his little brother. Allen," content until this point to be left out of the conversation Allen

15

looked at his Grandpa.

"Yes," he replied.

"Can you come and get your coin," bowing his head a little, Allen walked up to the man that tried to remove him from the room. He quickly reached up and grabbed his coin. As he walked away everyone could see that the coin he picked up was now the brilliant blue of a droplet from the deepest, truest, part of the sky. Kinsami suddenly gasped as he spied what now sat in Adaman's hand.

"An Empty!" Kinsami said. Kinsami had spent years in his family's library studying the power of Will. He was intrigued when he found a section on people with no colour and knew instantly what Gregory was the moment he saw the coin. A sudden chill ran through his body. If this boy next to him was not an idiot he would be the most powerful person in existence.

"Yes, Kinsami," Baras confirmed. "Gregory is an Empty."

"What is an Empty, my Lord?" Lavi asked. Her voice was soft and sweet to the ears.

"An Empty is a person that has no elemental alignment," Celes told her. "You are green with an attachment to the element of wind. Some people will have two or three alignments though one is always dominant. Gregory has none. Ability-wise though, an Empty can pull in any colour and use it as they see fit. In other words, Gregory is everything and nothing at once. An Empty has not been seen in over a thousand years and statistically will not come again for a similar period of time." Lavi looked at Gregory with awe while Kinsami's dark look had not left his face since seeing the coin.

"Now you know about Gregory and the reason he has been granted access to Eckhart," Baras said. "You have all been given access but acceptance will be at a cost. Lavi and Kinsami, each of you have shown great ability in your colour and have also been affected directly in this test by Gregory. For this reason, you have been allowed to know that Gregory is an Empty. If you enter Eckhart however, you cannot speak of this to anyone else, otherwise the price will be expulsion or worse. If you don't accept you can walk away now." Lavi was already

16

nodding with agreement, but Kinsami ignited.

"There's no cost to enter the halls of Eckhart, or any castle for that matter," he said barely containing his anger. "This is how it has been throughout time. My family for generations have walked these halls and learnt the art of Will. I will not be denied this honour so that your family can remain in the shadows... Lord... Baras. I will not make such a promise."

"Then leave," Baras said coldly. Kinsami looked to Celes and Adaman. "Do not look to the other Lords and Ladies for help. Eckhart is my castle and mine alone. I choose to admit or deny anyone as I please. Your honour means nothing in these halls. Your ability means nothing within the castle walls. Everyone, once inside, is equal. You will accept these terms or leave."

Kinsami stared for a minute more. Every essence of his being wanted to fight. Finally, he hung his head in agreeance. He made a promise to himself that he would never accept Gregory as an equal and would never lose to him.

"Good," Baras said. "Now, Gregory, will you be so kind as to put out the flames above us?"

"This shit is real isn't it?" Gregory asked his Grandpa.

"Yes," came the simple reply.

"I... I don't know how."

"It's all to do with the mind, Gregory. This'll be easier if you close your eyes." Gregory did so. "Now, picture the flames in your mind. Picture them changing down to orange flames. Picture the intensity getting weaker. Watch them start to flicker and finally die. Keep this visual running through your mind. You need to want this to happen. When you feel you want what you see enough, speak a command. *Cease* will do."

Gregory followed the instructions, fuelling his Will with the want to help his Grandpa. "Cease!" He commanded.

Baras waited a moment watching the flames glow orange, struggle and then finally die. He then looked to Kinsami. "Kinsami, do you still wish to show off?"

Kinsami grinned a wicked grin. He looked to the roof and clicked his fingers again. This time a spiral of flames burst from his hand igniting all the candles. Geysers of flame metres in height danced on the wicks for five minutes before burning out. He seemed pleased for the first time since entering the room.

"Welcome to Eckhart Castle," Baras said to the three.

The old pickup attacked the rugged terrain with little effort. There were no tracks that it was following but it bounded along regardless. A random tree or rock may have acted as markers but there were never any adjustments to the direction that they drove. The only constant was the wall of mountains that had been slowly growing over the past two hours until they now loomed far above.

The boy, Dirk, was getting restless from this unexpected and definitely unwanted trip. He was at an age of about sixteen with sandy blonde hair, and had a solid build below a blue shirt with a popular animation pictured on it. His arctic blue eyes looked distant and sad. He had not meant to hurt Billy as badly as he did. He just couldn't let Billy bully his classmate anymore. Each day it was the same – Dirk watched Billy steal any lunch money the boy had, the boy would be pushed into the dirt, he'd be tripped in the hallways by other boys doing Billy's bidding or at least too afraid not to. Too add to it, the classmate would get dunked into dirty troughs or at the very worst Billy would go so far as to trip the boy onto busy roadways.

Dirk remembered the look on his parents faces as the police explained what he did to Billy. Two broken arms and bruised from head to toe, Billy was now on a hospital bed in a coma. His mum looked shocked and had lost all colour in her face, while his dad had a stern expression with a fist to his mouth, thumb on lips. When they had finally arrived home, Dirk's future unsure, his parents sat quietly in the lounge. They didn't speak to or look at him. They didn't even talk to each other. They were lost in their own thoughts about what had happened.

Dirk went to his room and sat in a chair by the window overlooking the street. His neighbours never came out of their houses except via the electric garage doors and then only within their cars. His room was rather plain. It had a simple bed with black and white striped blankets, the chair he sat in, a small desk and a white cupboard for his clothes. The walls were blue with white carpet and ceilings. The only hobby the room showed for Dirk, was making model aeroplanes. He had hung each one crafted from the roof, with a total of thirty one.

As time went by and the sun started to set, he found himself drifting off to sleep. A knock at the front door got his attention. He looked back out the window and saw that there was an old, red pickup parked in his driveway. The sky was still dark but he could see that the eastern horizon was starting to brighten. He feared that the pickup belonged to Billy's parents. Listen at his door, Dirk couldn't quite make out the words. The conversation went for five minutes before his fears started to come to fruition.

"Dirk," his mum called. "Could you come out here for a moment?" Dirk didn't know what to do. He could hide out in his room and hope that everything would blow over. This he knew was impossible as his mum would come find him and bring him out. Better to come out on his own accord. Opening his bedroom door, Dirk walked into the lounge room. It wasn't Billy's parents standing with his own. In fact, he didn't know who the old man was. The old man had grey hair, both on his head and on his face. The hair showed evidence of thinning but apart from this the man still had a middle aged complexion.

"Dirk," his dad spoke. "This is Baras. He is the headmaster of a private school for special youths. He heard of your circumstances and has come to offer you a place at his school. He has already talked to both the police and Billy's parents. No charges will be pressed if you leave town with Baras."

The argument that followed was heated and in the end, Dirk left wishing his parents the worst. Storming out of the house, he walked to where the pickup was. Feelings of anger and sadness threatened to over. They came to a head with Dirk kicking the pickup's tyre. The old man had brought out a bag of Dirk's belongings and they left immediately.

Now, after hours of riding in the pickup and his feelings settling, Dirk understood that his parents only had his best interests at heart. He wished he could take back the words he said in anger.

"They understand, Dirk," Baras said as if reading his mind. "Your parents were happy that you fought to stay with them so much. They love you, Dirk, and this has been just as hard for them. Don't let recent events get you down. You are going to find that this school will give you a perspective of the world not many people get to see."

Dirk didn't answer. He had no intention of talking to the old man that uprooted him from the world he loved. Instead, he watched a cave grow in the mountain range. This he knew was where they were aiming for. The pickup entered the dark cave without slowing. Headlights lit the area ahead and Dirk was surprised that the tunnel had smooth walls and curved ceiling. Definitely man made.

It was only moments before they had passed through and were out under a clear blue sky. The area they entered was a crater of a super volcano capped millennia ago. It was miles wide in every direction with green grasslands, forests and a lake. Looking over the terrain Dirk saw rolling hills suddenly drop off into random canyons, and against one wall a marshland ended in a miniature desert like area. Close to the far wall was a castle of archaic decent. He wondered who could have built this structure here as no history lessons or museums spoke of a castle so close to where he lived.

The vehicle drove within a hundred metres of the large wooden doors used to enter the halls of the grand structure. As dirked stepped out he could smell the salt in the air and could hear somewhere close, ocean waves crashing against rocks. This was impossible though as there were no oceans within fourteen hours of his home. They couldn't have been driving for more than six. Dirk took his bag out of the pickup and then without another word the old man drove off. Dirk watched the vehicle leave.

"Great," he said to himself. "The old man could have at least showed me where to go."

"That's my job," a soft voice said behind him. Dirk jumped and turned to see a woman standing where no one was moments before. The woman was tall and slim with long black hair and dark eyes. She had a suit like his teacher would wear. Official but a touch out of place. "I shall take you in, show you to your classroom, and then after class, if needed, I'll take you to your dorm so that you can settle. If you leave your bag by the entrance someone will see it to your bed. Dirk McDougal, welcome to Eckhart Castle."

Chapter 2

Prior to coming to Castle Eckhart, Gregory had never lived away from a family home. It took him only a couple of days to find his feet and become comfortable. All around the Castle grounds, Gregory saw things he once thought impossible. People had started fires without fuel, made a small thunderstorm inside a room and even bent light enough to make small objects shimmer almost out of sight. Gregory had come to accept that Will could be used to do the impossible.

At night, Gregory practiced alone in his room but had yet to work it out completely. Some of the other students on the grounds said that they picture themselves filling with the colour of their coin, then from that point, use their Will to determine what it becomes when it is released. This didn't help Gregory, however, as he was an Empty. He didn't have a colour, so what did he picture himself filling up with?

Kinsami surprised him. He had made it known Gregory was his rival, yet he didn't once reveal the strength Gregory held. People tried to pry at times, asking Gregory what he had done to spark such passion in Kinsami, when no one else was on his radar. Gregory just shrugged and walked away. Soon no one would interact with Gregory. Everyone believed he was powerful, and with the way he acted, possibly dangerous.

Now, he sat in a classroom for the first time with twenty-seven other students. He placed himself in the back corner of the class, more to get away from people staring than any notion of being a badass. He looked around the room. Beside the door to the hallway was an emergency wash sink and first aid bay. Gregory thought, this shouldn't be in a place of learning. The desks were single seaters with a lid that opened to a hidden shelf. This shelf had instruments Gregory could not discern, but he accepted that as his new world.

Kinsami was seated in Gregory's class, right in the middle. He liked to have everyone around him. Gregory also noticed Lavi was in his class, she sat in the corner at the front, closest to the door. She liked to get away quickly with little interaction. These two knew his secret and would interact with him but he could not call them friends. Not yet at least.

The teacher walked in and the room went quiet. He was big and not in a tall way. Gregory started to remember insults he had heard somewhere but couldn't quite place it. He immediately reprimanded himself for the thoughts. The man was probably the nicest person for all he knew.

"Okay class," the teacher said. As he spoke, parts of him started jiggling that shouldn't be moving. "I'm not here to get to know you. I don't care about your colour, your heritage or your ability. To me, you are all nothing. I am here to make you something. Some will get it. Others won't. I take no responsibility for laziness, stupidity or inability. That's all on you. Any questions... none? Good, let's get into this."

Okay, maybe not the nicest person, Gregory thought. A knock at the door drew the class's attention. Standing there was a boy in a blue shirt, dark jeans and sandy blonde hair. He looked shy and Gregory realised that he had not seen the boy on the grounds before. It must be a new kid.

The teacher looked at him, annoyed at the disruption. "You're late for your first day. Thank you for your demonstration at what laziness gets you."

"I only just got here," the boy protested.

"Exactly and that makes you late. Class as you can see there is a little stupidity in this one too." The boy started to look annoyed. "Probably a pale coiner."

"Whatever you're calling me I'll make you eat your words," the boy was passed annoyance and had a dangerous look on his face.

"Well then make me eat them. Wow me. Show me the best you have and the class can judge as to whether my words are to be eaten or not. Even better, move the eraser on my desk with your colour. A task even the girl at the front there could pull off," the teacher said motioning to Lavi.

"With my colour? What the hell are you talking about?" the teacher looked stunned.

"Three in one - Laziness, stupidity and inability. You are going to go far," the teacher said sarcastically. "What is your name?"

"Dirk McDougal," the teacher looked through his list and his eyebrow raised a little as he came to Dirk's information. "Take a seat in the back," he said pointing to an empty chair next to Gregory. Dirk didn't move. "Is there a problem?"

"Why should I listen to a bully?" Dirk said quietly. "You clearly have no respect for your students and won't inspire any of us to achieve anything."

"Take your seat now, Dirk," the teacher matched his tone.

"Yeah, take your seat, Dirk," another student had stepped over to where Dirk stood and grabbed his arm. Dirk responded simply by throwing him across Lavi's desk and into a smug looking boy two rows back. He apologised to Lavi, who blushed nodding furiously. The first boy got to his feet and with two others rushed Dirk.

Gregory was intrigued with the brawl that followed. He noticed the teacher had not stopped the boys, but also noticed he was negating any build-up of Will in the brawlers. Isn't it funny how a thought or memory could suddenly come to you in the most unusual of circumstances, Gregory thought, remembering what Celes had said about him in the testing room of the museum. An Empty can fill themselves up with any element. He laughed aloud as it was so obvious. He saw Kinsami grinning menacingly as the other boys fought close by. Guess I'll try red, Gregory thought, visualizing a velvet swirl moving around him. It drew in close, clinging to his body. He watched it move below the surface of his skin filling every part of his insides. Now what to do with this... revelation?

Suddenly, the room became silent. Gregory could see the fight was still going on to the jeers and cheers of the rest of the class, but he couldn't hear it. What he could hear was a static, like that of a radio not picking up a channel. He looked around for a source but nothing was standing out. Every so often a sound, like a voice, tried to come across but he couldn't make anything out.

A body crashed into his table sending Gregory into the back wall. As he collided with the wall the red energy that he drew into himself came bursting out in a powerful rage. The wall exploded with a loud roar stopping the fight instantly. The

24

teacher was yelling at Gregory and the boy atop him as to which one of them destroyed the wall. Kinsami gave Gregory a dirty look and a few students picked up on this. Gregory's infamy had just grown with no real action on his behalf.

"Special youths?" Dirk said mortified. "They're a bunch of lunatics if they bring explosives to class."

"Okay everyone, back to your seats," the teacher said. "Let's calm down before we move on to the actual lesson."

Gregory moved the dazed boy aside and readjusted his table. The rest of the class settled back into their chairs. Dirk wearily moved to his desk next to Gregory, eyeing off the boy. This could be the boy who has dangerous items and Dirk worried for his own safety. Tomorrow he'll need to secure himself another desk.

"Now remember the seats you have chosen today. I don't like change and this is how you are going to stay for the rest of the year," the teacher said. Dirk's spirits immediately dropped. "For today, let's go out to the fields in the sunlight and fresh air."

The class stood and filed out the back of the building. Clearly, the adjoining class was doing the same, as they now had a room full of rubble. As Gregory was walking out the teacher suddenly grabbed him by the chin and looked into his eyes as if studying them. "Come see me after class." He released Gregory and walked out first.

The fields behind Eckhart were rich and healthy. They were not mowed but the grass didn't grow above a few centimetres. As the class found a spot with a little shade provided by a tall oak, Gregory found that the grass was extremely comfortable to sit on. The rest of the class sat in an arcing shape around the teacher.

"My name is Mr Sir..." the teacher said. "At least, that is what you can refer to me as. None of you has earned the right to use my proper name. Today I'll give you a history of Will and the basics behind it. I expect that no one will talk while I am. Agreed... good.

Will has always been a tool to wield as the conscious mind saw fit. It is not just humans that have this ability, but

25

everything that can think and form a mental image. It is rare in animals though, as they think in a different way. 700 years ago a giraffe had a calf with a disability that gave it trouble lifting its neck. This giraffe was a yellow and could bend the trees using its Will so that the calf could eat easier.

Every religion on this earth stems from people who have or have witnessed others using their Will to perform seemingly miraculous feats. Gods were regular people with strong colours or even Empties." Both Lavi and Kinsami gave a quick glance to Gregory. "For anyone that doesn't know, an Empty is a Will user that has no colour. They can manipulate any colour and therefore do anything like the Gods of legend. Humankind has great ability but we are also very ignorant and things we don't understand will be shaped, changed or even over ridden by active imaginations. As an example. Dirk, explain this lesson to us in your own words."

Dirk couldn't believe that he had been singled out for a second time but then again that's what a bully would do. Once they have you in their sight, that's it. He would show this bastard though. He had been listening to the lesson and he got the idea... Just not the context in which it was being used.

"You speak of a theory in the capabilities of humans and animals using religion as a base reference as they speak of miracles and inhuman ability. Also, many animals are portrayed as demons in these religions and as the demons have... shall we say magic to make it easy... then animals must, therefore, be able to use magic also."

"A very in-depth answer after hearing only a few statements. Thank you, Dirk," Dirk smiled thinking he hit the right answer. This was short lived, however. "Thank you, for proving my point. Class, not only did he immediately state that what I said, being true and direct, were just theories. He also started to change the fundamental elements of my statement, being Will, to suit his own ideas, calling it magic. The word magic will invoke different meanings, different visuals in different people and the avalanche of incorrect information will grow as it is again passed on."

"But what you speak of are just theories. Everyone here

knows this to be true." Dirk spoke up looking at the students around him. He immediately started to doubt himself. Staring back at him were faces of stunned disbelief. "Is...Isn't it?" The class laughed. Gregory sympathised with him as he was in this position only days before.

"Dirk, I read some quick notes on you after you entered. I know your background and lack of training. For now, it'll be best that I show you the power of Will." Mr Sir closed his eyes for but a moment and then looked straight at Dirk. Lavi didn't know why she acted in that moment. She felt green Will in the air and her body responded by jumping in front of Dirk and producing a clear solid barrier.

Letting out a burst of air, Mr Sir directed it straight towards them. This hit Lavi's barrier with such force that she was pushed back into Dirk who held her protectively and braced himself in the wind. Once the onslaught died away, Dirk was surprised they had been pushed metres back from where they originally stood.

"What did you do?" Dirk asked as he let go of a blushing Lavi. She quickly went and sat down again.

"Come see me after class, Dirk," Mr Sir said. He turned back to the class. "The history of Will is all around you if you would only see it for what it is. It has always been here and shall be long after we have returned to dust. No one, though, has ever truly understood all the mysteries that Will holds.

The coin is one such mystery. Why are we born to a specific coin fragment of Will? Why have we never truly succeeded in breaking past a three colour mastery of the five basic colours? Why are there Empties with no colour to their coins? The more time you spend here and grow the more advanced classes you'll take. I have only scratched the surface of what is possible in this world.

The way we use Will is simple. Fill yourselves with the colour of your coin. When you feel you have the right amount, focus on what you want and then will it to be with the colour you have gathered. Keep control as you exhale your Will or things may go very wrong such as walls being blown... Who... Dirk!" Mr Sir yelled at the boy as he sat with a furrowed brow.

Dirk had followed Mr Sir's instructions trying to gather colour and conjure his Will but at the last moment felt a sudden drain. Mr Sir had negated his Will build up in time. "I said see me after class." A loud chime flowed down from the bell tower at the top of the castle. "Which happens to be now. You and Gregory stay back. Everyone else, get lost."

The two boys watched their classmates leave. Each felt nervous as neither really understood why they had been asked to stay back. Mr Sir looked at them both, then decided that Dirk needed to go first. Gregory's issue being a personal matter. Well, Dirk's was too, but Mr Sir had already made it a rather public matter.

"Dirk, you have not been introduced to this side of reality before. In fact, you have given little interest in the subject, even as a theory. You are smart and will attack your problems head on. I want you to picture a coin in your pocket big enough to just fit in a closed fist. Once you have that picture in your mind reach into your pocket and pull out the coin."

Dirk didn't quite trust the initial compliment but did as he was told. He jerked as his hand touched something solid, round and flat. A little part of his mind still didn't believe the concept of Will, but the moment he pulled out the coin his reservations vanished.

"A strong yellow like the summer sun," Mr Sir said. "This is your colour and means that you have a great affinity with the earth element. It is highly possible for people to grow minor affinities to other colours but this is the colour you are going to excel in. You saw that I could use the green, air element, but this is not my coins colour. I am purple and excel at things of the spirit. This allows me to negate the build-up of colour and break a person's concentration before they can use their Will. I did this in class with a number of students looking to harm you, also when you so stupidly attempted to use Will with no real focus on what you wanted to happen. You could have destroyed this entire area.

I need you to work on small things until you get the feel for it. I can see that you understand the basics of bringing your Will to reality. You need to learn to visualise exactly what you want before pushing your Will out. When you leave here, gather a handful of soft dirt and take it straight to your room then dump it onto your bedside table. Each night before going to bed I want you to visualise the dirt moving into specific shapes of your choosing. Think things like a sphere or a cube. Once you are comfortable with this, start to conceive harder and harder shapes. This will help you immensely. Now you can leave too." Dirk didn't need any more of an invitation and took off. He did make sure to get his dirt.

"Gregory, what is your eye colour?" Mr Sir said shifting his attention to the boy

This definitely wasn't what Gregory had expected. "Blue," he replied

"And the transition to yellow, is this you're doing?"

"What do you mean? My eyes have always been blue. They aren't changing."

"I'll take that as a no then," Mr Sir sounded pompous. "Your eyes are definitely changing to yellow. It is only a small amount at the moment but soon you and others will be able to see it. I only noticed due to my colour and ability. Have you used any objects imbued with Will? They could be anything where something strange happened." Gregory thought of the mirror in his Grandpas attic. He was thinking about his eyes at the time it started to glow,

"Actually, there was a mirror that started to glow really brightly. I told myself the sun had hit it."

"That may be the item and, having no knowledge of Will, you may have set it off accidentally. I know of your coin Gregory. Baras told me, as well as others he trusts. Do not bring it up with just anyone though, unless you know that Baras has told them first. By now I would think that you have realised you can fill yourself with any colour and use it. Something that is little known about an Empty is that you don't even need to fill yourself with a colour. Remember this, as one day it may save your life. You can use your Will as you want with no build up at all. In truth, it is the reason why Will users with no coin colour are called *Empty*."

"I had only worked out I could use any colour in class. I'm

sorry for the wall. I was in the middle of gathering red to make a small floating fire when... when I got distracted." Gregory was going to talk about what distracted him but he decided against it.

"The wall will be fixed before you even leave the grounds. I should have stopped it but I was distracted. At least you can see the dangers behind Will. In any case what colour do you want your eyes to be? Blue or yellow? I can leave it or correct it."

"I'll leave them to what they are doing," Gregory said after a moment's thought. "My Will set it off and somewhere in me chose this new colour."

"As you wish. You can leave now. Remember what I said to Dirk and practice with little things. I shall see you for tomorrow's class."

Gregory nodded and walked off to the castle.

"I know it was you, Gregory," Kinsami said referring to the wall in the classroom. Gregory had only just arrived inside when he was ambushed by this self-proclaimed rival. "Why would you show off like that when you should be protecting your secret as I need to?" Kinsami was still fuming over the fact he was being forced to do something. He would never forgive Gregory for being placed in this position and would do everything to push him down where Kinsami believed he belonged. Deep down, the show of power in someone so clueless scared Kinsami. What level could he reach if he had even a little training?

"I didn't mean to blow the wall up," Gregory admitted. "I'd only just worked out how to draw in colour. I lost focus when I got knocked back."

"You have too little control to wield such power. You should not have been the one to be given such a gift. You are going to hurt someone if you keep trying to use your Will. You should just leave Eckhart."

"I'm not going to leave, Kinsami," Gregory said then started walking away.

Kinsami levelled his eyes at Gregory's back. "You're making

a stupid mistake."

"Then I must be stupid," Gregory replied. He found that short, off handed remarks were best to deal with Kinsami and also riled him up.

A sound came from around the corner of the hall. A scuffle which Gregory placed as living beings wrestling. He ducked his head around the corner and saw four boys ganging up on one. All five were from class and he couldn't blame the four for what they were doing. It was Dirk who they were pushing around after all. Mr Sir had placed a target on the new kids back and any bully would try to hit that mark.

It was not in Gregory to stand by and watch someone go through such abuse. Stepping out, he noticed the dirt scattered across the floor and realised that it was Dirk's homework. What startled Gregory even more was that Kinsami was walking out beside him.

"What?" Kinsami said. "You'll only hurt yourself or the boys against you... well, you'll only hurt yourself and I want to be the one to take you down."

"Whatever Kinsami, but since you're here let's do this. Hey! Leave him be!" Gregory bellowed at the boys. They looked up and hesitated but soon ignored him, until they also saw Kinsami. He scared the boys enough to move them along.

"We were just finishing anyway," one of the boys said. "See you around, Dirt." As they walked off Dirk steadied himself and made to give chase.

"Dirk, we aren't going to save you a second time," Gregory told him.

"I didn't ask you to help me. I was doing fine."

"Says the grazed forehead, bruised arm and..." he poked Dirk's chest enabling a small yelp. "Anyway, it looks like you have enough dirt to clean up here... Dirt... I get it now," Gregory said with a laugh. Dirk shot him a deadly look and Gregory laughed again. "It's one thing to get hot headed over a few punks but it's another thing to get angry at a friend for a couple of jabs."

Dirk kept the look for a few more moments then smiled. "Friends then," he replied. "Where do they keep the dustpan and broom?" Kinsami laughed long and loud.

"Seriously, just visualise the dirt rising to form a floating ball. Pick it up from out of the air. You two are as bad as each other." Kinsami replied.

"I forgot about that. I'm still getting my head around the fact that the force of Will exists. I doubt my ability though," he admitted.

"Just do as the teacher said and you'll be fine," Gregory told him.

Dirk decided to give it a try. He pictured the colour of his coin. Within his mind, the ground started to glow in this colour. It climbed the walls and painted the roof. Focusing, Dirk started to draw the colour up through his shoes, into his legs, through his groin, passed his stomach and into every fibre of his body until he shone golden yellow. Absorbing most of the colour, he decided to leave some in the dirt. He had remembered a theory on quantum entanglement and thought that it may help. This theory was about particles that were paired and acted in similar ways over great distances or something to that effect. Dirk decided that the colour coursing through him was paired to that of the colour in the dirt on the ground. This, therefore, would be beneficial for both himself and the object he was going to use.

He pictured the dirt lifting off the ground, rotating like a galaxy in the air and slowly converging into a sphere. Two more times, Dirk ran through the visual in his mind. Once he got the motions down and focused on what he wanted, he willed it into existence. Though, still a bit rushed.

Levitating, the dirt flew into the air in a massive spiral. The outer limits were stretched so wide the dirt was hitting the walls of the hallway along with Gregory and Kinsami. As the boys held their arms across their faces, the spiral started to slow and converge on a central point to create a kind of lop sided ball. The spin was still creating a wobbly mess as Dirk caught the ball. His hands were thrown in awkward directions as he tried to contain his dirt. It was another minute before Dirk tamed the momentum and could loosen his grip

"Maybe I need to work on that," Dirk said beaming from ear

to ear, happy he still succeeded. "Thank you both."

"You're welcome," said Gregory. Kinsami just grunted.

"What's your problem," Dirk asked Kinsami.

"Don't worry about Kinsami," Gregory said punching the new boy in the arm. Kinsami was both shocked and livid as Gregory revealed his name. "He treats everyone like this," leaning in close to Dirk, Gregory had his hand up to his mouth. "He is better than everyone."

Dirk caught Gregory's wink and smiled.

"Gregory, you can't just go around giving out people's names like that. A name has power and I don't give it out lightly," Kinsami scolded.

"Gregory... Kinsami... Well I had expected an introduction from my new friends but I guess that'll do," Dirk smiled at each. "I'm Dirk McDougal."

"Forget it Dirt," Gregory said. "Name's stuck now."

"And I need not know the name of someone inferior to me," Kinsami answered. "You need to prove yourself worthy of me for me to ask of your name."

"You were serious, Gregory?" Dirk remarked. Gregory nodded. "Ok then Kinsami, tell me how I can prove myself to you and I shall. Still, I think you're all talk."

"Come with me and Gregory," Kinsami said. "We meet today. It'll be more comfortable to talk in a room... and more private."

"Is that today?" Gregory asked. "I thought you only wanted to rouse on me when you waited for me in the hall." Kinsami shook his head and kept walking.

"What's this meeting?" Dirk asked as he caught up with Gregory.

"When we were admitted to this school we had an entrance exam. Three of us got special acceptance to the school. Kinsami, myself and one other who'll be waiting for us. We agreed that we would meet once a week after class. Today is that day," Gregory told him. Kinsami walked out in front happy to be excluded from the conversation

"Why?" Dirk questioned.

"Why what?"

"Why did you decide to meet with them? Kinsami doesn't seem to like anyone that much. It seems to me that the meetings are going to get old rather quickly. You'll lose things to talk about and there'll be a lot of awkward silence. That or you'll kill each other."

"Actually, it was more of a stipulation placed on us by the headmaster. He chose us three above all others to be here and told us that we may learn a thing or two from the differences each of us has to offer. He asked that we meet and talk about ourselves, our week and all the trials and tribulations we are finding. We agreed on a trial basis. It may end as you say but we are going to give it a shot." Gregory explained.

"The headmaster... old with a young complexion, thinning grey hair, drives around in a red pickup?"

"You've met him?" Gregory sounded shocked.

"He came and picked me up from my house when I was in trouble and brought me to this school. I don't really know what's going on," Dirk admitted.

"Yeah, I'm only a few days ahead of you. Everyone else here seems to know a world that you and I have never entered."

Dirk nodded.

Kinsami had stopped at a door and was waiting for the other two. The boys had walked down a few hallways to the dormitory wing. Dirk was noticing the girl to boy ratio in the hall was heavily favouring the girls. In fact, they were the only boys anywhere in sight. Girl's dorm was his immediate thought.

"Dirk..." Kinsami struggled with the word. "You can knock on the door for us."

"Wow, I didn't realise it was so easy to prove myself to you," he said sarcastically.

"Just playing with our host," Kinsami replied with a smile.

"Okay, okay," Dirk said. He walked up to the lime green door. There were no marks, etchings or signs on the outside of the door to show the occupants name. He rapped lightly. There was a commotion inside as someone ran up to greet them.

"You boys better have a good excuse for being late." the door swung open and Lavi was standing there with a look of annoyance on her face. She was wearing a frilly blue dress that fell to her ankles and her red hair was tied in a ponytail. Her hazel eyes connected with Dirk's. Immediately, she retreated into her shell. Blushing furiously at Dirk, Lavi wondered how a boy she had seen only once in class had found his way to her door.

Dirk was equally stunned. He knew that this was a girl's dorm and that a girl would be opening the door. Why though was it the girl from class that seemed to shine above the rest? He noticed her as he sent the other boy flying. She seemed so innocent and fragile compared to how she does now. When she protected him though, he saw the strength she possessed and for the briefest of moments, as she opened the door, he saw a fire inside her that matched her hair.

"Make way," Kinsami said barging past the two awe struck teens.

Gregory followed him in. "Lavi opens up after she gets to know you," he told Dirk on his way past. Lavi looked to the ground then flittered back to her seat. Dirk walked into the room. The room was a typical girl's room. Chester drawers with a large mirror and a scattering of different makeups, pink lacy bedspreads and matching pillows. On the walls, were posters of popular boy bands and in the middle of the room were a few small seats around a coffee table. As the boys entered they made straight for the seats.

Lavi moved close to Gregory and spoke in hushed tones. "What is he doing here?" she asked.

Gregory looked at Dirk. "We ran into him and a few boys having a bit of a disagreement in the hallway. I think he may have impressed Kinsami with some raw power. Kinsami invited him with the pretence of putting up some challenge or another."

"He is a ruffian. You saw what he did to those boys in the classroom... and you said he was fighting just now with some other boys too."

"The same boys. Dirk is actually rather nice and has a strong sense of justice. Yes, he does get carried away with a defensive offence when he could just let things go, but he won't seek out trouble himself. Was it not you that saved him from the teacher's assault? Just give him a chance Lavi."

"He has one chance in this room. If he makes any trouble he can leave."

Gregory noticed that Lavi had not taken her eyes from Dirk. He started to see something she hadn't yet realised.

Lavi bounced over to Dirk and offered her hand. "I'm Lavi."

"You're also beautiful," Dirk replied without thinking. His hand paused mid-air as he realised what he'd just said. Lavi's face went bright red and she backed off, sitting on the floor behind her bed a little bewildered.

"Well you know how to make people feel comfortable," Gregory said slapping Dirk on the shoulder laughing.

"Should I leave?"

"No, you're okay. She'll pout around for a bit then come back out and join us."

"You seem to know her well."

"Not really, Dirk. I just knew a girl like her."

"If you three are about done I want to get this over with," Kinsami cut in. "Lavi, come over here."

Lavi was in two minds about obeying, but in the end came back to the seats. She wouldn't look at Dirk anymore... She couldn't help but look at Dirk.

"Where do we begin?" Gregory asked.

Dirk was the one that answered even though he wasn't originally part of the group. He just thought about the things he wanted to know and that may help him grow within the school.

"How about we start with where we are from and the type of training we have had in the power of Will?"

"As good as any place, I think," Gregory agreed. "I'll start us off then. Kinsami would like to think otherwise but up until only a few days ago I knew nothing of this world. I was in the position Dirk was. I never dreamt that such power existed. I spent my childhood scared of my own shadow. There was one occasion while exploring in the attic of my grandpa's place over a week ago that I found some objects I thought were just basic objects. I accidentally activated one and found out that I was

36

still a scared child running from shadows."

"What did you activate?" Lavi asked looking intrigued.

"I found a mirror in an old chest. I was looking at myself thinking how I didn't like my eye colour. The mirror started to glow brightly. That's when I ran and told myself the sun must have hit the mirror. Now my eyes are slowly changing to a new colour. I can't quite see it yet but Mr Sir confirmed it."

"He's a grumpy, old bastard," Kinsami said. "But the turmoil he causes is fun to watch'

"You really have a dark soul, Kinsami," Dirk told him. Lavi narrowed her eyes watching the exchange closely. "Do you have no compassion for anyone else?"

"I'm not here to make friends and bend over backwards to suit others. At least I'm not stupid like you and Gregory," Kinsami said. Gregory let the comment go but Dirk looked like he would jump across the coffee table at Kinsami.

Lavi was waiting for this and cut in. "Boys! Either take your dribble outside or shut up. Gregory has the floor." Dirk settled a little and Kinsami seemed to simply shift his focus to Gregory, ignoring Dirk. "What colour are your eyes turning, Gregory?" Lavi asked.

"Yellow. Apart from this one accident, the entrance exam and blowing up the wall I have yet to be able to do anything real with my Will. I didn't even want to blow the wall up in class. I just lost my focus as I was knocked over. I wanted to create a floating flame with the red I drew in."

"So you're a red?" Dirk asked. Kinsami smirked as he looked at Gregory. Lavi looked away.

"Not quite," Gregory coughed. "As Mr Sir said. People can often times manipulate more than just the one colour."

"So what colour is your coin? Will you show me like I did for the teacher? Could we all bring out our coins?" Dirk asked enthusiastically. Now that he knew about Will everything was exciting.

"Yes, let's do that. I wouldn't mind judging how strong we all are." Kinsami was secretly thinking that if Gregory was the one to show who he was to another, that would leave it open for Kinsami to tell whoever he wanted. Kinsami could then argue that whoever Gregory told couldn't keep it to themselves. Reaching into his pocket, Kinsami pulled out his coin and placed it on the coffee table. The rich red was alive. Shimmers of crimson and scarlet ran over the surface with arcs reaching off the coin like solar flares from the sun. Kinsami didn't need to boast with a coin like this.

Dirk was impressed with the coin and brought his out next. Remembering what Mr Sir said to conjure the disc, he dug into his pocket and pulled the coin out. After having such a rich colour outside, it was now a pale yellow. As he placed it down Kinsami laughed.

Gregory looked confused knowing the true colour the coin possessed. Reaching over, Gregory wiped it. The surface was gritty like sand, and as he wiped, sand was brushed to the table, showing a rich, earthy yellow below. Kinsami sat back with his arms crossed.

"Fine. Lavi your turn. Show us your coin," Kinsami commanded with chagrin.

"I... I shouldn't. Mine isn't just a colour," she said a little worried.

"Nonsense. I've brought mine out and flames leapt through the air. Dirk had sand encrusted upon his coin so dense it covered up the colour. What is yours going to do? Float around the room on a little wisp of wind. I'm not afraid of a ghostly coin."

A switch clicked in Lavi's head and her whole demeanour changed. She looked at Kinsami with a wicked smile. "Remember those words, Kinsami."

Lavi concentrated for a moment before her hazel eyes became sure. Suddenly the dress she was wearing started to flail about wildly. Dirk looked away embarrassed as it lifted up randomly. Lavi took hold of the coin within the dress and pulled it out into the room. She opened her hand and gale force winds filled the enclosed space circling a glowing emerald coin. It did not affect her in any way but the boys were ducking for cover at the edges of the room where the wind was less condensed. Lavi closed her palm again and straightened her dress. The wind died down instantly.

"Beautiful and strong," Dirk commented to himself. Lavi heard him and with a squeak from her lips, switched back to her quiet, shy persona. Gregory and Kinsami picked themselves up and sat back in the chairs.

"Let's not do that again," Kinsami said, eyes settling on Gregory like a wolf to its prey. "How about you, Gregory? What's your coin look like? Dirk would love to see it."

Gregory shot him a filthy look. "No, I don't believe I'll be bringing it out today," Gregory told him.

"Please, Gregory," Dirk said. "I won't tell anyone if it isn't anything special. I couldn't judge you even if I wanted to. I just don't know."

Kinsami was still smirking.

"Okay, Dirk, but just know that I'm sorry," Gregory said knowing he was about to lie to his new friend. Dirk started to picture something as dramatic as Lavi's and was now starting to regret pushing the point. Gregory thought about his coin and then started to picture Allen's blue coin. Once he had the colour in mind, he added an elemental emphasis. Reaching into his pocket, Gregory pulled out his coin and placed it on the table. He wiped away the dampness from his hand. Lavi and Kinsami both did a double take as they saw it. The coin was not that of an Empty, but of a blue. It was as deep as an ocean and was spewing water out in a bubbly stream. The water started to cross the surface of the table and hit the other coins. As it hit Kinsami's, the water turned to steam with an audible hiss. Crossing further along the table to Dirk's, the water started to combine with the sand, being absorbed to create a gritty mush. Kinsami, openly annoyed, stated one absurdity after another taking back his coin and stalking out of the room.

"That was nothing to apologise for, Gregory," Dirk said. He didn't realise what occurred behind the scenes.

"I felt it w..." Like in the classroom a static sound grew in Gregory's ears blocking out the world around him. He could see that Dirk was trying to talk to him but he couldn't make out what was said. He started hearing voices in the static but couldn't concentrate on it. "I need to go," he said not knowing if any sound came out. Walking from the room, Gregory left Lavi and Dirk. The two glanced into each other's eyes for a moment before they both looked away quickly.

Out of the room, Gregory tried to listen deeply to what was being said. It was still too faint to make out until finally, two words came across. "Entrapment Spell'.

Gregory thought it weird that a spell would exist. That was in the realm of magic and not Will. Will doesn't rely on spells to do anything. He decided that he would seek help on the subject.

Chapter 3

Perception of time and space was warped. The realm here was grey and misty. No colour could be seen, no temperatures felt, no time passed, no day or night. Just an endless abyss of nothing. If you looked up, you would be lost in the swirling grey long before you ever saw the sky, if sky there was. The ground below was barely substantial grains of ash and sand. Longevity was the only thing in abundance and the group of thirteen knew this all too well.

They had difficulty remembering younger times and had lost count of the days gone by centuries ago. All they knew was that they once lived out normal lives with friends and family. They were introduced to the power of Will at a young age and were shown secrets and tips passed down through their families. They started to become fluent and gained more control over the feats they attempted. The day finally came when they were granted admission into Eckhart Castle. Such an easy test lighting a few candles and having them burn for a period of time. They were admitted easily.

Eckhart fast became their home. They found the lessons both entertaining and enlightening. Using what they learnt in class their abilities grew ten-fold. They found each other. Some from the same classes, others from around the Castle. There were more back then and they became fast friends. They hung out and shared themselves mentally, sometimes physically, with each other. Their futures were bright.

Tragedy hit the castle. Flames, death, screaming. These memories were still strong in their hearts. They did not cause the events that took place so therefore, why were they being punished? Cast out into this empty void with no hope for a reprieve. They gathered together for comfort and support. In time their hearts became dark and cold with no kindness towards those who trapped them in this place. They practised their abilities nonstop as they felt no fatigue in this realm.

Finally a breakthrough. A purple opened a window that could view the realm from which they came. Everything was different. Technology, craftsmanship, style, structure.

Everything was from centuries before they were born. This window had been opened onto the past. They found that they couldn't change what time the window showed either, only the places within that time. They had to sit, watch and wait for something or someone that could release them from their turmoil. Until finally...

"That's the boy there," the first said pointing to a brown haired teen getting out of a red pickup with a younger boy and an older man. "He was the one that saw me using the mirror."

"He doesn't look like anything special. Keep an eye on him and if he proves to be noteworthy let me know."

"Hang on, Five. Do you recognise that place?"

The one titled Five studied the area before her. "That's the museum!" She exclaimed. "We'll get to see his coin."

The man and woman waited for a bus load of school kids to enter the museum before the boy of interest could. Watching the interaction between the boy and the doorman, they finally saw him pull his coin out.

"He's a fucking Empty! I hope you marked him."

"Of course I did. The first person in God-knows-how-long breaks into our realm and you think I would just let him flitter away? I marked his eyes. It would have seemed like a bright light to him and he may not even remember the interaction but the mark is growing in him and the link to me becoming more powerful. I hid the mark behind a colour change. It'll be impossible to lose him and soon we'll be able to speak with him."

"Good work. Keep on him and see if you can get a message out."

Gregory was at a loss to what was going on. This was now the second time he had heard the weird sound that drowned out everything around him. The second time felt stronger, more engulfing. That and he heard two words out of the jumbled mess. Entrapment Spell. He was sure that his teacher would know what this meant, but he got the feeling he shouldn't disclose the whole truth behind what had been happening. He didn't know how serious it could be and didn't want to get in the middle of anything just yet.

After wandering aimlessly for twenty minutes, Gregory realised he didn't know the way to the faculty quarters. Sure he could try the classroom but that was most likely in the process of being repaired. Spotting a young woman in a suit close by, Gregory decided to ask if she could help him.

"Excuse me," he called out. The woman turned to look at him. "I don't know if you can help me but I am looking for Mr... Sir."

"I'm sorry I don't know that name," the woman replied. "Is he a teacher at the castle?"

"Yes. You would probably know him by his weight alone', Gregory's mouth twitched. "I'm not trying to be offensive. It's just the best description for him."

"It's okay. You're talking of Mr Patel. If you go into the building across the way," she said pointing to a small, round structure near the castle walls. "His floor is the second from the top."

"His floor?" Gregory looked surprised.

"Yes, all faculty members have a floor to themselves."

Gregory thanked the woman and started to jog towards the building. The structure looked to be made of stone with eight floors and a twelve-metre diameter. The doorway into the building was flat and metallic. There was a split down the centre and no visible handles. It looked like the doors of a lift. Gregory's thoughts were proven correct when he spied a button to one side and pressed it. The doors opened with a ding and Gregory stepped into the small square room. There was another door on the opposite side that would lead into the room of the chosen floor. He looked at the buttons inside and chose the second button from the top. Gregory believed that the lift would wait for the owner to allow the occupant entrance to their home but after a short ride up the doors opened and Gregory was left looking straight into the room of Mr Sir.

The room was not as Gregory would have imagined. He thought of food scraps over the floor and on lounges, to which there would be plenty of. He pictured a big TV on one wall and all the creature comforts one could fit into a home. Gregory was far off the mark and he realised this was because he labelled the fat man into a lazy slob category. He made this assumption so easily and reprimanded himself for it.

The room he looked into was immaculate. Not a thing was out of place. There were shelves full of books near one wall and a desk at which Mr Sir could sit and read. The area was open planned and the study flowed into the entertaining area, which flowed into the dining and kitchen. The entertaining area had two long couches with a glass coffee table in between. The kitchen was not overly large with basic bench space, oven, sink and fridge. There was no dishwasher or microwave. A small table set for a maximum of four was positioned just off the bench. The walls to the outside intrigued Gregory. They were definitely a work of Will as seemingly there were no walls at all. Just endless views all around. Gregory coyly stepped inside looking for Mr Sir.

"Mr Sir," he called. A rustle came from a back room and a moment later Gregory saw his teacher come waddling out. *"Walking out'*, Gregory thought, correcting himself. These rude thoughts seemed to come unbidden to his mind. Then again it is just his thoughts. Who are they harming?

"Gregory, what brings you here? Class ended not so long ago."

"I have a simple question, but it has been bugging me, so I've come looking for an answer."

"It doesn't sound as simple as you make out," he waited. "Well? Go ahead."

"You say that there is no such thing as magic."

"Yes."

"I hear people talking about spells around the school grounds. I would have thought that things like spells were in the realm of magic and not that of Will."

"This is true." Gregory looked at him quizzically. "Speak up boy. You have yet to ask me your question. If you're just going to go around making statements I already know then you can leave me to my down time."

"Do spells exist?"

"Not in the way you're thinking," Mr Sir replied. "I don't agree with the use of the word but it all comes down to the way our minds work. Take Dirk for example. Before he knew what he was talking about he had decided that the power of Will could be dumbed down to *magic*. Early users of Will used names like water breathing spell, flying spell, and earthquake spell or if you want to go down darker roads torture spell, entrapment spell and choking spell for their actions. I detest that we are now stuck with the names created by those simpletons of the past."

Gregory was surprised by how easily an opening came up to talk about the entrapment spell. "Do people really do those sorts of things?" He asked delicately. "I mean I can understand flying and water breathing but torture and entrapment. I don't even know what an entrapment spell would do."

"And its best you don't," was all the answer he got. "Run along, Gregory. I'm tired of playing babysitter to you and your unintelligent mind."

Gregory was ready to argue the point but decided better of it. He walked back to the elevator and pushed the button to descend.

The atmosphere of the room was hushed and unsettled. It had been twenty minutes since Gregory and Kinsami had left, but Lavi found that she couldn't move from her chair. She was having a lot of trouble even looking to the left. Not because someone was using their Will to bind her or any other logical reason but because, no more than two feet away, was the new boy.

Dirk was sitting up straight, hands on knees and looking slightly to the side. He too had not moved at all, it was as if he mirrored Lavi. She couldn't determine why he was still here and she didn't want to break the silence that had formed. Thinking it more comfortable than if he was speaking. That, and she didn't know what to say to a boy like him. She could feel that her face was a little warm.

Dirk, on the other hand, had a million and one things running through his mind about the situation. Should he stay?

Should he leave? Should he talk to Lavi? If so, what would he say to her? He had already acknowledged and accepted that he liked her. This day was so different to any other he had lived before. It started out like it was going to be one of the worst and now was ending as one of the best. He had never met a girl that had moved him so much, so quickly. He wanted to live in this moment but didn't want to miss the opportunity to talk to her. If he talked to her though would he scare her away?

Finally, he decided to take the risk and talk. Dirk looked at Lavi and the movement made her look up at him. Nope. He looked away. He definitely wasn't ready for those eyes. He didn't even know what he was going to say.

Okay, ready yourself, Dirk thought. Those eyes are going to meet yours again. You have seen them. You have gauged the force they have. You can hold them. Now go. Dirk ordered himself to look at Lavi. She looked back his way, though a little confused this time. Almost losing to her eyes again, Dirk steeled himself at the last moment, right before he lost the ability to think let alone speak.

"I guess they aren't coming back," that was it? That was the big talk you had lined up? His mind chided.

"No..." Lavi said in return.

"I mean, I knew they weren't coming back by the way they'd left. I don't even know why I needed to bring it up."

"Why have you stayed so long then?" Lavi asked him worried at what the answer may be. She had confirmed on two occasions that he was a ruffian prone to fights. What other dark, twisted or dirty secrets may still be in his personality. She saw him think for a moment and then look at her with determination.

"When I followed Gregory and Kinsami I really believed that I was going to gain some deeper knowledge into this world. I have been in the dark about the power of Will and how to use it up to this very day. It is an amazing gift I have been given and I want to learn everything I can.

Then we arrived and you opened the door. I was stunned, to say the least. I have constantly noticed you around the grounds. First in the classroom where I may have given you a fright and then when you came to my defence against the blast from Mr Sir. Now, beyond all belief, I find myself alone with you in your room. You have been on my mind from the first encounter and I guess I just wanted to make the most of the time available to spend with you while I could," Dirk took a deep breath. "I like you, Lavi."

Only for a moment did Lavi look moved by Dirk's confession. Her awe was replaced by her own look of determination. In public she was always worried about what others thought of her. She would lock herself away behind a wall giving little to be judged. Now, with just herself and Dirk in the room, and no one else to judge her, she was focused on what he'd confessed and her own thoughts about the situation. Lavi was uncharacteristically calm.

"I don't know you, Dirk," she said. "As you have indicated we've only just met for the first time today and these are the most words I have spoken to you so far. You say you like me? You don't know me. All you know is that this form before you is pleasing to the eyes. Sure, I won't lie, you have a pleasing form also but that doesn't mean much, if anything. The deep feelings within you, the things you like to do, the way you interact with others and how you connect with the person I am. These are the things I place with the most importance when someone says they like me. If we don't match then there is only heartbreak ahead."

"So what do you see when you look at me?" Dirk asked. He was expecting she may turn him down but he hadn't heard that yet. He knew what she was saying. She was guarded and didn't want to get into something she wasn't sure on. He just needed to know where he stood so that he knew where to start.

"Here is what I know about you, Dirk. You get into fights. That's it and it doesn't make me want to be with you very much. You know even less about me. What are my hobbies? What do I like to eat? What picks me up when I am down? You don't know anything so don't say you like me." This was the answer Dirk was after and he smiled. "Why should that make you smile?" Lavi asked.

"I haven't asked you out. I said that I like you, but I didn't need an answer from you. You gave me your answer though, and I am happy that out of all that, I wasn't rejected," Lavi went to argue, but Dirk kept going. "You said I looked good and that you didn't know enough about me to be with me. I'll change what I said though. I do not like you. I am liking you. Yes, it started with a physical attraction but all romance does. I've seen you be girly and bashful, protective and courageous, strong willed, smart and centred. These are characteristics I like. I want to get to know you more and let you into my world."

This time Lavi couldn't find the words. She just sat with her mouth slightly open, as if about to speak.

"I think, with the meeting over, I will retire and leave you to whatever you like to do," Dirk said before getting up and letting himself out.

After the shock wore off Lavi blushed. She ran and dove head first into her pillows.

"Okay class, are you ready for your exam?" Mr Sir said the next morning. The class had returned to the room to find that the wall Gregory destroyed was now completely repaired. There was not a scratch upon the surface. No one really cared though, as they knew Will users repaired it within seconds.

"But it's only the second day and yesterday wasn't very informative," said a girl with pigtails who sat in the middle of the classroom. "How do you expect us to do well in an exam?" Others joined in and started throwing out objections. Kinsami stayed calm within the turmoil. He was prepared for any exam that could be given.

"This shall be similar to the exam that was taken to enter the castle. I wish to see the extent of your power myself."

"Did you want us to take the exam here?" Dirk asked. "I'm worried I may destroy the place completely if I'm to use the full extent of my power."

"Ah Dirk, I didn't see you there," Mr Sir said. "I had thought you may be late again. You're right though we may lose a chair or two if you unleash the raw energy you have stored inside. That's why we're going back to the fields again." The classroom burst into laughter.

"Good one, Mr Sir," one student said.

"Yes, the chairs'll be safe from Dirt outside," said another.

Dirk looked to Lavi, and seeing her eyes on him, he decided to take it on the chin. He turned to Gregory who was just smiling. Dirk found himself smiling back.

"Okay, calm down class. Take what you need and get to the fields where we met yesterday."

The students started packing their things and filing out of the class. Dirk waited for Gregory to be ready before he started walking out. He was happy that he'd made a friend in Gregory.

"Thanks for the support back there, Gregory," Dirk said as they were walking out. "It calmed me down a lot. At my last school I was a bit of a loner and was targeted from time to time. In these moments I defended myself. Today, thanks to you and one other, I came out the other side happy. I realised their words were nothing but sound with no true power."

"No problems," Gregory didn't realise that he had done anything significant but he could see that Dirk was grateful for whatever it was he did. "Who was the other person?"

"That doesn't matter right now," Dirk said quickly.

"What, no fighting today? I feel I've learnt less about you, Dirk," Lavi said. There was a wicked little grin on her face. Gregory looked from Lavi to the now crimson expression upon Dirk's face.

"Oh my god!" Gregory exclaimed. "Did you two kiss when I left the room?" Both Lavi and Dirk looked at him in shock.

"No!" they both said in unison. Lavi continued steering the conversation away. "What happened to you by the way? You seemed to be in a daze as you left."

"Sorry I was..."

"Hey!" Mr Sir shouted from down the hall. "I know Dirk is with you but can you speed it up a bit. We're all waiting out here."

Gregory was glad that he didn't have to continue with a lie he hadn't fully formed. The three ran down the hall, to where Mr Sir waited, and out the door. It was a miserable morning. Dark clouds encompassed the area threatening to rain at any moment. Soft rumbles of thunder echoed across the fields. The three moved to where the class was seated, by the tall oak tree, and sat at the end. Mr Sir walked up.

"Thank you, Dirk, for volunteering," he said. "Get up here and show us what you've got."

"I didn't say anything," Dirk protested.

"What happened to *I'm going to destroy the whole classroom because I'm so awesome?*" Mr Sir pushed him. "Either way, you're up so front and centre."

"Fine," he said walking out to the front of the class. "What do you want me to do?"

"It doesn't matter what you do. Just face the other way and make it something *spectacular.*"

Dirk turned around and focused. He understood the basics of using earth now. He also got ideas, on what could be possible, from the library late yesterday afternoon. He read up on some famous yellows and why they were remembered. He still didn't have full control, or knew whether what he did each time was correct, but it was working. He thought for a moment about what he could do before an image came to him. He grinned.

Dirk pictured the colour all around him. In the trees, the blades of grass, the small animals hidden from prey and the castle itself. The area that was covered by his colour stretched for miles. He knew that he would need a lot of colour and focus to complete what he had planned. No one would doubt his power after this. In his mind's eye, he pictured a fountain spout from the ground, gushing out a bright yellow stream. It continued to fill the whole area with yellow. Soon it was seeping into the ground soaking deep below the surface until an inverted dome was created.

He was ready to begin. He would lift the area for miles around into the sky. The castle and school grounds would be upon a floating island. The fountain continued pulsing out colour and he drew this into himself until he felt that he would burst. With his focus set, he willed his grand design into existence. The ground started to shake and he knew everything was set perfectly. Dirk slowly raised his arms to the sky. The ground though did not lift up as planned. Instead, a small stone before him started to rise half a metre. He let go of his Will, confused by the outcome, and the stone dropped.

"Calm down, Dirk, you almost killed us all," Mr Sir said with a sarcastic tone. The classroom erupted into peals of laughter. What they didn't know was that Mr Sir was being serious. He sensed the power in Dirk and got an idea of what he was about to do. He knew that the boy could have pulled it off if he had thought of every avenue for its success, but he didn't want to risk that. Dirk was about to throw the whole area into the air. He may have flipped it squashing the entire class or sent it too high freezing or suffocating everyone. Mr Sir saw the risk and pulled back everything but the smallest amount of Will. This gave Dirk just enough power to raise the stone... A shiver ran through Mr Sir. The stone had flipped. Dirk looked ashamed. He walked back to his spot and sat without a sound.

"Alright, Dirk raised a stone. Now we have seen our best let's all strive to beat it," more giggles. "Kinsami, you're up. Do you think you can do any better?" Kinsami scoffed and got to his feet. He glared at Mr Sir who levelled him with an unimpressed look.

Without a word, Kinsami stretched out his arm towards a distant cliff face. Flames spun from shoulder to palm as he focused his Will. The cliff burst into a stream of lava, flying high into the air, over the castle and arcing back to land before Kinsami. Using his Will to manipulate the temperature, Kinsami cooled the arched lava to a point where it became solid rock.

Everyone was clapping and cheering at this feat. It took a lot of control to hold lava in place over such a long distance, then to keep it in shape while it cooled was phenomenal. Everyone was impressed.

"Well, it's no floating rock, hey Dirk?" Mr Sir commented leaning towards the boy. Dirk just grumbled to himself. "Lavi, Did you want to show off or are you content keeping what you're doing to yourself?" She suddenly looked up at him and then just smiled looking back down. "So be it. Sebastian, get up here."

A skinny, little boy with black hair got up and walked to the front. It was surprising that someone of his stature was the same age as the rest of them, Gregory thought. Though the kid didn't fit in with the class, what he couldn't get over most was how confident the boy looked. The boy took no time at all to gather his Will, instead he dove right into pushing it forward. A mist descended over the crater, blinding everything to within a metre. It settled in around them for several minutes before being sucked into numerous water spouts on the field. With the mist gone, the class was awed by Sebastian's presentation. The nine water spouts continued to ravage the fields for three minutes more before Sebastian let them die away. Little evidence of their existence was left as the water sunk deep into the earth.

"A strong blue presence. Thank you, Sebastian," Mr Sir said. "Who else likes to play with water...? Gregory, get up here."

"Water?" One student questioned. "Yesterday he blew up a wall. How is that water?"

"Clearly, you need to learn more, Sarah. Almost any colour can do the same thing. You just need to have an understanding of your own colour and work out how to manipulate it. Let's take a less destructive activity, such as levitating, and apply it to each colour. Red: use heat to create a lighter than air field around what you want to lift. Blue: Using a similar concept but substituting lighter than air water vapour. Purple: A spiritual approach can be harder to comprehend but it involves using what is perceived as a soul to lift yourself or objects up. Yellow: Create two opposing magnetic forces within the object and that which you are levitating from. Dirk seems a natural at this. Green: If you don't know I'm not explaining. Gregory, get up here and stop stalling."

Gregory walked to the forefront and looked at the class. He noticed that Dirk was passing Lavi a note which she accepted but didn't read, instead she placed it in her pocket. Everyone else seemed to be watching Gregory intently, waiting for him to fail. He was going to make this big. He knew the fat bastard couldn't... Gregory stopped his thoughts and recorrected them when he noticed himself making negative slurs. He knew, *Mr*

Sir, couldn't stop him like he did with Dirk. Gregory didn't need to build up his colour. No one else seemed to notice, or maybe they weren't looking for it, but Gregory always saw when Mr Sir nullified peoples Will.

Having an idea ready to go, Gregory just willed it into existence. This felt nothing like anything he had performed when using a colour. This was born straight from within and belonged to him alone. One moment the fields were clear and the next, the whole crater was full to the top with water. The class had a large bubble of air around it, with a corridor that lead to a similar bubble around Eckhart Castle.

Gregory smiled inwardly when he saw the terrified faces of the students and the blob of a teac... and the teacher. I've got to stop doing that, he thought, correcting himself again. Mr Sir shook himself out of his shock and rounded on Gregory.

"That's extremely dangerous, Gregory. You need to take it away right now."

"Why? Didn't see this one coming with enough time to stop it?"

"Gregory. Today's lesson is to gauge strength. Not show off, make a mistake, and kill everyone." Overhead a whale passed by sending out cries of sorrow. "Did you take this water from the ocean?!"

"It seemed like a logical choice, wouldn't you think? I did need a lot of water for what I wanted to do."

The class, if not shocked already, where now going crazy. To fill the area with water was a massive achievement and rivalled even Kinsami. But to relocate this much water and a whale instantly was almost unbelievable.

"Gregory, that whale is crying out for its calf. You need to send the water straight back to the exact location you took it from now before they are lost to each other forever. Not only that, the sudden relocation of so much ocean water is going to cause major tidal problems for coastal towns."

"Okay, okay," Gregory made a motion with his arm and the water, and whale, were gone. Dirk was the only one not looking at Gregory with a respect for his power. Rather, he was thinking how he could also achieve such a feat.

"I think that is too much for today's lesson. Everyone retire for the day and meet back in class tomorrow. Get out of here," Mr Sir said.

Kinsami was going out of his mind as he watched everyone leave the area. He alone stayed on the grass under the tall oak. This had been his chance. After the failure of the device, due to Gregory, at the entrance exam, he saw this as a second chance to show everyone he was the best. Gregory once again stole his thunder. And not even by a small amount. Gregory completely overshadowed his Will as if Kinsami was a pale colour. He would not forget this and definitely wouldn't forgive the loss of honour.

As Gregory walked across the field a familiar sensation came over him. The silence of everything around him combined with a scratching noise, like an out of tune radio. It was as if he was in two worlds, he was with a group of students strolling into the castle, but at the same time, alone with the overwhelming hold these sounds had on his mind. Moving down a hallway, Gregory entered a secluded room. This brought about something he hadn't experienced before. There was a faint clarity behind the scratching noise.

The room itself wouldn't have enhanced any signal as it was a room designed for study. Desks were set against the walls and lounges throughout the centre were arranged in various positions conforming to the different ways people were comfortable studying. As Gregory moved across the room towards a window, the clarity sharpened even more. He was surprised to hear the words "Hello' and "Gregory' as if someone was trying to talk to him. Coming up against a wall in the direction that gave sharper clarity, Gregory jumped from an open window before moving on.

The area he was drawn too was beyond a courtyard with a garden that held a large assortment of flowers. Gregory saw different varieties and colours all thriving within this small area, and even some species that shouldn't have been growing this time of year. He couldn't help but appreciate the work that had gone into its upkeep. A voice brought him out of his

54

wonderment.

"Hello, Gregory," it said. "Are you able to hear me?"

Gregory looked around but couldn't find anyone that belonged to the voice. "I can hear you," Gregory replied. "Where are you? How are you doing this?"

"I am talking to you from a different realm. I know you caught the words *entrapment spell* last time I tried to reach you. You have no idea how long it's been since I've spoken to someone other than the few people on this side."

"There are more of you there? What is this entrapment spell?"

"Gregory, I don't have much time so please listen to what I have to say. You'll have to research the entrapment spell yourself. A long time ago, centuries in fact, me and thirteen of my friends were caught in a creation of Will that went awry. We were close to the Will user when they let out a burst of Will that engulfed us and cast us into a void. There is no time here so we won't die. There is no hunger or temperature or day or night. There is nothing but the grey empty landscape."

"Over time we have grown in power. Still, we could not find a way to escape the torturous world that the emptiness has brought us. That is until you opened a small crack using a mirror."

Gregory thought back to the mirror in his Grandfather's attic. Memories he had forgotten came to him. These were of cold, dark eyes staring at him through what looked to be a tear in the glass. "Was that you I saw?" He asked.

"No. It was another from my group. He told me that he made contact with you. We've been watching you and know what you are." Gregory became a little uncomfortable. "I know you want your power to remain secret. I can't even begin to imagine the pressure you must feel to hide who you are. Though, that is a small compared to the suffering we've felt over the course of our entrapment. I ask that you help us."

"How can I help?" Gregory asked after considering everything that was said and feeling sorry for those who were trapped. "I wasn't aware that Will could be used in such a way to make this happen.

"All I ask is that you look into what we were caught up in and see if there is anything that can be done, whether from your side or ours. We just want to be able to live our life again."

"I'll do what I can. How can I let you know what I find?" Gregory asked, considering he may not have another chance to speak to the voices.

"Please forgive us for recent attempts to contact you. We're still learning how to do this ourselves, though are becoming better and can now choose the timing. We'll watch and try to contact you at convenient times... And Gregory?"

"Yes?"

"Thank you," the voice said. Gregory felt the voice depart and started to hear his own world. Birds were chirping and bees were buzzing in this garden of such beauty. Gregory stayed a few minutes longer before going into the building. As he was climbing inside, he ran into a group of boys from his class, almost falling over them.

"See, here he is," one said as he grabbed Gregory, stabilizing him. "I knew he entered one of these rooms." Gregory noticed that they were the same four boys that were picking on Dirk.

"Look, I don't want any trouble from you guys," he said trying to sound brave, but he was far more afraid than he let on.

"Gregory," another said. "No one's going to be giving you any trouble, not after the stunt you pulled in class today. That was by far the greatest thing we've ever seen."

"You even beat Kinsami," the third said.

"We didn't think anyone could do that," the fourth boy added in. Gregory was getting an idea of how they perceived him, giving him a sense of relief and more confidence in the situation.

"What do you want then?" he said over emphasising his annoyance.

"We want you to join us," the first replied. "We want to hang out with you and get to know you more."

"I'm not about to start dating you. Leave me alone." With that Gregory walked off and didn't look back. The boys didn't dare follow.

"Now what are we going to do?" one of the boys said as Gregory walked away. "We need to get him on our side to elevate ourselves within the school."

"It's okay, Edward. He seems socially distant. We just need to play on this and build his self-esteem a bit. He'll come around." The boys started walking through the halls towards their dorm rooms. They decided to hang out in whoever's room they came across first. Once there, they would begin their daily ritual of talking about girls and criticising anyone they deemed deserving.

"But what if he never comes around, Stuart?" Edward asked. "He's been hanging out with Dirk and Lavi a lot. I've even seen him with Kinsami. He doesn't seem to know the right type of people to surround himself with."

"Then we'll guide him to the right type of people," Vincent, the third boy said. "Kinsami sees him as a rival and we've seen why. As for Dirk and Lavi, they'll be easily disposed of after today's events."

The boys walked past their classroom and the fourth boy, Malcolm, stopped by the doorway. He noticed a figure inside and was curious to see who it was. To his surprise, it was the subject of their recent discussion, Dirk.

"Speak of the devil," he said. The other boys heard him and only just noticed that he'd lagged behind.

"What's that, Malcolm?" Edward asked.

"It's Dirt. He's in the classroom practising."

"Well he definitely needs it," Vincent said with a grin. The group of boys moved to the door and after watching for a moment, they entered, locking the door behind them. Dirk was so focused on what he was doing that he didn't hear the boys enter. It was only when the group was directly behind him that he realised.

"What do we have here?" Stuart said walking over and inspecting the pile of rocks in front of Dirk. "Playing with rocks again... But wait, this is far too many for you to use. Isn't that right boys?" the boys all nodded.

"What do you guys want?" Dirk asked, looking at them one by one. He had no doubt they were about to finish the fight that was interrupted yesterday by Gregory and Kinsami. This time though, he wanted to settle it without the use of his fists. He had Lavi on his mind and wanted to be more of the person she wanted.

"We're here to help you, *Dirk*. We don't want you to strain that small mind of yours taking on more than you can handle." Vincent leant over and picked up most of the rocks. He bounced the stones on his palm a few times, then clenched his fist around one before throwing it out the window, shattering the glass. Dirk knew that no one would come to inspect the noise. The amount of times Will manipulation went wrong, breakages were common place.

Closing his eyes, Dirk imagined the stones that broke the glass. By following the colour ritual he had developed, he brought the stones back, maybe with more force than he meant to. They raced back through the shattered window and hit Stuart in the chest, sending him to the ground gasping for air. The other boys stood, mouths wide.

"Sorry, I thought I would bring a few back. Just in case I became more adept." Dirk was relaxed, ready for the imminent attack.

"Oh, you're going to regret that, you bastard," Edward said.

"I don't think so. This fight is going to happen regardless so can we get it over with."

All the boys looked angry now. One of them looked at Dirk with a focused expression on his face. Moments later Dirk found he couldn't move the way he wanted. His arms slowly extended out wide against his minds instruction while his body was frozen in place.

"Cowards," Dirk said. "Do you need to constrict my movements to feel comfortable in a fight?"

Insulted, the three remaining boys descended, taking up positions around Dirk before physically beating him. With each punch or kick, Dirk let out a groan of pain. Muscles in his face clenched and he couldn't keep his eyes open. They started to slow down as Stuart was finally lifting himself to his feet.

Walking over to the constricted boy, Stuart glared at Dirk. "After today you'll know your place," he started. "We will remind you anytime you step out of line. You are the bottom of the pack, Dirk. You will leave Gregory alone. You will stay quiet in class. Your existence is meaningless and you shall accept this. You can give up your training also."

Dirk gave him a look that suggested otherwise so Stuart started punching his face. He did this until Dirk was almost passing out. They let their focus of Will fade and Dirk dropped to the floor.

"You can expect that each time you give me a defiant look." Stuart turned around and walked out. Edward and Malcolm followed while Vincent stayed behind to kick Dirk one last time, then chased after the others.

Dirk laid there in pain feeling sorry for himself. He wasn't going to let the bullies break him but he would not retaliate. Firstly, he wanted to remove himself from their immediate vicinity and let them think they'd won. This required him to find a place to practice and better himself until he could walk these halls without worry. He wanted them to know he was the greater person in the use of Will because they wouldn't understand he was a better person within. This is all he could think of to remain passive in the situation.

Finally, Dirk pulled himself to his feet and made his way out of the building. Thinking about where he could find a secluded space to practice, Dirk decided he would leave the castle grounds by the large gateway and follow the wall. It was common sense that the wall would terminate at the cliff face being so close. When Dirk arrived at his destination it proved to be better than expected. The soft curve of the wall gave extra privacy and there were no windows to be seen through. Dirk smiled and sat back against the cliff face resting his battered body. This would do nicely, he thought.

Lavi sat at a desk in the corner of the library. The room was quiet and comforting for her. It was the opposite of her personality when around close friends and she enjoyed these quiet moments. No one else stayed in the large multi floored

59

room, instead they checked out what they wanted and moved to their dorm rooms or other places to study. Lavi liked the ambience in the library though. Sounds dissipated before they reached anyone's ears, allowing a space of perfect silence. The Northern wall gave the best views of the castle ground. While building Castle Eckhart, the Lord of the time had used his Will to make this wall invisible to all who entered the library. From the outside though, it was solid stone. This meant sunshine would fill the room giving students the best reading light.

Lavi was reading a crime mystery book about an ambidextrous killer who was killing women with no evidence left at the scene, and how a journalist was finding his life being drawn more towards the killer through his interactions with a psychic and his reporting on the story. Well, she was trying to read it at least. She'd read the same page for the fourth time, still not taking in the words.

"Damn you, Dirk," she said aloud, though no one heard. Yesterday, Lavi had read half this book and was looking forward to finishing it. Now her thoughts were being drawn back to that... that stupid boy. She made a mental note to yell at him later for disrupting her book.

She was constantly distracted by Dirk's note in her pocket. It would probably just read, *oh Lavi I love you, blah blah blah.* Pulling the folded piece of paper out, she sat looking at it before rolling her eyes and tucking it away again. Lavi picked up the book once more, and reading the same page two more times, she slammed it closed and fished out the letter. She read,

Dirk: My hobby is crafting model aeroplanes. I would love to fly one day. I believe it would be the greatest feeling in the world to be in the sky with nothing else but the clouds and the birds.

Lavi:

Dirk: I like to eat sweet bread and pastries. Also, ramen is up there as one of my favourites.

Lavi:

Dirk: When I'm feeling down, I find a secluded place to be by myself and think through my issues. I usually walk away

feeling better.
  Lavi:
  Lavi smiled softly.

Chapter 4

Yesterday was gone and a new day had begun. The castle was a buzz with daily routines. Students were getting to class with teachers hot on their heels. Ground keepers were busy cleaning the yards and repairing any damage the students may have done. They were always finished within a couple of hours and spent most of the day on whatever they fancied. They began another short shift late afternoon. Administration staff were ushering students and running notes around the place. In secluded areas of the castle, adept students were putting in years of learning to their practice with fruitful results.

With the day's lessons soon to start, the classroom was slowly filling up. Gregory was in quiet conversation with Dirk when Lavi had surprisingly come to the back of the class and pulled up a chair without saying anything. Dirk wouldn't talk about his new bruises when prompted. He just looked at Lavi and said he wasn't fighting. Gregory thought there was more to it but let it go.

Ten minutes before any lessons were set to begin Edward, Stuart and a few others showed up. Scanning the classroom, they found Gregory and crowded round him, blocking out Dirk and Lavi.

"Can't you see we're talking," Gregory said nodding at Dirk and Lavi. Contemplating overnight about how the boys may be thinking Gregory felt a surge of confidence. Knowing his display of power had made a strong impression in their eyes, Gregory thought they may be scared of him all the while being drawn to his strength like moths to a flame. It made him feel strong. It made him feel in charge. His whole persona changed the moment he was talking to them like he was looking down on them.

"It can wait, Gregory," Stuart said. "I want to introduce you to a few people. These are..."

"I don't care," Gregory said waving him to silence. Gregory was imitating how Kinsami had treated him when Gregory first tried to introduce himself at the museum. He noticed that Kinsami was watching the exchange with unguarded hatred in his eyes. Gregory had finally shown Kinsami without a doubt who was greater. "Your names mean nothing to me so don't bother and let me get back to my conversation."

"It's okay, Gregory," Dirk's voice sounded. "Listen to what they have to say or they may never leave us alone." Gregory nodded then looked at the group.

"We can all see that you're strong," Edward said in delicate tones. He was being careful with his approach. "We can all see that you have great skill and, forgive me when I say this, are naive in the way you approach it. We only wanted to offer you a place where you may get a number of different perspectives. A place where you can share in what we know and we can show you how to be greater than you already are. We can't say we are greater but we may see things in ways you may not have considered and therefore, be of some benefit."

Gregory thought about this for a moment and knew that it was a similar idea to what his Grandad had said to do with Lavi and Kinsami each week. The idea appealed to him but he wasn't sure he wanted to join this group.

"What are you going to get out of it?" he asked

"It's not often that greatness comes into a school. We thought we had found it in Kinsami but you have shown us he is insignificant in comparison. When people think about the great Gregory and all his exploits, and there will be plenty, we want them to know that we were also here at the beginning. A little slice of immortality in history."

Gregory found that he was enjoying the praise and attention but he didn't want to admit it just yet.

"Okay everyone, get in your seats and shut up," Mr Sir had stormed in at that time and stopped any further conversation.

"Let us know," Edward said as they broke off and walked back to their seats. Some even left the room as this was not their class. It amazed Gregory that they'd go to such lengths to be near him.

"They're really trying to suck up after yesterday, hey Gregory?" Dirk said to his friend

"Dirk! What part of shut up don't you understand?" Mr Sir yelled. "I swear you get more stupid each day."

Both boys went eyes front. After a moment Gregory tapped on his desk and Dirk looked across. There was a note saying *Fat prick never changes*. Dirk had an odd expression and shook his head. Gregory took the gesture to be an agreement that he didn't change, but Dirk was actually disturbed at Gregory's choice of words.

The rest of the lesson crawled by as Mr Sir dribbled on for the first time about real topics of learning. The whole time Gregory was counting the minutes and seconds before they could leave. He had seriously considered what the group had said and decided that he wanted to look into it a little more.

When the lesson finished and everyone started filling out, Gregory hung back. Dirk saw he hadn't moved and stayed back with him.

"What's the matter," he asked.

"I think I'm going to hang with the group of students who came in earlier," Gregory told Dirk. "I want to see if I can learn anything from them like they said. It's similar to what my Grandpa suggested I do with Lavi and Kinsami. I thought I'd give it a shot."

"Just be careful around them," Dirk warned. "Remember, some of them are the ones that've bullied myself and others in the past and I don't trust their character."

"Why not come with me and check it out too. You may even become friends. I know they'll listen to me if I ask them to."

"Don't get too big headed, Gregory. Remember someone that wants something will always tell you what you want to hear. A friend will tell you what you need to hear even if it's something you don't want to hear. Anyway, I'll let you make your own mistakes. I have somewhere to be."

"That's fine. I'll watch myself but I at least want to give it a shot. Tell me about your adventures after, okay?"

"Done," Dirk said before getting up and walking out. He was going back to the training ground he found the day before. The area was a calming, peaceful place for him.

Gregory walked out the doors and found a group of seven students were waiting for him just down the hallway.

"You took your time, Gregory. We thought you were living

in the classroom."

"If you only want to be throwing insults around then leave me be and I'll go to my room," Gregory wanted to see if they would risk him walking away. He smiled when they baulked.

"Gregory, come on. We're only joking. Let's go to the yards." the group turned and walked out to the courtyard of the inner grounds. Gregory followed them feeling like he was king. He had never felt so wanted before and regardless of Dirk's warnings, wanted to keep it going.

The courtyard was a massive area surrounded on all sides by the castle's inner walls. There were trees and benches, clear grassy patches, cemented walkways and cushioned meeting areas. The sky was clear like most days, and the sun's warmth penetrated right to the bones. He saw the group making their way to one of the cushioned areas.

The area was round so they could all see and interact with each other and Gregory settled down in an empty seat.

"So how do you do it, Gregory?" one of the others asked. "How do you do such great things with seemingly no effort at all?"

Gregory thought about it for a moment and decided he wouldn't reveal the secret he promised to keep. He knew that the students would go crazy over the truth and would worship him even more but he couldn't say for sure if they would keep it to themselves. How could he answer otherwise? If not one truth, then maybe another will suffice?

"I don't doubt myself in any way. I picture what I want then go for it."

"We all do that, Gregory," another student said. "You still outperform us. There are rumours that you are relatively new to the use of Will. People with this type of natural ability just don't exist among normal users."

"I'm not a normal user," this remark got their attention and they leaned in. He didn't clarify straight away. "In sports, academics and your everyday leisurely activities, you'll always have those one-in-a-million people who just get it and achieve with no difficulty. These people have the ability to raise those in the same field, or crush them completely with little effort.

Sometimes they have come from a lineage completely removed from the activity and other times they are, like me, from a gifted family."

"You? If you were from a strong family we would know," a girl almost spat. "We know everyone here and all the great families of note."

"Forgive Sarah, she likes to know everyone's business," Stuart interrupted.

"Well if you are from a strong family then what is your lineage, Gregory?" Sarah wanted him to try and prove her wrong.

"Why don't we just say that one day I could inherit this castle if I so chose." Everyone went quiet and just stared. Sarah had paled quite visibly.

"You are of Lord Baras' lineage?"

"Yes," Gregory said simply. He knew that this was enough to explain why he could be so gifted.

"Can you use any other colour? Children of tri-colour users have a greater ease of opening one or two new colours themselves."

"I hadn't thought of it," Gregory lied with such ease. This group of people were bringing out things in him he would not normally think or do. He never longed for the praise of others, but the honest look of amazement on each of their faces was fuelling a fire within him. The lying was another thing he wouldn't normally do. He didn't find any trouble lying to these people, though, as he knew they weren't the nicest of people and he felt he was above them.

"Why don't you try it then? The most any person has been able to unlock is their base colour and two others. Why not choose another colour and see if you really are a natural by using it?"

"I'm confident in my ability. Why don't you all decide on the colour and what I am to do?"

Sarah quickly waved the other six boys in. She was whispering and pointing to the wall at the eastern side of the courtyard with an impish little grin. The others finally nodded.

"We want you to take on the colour of green and make the

66

whole lower floor of the eastern wall invisible."

Gregory thought about this and was coming up at a loss of how to make anything become invisible with green Will. He couldn't just turn the bricks to air as that isn't technically invisible and it may take away the structural integrity of the old castle. Then it came to him. He would definitely be using green but he was going to cheat a little and throw in some blue.

"Looks like it's going to be too hard for the kid," Edward said to Sarah. "We may need to give him something easier for his first use of a second colour."

"Ha. I thought he was a natural. He isn't anything special," Sarah replied.

"Don't write me off just yet," Gregory said quickly. "I haven't used green Will before and was trying to figure out how it could work on its own. If I mix in some blue I can achieve what you have asked." Gregory didn't realise that using two colours at once wasn't as easy as he thought. The colours can easily mix and become something completely different throwing off the output of Will. The user needed to be adept at what they were doing.

"Go right ahead, Gregory," Sarah said. She was thinking up a number of insults for Gregory knowing that he could never succeed on his first attempt. Gregory, however, did not even take the path of gathering colour. He dove straight into willing his idea into existence as only an Empty could. The whole bottom floor started to shimmer and then suddenly disappeared.

Gregory wasn't ready for what he saw. He didn't know on the other side of the wall was the girl's dorm rooms and that he would strip away the privacy of everyone with a courtyard facing room. Some girls sat dazed, others walked to the wall and started tapping on the invisible structure. In two rooms the occupants had started to scream and dive for cover as they had been in the midst of changing. The boys were all whooping and cheering at this and Sarah, though shocked by Gregory's achievement, smiled at the ruckus he made.

The boys all moved to Gregory and were patting him on the back and cheering. Gregory couldn't help but be swept up into their emotion and found he was having fun. Directly in front of him, however, a student was not having any fun. Standing in nothing but a purple bra and underwear, a female student had thrown away modesty to allow her rage to build. Around her was an aura of red that matched the colour of her hair. She wore a look that could turn back a pack of wolves. If Gregory hadn't known her to be a green user he may have mistaken her for a red.

Lavi raised her hands and threw them forwards. Winds burst forth in front of her, but curled back as it hit the wall she couldn't see. Stamping her feet in frustration, Lavi had become angrier. She did the same movements but this time the force was multiple times stronger. The wall of her room crashed outwards freeing gale force winds to blow both the group of students and the stones that made up her wall, across the courtyard. Gregory recovered and looked back at her. She pointed at him then drew her thumb across her throat suggesting Gregory was going to be in a world of pain. The stones around the dazed group floated into the air before racing back to Lavi's room and reconstructing themselves into a solid wall. Gregory pulled back his Will and the walls all went back to normal. The others finally recovered and all sat looking at Gregory.

"What did you end up doing?" one had asked him.

"I don't know," Gregory said toying with them. "I don't want to give away all my secrets."

"Come on Gregory. Your skill is so far above ours we couldn't imitate that even if we tried." Gregory smiled.

"I charged the air throughout the eastern side of the building and out into the courtyard in front of the wall. Then I made it so the air held up small pieces of polished ice."

"How could that make a whole wall turn invisible?"

"Think you stupid worm," Sarah said. "The ice would be polished to create a sheen that would act like a mirror. If you have billions of mirrors floating around facing certain angles, our vision would be diverted in a way to create the illusion of an invisible wall. He is smart." Gregory's eyes widened at the compliment from Sarah then he nodded his thanks.

"I still don't get it."

"That's because you're a dumb arse," Gregory said to the boy.

"Whoa...," some of the boys sounded. Others cheered Gregory on. Gregory was running on a high and couldn't see the lines between right and wrong blurring.

The area Dirk found the day before had been dramatically changed. This was not a natural occurrence, however. Dirk's practice was making great progress at the expense of the landscape. He was levitating chunks of earth, burrowing holes into the cliff face, creating pillars of stone and turning rock to a clear glass-like texture.

While he was doing this, he started to get glimpses of something near the rock face that was not of his making. As he gathered the yellow he needed for another Will construct he saw it again. An obscure line upon the rock face was splitting his colour in two but there was nothing that could explain what was happening. He let the colour seep away without the use of Will and walked to the rock face. Creating colour once more, a clear line was evident. The rock face looked solid enough upon inspection.

He allowed the colour to fade away again but this time only to one side of the line. He followed it up in an arcing motion and found that the line came back down to touch the ground a few metres away. Stepping back and looking at the colour he found it resembled a crude door. Maybe that's what it was. Dirk willed the colour to drag the rock face into the earth below. The door-like stone slide into the earth with a low rumbling, grinding noise. The darkness within fled from the intruding light to reveal a tunnel - a reward for Dirk's curiosity. He wasn't sure if he wanted to enter but he didn't want to stop now. He stepped inside.

Immediately the area became dark, the light of the sun keeping to the entrance. Should no light become available, Dirk considered returning when he was more prepared. He thought for a moment and realised that given the right earthly elements he could make a phosphorescent effect. Thinking

69

back to his chemistry classes and straining his mind, Dirk remembered the mix he needed. After he drew out the elements with the power of Will, Dirk coated the cave walls with a phosphorescent glaze. The cave started to glow a soft green, lighting the path ahead.

The cave walls were smooth and reflective in the non-glowing areas. Dirk set forth into the ephemeral light walking under the stalactites hanging from the ceiling that must have formed thousands of years prior. The walk was easy with no pitfalls or jutting rocks to trip him up. The only effort was walking up a soft, climbing gradient. The sound of every foot fall echoed around the walls. He let out a *boo* noise for lack of a better sound and listened as it bounced continually from wall to wall slowly fading over time.

As he continued, the darkness changed into a different type of darkness, the kind you would find on a half moonlit night. There was also the roar of ocean waves somewhere up ahead. Remembering he heard the ocean when he first arrived, Dirk wondered why he never thought about this again. Continuing forth, Dirk allowed the phosphorescence to fade away as he came to what he believed was an opening of sorts. Dirk knew it wasn't going to lead him to the outside but he was curious as to the new type of darkness. Exiting the cave he found he knew nothing at all.

Dirk walked out onto a ledge three by six metres. The ledge was the only piece of land jutting from a sheer rock cliff face that dropped into an ocean far below. Waves crashed against the base sending a spray of salt water into the air. The ocean stretched out to kiss the horizon. Dark water moved to an unknown rhythm and reflected the crescent moon and stars above. The night troubled him terribly as only ten minutes before, and probably five hundred metres behind, it was daylight.

For now, he forced these thoughts out of his mind until he had the chance to talk to Mr Sir or another member of faculty that may know the secret to this mystery. Dirk didn't like the unexplained. Taking in the scenery for a second time he found such beauty in what he was looking at. He felt that he was blessed like no other student was for the find. He knew no one else was even close to finding this and immediately wanted to bring Lavi here. Turning back to the cave entrance, he wanted to savour the cliff side in small amounts. When he turned, he saw the glow of the phosphorescence. A thought of creation and inspiration struck him laying way for future plans. Should he bring Lavi here, she would not forget the experience.

Slowly he walked back to the glow of the cave and trekked down to the entrance. Noticing daylight was evident the closer he got to the opening, Dirk just shook his head towards the disharmony of time and space. He would need to walk the tunnel a number of times to determine the time differences and the way that time was passing at each entrance.

Kinsami sat cross legged meditating in his room. The windows had been blacked out so no natural light could enter. Around the walls were torches set with an endless flame of Kinsami's design. This gave the room a soft orange glow. Other than the mat Kinsami used to meditate on there was only a futon in the corner for sleeping and a small cupboard for his clothes.

A glowing aura had formed around Kinsami as he sat in deep focus. He had been practising each day with a flame cloak after having the idea placed in his mind at the entrance exam. Kinsami had been making good progress creating more and more of an armour like cloak around himself, getting burnt only twice. Slowly, he pushed forth his Will, as an incredibly unstable form would have been created from being too impatient and rushing it. The flames started in his fingers and toes. They spiralled around each body part making their way along arms and legs until they reached the main body. He twisted and shaped the flames over the rest of his body into the shape of samurai armour. Armour his father had on display in the Otoma residence.

Kinsami finally let out a deep breath and opened his eyes. The flame armour was complete. He couldn't feel the heat from the flames enveloping his body, but could see the paint on the roof starting to curl as the temperature rose. Kinsami

71

twisted and danced and was happy to see that the armour was following his every movement. Creating the armour to replicate his family keepsake was mastered days before and now he smiled greatly as the integrity and ability to wear his flames was accomplished. The final task he set for himself was to learn to focus the temperature at will. Kinsami was proud of his achievement.

He let the flames fall into nothingness and picked up some books for another lesson in class. Heading out the doorway of his dorm room he felt alone. Normally, Stuart, Sarah or another friend would be there to meet him and walk with him to class. He knew they weren't true friends, and didn't treat them as a friend would, but the emptiness of being alone stung. These days they hung out with Gregory.

"Gregory," Kinsami said aloud cursing his name. He'd been granted too much power with little knowledge on how to use it. He would never know what it was like to struggle to achieve everything you had. He would never fully appreciate the gift given to him. When Kinsami trained, beating Gregory was all he had on his mind.

Kinsami approached the classroom and saw Gregory and a group of his former friends walking in from the other direction. Kinsami saw Gregory flick the skirt of a nearby classmate using green Will much to the amusement of those around him. These two acts were new developments. Gregory had started to show abilities in a new colour. If he wasn't careful he may pass from being a normal colour user to someone significantly more like an Empty. The other development being that he was becoming like the other students. Cruel, uncaring, and was bullying others, all within a single day of hanging out with Kinsami's former friends.

Kinsami walked in taking his seat. Gregory had gone to his own at the back, finally leaving the others alone. Dirk tried to greet him but Gregory showed no enthusiasm in his response. This was going to get interesting, Kinsami thought to himself. Frustrated Dirk looked forward, ignoring Gregory.

The moment Gregory was waiting for came soon after as Mr Sir entered the classroom. "Here's the fat man. Welcome Mr

Sir," Gregory said with a highly exaggerated bow. Parts of the class erupted into laughter.

"He actually did it," one of them said to another. Kinsami knew what was happening because he had been in Gregory's position. The only difference was that Kinsami had honour. He wouldn't bend a knee to the desire of the mob.

Mr Sir stopped in his tracks, looking directly at Gregory. Flicking his hand at the boy, Mr Sir continued into the room. The class went silent and looked back at Gregory. He wobbled for a moment under the Will of the teacher then slumped forward over his desk with a vacant look in his eyes. He didn't move in any way. Dirk reached over to help him into a better position.

"Leave him, Dirk," Mr Sir told him. "He won't know what position he slept in and I believe he needs time to himself without being disturbed. That goes for everyone else as well," Mr Sir said pointing at the class. "Make any rude or obnoxious remarks about me no matter how true and you will get the same treatment. A sleep full of your greatest fears. And don't bother complaining to administration. Previous years have had no luck. Now, onto the lesson."

Kinsami silently admitted that he liked the teacher just that little bit more. Direct, to the point, and crushing any future attempts that may occur. It was the best way to approach life. The rest of the lesson went without event and soon it was time to pack up. Mr Sir released Gregory and he came to with a start. His face was pale and he was visibly shaking. After a moment his mind finally cleared and he started to look around taking in his surroundings. People were already leaving and he saw Kinsami getting up.

"Kinsami," Gregory called. "Wait a moment. Dirk, Lavi, you too if you could. I have something to discuss."

Kinsami looked ready to argue but when Dirk sat and Lavi moved passed him to sit next to Dirk, Kinsami decided he could spare a moment. He walked over and towered above Gregory's desk. Gregory placed his face in his hands for a moment longer remembering the nightmares he had just lived through with no escape.

"Well," Kinsami said.

Gregory finally looked up at the three. He wiped the last of the cold sweat from his brow and then went into it. "I'd like to have our arranged meeting early this week in the library. I have something I need to talk to you about and it's too big to keep to myself."

"Okay," this surprised everyone that Kinsami was on board, but as he continued it made sense. "I want to get it over with as soon as possible so I don't have to worry for another week." Dirk and Lavi agreed.

"Yes, but don't think I've let you off for yesterday, Gregory," Lavi told him.

"What happened yesterday?" Dirk asked.

"I'll tell you later, Dirk. I don't want to see you guys get physical."

"Come on, Lavi," Gregory said. "It was funny and anyway, that purple suited you."

Lavi's eyes went wild and she backhanded Gregory in the face. "Dirk, Kinsami, let's go," Lavi walked out of the room. Dirk looked wide eyed at Kinsami who just shrugged and followed. Dirk looked at Gregory, who was holding his battered nose with a sour look on his face, before he followed Lavi also. Gregory got up and walked behind them at a distance. Following them into the library, Gregory sat at a table of their choosing. Everyone remained quiet waiting for him to talk.

"I asked you here to talk about som... What?" The others started to laugh but Gregory couldn't hear them. He didn't hear the same scratching sound that usually accompanied the silence either.

Lavi leaned forward and pushed the middle of the table. A small circle in the centre moved inwards and with a rush of air, Gregory could hear again.

"You don't come here much do you, Gregory?" Dirk asked. Gregory shook his head. "The room has a strong sound dampener. There is no noise unless you press the button at your table. Then it's only for the people sitting at the table."

"That's excellent. I only chose the library because few people come here and I didn't want someone to overhear."

74

"Before we get into this, there is something that is bothering me," Dirk said. "Your eyes, they have been changing colour over time."

"I noticed that too," Lavi said. "I thought I was seeing things to begin with, but it has become more and more obvious."

Kinsami reached across the table and grabbed Gregory under the chin turning his face towards his own. He looked intently into Gregory's eyes. He saw the blue eyes he knew were Gregory's but within the blue were swirls of yellow. After a moment, he pushed his face away.

"Yes, they're changing to a yellow," Gregory admitted. "I found some enchanted items at my Grandads and accidentally started the change somehow. That was the first time I had used Will and it scared the hell out of me. Mr Sir offered to correct what I'd started but I chose to let it be. I never liked the blue." The others nodded and then were over the new revelation once it had been explained.

"So what's the big news that you can't keep to yourself?" Kinsami asked. "We aren't getting any younger here."

"I am hearing voices in the walls," Gregory came right out and said it.

"So you're going crazy?" Dirk asked.

"It's not like that."

"You just told us you're hearing things. How are we supposed to take it?"

"People have been contacting me from a separate realm. They were trapped there hundreds of years ago through the misuse of Will and have asked for help to get out."

"Why is it only you they can talk to? How long has this been going on for?" Kinsami asked.

"It's been going on since I blew up the wall in class. They interrupted me as I was building Will and threw me off. They're talking to me because I found an instrument in my Grandads attic that opened a hole to their realm. Ever since, they've been reaching out to me and I finally got to talk properly the other day. These people need our help. I'm asking if you'd help me free them."

"What are we looking for?" Lavi asked.

"There was another reason I asked you to the library. Could you help me look for information on something called an entrapment spell? This is what has trapped them."

"No offence, Gregory, but how do you know they are good people and didn't deserve what they got?" Kinsami asked. "An entrapment spell is like a prison and a prisoner will say anything to get out of their cage. I'm not going to help in this affair and you need to stop also."

"For once I'm with Kinsami," Dirk followed. "I don't feel comfortable with this."

"What about you Lavi?" Gregory asked looking at the red head.

"I'm unsure, Gregory," she said. "Let me think about this. If there are some people trapped who genuinely need to be rescued, there would be no hesitation. If Kinsami is right and we are letting out criminals then I don't want to help. Look into who they are and research carefully. If they are good people come back and ask again."

"Whatever!" Gregory almost yelled. The others jumped at his tone. "I don't need any of you anyway. Just piss off and don't bother with these meetings again. If you won't give me a little time, I don't want any from you."

"Fine by me," Kinsami said walking off. Dirk and Lavi looked at Gregory and then at each other. They shook their heads and got up.

"Just like I thought. You can just piss..."

Lavi hit the button on the table muting Gregory mid-sentence. She walked off with Dirk.

"Lavi. There is something I want to show you," Dirk said as they exited the library.

"What is it?" she asked

"I found a place that is secluded and would like to invite you."

"Like a date," she asked becoming a little bashful.

"No, no, noo... Well, yeah a bit. Would you like to?" Dirk asked looking down embarrassed.

'...Okay," she said. Dirk looked up at her with a smile on his face.

"Well come on," he said taking her hand. She pulled her hand away.

"Not right now, Dirk. You need to allow me to prepare for a date. It's every woman's right."

"Sorry," Dirk said. "It is just time sensitive and I got excited. How about this time tomorrow? We could meet right here."

"It's a date," Lavi said with a wink.

Gregory was annoyed that his so called friends wouldn't help him. He was yelling abuse at the top of his lungs allowing the library dampeners to steal the sound. It took him a few minutes before he started to calm down. With a red face, he looked around and didn't see another soul other than the Librarian who was busy sorting through some books.

"Well, if they won't help I'll just do it myself," Gregory said. He moved to where the librarian was and when he was within a metre started to hear the rustling of the books. The librarian's desk must allow for sound, he thought.

"Excuse me," Gregory said. The librarian didn't move. He was a short man with light brown hair and eyes. He was starting to get old and Gregory noticed that the man was missing a few teeth. Must be getting a bit hard of hearing also. Gregory saw the name tag on the man's red shirt. "Edgar," he said a little louder this time, waving a hand at him. The man looked up.

"Yes, young master?" Edgar said. His voice was old and had a whine to it. Now that Gregory had his attention what did he want? Gregory stared, his mind blank for a moment before it kicked back in.

"I am to research forbidden spells. In particular, I have to look into spells like the entrapment spell and give a talk on the history of it and how wrong it is."

"Mezzanine floor, row 8, book 2445. *Spells of Pain and the Bloody History That Followed,*" Edgar told him.

That was it? Gregory was prepared to defend his lie until the old man gave in. That felt too easy. Gregory made his way to the book mentioned. He located the spine and tilting it from the top, pulled it out. The books cover was one that would turn many away. People were being ripped apart to a high detail with the blood running to a bath where a young lady was bathing. Gregory looked away from the cover after confirming the name and brought it with him to a table in a secluded corner.

He looked through the index, and tracing a line down the list, he located the item he was after. Entrapment. He flipped to the page number listed and started to read what was entailed with the spell. Apparently, Kinsami was correct in that it was held for those who had done the most outrageous of crimes using Will. It was a type of imprisonment that could not be escaped from when inside. Not by a regular user anyway. From the outside though, it was easy to open the prison. All one needed to do was find the point at which the prison was originally created and then use Will to create a doorway to those trapped. Gregory was happy that he could so easily find the answers that he was searching for, but had now started to doubt the integrity of those he had been talking to. Both those he considered friends, and a book written without a need to lie, said the same thing and Gregory needed to be sure. Tonight he'd visit those who were trapped and question the kind of people they were.

Darkness had set in, Gregory now felt comfortable to speak to those who were trapped. He didn't know why he needed to sneak around, but like hiding the subject of the voices from others, it felt necessary. Keeping to the shadows, he passed through the hallways of the castle, turned school. Having never been out so late, the castle felt eerie at night. Shadows came alive and every noise echoed down the halls. Gregory ducked out of sight when he saw two people coming along the hallway.

Reaching the garden Gregory had made contact last time, he walked to the same spot. Without any understanding of how a regular user of Will could accomplish the task, Gregory proceeded as only an Empty could. He thought of a window between this world and the other. One where sound could travel through but nothing more. Once he had the image in his mind he willed it into existence. A shimmer of light flashed through the air in front of him, swishing and curling until it formed a perfectly round shape.

One moment, Gregory could see the back wall and the next he could see a grey circle. He did not know for sure whether he was looking into the right place until a face popped up. The figure on the other side tried reaching out but his hand and part of his arm disappeared out of sight. Gregory was a little disturbed by the fact that where the arm finished on the window, he could see the blood, muscle and bone cross section. Making a point to think things through next time, he tried to ignore the gruesome sight.

"What is this, Gregory?" The figure on the other side asked. This one question, and the voice that was used, confirmed to Gregory that it was the correct place. The figure was a weasely little man, far younger than Gregory had pictured. Possibly in his twenties. He had a hooked nose and bulging eyes that didn't seem to fit the shape of his skull. A unique look.

"I wanted to talk some more and found a way to open a communication link with a visual window. I still couldn't make a window to allow physical things through," Gregory wasn't ready to let them know he could free them. This window was enough to give him confidence. He knew he could let them out on a whim. If it came to it, he decided he would do it properly in case there was some mechanism that may block him.

"How can I help you, Gregory?"

"I wanted to learn a little more about you," Gregory confessed but he wanted to do so subtly. "What were you like before you found yourself in this prison of yours, and how did you even end up in there?"

"It is smart to be a little distrustful," the man said.

Gregory felt caught out. "No, I didn't mean it like that," he tried to sound convincing.

"It's okay, Gregory," the man replied. "If I was in your shoes I would feel exactly the same way. You don't know us. You don't know what we are like and the lives we have lived."

"I didn't mean to offend you," Gregory apologised. He was starting to regret he asked at all.

"No offence taken. We were a lot like you, Gregory. We were

Will users and even attended Eckhart to learn more of the art. We were friends who shared, loved, and dreamed together. We wanted to do something with our lives using our Will to show we truly lived. We don't know if we'll ever dream again now

One day without warning a group of people appeared at the castle. They started hurting, torturing, and murdering people. Students and teachers alike, they did not discriminate. Some of us made a stand and fought back. People who could hold their own were captured and taken to who knows where. It was in the chaos that we were imprisoned, possibly by the people that were destroying everything. One moment, my friends and I were fighting back and the next we found ourselves here in this lifeless, senseless, timeless world.

We have been trapped for centuries now. In time someone in our ranks found a way to open a window like you have now. This allowed us to watch the outside world. The window that was opened was from a time long before we were born. The world beyond moved at the same pace as the world we find ourselves in and we couldn't shift the timing. We watched countless years go by until we found you. An Empty that may free us from this hell we've found ourselves in."

"I didn't know it was as bad as all this," Gregory said. "I am sorry to hear that you have gone through so much negativity. Please hold on just a little longer and I will free you from your cage."

"That is all we ask, Gregory. To be once more in a world where we could know heat on our faces or the cold crisp winter breeze. To know the taste of food and the passion of a body against your own." Gregory blushed.

"Maybe you could help me help you. Where were you when you found yourself trapped? I may be able to track back from that point and find some clues."

"We were in the yard by a big oak tree. Our teacher used to take us out to it a bit."

"I may know the one. I'll have a look around and see what I can do. Hopefully you'll be free very soon."

"I hope so too. Thank you, Gregory," the man looked over Gregory's shoulder and a very weird expression crossed his face. Gregory turned around to find a boy in his new group of friends looking at him and the hole in the air. Gregory quickly swished his hands over the hole and it disappeared.

"I was practising a new ability I learned today," he said quickly. "You know, push its boundaries and stuff." The boy nodded.

"You're really impressive, Gregory," the boy said. He was about to walk away but then as an afterthought, explained, "Me and a few of the guys are going to have some fun. Sarah is going to be there as well. Did you want to come along?" He mentioned Sarah like there was something there, but he couldn't work out what. Gregory thought about it for a moment and decided he would go. He wanted to move the boy's thoughts away from what he'd just witnessed.

"I'm in," he replied. "Just show me the way." The boy ran down the hallway with a smile on his face and Gregory followed.

Liam was troubled with what he'd just experienced. When a new window opened in this empty realm he raced over and tried to escape. He was disappointed that it didn't allow any physical substance to pass through. When he saw Gregory on the other side he knew straight away what was happening. Gregory was having doubts about freeing them and this was the crucial conversation he was waiting for. The conversation they had all prepared for no matter who was there to take the call. He was surprised that it didn't come sooner, but Liam felt he'd eased Gregory's doubts and set him back on the path to freeing them.

What Liam found troubling though, was that the boy who walked in on them had been in this realm with him also. Liam was, in fact, looking straight at him. If Edward's younger self was in the castle, it meant they had almost come back full circle to their own time. He knew that it wasn't long until the castle would be attacked and they would be trapped in this realm. If only he could change the past, but he knew that the paradoxes it'd create wouldn't allow for this. If he saved himself from being trapped, there would be no one stuck in this lifeless land that cared enough to save his younger self when the time came. He couldn't save himself and not save himself at the same time. He needed to let his younger self's life play out as it already had for him.

"Edward, come here," Liam called out to the older doppelganger.

"What's up? Who was that?" Edward asked having watched the conversation progress

"Do you remember the talented kid we used to hang with and get to do mischievous things? Lord Baras's Grandson."

Edward nodded after a moment's thought. "I have a recollection."

"What was his name?"

"Was it Graham..? Geoffrey..? Grego... Holy shit it's him!" As the name sprung to mind, a picture of Gregory followed.

"I saw you standing behind Gregory after he opened the window to this realm."

"I remember that," Edward said, his eyes were closed trying to think. "The next day we were invaded and then trapped in this realm."

"Do you know what that means then?"

"We are free tomorrow," Edward said with a wicked smile. "This changes nothing. We continue with the plan. Go tell everyone to be ready for when it happens."

"So what mischief are we getting up to tonight?" Gregory asked Edward as they were leaving the castle. Gregory knew it was wrong when they played pranks at other's expense but he was having fun.

"We are going to be fighting each other in a big battle royale," Edward said glancing back at the boy. Gregory came to a stop when he heard the plans. Slowing down, Edward turned to face him.

"We are going to be fighting?" Gregory exclaimed. "Are you guys insane?"

"This won't be the first time, Gregory. It is completely safe and it enhances our Will control tenfold each time we fight."

"I'll watch at least," Gregory said. "If it is as you say, I may join next time."

"Make up your mind when we're preparing. I'll ask you one more time before we begin. Say yes and I won't tell Sarah you were being a little wimp," he said with a wink.

"You've mentioned Sarah twice now," Gregory brought up. "What do you think is going on?"

Edward smiled. "She is telling everyone you are together." Gregory was taken aback and could not speak straight away. "From your reaction, it looks to be that this statement is untrue."

"No... Noo," Gregory finally spat out. He hadn't been thinking of Sarah in that way but now that it was brought up her image in his mind was different. Her black hair was now the colour of a midnight sky with a deep blue sheen, her pudgy little cheeks were cutely curved when she smiled, the eyes that were a basic blue now sparkled like a multifaceted crystal in the sun, her freckles only helped to enhance her features. "It's not that. I just didn't think she would be telling anyone so soon. Come on. Take me to where the brawl is."

Gregory collected himself and started to think about Sarah. He barely knew her but he was starting to think he wanted to. Maybe he would compete in the brawl if she was going to be there.

Edward led Gregory out to the same oak tree they attended for lessons. There was already a rather large gathering of students around, chatting in smaller groups. Edward walked to the circle of friends Gregory recognised and made himself some room to join in. Everyone became quiet when they saw Gregory approach.

"Gregory!" Stuart said louder than he intended. "We didn't expect you would be coming to the event. Sarah is here." Sarah looked over with a start and then at Gregory who winked at her. She allowed her face to relax into a smile knowing her lie was safe. Moreover, that she had secured a great catch with a strong future.

"I heard there was going to be a fight," Gregory started. After he said the next line there was no going back. He took a deep breath. "How could I stay away?"

"Someone is keen to get their arse kicked."

"No one is laying a hand on this face," Gregory said, pointing to himself.

"Why would anyone be trying to hit you, Gregory?" Sarah asked with a smirk. "You know we are going to be fighting with Will right?"

"With our Will? Isn't that more dangerous?" Gregory scoffed.

"Not if you use an elemental double," Edward supplied.

"A what?" Gregory asked. He still didn't understand what was going on.

Sarah just laughed long and loud. "So you were ready to come in here fists swinging at anyone that got close and not care if anyone got a couple in on you?"

"Yeah. That's what came to mind when Edward mentioned an all in brawl." Gregory rubbed the back of his head feeling oddly bashful in front of Sarah

"You're more of a bad arse than I thought," Sarah said with an impish little grin. Gregory found that the beauty he somehow missed before was even better in person.

"Explain the rules to me then."

"Take it from me, Gregory," Stuart stepped in. "I am the reigning champion at the moment. We use our Will to construct a fighter with our base colour... Or colours in your case. We continue to manipulate our fighter with our mind and our Will. We make them fight and try to destroy the focus of the other fighters. Last one standing is the winner."

"And this heightens your ability?"

"You'll see that it's not as easy as it sounds. Even for you. There is a lot to take in and keep your mind on. Check it out," Stuart nodded towards another group. They had constructed a fighter from red. It was barely a silhouette but was clearly the shape of a person with extra limbs. This fighter had four arms. "That rookie has brought out his fighter too early. Save it for the final moment and you'll have greater control in the fight."

"How many fights have you been in?"

"Probably eight," Stuart said after a moment's thought. "I worked it out after the fourth and have won ever since. It's

84

beginning. Watch for a bit longer and pull out a fighter when they start walking towards the centre."

Gregory watched as more and more people brought out fighters. Not all looked human, a green user created a reptilian-like fighter. Another student created a ninja warrior dressed in an ocean blue, representing his colour. Gregory got too excited and forgot what Stuart had said moments before.

Thinking of the type of fighter Gregory wanted to create, he noticed that no one had created a warrior in more than one colour. This, Gregory thought, might be an advantage to himself and therefor made a blue fighter in perfect detail. There was no haze around the fighter like all the others which displayed a blurry image. Gregory dressed his fighter in green robes, then made three balls of gale force condensed wind. He positioned one above, one left, and one right of the fighter. The balls of wind only came to him at the end of his creations birth when he saw other fighters brandishing weapons. Some had harpoons, others sais, and katanas. One student even believed a blade brimmed hat would be a good weapon.

Everyone around the arena was in awe of Gregory's creation. They had not seen a fighter in such detail with two colours before and were taking in the beauty of the creation. They also knew that Gregory was a beginner and some had him in mind as their first target. Those who create finely constructed fighters were trying to show their strength but did not realise by making a basic fighter, it is easier to control and hold together. Also, using two colours makes the mind work harder to manipulate the two colours. Seldom, could a dual colour user keep the fighter formed for so long.

The fighters started to walk into the middle of the arena and Stuart and Sarah both came to the outer ring of the field. Stuart created a simple figure with no weapons and of such a pale colour it almost looked white. Gregory couldn't see his colour at all. Sarah, on the other hand, constructed her fighter in a deep purple. It was still a simple fighter, but Gregory felt happy to see this glimpse into her world. He didn't realise just how far he fell. His own mind was working against him, becoming infatuated because of a single conversation with

Edward.

"Well, let's get this fight underway," someone from the other side said. "Begin."

All was suddenly chaos as fighters were running in and around the set area. Some had already started into one-on-one duels. Others took advantage of their distraction by cutting in and taking out one of the fighters before fading away again. Sarah and Stuart were fighting back to back seemingly helping one another. This would only last so long before they would need to face off against each other. Gregory didn't know that Stuart had an eye on him and was waiting for the right moment to strike.

Gregory saw a fighter coming up on his right. Instead of facing him though, he used one of the wind balls, sending it into the fighter and destroying him completely. He needed to dodge another fighter that had snuck up on him, the ball he was currently controlling stopped mid-air. After a successful dodge, he sent another ball into the new fighter before bringing both the balls back to his own. He was having trouble controlling everything at once and found he had hindered himself with so many objects on this battlefield.

Stuart knew this was going to happen and found his opening sooner than expected. After fighting off another competitor he noticed Gregory's fighter was frozen and two balls were whizzing around attacking other fighters. Stuart sent his white fighter to take out Gregory. Noticing the attack too late, Gregory's fighter exploded into a rain sparks.

Gregory felt bummed, not making the top ten and moved back to the oak to sit down. He was surprised when a grumpy Sarah sat down next to him soon after.

"What happened?" Gregory asked.

"That bastard, Stuart, was supposed to protect my back until the last ten were made clear, then it would be all in after that. He left me alone to take you out," Sarah punched Gregory in the arm to show she wasn't happy with him either.

"Guess I was too good a target to pass up," he replied with a smile.

"Steady boy. Don't go thinking you're all that just because

you have two colours going for you."

"You seem to think there is more to me with the rumours you started." Gregory noticed the blush creeping across her face. *Damn she was cute,* he thought.

"Thank you for not calling me out on that, Gregory... Why didn't you by the way? I'm sure it would have come as a shock."

"It did... When Edward told me," she narrowed her eyes then glared at Edward who was still battling. "In that moment I realised I had never truly looked at you. What I found was beauty in its most pure form," he paused for a moment to gather his courage. "I would like to ask you out officially, Sarah. Would you be my girlfriend?"

"Of course, Gregory," she had a soft smile on her face but inside was one more cunning. Everything was going to plan. Edward wasn't going to comply to begin with but he came through in the end. Gregory acted just as she thought he would and now she needed to keep things as they were to build a grand future for herself.

Gregory was over the moon. He couldn't believe how this night had turned out after how it started. First, those who he thought were friends turned their backs on him. He had a visual conversation with people in another dimension. Now he had a girlfriend. How could this night be any better? Gregory heard a long, despairing moan come from the fighters. As he looked towards the fight he saw Stuart on his knees and Edward bouncing around, fists pumping the air. The battle was over.

"Serves him right," Sarah said.

Gregory laughed. "Yeah."

He reached over and took Sarah's hand. She held his right back. Her hand was soft and small in his own. It set him ablaze and he realised the night had just gotten infinitely better.

Chapter 5

Brushing her red hair, Lavi watched herself in the mirror as she prepared for the date, wanting everything to be perfect. Upon the desk sat the letter Dirk had written. She read it multiple times the night before and had finally written in her answers, blushing with every pen stroke. She had accepted she was attracted to Dirk before she'd even spoke to him and more and more, she found him to be a nice, handsome, genuine guy. The letter was the first step to truly letting herself feel it.

Manipulating her hair into different styles Lavi decided she would leave it down today. She reached for a little foundation with neutral tones and applied it to her face. Next, she added a soft pink blush to her cheeks. She hadn't had many occasions to apply makeup to herself but she liked how her face was transforming in the mirror. The eye liner was a little tricky but she made the lines perfectly. Lavi almost poked her eye with the mascara brush but finally lengthened and darkened her lashes.

Lavi felt beautiful and was almost ready to see Dirk. All she had left now was to wriggle into her dress. Getting up, Lavi looked at the red dress she'd laid out on the bed. Suddenly, she looked back at the makeup kit and realised she hadn't put on any lipstick. Picking up a deep red to match her dress, she smiled and held it to her chest trying to imagine Dirk's reaction when he saw her. Winding off the cap, Lavi drew it across her lips before kissing the air a few times and inspecting her work. Now she was complete.

Lavi started walking towards the door. As she reached for it she felt a draft. Where was her head? The dress was still on the bed and she almost walked out into the hallway in her red underwear. She shook her head and walked to her dress. Fiddling with the small handle, she unzipped the back of the dress and stepped into it, pulling it into place. Finding difficulty reaching the zipper once more, Lavi used green Will to do herself up.

One last time, she looked at herself in the mirror, twisting to glance at her rear. She knew she was stunning. Grabbing the letter, Lavi folded it to hide away in her bra before she skipped, almost floating, out the door.

There were no classes today and the wait for the promised time was almost too hard to bear. She had walked to the library and back to her room seven times already just to see if Dirk may be there early but was let down each time. The carpet was having trouble keeping its shape with the amount of pacing Lavi had done. Even now she was still early but she couldn't stay away any longer.

She rounded a corner with thoughts on what could be instore for tonight, so didn't see Gregory coming the other way. Lavi walked headlong into him, bowling him over. Gregory landed with a thud and shot her a dirty look.

"Get your head out of the clouds Lavi and watch where you're going," Gregory said with poison in his tone.

"Either you were distracted too and now a hypocrite or were fully aware and clumsy as fuck," Lavi lashed out, not in the mood to take his abuse today. She had been very wrong about Gregory also. In the beginning, Dirk was perceived to be the bully prone to fights. She could not see the nice person he was. Gregory on the other hand progressed in the opposite direction. He started out as nice but became a jerk as time went by. He had joined a group of bullies and started showing his true colours with how he treated and talked to people.

"You going to see Dirk?" Gregory asked noticing the dress and makeup.

"What of it?"

"Thought you didn't like him. You could come with me instead."

"What makes you think I want to do that? You have become more of a jerk these days. You poke fun at people's natural features and play pranks that are degrading and could cause mental scars. You are a bully Gregory and I don't want to be with you."

"It's not with me exactly," he was angry at her on the inside for the way she had just spoken to him but wanted to be nice. He was trying to gain her help after all. "I've worked it out."

"Gregory just spit out what you want. I have somewhere to

89

be and you are holding me up."

"You know what, you're a bitch and you look like a slut. I wanted you to come and help with opening the way for the trapped group to be free but fuck off and go slut around." Gregory vented at her and stormed off.

Lavi was crushed. She'd made herself look beautiful for someone close to her that she wanted to be the girlfriend of. She wasn't like that at all. Her eyes teared up and she quickly fanned them so that her mascara wouldn't run. She walked on now missing the bounce in her step. As she reached the entrance to the library she found Dirk was there waiting. Lavi stopped at a distance before he saw her and just looked at him. He was reaching with his hands, moving them in odd ways while talking to himself. He paused and then started again with different lip movements. Lavi realised he was practising what he might say when she arrived.

She smiled so deeply that all the worries Gregory gave her vanished instantly. Now she was tearing up for more happy reasons. Why did girls even wear makeup? It's so hard to maintain. Dirk was wearing a simple, pale yellow shirt and blue jeans. To Lavi, he was handsome just as he was. When he looked up and their eyes met she could not hold the gaze due to the intensity of feelings that swept over her. He ran over and his hands started moving. She wasn't looking at him and didn't hear anything either. She looked up and saw a goldfish, mouth opening and closing with a lost look in his eyes.

"Welcome," he finally said. Lavi could hardly contain her giggle. "What?"

"That's your big opening?" She said laughing loudly. "You stand there for five minutes working on a greeting accompanied by gestures and you settle for *Welcome.*" Dirk was stunned and a little embarrassed that she had seen him that way. Especially with the fact that she was laughing at him for it.

"I had so many different lines in mind and had just settled on the perfect one when I saw you."

"So what was it then," she asked still smiling.

"That's the problem. I saw you," he told her. She raised an

90

eyebrow at him. "The moment I saw you my mind scrambled. Even now I don't remember what I had decided on. You are so beautiful, Lavi. That dress, your hair, the way your face is alive. I am lucky to have experienced such beauty in this life."

Lavi was overwhelmed by the compliments. "It isn't too much?" She asked looking for reassurance. "Gregory said some mean things earlier. I was feeling a little down for it." Dirk's brow furrowed a little.

"Gregory has been changing little by little over time to a point where he now doesn't care what he says as long as it inflicts either pain or discomfort. I look at you and see beauty. I look at you and see the brightness of this world. I look at you and warmth creeps inside chasing away the cold that was left over from a time without you."

"You're just biased."

"No, Lavi. It is not a bias. You are beautiful. You have enhanced it with your makeup and dress but even without these things, you are beautiful."

"I don't believe you," Lavi said. "I know you are biased. I look like a slut. I feel like a slut. I've done too much."

"Gregory called you a slut?" Dirk asked. Lavi just nodded. "I am going to approach this from an odd angle. I want you to listen to what I say carefully in full and accept it. You are ugly." Dirk saw her eyes almost break. "Listen to it all. You are ugly. You are beautiful. You are plain. You are exotic. You are funny. You are boring. You are skilful. You are clumsy."

"Are you going anywhere with this," Lavi asked confused. Dirk put up a hand.

"I could never be like her. She is far above me. She is pathetic. She is below me. She is a slut. She is a prude. She is innocent. She is experienced. You are all of these things, Lavi, as there will always be someone to think something different of you. You are every possible thing there is to everyone else. All that matters is what you try to be. It doesn't matter what I think. It doesn't matter what Kinsami, Mr Sir, those jerks from class think and it especially doesn't matter what Gregory thinks. It only matters what you think you are. Don't let others influence that, just continue being you."

Lavi listened to Dirk and slowly, what he said started to make imperfect sense. She agreed with him. She'd heard many names being flung around at different people and none were ever completely true. Or false for that matter.

"Dirk, you're wrong."

Dirk's shoulders sunk. "I may need to hit a certain someone later."

"No, Dirk. The reason you are wrong is that it does matter to me what you think," she was smiling again. Dirk breathed a sigh of relief. "So where is this special place that you've found?"

"Come with me," Dirk took her hand, leading her through the halls and out to the area behind the wall. Lavi could feel the warmth and strength of his hand as it held hers. These hands were a little rough and larger than her own. Just the touch of his hand was enough for her to lose herself in the moment. So far gone was she that a cold, emptiness filled her as Dirk let the grip go. Looking around, Lavi realised she missed the whole trip and couldn't quite work out where she was. Lavi could tell that they were at the base of the castle walls and next to the cliff face so she could deduce a general location but not an exact one. This special place was rather plain but Dirk found something in it.

"This is the place that I come and train myself with the use of Will," Dirk told her. "I had found at times I didn't get along with the other boys and this was a secluded area for me."

"You could have told me we were coming to see a training ground," Lavi said with a dissatisfied look on her face. "I may have chosen my attire differently."

"This is not what I wanted to show you," he said quickly. "This is the beginning and where I made my discovery."

"Oh?" Was the only reply he got.

"As I said, this was my training ground. I would build my colour around me and then Will it to do many different things. In time, I noticed that my colour wasn't... umm... connecting properly in specific areas on the rock face."

"What do you mean?" Lavi asked.

"Whenever I pictured my colour building... Think of two

pieces of paper sitting next to each other. If you were to take a pencil and colour the two pieces in the same colour you would still see the line that divided the pages. The same happened for me on the rock face. I started to notice that when I imagined my colour around me, before I drew it in, there was a distinct divide on the rock face. I could see lines like the divide between the two pieces of paper. I allowed the colour to fade on one side of the divide and was left with an archway. This archway I found to be a door."

"Your colour showed you this?" Does the colour not exist in our own mind? How could you recognise this divide without prior knowledge?"

"I don't know," he admitted.

"This would mean there is so much more to colour than previously thought. I had believed that colour was only the imagination of your own to help prepare yourself to use Will. The way you speak of it is like it has substance and comes from the land itself not just your mind."

"Why don't you try it then, Lavi," Dirk said before walking up to and drawing a line on the rock face with his finger. "Watch your colour specifically at this point here and try to see what I am talking about."

"I don't picture colour the same way you do. You picture it in the land where as I picture it in the sky. I use Will to move air and therefore it is easier for me to picture the colour where I shall perform."

"Try it anyway around the archway," Dirk insisted. "I would like to see if you notice anything."

"Okay, I'll have a look," Lavi gave in. In her mind she brought forward an emerald spectrum into the air around her, she watched it build in tone and texture and pictured it moving with the breeze. After building a large amount of green she looked to the spot where Dirk had indicated. At first, she didn't see anything on the cliff face, she knew she wouldn't. She did not form colour like he did and therefore it would never work.

As she was about to dismiss the colour build up and admit defeat she saw something strange of her own. It was not on the rock face but in the air. The green Lavi had built was curling in at both sides of where Dirk had indicated, then was blowing back towards her as if a soft draft was coming from that spot. She looked along the path of where her colour was doing this and could see the arch Dirk must be talking about. She walked to where it came back to the ground on the other side.

"It comes back down here," she said to Dirk after letting her colour fade. Dirk smiled at her.

"Exactly that."

"That's incredible, Dirk! The colour really does have some sort of substance that has yet to be explained. It isn't just a visual aid. In fact, I would go so far as to theorise that we are using Will to bring forth the colour and using the colour to do as we please."

"A lesson Lavi?"

"Aren't you at all intrigued by this? You've made a massive discovery," she was excited, to say the least.

"Calm down," Dirk told her. "I haven't lived a life in the world you know. I don't know what the boundaries are and therefore cannot fully grasp the significance. As I learn I am accepting it as my new reality. Everything is exciting in its own way."

"I guess that makes sense."

"Besides, I brought you here because I had something to show you. It's not the training ground or the lines on the wall. It's not even the fact that those lines make an archway I have called a door. It is what is beyond the door that is my find."

Lavi didn't even think about that, she was getting too involved in the details of what was found. Now she was getting curious as she looked to the archway.

"Only a yellow would be able to open this as intended as it is solid rock. It may not be an accident that you found it."

"It may be a secret only a yellow could discover but it was by accident, and circumstance, that I had found my way here. Let me open it for you. We're starting to run out of time."

Lavi thought the last remark was a bit odd, but then again, they were an hour from sunset. He possibly wanted to be back by nightfall. She watched the concentration on Dirk's face for a moment before a soft rumble announced the opening of the cliff face. It didn't swing open like Lavi had thought it would, but sank into the earth below. Behind the wall was a cave lit up by phosphorescence. It wasn't just the green variation either but blue and red hues could be seen inside. Dirk walked to the entrance and bowing back at her extended his hand.

"If I may," he said.

"You want me to trust someone I barely know to take me into a cave for who knows what?" Dirk wobbled a bit, taken off guard by the remark. Lavi giggled and took his hand. She gave him a cute smile as he straightened. He couldn't help but smile back. They entered the cave and walked along the path Dirk had come to learn. Lavi was mesmerised by the natural formation of phosphorus and how the colours intertwined and played with each other. She was dumbstruck though when she came to a point on the pathway where the phosphorescence perfectly formed *Dirk 4 Lavi.*

"This phosphorescence is of your doing!" She said incredulously.

"Well, when you said I had to wait another day, I got a little impatient and decided to decorate."

Lavi couldn't reply but stared in awe at the cave walls around her. She started to notice that the colours didn't just blend into each other in random patterns, they actually formed murals. There was the ocean with dolphins leaping. There was a sunrise with a hawk flying by. There were landscapes and star systems, rivers and rain. Dirk had put almost everything conceivable on these walls and it was all for her. She held his hand tighter as they moved forward.

Lavi was not prepared for what she saw next though. She heard the ocean long before she saw it, but to walk out on a starlit night sky with a moon hanging just above the horizon was unbelievable.

"How long have we been walking for," she asked Dirk. She couldn't know for sure as she had been so distracted.

"Not long Lavi. The magic of this place is that the time of day is flipped from our own. It took me a couple of trips to find the timing to be accurate but it's why I was so stuck on timing."

"It's amazing, Dirk," Lavi said walking out on the ledge and looking around mesmerised. "It's so beautiful."

"I thought you would like it," Dirk said moving to the ledge and sitting with his legs hanging over the side. Lavi bounced over and sat next to him. Neither of the two said anything. They both found that they were lost for words all of a sudden. If she couldn't talk, Lavi decided that she would express herself in other ways. She slowly laid her head on his shoulder, smiling inwardly when she felt him jump. He put his hand around her back, the feel of it sending tingles across Lavi's skin.

They sat in silence gazing across the moonlit ocean scenery. Lavi was melting into the warmth of the body beside her and did not want to come back to reality. She was brought back to conscious thought when glowing objects started moving out of the cave and into the night air. The phosphorus was being formed into shapes such as unicorns, faeries, dragons and loads of other mythical beasts, to dance amongst the stars. She looked at Dirk who was already smiling at her.

"How long can you hold your creations?" she whispered as if anything louder would break the spell she was under.

"I have already set them in motion. I am not controlling them. They'll fade upon sunrise." Lavi was amazed, to say the least. He had brought these creatures to life and didn't need to control them. She could only put it down to his inexperience that he just made his own rules.

"Who are you," she whispered again.

"I am a man in love," he whispered back.

"Follow me," she then said. Standing up she leapt from the cliff face into the open air.

"No!" Dirk cried reaching for her. His heart was racing as he watched her fall for a few metres, but froze when she made a swooping curve into the sky, defying the very gravity that held everyone else down. He could only sit, mouth hanging, as she chased and played with the mythical beasts he brought to life. She rolled onto her back and gestured for him to follow. "How?" He called out.

"Remember what Mr Sir said. A yellow user would manipulate the magnetic force of the world itself to raise objects or yourself. Will yourself to be a similar magnetic force to the world and fluctuate the strength of this to rise and fall."

Dirk remembered Mr Sir mentioning that in class but he only thought of other objects. He never imagined he could raise himself using the same technique. Lacking the confidence Lavi had, Dirk stood on the cliff side and drew in the yellow. He pulled it all into himself and pictured himself glowing yellow. Slowly, Dirk willed his magnetic field to be an opposing force to the Earth, raising the intensity until he felt himself start to want to lift. Dirk thought this must be the weightless feeling astronauts felt. Putting a little more intensity into his Will he lifted from the ground.

Dirk started laughing hysterically. This was a dream he'd held since he was a child. Dirk believed that he would need to become a pilot, and now finding that it was so simple sparked an emotional overload that came out in laughter. When he started to settle down he worked on moving forward. This was a much harder thing to achieve but through a little trial and error, he found that if he made his base a stronger opposing magnetic force and his top half an equal magnetic force he could start moving around by leaning in the direction he wanted. Finally, Dirk got the confidence to move out to Lavi.

"Took your time," she said. Lavi saw his eyes were tearing up. "What's wrong, Dirk? I thought you would enjoy this."

"I do. I'm so happy. I brought you here to give you a beautiful night but you have given me so much more." He flew over to Lavi and took her in his arms.

"You have made me just as happy, Dirk," she said looking him in the eyes. In a moment, moved by all that had happened and the proximity of the girl before him, Dirk leaned in to kiss her. To his joy, she moved up towards him. As the sun broke the horizon Dirk and Lavi shared their first kiss. The phosphorescent beasts burst into glowing sparks around them before fading away.

Lost in the moment, Dirk let go of his Will control keeping himself aloft. Lavi caught him as he fell, and though she couldn't hold him up, gave him the time to Will himself aloft again. They both flew to the cliff side. As they landed they both started laughing in an embarrassed pull of emotions. Each had gone beet red.

"Thank you, Dirk," Lavi said hugging him once more. "If I had of listened to Gregory I wou..." Lavi's face drained of colour.

"What's wrong?" Dirk asked worried by her sudden shift in emotion.

"Gregory... He told me he had worked out how to free the people he mentioned. He was on his way to do so when I ran into him."

"Stay here," Dirk told her, taking her hands in his and talking directly to her. He knew it was unwise for Gregory to be pushing forward with releasing these people. "It'll be safer for you. Okay?" Lavi nodded. Dirk turned and ran back down the tunnel.

Something was wrong. As he had done each afternoon, Kinsami had retired to his dorm to meditate, to calm his mind and strengthen his focus. He sat upon his floor mat using the words his family passed to him to clear one's mind, but he could not find calm today. The hairs on the back of his neck were tingling and he couldn't shake the feeling something big was about to happen.

The sun had set outside his window. The last shafts of light dying into a twilight grey. Becoming restless from the constant uneasy feeling, Kinsami decided he would walk the castle grounds. He wanted to quell this feeling by showing himself there was nothing wrong. At times, night was archaic in the castle. They had electricity and lighting but this was hit and miss. Tonight, it would seem the latter was true as the sun gave no more light. Kinsami willed two small balls of fire into existence that slowly circled him, providing an ephemeral glow where the globes in the roof were failing.

As he rounded a corner a figure bowled him to the ground in a tangled mess of arms and legs. The figure, however, was far too quick to their feet, patting their chest to put out a small smouldering flame that caught alight when they ran into one of his fire balls. Kinsami brought the other ball forward and found Dirk standing before him.

Dirk looked down, recognising Kinsami. "Sorry Kinsami," he said offering a hand.

Kinsami patted it away and got to his feet. "Why the hell were you running around blind corners like the world was on fire?"

"Because it may very well be soon enough. Have you seen Gregory?"

Suddenly, Kinsami knew what this uneasy feeling was. "That dumb, impatient bastard. Tell me all."

Dirk started to explain what Lavi had told him. Gregory understood what was needed to break down the barrier and free the trapped group of people. He mentioned the argument between Gregory and Lavi, with Lavi not wanting to help him and Gregory storming away saying he would free them himself. Kinsami listened carefully, a stern look upon his face.

"We need to find him," Kinsami said. "He is playing with everyone's lives and we don't know who is going to be walking out from the other side."

"I agree, Kinsami. Is there any way we can cover more ground quickly. I don't believe we have much time."

"If you brought along your little hurricane she could have charged the air feeling out Gregory no matter where he was. As it's just us we may need to leg it."

"I left Lavi in a safe place. Why can't we do anything?"

"I have yet to learn anything in the red that can help and well... it's you."

Dirk just gave him a dirty look. "We're wasting time Kinsami. I could try and charge the earthen elements around us the same way that the green would work and seek his passing."

"If you think you can then go for it," Kinsami said.

Dirk had no doubt he could do it and started to build the colour all around him. He saw in his mind the castle halls, the classrooms, the dining rooms, dorm rooms and the outer yards. All was yellow and bright. He was about to will the colour to work for him when it had been sucked away. He tried again and this too was sucked out into the fields to disappear.

"Kinsami, quickly build colour all around the castle fields!" Kinsami heard the urgency in his voice and decided not to argue. He built a deep crimson everywhere he could think of.

"That's strange," Kinsami said suddenly. "My colour is getting drained away towards the old oak we take outdoor classes at."

"Let's go!" Dirk started running down hallways, passed classrooms and out into the night air.

"What's happening, Dirk?"

"Gregory is there and whatever he is doing, it is big. He's started something and it is draining all the colour around it."

"But colour doesn't have substance. It is a part of my mind," Kinsami argued.

"Trust me there is more to colour than you know."

Kinsami was about to argue back when the old Oak tree came into view. What rocked him was a spiralling dome spinning a kaleidoscope of colours visible to the naked eye. The dome was physically affecting the earth, air and tree nearby. Within the dome, Dirk and Kinsami could just make out the form of Gregory. They ran over to the dome but as they got close were knocked back by an invisible force. Dirk got to his feet again and moved closer with caution.

"Gregory!" He yelled with all his might. "You need to stop this." There was no response from inside the dome and Dirk tried to produce forms from Will that could help but couldn't keep his colour long enough to work anything. Fireballs flew past him to explode against the dome. This didn't affect the force before them in any way.

"I can't build enough power," Kinsami said. He felt completely useless. "I can't do anything."

"Try building the colour at a great distance away and then will it into a greater force."

Kinsami did this and couldn't believe Dirks suggestion worked. He decided to go all out with destructive force. Dirk first felt Kinsami's Will as a rumble in the earth. It grew harsher and fiercer until the earth blew apart in an eruption of lava and fire where the dome stood moments before.

"Kinsami, you're going to kill him," Dirk squealed.

"I can't hold back, Dirk. It's either all out or nothing."

When the eruption settled down and the area cleared Dirk and Kinsami fell into despair. The dome before them had not been destroyed but spun as fast and as strong as ever. The earth around the dome was completely destroyed but within was as if nothing had happened. Seeing Gregory raise his arms Dirk ran forward. The dome burst into electricity that ran through the air. The force sent Dirk spiralling across the field and up against the castle walls knocking him out cold. Kinsami looked at the area where the dome had sat. Gregory was standing before a rip in the air metres wide. The edges of this dimensional split were rippling with raw energy sending out sparks and lightning bolts. Figures moved in the Grey centre. Kinsami had failed.

Gregory had succeeded. He was standing in front of the rip he had created looking at the figures coming towards him. They stepped through the portal into the world of life, touch and sound. Gregory was grinning at what he had done but as he looked from person to person the smile turned to confusion.

"You?" he said to the group. There was no time to say any more when a burst of Will blew Gregory far off to the cliff face in the south.

"Go," a voice at the back commanded. The group split up and ran towards the castle yelling and hooting. Three stopped before Kinsami with a dangerous look in their eyes.

"You shall be the first to die," one said. Kinsami thought they looked familiar but couldn't place them.

"You can only try," he replied calmly. This was more to his liking. A person of substance was before him threatening him and he knew he was skilled enough to hold his own. With a quick burst of red Will he cloaked his body in a flame armour of samurai design. If this surprised the opponents before him it didn't show. They started throwing everything they had at him but nothing could breach his armour. Water sizzled and steamed, earth melted, air fed the armour, fire did nothing at all and none could utilise the purple.

"Let him be," the first voice said. "Go have your fun." The

two men ran around Kinsami and off into the castle. Screams were filtering over the walls and flames could be seen burning in different areas. Kinsami stood his ground and faced the woman giving the orders. She was not overly tall with black hair and blue eyes. She had a wicked smile at their reunion.

"I had chosen you to be my boyfriend when I was young," she told Kinsami. "But when Gregory showed he had more power than you in our class lessons he became my new target. Yesterday, the girl I was finally trapped him."

"Sarah? How?" Surprise was an understatement for what Kinsami was feeling.

"I'll find out the answer to that riddle tonight. For now, why don't you join me? You would be a great asset to the group."

"Join you in what?"

"Bringing down Castle Eckhart and the remaining castles. They belittle and hide truths from us that could enhance all our lives."

"How do you know this?"

"We have watched from our prison. We have seen the evolution of this castle first hand."

"Forgive me for not believing you but right now your group is out murdering everyone I know," Kinsami said with a stern look.

"Not everyone, some are being taken captive. It doesn't matter if you believe me or not. You either die sooner when your cloak runs out of puff or you live a life alongside us."

Kinsami knew what she said would be the most possible eventuality and wasn't prepared to die just yet. Neither, did he want to lose honour by bowing to this girl's wishes. In the end, life won out.

"I'll join you," he stated. "But know this. I will not be killing anyone, I will act at all times with honour and should I get the chance I will take you down."

"Spoken like words from a movie," Sarah said clapping. "So scary. Drop your cloak if you dare and join me for a walk."

Kinsami had trouble trusting her but dropped the armour. He started walking to her but when he saw her walk back into the still raging rip in the air he hesitated. She turned and

102

gestured for him to follow. Cautiously, Kinsami approached the portal and reaching out with a hand put his fingers through. Sarah caught his hand and dragged him in. Kinsami instantly became numb. He had little left of the five major senses and was starting to fret.

"Oh stop that Kinsami. It doesn't become you. This is the hell we have lived in for the last few centuries. You'll adjust to it eventually, but you won't be here long enough."

Sarah drew in her Will and opened a window out onto the savage scene below. "Now where are you, you bastard?"

Gregory opened his eyes and reeled back from what he saw. He was lying on his stomach on a stone shelf. His arm and head were dangling over the side and the straight drop of hundreds of metres was not something he liked waking to. The shelf was small and there was no safe way on or off. He was lucky to have even landed where he did without falling to certain death.

He looked further out into the area below. In the dark of night, the flames that ate Eckhart castle were visible for miles around and this cut straight to Gregory's heart. He had caused this by ignoring the warnings of his friends. Could he think of them as friends? They probably didn't view him as such for the things he had said and done lately. He thought back over the means things, the pranks, the lies and the bullying. When did I become this person?

Gregory willed his physical form to change. He shimmered and twisted, dematerializing and becoming a breeze. A breeze Gregory could control, blowing straight back to the castle.

Swirling into the centre court yard he formed back into himself. All around him was chaos and death. Every broken piece of the castle was a chipped piece of his heart. Every mutilated body was a dying piece of his soul.

Gregory walked through the turmoil and listened to the screams of students he had shared the grounds with. His mind echoed the turmoil around him. He had no coherent thoughts as he floated through Eckhart. Where was the defence? Where were those who were fluent in the use of Will to fight back?

Where was his Grandfather?

Two students ran into the courtyard followed by five men and one woman Gregory had freed. They became trapped against a wall, crying and hysterical. After mere moments of being crowded in by the group of murderers, one student burst into flames. Their screams would haunt Gregory for a long time to come. The group stepped aside as the burning figure ran helplessly around the courtyard. Gregory stood transfixed watching with no ability to do anything for them. He was psychologically frozen.

The second student fell to his knees screaming at the death of their friend as one from the opposing group stepped forward.

"Let me drown him where he stands," he said to the others.

"No, you have killed far more than anyone else. Let me rip his insides apart organ by organ, tendon by tendon."

"And what makes you think you get to have so much fun. I could melt off an arm here, a leg there. Piece by agonising piece, I could melt him down over the next hour."

The boy was mouthing the word no over and over again while crying and shaking hysterically. He had soiled himself in fear of the torturous deaths that were on offer. He wished he was back home away from all of this.

"Step aside boys and let me show you how it's done," the girl in the group said. She turned her attention to the boy before her. "This will not be pleasant for you."

"Please don't do this," the boy squeaked.

"Now where's the fun in that?" She drew in the yellow she had been building and willed a deadly creation into existence. Dirt started swirling around the boy, forming a sphere solid and strong. It enclosed the boy completely leaving a crack in the front big enough to reach out an arm.

He had started screaming louder and was trying to reach out of the hole in the hopes of breaking free from this hollow, dirt sphere. Slowly the ball shrunk around the boy becoming tight to the skin but not crushing him. The girl started twisting her creation gently until she heard sickening cracks of bone. On each crack she would twist her creation in another direction. Soon, like a bag of popcorn popping in a microwave, the cracks were few and far between. The boy inside was silently screaming in a pain so unbearable he was almost blacking out. In the end, the girl drew her sand in over his mouth and nose suffocating him.

Dispersing the dirt she flung the body across the courtyard to land, by accident, at Gregory's feet. Gregory stared in horror at the mangled, bloody mess that had once represented a person. Fear crept into his whole body numbing his conscious thought. The group had watched the body fly through the air and their eyes brightened as they saw Gregory.

"Another one," one said. "This one's definitely mine. You pricks have had your fair share."

"Seems a bit of a small fry anyway so why not. You can take him."

The first started to draw in his colour getting ready to use his Will. At the point he felt he was ready he set his vision of pain into motion on Gregory. Gregory's body tightened in anticipation of what may occur but found nothing had happened. The man ahead of him tried again to get the same result.

"It's not working," the man said.

"You're probably just useless," said another. "My turn." He went through the same process as the first and again nothing happened. Gregory looked up at the group with tears in his eyes.

Suddenly a giant form appeared before him. With a burst of Will, the group toppled, holding their heads as waves of pain overcame them.

"We need to go," Mr Sir said turning to Gregory. Gregory didn't move but just slowly looked at him with empty eyes. Mr Sir shook him. "We need to move now! Get a hold of yourself."

Still nothing. Mr Sir picked Gregory up and flung him over his shoulder. He ran into the castle and down the hallways. Blocking the use of Will by the group terrorising the castle had been extremely difficult and he almost couldn't save Gregory.

Mr Sir had saved a handful of students already and was keeping them safe in his personal room on the castle grounds.

He had set the lift to only operate on his command. He could believe that Gregory lasted this long being an Empty but that lost, lifeless look in his eyes. Seeing the two students die must have crushed him. Gregory was dead weight and before long Mr Sir found he needed to rest. He escaped into an empty classroom and placed Gregory down gently, out of view. He too crashed down with a thud catching his breath.

Suddenly, Gregory seemed to come back to the conscious world. He was blinking rapidly and looking around trying to get his bearings. He didn't know how he got here or why the group doing so much destruction had let him live. Mr Sir reached over and grabbed him by the arm startling him.

"Gregory, are you..." He started but Gregory Flung his arm away and retreated back from him.

"Don't touch me you fat, disgusting bastard. You are a bloated mass of corruption and shit. I wish you would just go die!" Gregory's face suddenly went white. It was as if something deep inside him was resonating with the words he had just spoken but he couldn't capture the feeling. Echoes were bouncing around his mind. The same words but with different voices. His mind snapped under the pressure it felt and he fled out of the castle into the night.

Mr Sir was shocked by the words that came from Gregory's mouth. All his life he had known his faults and every time someone made fun of him it cut extremely deep. This fresh attack from Gregory so malevolent and painful was his last straw. Mr Sir could not find the enthusiasm or Will to get up again and stayed slumped against a desk. He stayed slumped as noises rumbled down the hallway outside. He stayed silent as figures entered the room. He gave up when everything went black. Life had been a cruel mistress.

Gregory didn't know where that explosion of words had come from. He'd been feeling deeply sad about what he had brought upon the castle. He was frightened and numb to the core but the words he said to Mr Sir came from a deeper place. Thinking back, Gregory remembered all the bad thoughts he had about the man, all the times he paid out on him to others

106

and then even to his face. The climax of his interactions with Mr Sir felt like it was needed but he didn't understand why. Gregory knew it had nothing to do with the man, rather, it was due to Gregory's own faults and hang-ups. Why did it ease his own faults to make fun of others?

Gregory let the trail of thought go and kept running not thinking of where he was running to. He rounded a corner and almost ran head first into one he had freed. The person rounded on him and started to build his colour. As Gregory had no need to build colour he used his Will instantly to rip the person apart and kept running even as a shower of blood stained the walls.

He found no other threat as he made his way over the castle grounds. The turmoil had dug deep into Eckhart and Gregory found he was now on the outskirts of the castle grounds. He found himself walking outside the walls close to the old oak tree and saw the tear in the sky. It was as strong and powerful as ever and was a physical representation of the tear he felt in his own soul.

He was readying his Will to force the portal closed and didn't want to cut corners. He pictured a rainbow of colours formed from the fundamental five as they mixed. He drew this into himself and readied his Will. Focusing on the rip and putting all his feeling in to see the rip close tight, he willed it so. The electricity surging around the outer edges of the rip glowed and surged with great intensity. Gregory had to shade his eyes against the light created.

"You made it too strong, Gregory," Dirk said with a cough. He was dirty and leaning to the left holding his side. "Have you found your old self yet?"

"I'm," Gregory couldn't find the words. He just shook his head and looked away.

"Welcome back," Dirk said putting a hand on his shoulder. He looked at the scar in the air. "We'll close it, Gregory. Don't worry about that."

"I threw everything at it just then," Gregory said in despair. "How can we close it?"

"We'll work it out, Gregory and then we can deal with the

freaks inside."

Gregory felt a weight on his back and a swirling in his stomach as he thought of the ferocity he had caused. He could feel the flames, see the destruction and crumbling buildings. He remembered the deaths he had witnessed caused by him. And Mr... Mr Sir. Gregory threw up.

The sun was warm and toasty this morning. It caressed the whole body burrowing its way deep into the muscle tissue. Lavi was completely relaxed lying on her stomach with her zipper down exposing her back. She hoped Dirk would return soon. He could give her a massage, and rub her feet. That would be nice. She was also getting sleepy with the warmth of the stone shelf below her and the fact she was sunbaking under the sun, which should be the moon. Where was he?

Lavi was getting restless waiting for her boy, she smiled. Getting to her feet, she zipped the red dress back up before pacing back and forward on the cliff side staring at the cave. She walked part of the way towards it then with a sigh walked back to the edge and sat down again. She tried to relax but couldn't find a comfortable way to sit or lie.

"Damn you, Dirk," she said and got up, walking to the cave entrance. Taking a deep breath she entered the dark hole in the wall and walked the glowing pathway. She took the time to take in more of the murals Dirk had created for her. She was deeply moved by all that he had done and it fed the flames of love that had already been growing within her. She was starting to feel that she had now been ruined for any other guy she may ever meet. Her feelings were too deep and too strong that she couldn't fight them any more than she could change her natural colour of Will.

Something itched within her nose. It was acrid and she sneezed from its body. How had smoke made it into the cave? Pulled from her daydreams of Dirk she heard the nightmare beyond. Screams started to filter into the cave and bounced around the walls. She could also see a glow at the end of the cave mouth that shouldn't be there. She knew immediately that this was the source of the smoke and ran to the entrance.

The scene outside was beyond her worst nightmares. Blood and bloated bodies scattered the fields. She could see flames higher than the walls themselves licking at the night sky. Lavi ran out into the fields following the curve of the walls until she saw the old oak. She stopped as the great tear came to view throwing lightning in every direction. She had never seen anything like this before but knew that whatever Gregory had done this was the result.

She saw a group of students run out from the castle walls with another group hot on their heels. The second group were yelling threats and hounding the first. They came to halt as the group of students they had been chasing suddenly disappeared into a new rip. It had opened right before them and looked like it was manipulated to engulf the students before closing again.

Dumbstruck the second group noticed two figures standing close by. They started chasing after them now and a new rip opened up behind the two. Lavi saw that it was Gregory and Dirk with the latter being dragged into the new rip by the prior. Another woman ran out of the original rip hurling fire at the two. She was angry.

"Dirk," Lavi found herself calling. Her words reached Dirk and he looked at her, his eyes terrified to see her there. He moved to the entrance of the rip again but it closed before he could exit. Dirk was gone from this realm. The angry woman turned and looked at her with a deadly glare.

Sarah stood in the realm she had spent the last few centuries in with a window open on the terror of Eckhart castle. She had focused it on a specific group of students that included herself. She knew that she could not change what already was but she could definitely find the person who trapped her and make them pay.

She didn't fear that Kinsami was left to his own devices behind her. He was a man ruled by honour and what was right. She was safe in the fact that he wouldn't attack a woman's back. He would face his opponent one on one and she knew that with the years of training she had endured in this realm he would be no match for her.

She watched her friends as they were when they were young. She even remembered the fear she felt back then as she fought back to back. They had relied on the colour fighters they used in their little brawls to fight for them while they made their escape. The all in fights they would hold on random nights were nothing compared to the true terror that a real life and death battle brought.

Knowing what she knew now it was not a true life and death battle, for those fighting wouldn't risk killing their younger selves. The paradox that would create was too much to think about. All they did was pretend to fight them and chase them through the campus. Sarah knew all the moves they would make and watched them make their way to the old oak tree just outside.

"This is it," she said getting up close to the window but pulling the view out to take in as much of the field as she could. "Come out, you bastard?"

She saw the two figures close by and immediately recognised Dirk and Gregory. Colour drained from Sarah's face as she realised what was about to happen. Gregory opened the rift that sent her to this hell. He then opened one behind himself to flee from his actions. The anger that built within Sarah was sudden and strong and caused Kinsami to take a step back. She raced out of the portal and with Gregory in her sights, she let fly fireballs of awesome strength. These passed through the empty air as the rip closed in on itself.

Turning around in frustration Sarah's eyes fell on Lavi standing across the field. Lowering a wicked gaze locked straight on her, she decided that Lavi was going to relieve her frustrations that Gregory thrust upon her. She approached the girl not once looking away. Lavi stood her ground and faced the girl that approached her.

"A red head in a red dress. How cliché. You've tarted yourself up tonight, Lavi. How many boys have you taken so far?"

"Sarah?" Lavi said recognising the girl. "What's going on? Why are you doing this?"

Sarah just laughed at the girl not bothering to answer the

110

questions thrown at her. She built up her colour and ripped the dress right from Lavi's frame. Lavi stood as she had when Gregory made her dorm room wall invisible. Now was not the time for modesty. Now was the time to fight.

"I knew you were a slut," Sarah commented.

"Fuck you."

The carnage below the cliff face echoed over the land. The fires that sprung up in the castles grounds lit the night sky. Baras stood watching the turmoil not making a single move to help those under his care. His face was neutral and he almost looked intrigued at how the night would turn out. In his hand was a phial that glowed a soft white glow. He was holding it forward facing the open top towards the castle. Small white lights would flutter up to the phial at random intervals entering the seemingly bottomless glass. The purple robed Adaman walked up behind him.

"Baras. Word reached me through the mirrors. I came as fast as I could." He looked at Castle Eckhart burning below then back to Baras. "What are you doing?"

"I am gathering the soul data of all those that have lost their lives to feed back into the Veritas Rerum," he said simply.

"You and that stupid device," Adaman said displeased with the answer he received. "You have an obligation to the students below. You need to help them, Baras. We don't have time to be playing with silly little fancies."

"I cannot do anything, Adaman. When I was younger and the castle was attacked, the Lord Baras I was to become didn't lift a finger to help the people of Eckhart. Therefore, I cannot lift a finger today," Baras replied cryptically.

"If you aren't going to help them than I shall," Adaman said with disgust. Adaman turned and made a move for the edge of the cliff. Baras grabbed his arm as he was about to fly down. Adaman looked at Baras's hand gripping his arm then straight at Baras. "Why?"

"If you go down there and happen to kill either one of my younger selves already there, you'll risk destroying time and space itself. I have worked too hard to get everything just right for this one event."

"How old are you?" Adaman asked as the true weight of his words sunk in.

Chapter 6

In the grey, lifeless realm, there was nothing. Mist blurred anything within a few metres ahead. The ground was shifting and reshaping itself as it was made of little substance other than grey ash and sand. No sounds proclaimed life and no movement caught at the corner of one's eye. In this emptiness, nothing could be found.

Dirk had fallen to his knees before the empty air previously holding the rift which metaphorically dragged him into this realm. Gregory did the literal dragging. Dirk reached out groping at the vacant space hoping he just couldn't see the portal but could still pass through. His heart sank as nothing happened.

Lavi had looked so scared as she had seen him escaping to this deserted land without her. He had rushed for the opening the moment he saw her standing just beyond the field. Dirk couldn't think of what must have occurred after the gateway closed, the thought was too much for his fragile state of mind. He couldn't bear to be alive in a life she was not in.

Dirk looked back at Gregory who was always at the edge of his field of view. He wanted to run. He wanted to look for an exit that would lead him back to Lavi and the world he had come to know but that was panic calling him. That was the whispers of hysteria and Dirk was smarter than to listen to these voices. He absolutely must stay with Gregory for he was the only one who could open a portal. If those that were trapped couldn't even escape after centuries, and there were a number of them with many different abilities, then what hope did he have? Gregory was his key. He walked over to where the boy sat.

"Leave me, Dirk," Gregory said softly. His eyes were red rimmed and he wiped an arm over his dribbling nose.

"No!" Dirk said with strength. "You have been sniffling and bitching and feeling sorry for yourself for what has felt like the last two hours. Since you ran away from your troubles you have been sitting like a little bitch blubbering everywhere believing that it will help you somehow."

"Dirk, just leave me alo..." Gregory started, throwing an arm back.

"No, I'm not done yet! You have stranded us here. Sure you may be selfish enough to waste away your years in this realm that mirrors your soul right now but I sure as hell am not ready to be stranded along with you. You have dragged me away from life, from Eckhart and from Lavi."

"She is dead by now," Gregory said his eyes remaining low. Dirk lifted Gregory by the collar and punched him in the face.

"You don't get to talk about her, Gregory. Especially, if you're going to say shit like that." Dirk's eyes were shimmering from the tears building. "I want you to return us, Gregory. I don't care if you wander off and die once we return. You can do what you want but you will return me. I won't spend my days in this lifeless world you have slithered off to because of your fuck up. Lavi is alive. I will find her and I will save her!" He was forceful in his delivery more to try and convince himself and to stay hopeful. She was a strong girl after all and he did not see her die. Gregory sat staring at the ground a little longer before he responded.

"Leave me, Dirk," he said. "Leave me alone! Leave me alone!"

Dirk grabbed him by the shirt and drew him up to his feet, slapping him hard across the face. Tears were falling from Dirk's eyes now and he was getting tired of Gregory's shit. He spun him around and pointed at the air.

"Open it now and I'll leave you alone," Dirk whispered with great intensity.

Gregory's shoulders slumped as he gave in. He gave focus to his Will and opened a rift before them. "Now leave me be, Dirk. You have your exit."

"Thank you, Gregory," Dirk said before throwing Gregory through the portal. Like he was going to leave such a useful asset before knowing where or what he was about to land in. Dirk walked forward and stepped through before the rift closed in on itself. He was looking forward to a bit of sun and warmth over the nothing he was currently experiencing. Dirk looked up and his heart dropped.

114

"What do you mean you haven't found him yet," Sarah was fuming. She had back handed the man she was talking to after hearing less than acceptable news. The man fell to the ground and scurried away. After Gregory's escape, she had done nothing more than look through a window of her own creation. One that could view anywhere in the world. She was searching for signs of him. Anything that would show an indication he had been there. She was watching his known hangouts including family residence and friends' homes. Nothing would stop her from seeking revenge for being caged in another realm. He did this to her.

Dirk, though, was a conundrum. Little was known about him save what they had known at Eckhart. This was little other than he had no ability with colour or Will and liked the girl Lavi. Sarah paused in thinking about Dirk momentarily, as she remembered the look on Lavi's face after she crushed her effortlessly outside the castle.

Maybe, Gregory was holed up at Dirk's house. It was a big world though and the net casters would search everywhere soon enough. They couldn't hide for much longer.

"It's a small planet, Sarah," Stuart said. "Unlike the endless space in the void, we have already scanned the planet numerous times with our nets. They just aren't here."

"They can't have just disappeared, Stuart," she almost yelled. "Look again and look for any anomalies that may be shielding them from the net-works. I want them found."

"We've already looked."

"Look again!"

Stuart just shook his head and walked out. He knew better than to argue with Sarah while she was in one of her moods.

"Go easy on them, Sarah," someone behind her said. He was dressed in a dark, hooded robe with shadows covering his face. "It's not going to achieve anything to push them to breaking point. We've just gotten free after all and pushing some of them may very well push them away. Their greed for the spoils of this world would be high at the moment."

"Then what do you suggest, Edward? Should we all go on a

holiday to the beach and forget the turmoil that we've been put through?"

"I'm not saying that, Sarah, and you know it. I want nothing more than to see that bastard suffer. Still, a day is a small gift to give for the group to adjust. Let them relieve themselves of all those pent up urges that they could only dream of before. Then, they will focus more on your one dream. We will find him. A day for him may just make him lax enough to come out in the open. Win-win and you lose nothing but one more of the tens of thousands of days we have already given."

Sarah pursed her lips as if agreeing would undo her. She was prideful and her next words were not easy to give up but the risk of losing a chance at making Gregory pay was too much to gamble.

"Make it so," she said in soft words.

"I thought you'd make the right choice when you realised what was at stake."

"You didn't give me much choice. I want Gregory blood eagled upon the centre cross of the great hall. He can be an unnaturally long lasting reminder to all who induce pain onto others that it will not be tolerated." Edward looked at her oddly but said nothing of the obvious hypocritical statement. "Anything that may risk this happening I will avoid."

"It's why you chose me for this position. We have the same wants and I am not as rash as you," Edward stated. Sarah gave him a dirty look but he just smiled. "What are we going to do about your guest?"

"Kinsami? He's no threat to us. I know that I've grown far stronger than he ever could. If he rises up I'll put him back down."

"Be careful with him, Sarah," Edward warned. "He is a man of honour and pride. If cornered he will strike out and he is not without ability. You yourself understood that the three who opposed him outside the rift were about to die."

"He is a snake in a house of tigers," she said dismissing the problem. "Venomous, yes, but he is no threat to my end goal. We just need to bring him deeper into the group of tigers until he believes he is one. If he bites he will bite with pride and honour leading his choices. It makes him predictable."

"I hope you don't come to regret these words," Edward told her.

Sarah just waved him away. He was becoming a nuisance.

"How shall we treat him?" Edward asked, gauging her annoyance

"He has free reign. Do not mock or pick a fight with him. As far as anyone is concerned he is one of us."

"And if he proves unworthy."

"Kill him," Sarah said, eyes becoming malicious.

"Your Will, Five."

Dirk's heart fluttered wildly as he looked to the sky above. He couldn't believe the incredible sight that was visible to him and how it shouted that he had not yet made it home. All around was greenery. There were grassy hills, shrubs, trees and flowers of incredible colours. A strong river ran through the heart of the land he'd found himself in and spewed out into the ocean almost as far as the horizon away. All of these landscapes told him he was home, that he could find the entrance into Eckhart castle and be reunited with Lavi again. Why did the sky have to tease him so?

In the heavens were both incredible beauty and unimaginable destruction. Three bodies... four bodies now made their home in the deep blue sky above. The sun shone as it always had, warm and bright. It could cheer any morbid day. The day time moon, out of sync with the night rotation, was three-quarters across the sky and half full. The night would be light when it recovers a more normal rotation.

What worried Dirk though were the twins. In the sky, a planet twice the size of the moon had cracked down the centre with each half moving away from the other. Flares of cosmic dust had curled and danced in circular motions from the central point of the explosion. One-half was mostly visible as if it wasn't missing the other, whereas the other laid bare the scar across its core. Large purple crystalline structures were scattered throughout its inner being.

This beautiful, enchanting chaos tore at Dirk's soul like

someone had sunk hooks into his skin and was dragging him away. The haze of the atmosphere gave it an ephemeral look and he almost let himself believe that this was home and that Gregory was playing a prank on him.

Where was Gregory? Dirk looked around and spotted him some distance away. He looked ragged as he moved closer to the water's edge. Dirk called out to him but Gregory ignored the call and at some undetermined point used his Will to erect a house of iron and steel. He locked himself inside melding the door back into the walls once it had achieved its purpose. Running over, Dirk started banging on the walls.

"Gregory, we aren't home yet," He called desperately. "We need to jump again." Dirk's pleas were met only with silence. He tried numerous more times but got nothing from the house. "I hope you rot in there, Gregory," Dirk finally said before giving up.

With an unknown landscape around him, Dirk thought it best that he explored the area. He couldn't be sure how long Gregory was going to be sulking and may need supplies to survive an ongoing stay. Also, he wanted to check surrounding areas for any danger that could be lurking in the shadows. An image of Lavi came to mind.

"I'm coming, Lavi," he said aloud. "Just hold on a little longer. With renewed determination, he took his bearings and walked into a woodland area close by. Here Dirk knew there would be dried twigs and logs to make a fire. This was going to be a necessity as he had spied no man-made structures other than Gregory's.

There was an eerie silence within the woods. No animal noises could be heard and even the rustling of the trees seemed muted. A soft mist hung under the canopy above. It stuck to Dirk and made him perspire at a greater rate than he normally would. He walked in as straight a line as he could and at every three trees dug his heel into the ground indicating a way back. Dirk was getting more and more concerned the deeper he walked. It wasn't just the lack of sound but also the lack of items to scavenge. He had yet to see one rotting trunk, one broken branch, one tiny twig. It was as if someone was

118

cleaning the forest as it shed its excess wood.

Dirk decided he had come far enough and turned to walk back. He started following the heel print pathway he had created. After he had passed the first two however the heel prints seemed to vanish. Dirk couldn't find another. He would move forward a few trees and finding flat undisturbed earth went back to his last mark to choose another direction. Dirk did this until he had nowhere new to go and was now terribly concerned. In his peripheral, he caught a movement ten metres back. He looked over but nothing could be seen.

"Gregory? Is that you?" He called. "Come out." Another movement in his peripheral. Dirk didn't look straight at the movement but could just make out a shadow half Gregory's size in the woods. "What are you doing?" Balls of light no bigger than his fist started to float out of the earth and the trees. They lifted up all around Dirk creating a magical quality in the woods. He reached out to touch one being mindful always of the shadow at the side of his sight. Dirk suddenly felt dizzy. He fought to stay upright but the forest floor seemed to drag him down to lie in the soft moss. Finally, he could keep his eyes open no more and fell into unconsciousness.

Dirk awoke with a start. He found that he was lying on a stone slab bed in a clearing surrounded by woods. His wrists and ankles were being held down by strong vines. All around him little creatures were leaping and dancing. Crimson in colour they were the height of Dirk's waist. They had a second reversed knee giving them a spring in the dancing. The creature's toes and fingers were just two taloned wedges on each appendage. Small wings curled and swayed as they played in the circle around the slab and a tail with a triangular end kept balance. Each face had its own form of ugly. The nose was squashed into the area between their yellow shimmering eyes. Lips that were pulled back barely hid hundreds of sharp fangs in each mouth. The sides of the head held massive ears. They looked like little demons but Dirk had learned a bit about mythical creatures and pinned these down to be Imps. Mischievous little bastards that were getting ready to eat.

Dirk let his eyes wander as he thought of what to do but was instantly struck with a new engulfing fear. One chunk of the planet that had split in half was in view above Dirk. He had seen the twins earlier and was unsettled by them but now with one twin covering almost a third of the sky, he feared it may soon collide with this planet causing great devastation.

Dirk struggled with the hand and feet restraints but couldn't budge them. He didn't have time to spend dealing with these imps and decided on a quick and direct approach. He started to picture colour and was taken aback when the yellow he wanted was filtering in as a brown sludge. He put it down to the world itself and the variations in the habitation. How then could he work his Will?

He didn't have long at that point as the imps felt the peculiarity of Dirk and immediately started baring fangs. Dirk thought it was comical that they chirped like a bird to show aggression. They started to move towards Dirk with wings spread. Dirk reacted without lateral thinking. He pictured himself glowing with yellow and willed this colour to break his bonds and give him flight. Subconsciously, Dirk realised the only substance from his home world was his own body. The colour he drew from it would be true.

Floating above the little devils Dirk saw the annoyance and frustration in their faces. One had tried to lift himself into the air with his wings but fell back hard. The wings, it seemed, were for show more than being usable. Others started to create the little floating balls that had caused Dirk to fall unconscious but something else caught their attention as they started to look from one to another. They suddenly dashed off into the woods and out of sight.

Where the woods had been quiet before chaos had taken hold. Birds took flight above the canopy and deer ran alongside wolves in a bid to escape some unforeseen force. The trees themselves were vibrating. Softly at first but soon they were seen to almost be swaying down to their very roots. Darkness grew over the land and Dirk looked up to see the half planet racing past just outside of this planet's atmosphere. He knew this wasn't going to be good and he flew above the canopy. Spotting the river they had landed beside, he flew to that point.

Dirk felt that he wasn't going to stay afloat indefinitely with little colour but he did what he could to use minimal amounts of yellow to stay up.

On the horizon, a haze started to grow and Dirk was having trouble working out what could be so big as to raise the horizon. Clarity of thought was soon to follow as he saw the shore line of the ocean. The shoreline that was now miles away from where he had seen it some unknown time earlier. His face was pale and he almost passed out from the overwhelming impending doom. The three-mile high wave was created by the gravity pull from the chunk of planet passing by and was now closing at an incredible rate.

Dirk's heart leapt as he spied Gregory taking in the scene before him. If he could reach the boy then they could jump to safety and hopefully home. Dirk called out to Gregory but he was out of range and the roar of the ever closing tsunami drowned out his voice as it still may drown him. Gregory spread his arms out and a rift opened on the ground before him. Dirk swore as he watched the boy jump in knowing that he was running away again. Putting the last of the colour he could draw behind himself, he used it to thrust forward in a great burst at the slowly closing hole.

The wave was towering high above Dirk but he was focused on the small hole which would lead to safety. Too late and he would have no colour to save himself. The leading water engulfed the rift as Dirk splashed through, passing into the portal as it closed. He found himself torpedoed into a new sky before gravity reversed him and he fell a short distance to the earth below. The rift, nowhere to be seen. Gregory, though, was standing before him.

"That was close," Gregory said down to Dirk before moving away. Dirk clenched his fists and stood eyes locked on Gregory's back.

There was a drip. *Ping... Ping... Ping...* It was rhythmic and consistent. It splashed against the rocks below and echoed throughout the room. Each droplets life was short and exhilarating. From the moment it clung to the ceiling, fearing to let go in anticipation of the freefall, to the moment it found itself speeding towards the floor, the droplet took in sight, sound, light, and feel. The joy of life as it came into existence was incredible and it tried to absorb everything. Finally, as it came upon its death the droplet gave out one last, long cry for life. The circle of life and death continued.

Lavi found the noise annoying. Day and night the insistent metronome continued to bug her. She believed without a doubt the droplets only reason for existence was to drive her crazy. Lavi curled up on the rocky floor of her cell trying to stay warm. She had been trapped behind these bars for the last three days since the attack, dressed only in the red underwear she had daydreamt about teasing Dirk with. She had bruises over her body and was weak from lack of substantial food.

The fight with Sarah had been surprising. She had her doubts about winning as the girl was skilled and flaunted her ability often around the castle grounds. Still, to be beaten so quickly and effortlessly was heartbreaking. The only consoling fact was that she didn't have all the facts. She knew Sarah to be a purple at a soul level, and the red she displayed efficiency in showed her strength. Lavi believed that was the extent of her power but when the Earth itself started punching into her she knew how wrong she had been. Sarah had opened her third colour and showed formidability in all three. A mistake she wouldn't make next time.

She looked around the dungeon at each inmate. The cells were made of bars alone so there was no privacy at all. By the look of everyone, no one actually cared. Each had had their spirit broken whether at the horror filled night in Eckhart or the abuse brought upon them by the invaders. Lavi had been the only one who had not been taken from her cell. She didn't know what had happened to the other inmates but she could guess. Some returned with torn and tattered clothes, others with bruises and fresh wounds.

Lavi then looked to the one guard in the room. He was dressed in a simple shirt and jeans and was resting on a chair seemingly asleep. Lavi wouldn't fall for that again though. The man was a spirit user adept not only at blocking the use of Will but directing it back at the user. She remembered the pain she felt as she'd tried to pry open the bars only to have that force directed back at her ribs. The force managed to crack two as she released her Will all the while screaming. A hand reached in behind her and touched her shoulder. She jumped from the warm sensation.

"How are you feeling," a girl whispered.

Lavi tried to talk and at first, her dry throat didn't allow her. She swallowed and tried again. "I'll get by," came her raspy voice.

Rolling over she looked at the girl who'd given her such sympathy. Lavi recognised her as Michelle, a red from the class above her. The girl had brown curly hair and a large black eye that corrupted her sparkling auburn eyes. She was smiling though there was great sadness in that smile. Michelle wore a dark full-length dress that'd seen better days. "What about yourself? Are you..." Lavi swallowed again. "Surviving?"

"Don't worry about me," she replied. "I'll take some down with me. Until then just try and stop me." Lavi nodded her understanding. "Have you thought of anything that could help us get out of here?" the girl asked hopeful.

"I have the makings of a plan," Lavi confessed. Having endured the torture the droplets gave her mind, she let her thoughts run wild with ideas. She had settled on one but couldn't do it alone. "I had been finalising an idea but until you talked to me I had thought it unachievable."

"Oh?" Michelle expressed wanting to know more. Lavi crawled over to the bars and kept her voice low.

"Well, I can..."

"Shh! The guards," Michelle said suddenly. The door to the room had opened and three men walked in. Like everyone, they were recognisable and this made Lavi sick as to why these students were acting so. They walked up to Lavi's cell door and grinned at her. Lavi knew that it was her turn to be taken, but to what? Torture or abuse? The door swung open and the men secured her, dragging her out of the cell. She'd tried to use her Will but understandably it had been blocked.

Please be torture.

Dirk's hand was sore. He hadn't held back when he gave Gregory a right hook. The boy lying before him had taken the hit with little reaction. Gregory fell back from the force but now just lay there with a blank expression upon his face. Dirk was going to give Gregory exactly what he needed and that was the cold hard truth.

"*That was close!*" he mimicked. "You gave no thought to me whatsoever. You only thought of yourself and what you wanted. You were running away again and you condemned me to death on a world far from home."

"You got through didn't you?" Gregory mumbled.

"You better not be about to start talking back to me, Gregory. You need to hear what I have to say so shut up. It was no thanks to you that I survived the dangers of the last world. You hid away to sulk. I was attacked by imps, found that I could not produce colour sufficiently and escaped both an earthquake and a tsunami. I watched you step from the stone shelter and, believing you would try to help someone you had once called a friend, had my hopes crushed as you ran away."

"At the castle as well, you changed under the influence of those who were bullies. You started to believe that to be popular meant you had to be like them. You started to crave it and your ability to see right from wrong was lost. I think that's why you sought us out. You asked for advice from a group of friends you trusted deep down yet upon hearing words that were not what you wanted you turned your back on us. You proceeded to kill almost everyone at Eckhart. Sure it wasn't by your hand but it may as well have been. You were selfish in your decisions and because you had no ability to think of anyone else on such a huge matter you destroyed so many people's lives... Ended so many people's lives."

"Yes it was me who caused the fall of Eckhart," Gregory had tears trailing down his face. His nose was dribbling. "I watched as students were killed in gruesome, horrifying ways and could do nothing to stop it."

"And so you should watch your creation play out," Dirk had no sympathy at this moment. "I hope that these memories stay with you all your life. You are a murderer, Gregory!"

"What do you want from me, Dirk? I can't bring back those that have died. I can't fix the destroyed castle. I can't take back the words I yelled at Mr Sir... I can't return Lavi to you."

At the mention of Lavi's name, Dirk grabbed the now kneeling Gregory by the throat, picked him up into the air and then drove him back into the ground. Dirk leaned in close to Gregory and looked him straight in the eye.

"Now you listen to me, Gregory, and you listen well. You can never speak of Lavi again. She is alive and I'm going to save her. Now, you have two choices. One, you can hide away and sulk for the rest of your life however short you choose it to be. Two, you find some shred of the boy I had met at Eckhart and we return to the castle to start to make amends and crush the invaders you so warmly welcomed. Either way, you are going to return me to Earth." Gregory shoved Dirk from him. He still had tears in his eyes as he got up.

"You can't push your wants and needs on me, Dirk. I've told you before to leave me alone and I mean it this time." Gregory didn't need to draw in colour as an Empty and willed himself to shimmer from view.

Dirk's expression was dark. "Fuck, Gregory!" He yelled at the air. "I'm giving you a chance at redemption. If you keep running away you'll never again pick up the life you've lost... Fuck!"

Dirk rammed his fist into the ground out of frustration and rage. He knew that this was still not home and was powerless to do anything. On the horizon in all directions was a great wall of wind that stretched into the heavens. It was slowly rotating as if it was a massive tornado a hundred miles wide and he was in the calm eye of the storm.

Thinking about the trouble he had on the last world Dirk built colour all around him. It was not the true yellow of home but it sparkled and looked promising. Having not raised his fist from the ground he focused his Will into the point of impact and let the power free. The ground compressed for a three-metre radius around himself into the earth a half metre. Exactly what he had willed to happen. At least this world acted like he needed it to.

Feeling vulnerable in the open and not knowing where Gregory could be, Dirk started walking. He didn't want to climb the hill behind him either and was hoping Gregory may be feeling the same. It was amazing how this world, and even the last, had resembled the world on which he called home. The grass was still green, the sky blue. A trail of ants distracted him for a moment. Fundamentally, they were similar in shape but instead sported blue and red stripes on their abdomen and thorax.

Dirk stepped over the marching line and continued on down his make believe path. He was starting to calm down and his mind was looking for answers to the situation. Could there be a yellow equivalent to jumping worlds? Possibly, but he didn't know the fundamentals enough to even try to pull off something like that. How was it Gregory even knew what he was doing as a blue? Maybe, that was why he kept landing in random worlds.

Dirk was so distracted by this line of thought he almost didn't see the monstrosity standing close by as he rounded a small rise. A beast the size of a lion was standing before him. The body matched a lion's in both muscle and colour. Large talons raked the ground before the beast, cutting deep into the dirt. Dirk trembled at the thought of those things digging into his flesh. That was however where the lion ended. Dirk found himself staring into the eyes of an eagle. It had a wickedly hooked beak and dark brown feathers down to its neck. Great wings curled out of its back and a feathered tail was swaying backwards and forward.

"A Gryphon!" Dirk said aloud. "Why do I keep running into mythical beasts?"

The Gryphon leapt into action closing the distance between them with incredible speed. It had let out a terrifying screech as it bounded forward on powerful legs. Dirk barely had enough time to gather any colour let alone think of a proper plan. He willed the beast to be pushed away with the earth itself. A pillar grew from the ground directly below the gryphon now only a metre away and raised it high into the air.

126

At the pinnacle of the rise, it was thrown up and over the side. Immediately, the gryphon spread its massive wings and started to circle Dirk more wearily. Dirk took this time to build ample amounts of his yellow lifeline. He produced a simple plan in his mind and then waited for the beast to approach. Moments seemed like hours as the Gryphon circled above. It didn't approach again, as if it was afraid of Dirk.

A shadow darkened the ground before Dirk and he instinctually leapt to his side rolling awkwardly. Another Gryphon, smaller than the first, had crept up behind him and pounced, missing Dirk with its razor sharp talons by a hair's breadth. Dirk put his plan into action using a small amount of his stored colour. Spiny pillars grew from the ground around the young Gryphon. Crisscrossing, the spines lanced the beast in multiple vital points. The beast immediately went limp.

From the air above came that same ear piercing screech. The first gryphon was streaking through the air with front talons extended to dig into Dirk. The dive gave it great speed and Dirk reacted instantly willing more spines to curve up into the air at the beast. As Dirk tried to pierce its flesh the gryphon twisted and turned seeming to manoeuvre around everything Dirk could throw at it. On it came. Dirk grew desperate.

Letting his Will free as his imagination ran wild, the ground became less solid. The earth spun around Dirk like a small twister growing in size and intensity. Suddenly, it burst onto a course straight for the approaching gryphon. Curling up and around the beast, giving no exit, the earth engulfed it completely. Dirk looked at the sphere of dirt in the sky holding a Gryphon at its heart. He reached his hand into the air and as if holding the ball he slowly squeezed his hand shut. The ball imploded in on itself to a shower of bloody mud. Dirk let the ball fall to the ground and looked around for any more threats.

Finding none he amped up the search for Gregory. No cutting corners this time. Dirk ran back to the hill and climbed the soft gradient. As he approached the peak he saw a now visible Gregory kneeling at the edge of a ledge looking out to the fields beyond. He was watching intently as something had caught his attention.

Gregory was running away and he knew it was true. He was a murderer. He did destroy the futures of so many people in one fateful night. He had bullied kids and played pranks on them. He was rude to people and at some point, he had grown to believe he was better than everyone else.

With all this being true he was still human, wasn't he? Was he not allowed to feel sorry for what he had done? Could he not try to change? Everything Dirk had said was true and Gregory was overwhelmed. He wasn't thinking when he ran away yet again. He could think of nothing more than to disappear and flee the word assault of Dirk. Gregory watched the path Dirk had chosen before heading in the opposite direction up a hill. His thoughts were stuck on the dreaded night of death and this weighed him down greatly.

Reaching the summit of the hill he looked out over the field and saw movement. Surveying the scene, Gregory forgot his troubles for a moment. Gregory was above a cave of some sort and there were four people organising fortifications. They looked like they were warriors. There were four very distinct weapons for the four people either slung to them or laying close by. One large brute carried a double winged battle axe, another younger male with brown hair and leather armour sported a spiked chain mace. The two women did not have any weapons on their body but in no way did they look defenceless. The red haired woman looked especially capable in her armour. Gregory guessed the lance resting against a rock was hers. Therefore, the beautifully crafted bow of yew must belong to the dark haired woman. In many ways, she reminded Gregory of Sarah. A painful point and Gregory avoided looking at her.

Suddenly, Gregory noticed the terrifying creatures as if they just appeared out of the air. They looked like lions except for some noticeable discrepancies. The heads were fierce lion heads with great manes of varying shades of black and brown. The body though had shaggy matted fur with spindly, hooved legs. The most disturbing body part was where the tail should be. Each and every beast had an emerald snake in its place curling and hissing as if it were alive and had a mind of its own.

They approached the four warriors and Gregory got ready to act. He wouldn't let anyone else die while he watched. He knew that the warriors would be able to take a few of the beasts with them but there were over twenty and that was far too many. The beasts got closer and Gregory was about to act when someone came up behind him, wrapped an arm under his chin and put him in a headlock.

"I've finally caught up with you," a familiar voice said. Gregory twisted his head a little and saw Dirk. "You're giving me nothing but trouble lately, Gregory."

"Release me quickly!" Gregory urged. "They're about to be slaughtered." Dirk released Gregory and took in the scene below. He could see Gregory tense as he was about to act but something odd caught his eye.

"Wait!" Dirk said quickly grabbing his arm.

"I can't wait, Dirk. Those beasts are closing in."

"No, look," Dirk said pointing to a girl with red hair at the lower edge of the scene. She was hugging one of the animals and nuzzling her face into its mane. The beast didn't react in a dangerous way. Gregory went white. He'd almost caused great harm again and why this time? Because the look of the beast scared him? Was that a good enough reason? He reacted by what he perceived was the truth from just looking at the beasts.

"They are chimeras," Dirk told Gregory. "A terrifying beast to look at but actually, they are herbivores. The goat side of them still can't digest meats. That doesn't mean they aren't dangerous but it looks like the people are at no risk."

"How could you know about them?"

"Though this may not be our world I am starting to believe that the beasts of myths and legends found in the history of our world come from here and other realms. I have come across Imps and Gryphon also. The latter is an extremely dangerous beast in this world so keep a lookout."

"They look like they are building fortifications for something."

"It's possible that there are others on this island and they may be in a feud of some sort."

"I can't believe I almost hurt them," Gregory said tearing up. "I've just been making mistake after mistake lately."

Dirk smiled. He saw some of Gregory's walls breakdown. He was finally starting to process things. "You weren't to know, Gregory. Chimeras are not a usual topic everyone studies. I only know because of a semester at my regular school where we studied mythical beasts of the world."

"Whether I knew or didn't know, wouldn't have made the act any less horrible. I was about to cause pain to the animals all because they looked dangerous. I didn't know what I was doing at the castle either and look how that turned out."

A screech echoed out over the plains and Dirk looked around the area for the beast he knew was to follow. Gregory saw the distress in Dirk's erratic eyes. He knew for sure this time that what was to come was definitely dangerous. An odd cloud like shape grew in the air. As it got closer the boys saw at least fifty Gryphon heading towards the cave, warriors and chimera.

The warriors reacted swiftly and gracefully pulling out weapons and shouting orders to the animals around them. They all moved into a defensive line with the dark haired woman notching an arrow to her bow. She drew back

"Still a bit far away for an arrow," Dirk said. Gregory felt a form of power coming from her. She loosed her arrow, and instead of arcing through the sky, it sped straight at one of the oncoming Gryphon.

"She's a Will user!" Gregory almost shouted before putting a hand to his mouth. Calming down a little he spoke more softly. "She propelled the arrow with Will."

Eight more times she let arrows fly and eight more times Gryphon dropped from the air. She ran out of time however as the beasts descended on the defenders. Straight away the battle was decided. Now it was just a matter of how long until the Gryphon slaughtered them all. Chimeras were picked up with the mighty strength of the gryphon, talons dug into their backs. The axeman downed two before being knocked back.

130

The man with the chained mace seemed to dance through the beasts swinging his mace in a hypnotising rhythm scoring hit after hit. The Gryphon, however, seemed immune to blunt force.

A scream came up from the red haired woman. Running in to protect a small Chimera, she now had a taloned paw through her chest. She was able to thrust the broken end of her lance into the Gryphon's eye and up into its brain. It fell upon her as she was lost to this world. Something triggered in Dirk upon seeing the woman's death and he jumped over the cliff face, flying towards the fight. He came to a halt mid-way, however, when great steel lances ten times the size of Dirk himself started to rain down on the fight piercing every remaining Gryphon. Everyone stopped where they were, looking back at the boy in mid-air and the other on the hill behind with arms raised.

Chapter 7

"Is it really okay for me to be alive?" Kinsami hadn't been able to find the calm in meditation he once knew. There was turmoil in his soul and he could not shake it. It was shame of life. His acquaintances, teachers, and staff at Eckhart castle were all slain and he sold out for the chance to live. Was that how it was? He told himself that he was going to take any chance he could to take down Sarah and the rest of the group but he was doubting himself. Sarah had turned her back to him and he didn't move. Sarah had been vulnerable and he didn't take the chance. Was he afraid of her? He was honourable enough to admit that this was true.

"Father. Mother. I am sorry. I have brought dishonour to the Otoma name," he said to the heavens. "I promise on pain of death and everlasting torment that I will make amends for this dishonour." Kinsami got up and willed the candles around him to fade out. There was light enough in the room with two hours before sunset and he was comfortable. Sarah hadn't mistreated him and made sure everyone knew he was under her command. He was given back his own dorm room at Eckhart with all his belongings. They were not his anymore though. They were Sarah's.

He moved to his door. Will there be guards? He didn't quite trust that he was free to be himself in this castle, which had now become a prison. He looked back at the window as a second option. If there were guards at the door would it not be correct to assume they would be watching his window also. Scared again, he thought. What's the worst they could do? Throw him back in the room?

Kinsami raised his head, steadied himself and walked out confidently into an empty hallway. This brought on annoyance. Did they not think him a threat at all that they would let him loose upon the castle grounds? If that's how it is Kinsami decided that he would walk right up to Sarah and demand what her plans for the future. He knew the people that had invaded, had gone to classes with them, trained with them. He knew the type of people they were and what they were capable

132

of. No one would be able to stop him.

This is what he proceeded to do. He knew that Sarah had holed herself up in the tower of Lord Baras. Was he honourable enough to be called Lord? No. He didn't try to help anyone in his own castle. He was not a Lord that Kinsami recognised. The shortest route to the tower was through the central yards, into the main hall and through the staff access stairwells in the back. As Kinsami walked out into the light, the warmth of the sun fell across skin that hadn't felt it in a few days.

He looked around and was amazed that the Castle had been repaired almost to its original state. The fires in his memories were extinguished. The broken walls and caved in roofs rebuilt. The dead did not litter the pathways as they had when they were slain, fleeing for their lives. A predicament Kinsami could've been in had he not bargained for his own. He realised he dishonoured not only his families name but each and every person that had died here. This weighed heavy on him and he sent an apology to the heavens, to all those who perished. Would they speak kindly of him to the maker as they passed on by? Surely not. He knew he would have sins to atone for. This, though, would be for another time in, he believed, a not too distant future.

Kinsami continued into the Great hall and out the back. He found the staff stairwells and tried the door... Locked. Kinsami focused on the door melting down through immense heat. He willed this so with the red and watched it take form. The metal door started to glow a deep red before wavering and folding over on its centre. Slowly, it spread across the floor to take on the form of a puddle. Next, he drew out the heat from the metal using his Will. This solidified the puddle to a form that Kinsami could walk across. He continued up the stairs that led to the tower of Baras.

"Halt," a man on guard said. "State your business."

"Fitz, I'm here to see Sarah," Kinsami told the yellow from another class. "You will let me through or suffer." Fitz smiled but said nothing as he opened the door and walked in ahead of Kinsami.

"Hey Five, you have a visitor." Sarah looked over and upon seeing Kinsami nodded. Fitz walked back out to stand before the door.

"Five?" Kinsami questioned. "I'd come here to speak to you assuming you lead this lot. If you are only fifth in charge I shan't waste my words on you."

"It is more a nickname than a rank," Sarah said smiling. "I'm in charge so speak your piece." Kinsami thought a moment. He knew why he was here but hadn't thought of the words he would speak at this point. He wasn't prepared so a direct approach was all he had.

"What are you doing here, Sarah?" He asked

"I am taking down the Castle system," Sarah replied simply.

"Is that all? You're going to come in here, destroy the castles and then leave? There must be more to it than that so forgive me if I don't believe you."

"There is," she admitted. "I'm also going to track down Gregory and make the end of his life excruciatingly painful. Other than that I will be living my life as I see fit."

"I look at you and I see the girl I knew only days ago. I can see you have changed but deep inside you're still the conniving, scheming girl I knew to distrust. You will have plans for '*living as you see fit*' and they won't be pretty."

"I think I should be offended but I am that girl. Don't get me wrong, I have lived for centuries beyond this realm already. I'll correct that which I see is wrong. This being the Castle system. And I'll correct that which wronged me. This being Gregory. Other than this I want to enjoy life. I was scheming for an easy carefree life and after countless years in a realm of nothing, I want this even more. I'm not a bad person at heart."

"Would a good person kill countless students and teachers without remorse or care?"

"Would a good person stand by and watch." Kinsami's face hardened. "Don't preach to me with your tainted heart. I have seen far more than you could ever know and am set on my course."

"Why would you tell me your plans?" Kinsami asked

"Because you're going to help me."

"You are nothing, Sarah. I will help you do nothing," Kinsami laughed aloud. Sarah smiled and brought all her Will to existence. It was not threatening or powerful but immediately the colour drained from Kinsami's face and he backed away two steps.

It was not torture.

The shell of a girl once vibrant and full of life lay curled up in the corner of her cage. Dirty, tattered rags now covered her abused body. Fresh bruises spotted her skin and red, raw sores ringed her ankles, wrists and neck where she had fought against the leather restraints holding her down. She fought three putrid masses of blood, skin and bone in the shape of humans, who took turns to smother and pierce her.

In those terrible moments, she was stripped of her life. Her joy was sucked away. Her love, laughter, purity, innocence and future were all ripped out and shredded. In their place, a darkness was forced in. Nightmares and day terrors, pain and hatred were all the husk of this girl now held. The world was now shadows and darkness.

Michelle was concerned for the red head as she had not moved for four hours. Moving over to the bars beside Lavi, she reached in smoothing the tangled locks. Immediately, Lavi backed away, screaming with visions of abuse. The guard looked over at the girl and chuckled softly. Michelle shot him a glare but he just levelled his eyes back at her, daring her to try something.

It took a full ten minutes for Lavi to calm down and she sat with a glazed look in her eyes. Though she occupied the space, Michelle could see that she wasn't there. She tried calling out to Lavi but couldn't get through to her. Michelle felt for her. She could see the abuse forced upon her and the physical and mental torment it still produced. Michelle felt ashamed that she only had to endure the torture. Her father was a close friend to the Lords and Ladies of the castles and they had tried to get non-existent information from her. They had hit her and burned her, drowned her and whipped her but she couldn't talk about what she didn't know. In the end, they dumped her back in her cage and she had been healing herself softly with Will so the guard didn't notice. Building her strength with the yellow she had spent years trying to wield properly. Red was her true colour. Now she was finally fresh and ready to move ahead on getting out. All she needed was Lavi and her plan.

"Lavi, please don't leave me," she said through the bars. "I need you now more than ever."

"It looks like your little friend has abandoned you," the guard said laughing. "You should give up hope too."

"Fuck off, Vincent!"

Vincent's expression hardened and he sent a burst of purple Will at her designed to cause excruciating pain throughout the body without physically harming the victim. Michelle doubled over, her mouth stuck in a silent scream.

"You really piss me off, Michelle," Vincent told her. "You always walked around with a high and mighty look on your face like you owned the castle. You need to realise that things have now changed. You need to treat me with respect or you can expect more of this." Vincent released the pain hold he had on Michelle. The girl sat gasping in great gulps of air as she could finally breathe again. She looked up at the bastard before her.

"What? You got something to say?" Michelle just looked away. "I didn't think so. Know your fucking place and we won't have any trou..."

Before he could finish his sentence, a great burst of air blew Vincent across the room and he hit the wall hard. A sickening crack could be heard on impact. Michelle looked from the still form of Vincent to the other inmates. Some were lost in their own thoughts and the rest looked just as shocked as Michelle was. She then looked back at Lavi. The red head had raised herself on one arm with the other outstretched. She had a deadly look on her face and was breathing heavily.

"Lavi!" Michelle was impressed and saw that she had given them the opening they needed to escape. She used her Will to heat and then twist the cage door open before moving to Lavi's cage. "Let's get out of here."

"Wait, don't leave us," another voice further in called out. "I don't have the strength to focus my Will."

Michelle looked over and twisted open the door to her cage and all other captives. Struggling to her feet, Lavi moved towards her own twisting door on unsteady legs. As she got to the opening she saw Michelle's eyes roll into the back of her head as she fell limp to the ground.

"Dumb bitch, do you think Vincent was the only guard positioned in this room," it was the girl that called out for help. She had physically struck Michelle on the back of the head. Bringing her Will to existence, she forced Lavi and the other captives back into their cages and reformed the doors. Lavi tried to bring her Will to existence on the girl but she found like before it was being blocked. The girl picked up Michelle with inhuman ease and threw her into her cage. Walking over to Vincent she booted him in the gut bringing out a cough from the man.

"Well at least you aren't dead," she said unsympathetically. "How could you let them get the better of you?" He didn't respond as he had lapsed back into unconsciousness. "Pathetic." The girl walked over to where Vincent usually sat and took his place.

Lavi's burst of resistance had faded, replaced by images of her abuse and the harshness of her reality. A great depression filled every fibre of her being and she broke down once more.

"I'm sorry Dirk," she sobbed as she knew she would be forever tainted. Would he still love her? She looked over at a rock close by and judged the sharpness of its edge. Her eyes glanced to her wrists.

"Now what do we do?"

"Now, we go say hello," Gregory told Dirk. Gregory willed himself to take the form of wind and floated down to the fighters and Chimera below. Dirk couldn't see Gregory but had an understanding of what he was doing. He too floated down to a point a few metres from where the fighters stood with Gregory, materialising next to him. A number of Chimera moved in front of the fighters and growled low to warn the newcomers to behave.

"If we wanted to harm you, we would have done so from the cliffs or at the very least allow the," Gregory hesitated looking for the correct name.

"Gryphon," Dirk supplied. Gregory nodded.

"Gryphon to continue their assault." The Chimera settled down a little and looked back to the human fighters.

"What do you want here?" The strong axe wielder walked forward to stand before the boys. Gregory could see the man was ageing but an aura of strength enveloped him. Gregory got the sense that should he say the wrong word the man would not hesitate to cut him down.

"We are travellers not of this land. We have become waylaid and albeit lost," Dirk shot Gregory a look. Gregory was happy that Dirk took over the conversation but a new kind of uncomfortable came over him at Dirk's remark. "On our way home. It was by chance that we happened across your group. My friend here conjured the lances that destroyed the Gryphon."

The man looked the newcomers over with suspicion. He had many questions for them but that was going to have to wait. One of their own had lost her life. His daughter in law and now was not the time for questions.

"There are a few things that I want to ask you but I am not in the mood right now. Don't get me wrong, I thank you for the help but I have a funeral to prepare. Wait for me in the cave."

It was not technically a command but the boys found they didn't want to disobey. Dirk looked over at the red head woman and emotions swelled within him. Thoughts of Lavi ran through his mind and tears came to his eyes.

"What was her name," he asked. Moved by the sentiment for someone he did not know the man told him.

"Her name is Karis... And mine is Mote." With that, he turned and walked back to where his kin lay. The Chimera had ringed her and the other two fighters were cleaning and preparing her body for a pyre.

The boys retreated to the cave. From the moment they entered it sloped softly away into the earth. At even intervals, there were torches in brackets upon the walls lighting the path

138

ahead. Gregory and Dirk both decided it was best to stay close to the entrance of the cave.

"Are you okay?" Gregory asked. "You seemed upset a moment ago."

"Yeah. The girl, Karis, made me think of terrible things that could be happening to Lavi. I don't think I could take it if Lavi was gone."

"I'm sorry, Dirk," Gregory said placing a hand on Dirk's shoulder. "For what I have said and done and for the situation we are in."

"I know you are, Gregory. You've been apologising ever since the night at the castle but this is the first time it truly sounded sincere and that you had the feelings to back it up," Dirk looked into Gregory's eyes. "You have nothing to be sorry about. Not to me anyway. We all make mistakes and I will forgive anyone that honestly sought forgiveness."

The boys sat in silence watching the funeral preparations not knowing what to say to the other. Outside the Chimeras would race off and drag back large logs and chunks of wood. The three warriors would then collect the wood and place it on a growing pile. The wood pile took the form of a large rectangular funeral pyre. At one point the dark haired woman walked into the cave towards a pale yellow sheet.

"What colour is your coin?" Gregory asked her. Gregory felt a surge of power from the woman and before he knew it a knife blade was lodged in the cave wall beside his head. His eyes were wide with shock as he looked from blade to woman.

"If you mean to mug me you would have an easier time getting coin from a horde of Gryphon," she didn't wait for a reply but picked up the sheet and walked out to Karis's body. She slowly wrapped the girl.

"I, I didn't mean..." Gregory was left mouthing nothings like a fish.

"This is not our world, Gregory," Dirk said. "You can't expect them to know what you're talking about."

"I guess that's true. I was just curious after I felt her use the power of her Will to accelerate the arrows."

"I couldn't feel anything," Dirk admitted. "Speaking of

which, how do I put this? What colour is your coin, Gregory?" Gregory's expression showed he was caught off guard by the question and he tried to lock down his face.

"I have shown you my coin," he said quickly. "It was blue remember."

"Invisibility, conjuring lances, water manipulation, portals, becoming the wind itself. Have I missed anything? How do you get all that from the blue?"

"I unlocked the green with Sarah..."

"We are far from home, Gregory. No one is going to know what you say in this cave. I should have proven you can at least trust me.

"Okay," Gregory submitted.

Dirk's eyes narrowed. So there was something Gregory was hiding. Gregory reached into his pocket and pulled his hand out, fingers gripping something. Slowly he opened his fist. Dirk was confused for a moment as the lack of natural light made it look like nothing was there. As his eyes adjusted he started to see the outlines of a coin deprived of any colour.

"What is this, Gregory? There's no colour in that coin."

"Mr... I'm sure it was touched on once or twice in class," Gregory replied looking a little sad. He still had trouble bringing up Mr Sir after the terrible things he said. "I have little knowledge of it myself only finding out about the use of Will days before you. From what I am told I am an Empty. Someone deprived of colour... No, not deprived. Someone that doesn't belong to any given colour."

"So what does that mean in regards to the use of Will?"

"Because I don't have a true colour I can use any form or mixture of colour I wish. On the flip side of that, I can use Will at a moment's notice without gathering colour."

"That's unbelievable. How many people are like you? And why are you hiding it? You could have really shown the kids at school with Mr Sir's silly little tests. Well, I guess you did," Dirk laughed. "You did far better than me at least."

"The emergence of an Empty is about once every thousand years or so. It is a rare event. My granddad told me about it and asked that I keep it secret. Lavi and Kinsami also know as

140

they were at the entrance exam with me and witnessed it firsthand. They too were sworn to secrecy on pain of expulsion. Speaking of the tests though you did far better than you think in the classes."

"In what way? I could barely even lift a rock."

"Mr...' Gregory hesitated when speaking of Mr Sir again. "Your ability was being suppressed." Dirk accepted what Gregory told him but noted the hesitation.

"You can speak his name, Gregory. I'm sure that whatever you had said he would forgive you for."

"I spoke to him cruelly about his weight. I told him that I wished he would die," Gregory said holding back tears. "Everything I had done to him. It was never about him but me. I wanted to be popular. I wanted to feel better than everyone. I wanted to feel higher than everyone. It was like if I was hurting him and others my worries were non-existent. In the end, I was the reason he gave up."

"I didn't know. But remember that feeling. If anyone ever tries to lay you low, know they are only running from themselves. It's not about you. You need never take it to heart."

Gregory felt a little better in himself though it still pained him to think about Mr Sir. At that moment they heard Mote cursing. The boys ran out towards them.

"What's wrong? Are the Gryphon back?"

"No boy," Mote retorted. "Damn wood won't catch. It's too fresh."

"Would you allow me to light it?" Gregory asked.

"Be my guest if you think you can."

Gregory nodded and without waiting any longer produced a blue flame of extreme heat floating above his upturned palm.

"What are you?" The brown haired mace wielder asked. "You destroyed the Gryphon like they were nothing and you can produce real flame from air."

"I'm just a boy far from home," Gregory told them. "Is there anything you would like to say?

"First light the wood. As the flame takes hold we shall say our prayer," the dark haired woman told him. Gregory placed the ball of fire into the base of the pyre and flames instantly caught, growing to engulf each tier. From equal points around the pyre, the three warriors took up their prayer.

> Lockpick guide our sister's soul,
> Her quest has now ended,
> Her life is now whole.

> Lockpick take her to your heart,
> She fought for the righteous,
> She gave all to the last.

> Lockpick throw her the grandest of feasts,
> She was loved in this world,
> Her life shall be missed.

> Lockpick now let her rest in peace,
> With her brothers and sisters,
> Who long since have ceased.

> Peace dear sister at your journey's end.

"You can be with Terinath now," Mote said. "Look after my son."

Gregory and Dirk watched on from the cave entrance. They didn't want to interrupt the funeral proceedings and waited patiently for the warriors to finish. Dirk was thinking about Lavi and how he might be able to get home to her again.

"How lost are we, Gregory?" Dirk asked the other boy. A worried look crossed Gregory's face.

"I don't know exactly," he admitted. "I'm not quite sure what I'm doing when we jump between worlds. I don't even use colour. I just do."

"I thought as much. Is there something that you think of when you jump?"

"Not particularly. I just have an idea of where I want to be and open the portal to make the jump."

"So you have a picture of earth in your head and you just go there. I think the problem may be the vagueness of the picture.

142

As you can see each world is relatively the same. Grass, trees, rocks, water. You may need to think of somewhere very specific. Make it somewhere you are familiar with, not including Eckhart. We don't want to be landing in the middle of enemy territory just yet. I think if you focus on a specific place you'll get the result you want."

"That sounds as promising as any other theory," Gregory said. "I'll give it a go next time we jump and hopefully it'll be the last time we need to look for Earth."

Dirk nodded and the boys lapsed into silence again. They watched the flames burn low until there was a glowing pile of embers remaining. The three warriors had remained standing where they were for the duration of the fire, with the Chimeras lying in a ring around the pyre. Gregory had thought that this was a grand way to honour the dead.

In this time the sun had set and was now rising again on the eastern horizon. The brilliance of a sun rise on earth was not echoed here though. The sun was but a hazy light behind the wall of swirling air. It would be hours before they'd see the sun break over the top. The three warriors, almost in unison, all turned and walked over to the cave with two chimeras in tow.

"I think it is time you told us who you really are," Mote said. "Amara here thinks you may be bandits trying to mug us. I believe that is unlikely. Golenath went so far as to suggest you may be Gods. I would like to hear the truth from you."

"What we said before was true," Gregory stated. "If only a fraction of the truth."

"Then what is the full truth? Your answer will determine whether we build more pyres or not."

"It may be no less than we deserve but I'll tell you our story," Gregory ran through the events leading up to this point. He told them about the admittance to the castle, the voices of those trapped, the use of Will, the night of terror and the boys jumping between realms. The three warriors remained silent over the course of the story, their faces emotionless.

"We asked for the truth and you insult us with children's tales," Mote said. His face was showing annoyance at the boys. "Magic is a fantasy."

"When Gregory asked what colour your coin was before," Dirk said to the dark haired Amara. "He had recognised the power within you and was only curious about the colour you fell under. Was he wrong in his assumptions?"

"I do not know about colours and coins," Amara replied. Gregory's eyes narrowed and Dirk grew worried. "But you are correct that I have the power." Mote turned to her stunned. Amara met his eyes. "It is something my tribe has kept secret or did you believe that my long range bowmanship was pure skill. I don't believe anyone can make an arrow curve in mid-flight."

"Did you know about this?" Mote asked Golenath. Golenath simply nodded.

"We are followers after all," he said. "We know each other inside out."

"Followers?" Dirk questioned.

"In our army, the greatest warriors in a respective weapon are given the title of Prince or Princess," Amara told the boys. "We are then paired to another as followers. I am the follower of Golenath. Golenath of me." The boys nodded that they understood.

"Mote," a deep rumbling voice said. "Do not forget that we of the Chimera can perform acts similar to what these boys have described, sending fellow Chimera across great distances. It is not a hard concept to grasp."

"What the actual fuck!" the boys said in staggered unison. Dirk continued. "Did that Chimera just talk?"

"Yes, we do have that ability," the Chimera told them. The boys just stood staring. "A small feat to what you're claiming."

"This is true," Dirk conceded laughing.

"Ok, so you roughly believe us?" Gregory started but Mote cut in.

"We never said that," Mote interjected.

Gregory just raised his hand to hush the large man. "You are processing what we have told you and we have accepted some truths from your side. Where does that leave us now?"

"If what you have said is true than you may be able to help us," Amara told them.

144

"In what way?" Dirk asked.

"We are actually stuck on this island at the moment. Mote and Karis took a one-way road to rescue us but we are just as stuck now due to the wall of wind you see around us. The Chimera could send us home but most attempts on past Chimera have left them brain damaged. If you can open the path home we would be in your debt." Gregory was about to object when Dirk grabbed his arm.

"We've had difficulties with freeing people who are in similar situations to you. Gregory mentioned the night of terror. He is still reeling from that mistake. How can we trust that you don't mean to harm anyone on the mainland?"

"We mean to harm plenty of people on the mainland," Mote told them. The boys' expressions hardened. "We're at war. Our capital is not far from being laid siege to. Our armies are at a disadvantage without their Princes and Princesses. If you can view it for yourselves then do so."

Gregory and Dirk looked at each other. Gregory was trying to think of a way to view other areas in a world he did not know the location of. If he opened a portal, how would he know that what he saw on the other side was of this world or another?

"How do you think we can do this, Dirk?" Gregory asked the other boy. Dirk thought for a moment.

"Think of cartoons you may have watched as a child. There was always some evil villain watching the good guys through a magic mirror or the like."

"Yes but if I open the field of view, will it be this world I'm looking at?"

"A good point but bring it back a little. Open the scene above our position. We can determine if it is us or not by whether what we do is mirrored in the scene we are watching."

"That'll work," Gregory agreed. He decided to act a bit more towards the dramatic. He swirled his arms around as if he was using some mystic arts and smiled a little as Mote took a step back. The ground started to dampen as pools of water were drawn to the surface. Ripples ran across the water and droplets started to pull away floating into the air. The droplets swirled

145

upwards, coming together before Gregory in a round, concave disk. Gregory then drew away the heat from the water freezing the floating disk and creating a mirror like surface. Dirk put palm to face and shook his head at the extravagance.

"Oh, power locked within my soul bring forth a...' Gregory was getting carried away and Dirk cut him off.

"Seriously, Gregory, let's not be show-offs," Dirk told him. Gregory pouted a little and willed an image of the world above their location to form on the mirror. Dirk danced around a little and confirmed that it was indeed them.

"That's definitely something," Golenath said walking up behind him. "That would be a useful trick in this war."

"That it would," agreed Dirk. "But we are fighting our own war at the moment and cannot give up too much time to this world."

"Pity," was all Golenath said about that. "If you move the image over mid mainland close by and then a little south you should see the war being fought." Gregory did so and found a town under siege from a large army. The defenders looked like they were in trouble. A blonde woman on the battlements was shouting orders as she repelled some attackers.

"Hey Mote," Amara said. "Looks like Shana's already made the battle and is in the thick of it."

"Of course she is. I couldn't have held her back if I wanted to."

"There is truth in that," Golenath said.

"Boy," Mote directed the comment at Golenath. "I know you are in a relationship with her but she will always be the one in charge."

Golenath just smiled. "By the looks of things they need our help sooner rather than later. Will you help us be free of this island now?"

Gregory looked over at Dirk who shrugged and nodded back at him. "How close do you want to be?" Gregory asked.

"What do you mean? We want to get off this island."

"I can place you at any given point. You decide and I'll put you there."

"Show me the area of the battle," Amara asked. She watched

the scene in the mirror and then pointed to a spot. "Right here."

"That is outside the wall, in the middle of a battle, you know?"

"I know," Amara said confidently. "Can you put us there?" Gregory didn't answer but put his Will into action. He split the air close by and the scene of a battle could be seen on the other side.

"Step through and you'll be there," he told the warriors.

"That simple?" Golenath asked.

Gregory nodded and the three warriors gave their thanks to the boys. They said their goodbyes to the chimera and collected their weapons before stepping through.

"Close the portal and the mirror," Dirk said.

"Why the mirror also?" Gregory asked.

"If something was to happen to any of them I'm sure you'll start blaming yourself again and right now we don't need that." Gregory accepted the answer and dispelled his Will.

"Shall we go then?" Gregory asked.

"I think so," Dirk replied. "Think of somewhere on our Earth you have a strong affiliation to and open a portal there." Gregory did just that and on the other side of the portal he could see his Grandpa's attic where he first used his Will.

"Well it's been fun," Dirk told the Chimera. "Should we ever get through our battles we may come back and visit you."

"You will be honoured guests," one Chimera said in a growling voice. Gregory just nodded to the beast and the boys stepped through the portal.

Chapter 8

The room was silent as Kinsami sat in contemplation. He had been incredibly stupid. To believe a girl that was now hundreds of years old was still only as strong as the girl he knew in her mid-teens was a massive oversight. She did not even attempt to attack him when she brought her Will to existence in the tower but Kinsami knew he was greatly outmatched. He did not even believe what she could do was possible. The fear he felt towards her was now justified.

She had continued to tell him about the castles and the hold they had over the population of Will users. She informed him of a barrier that enveloped the castle, the grounds and the fields beyond. A barrier that seeped into every crevice within. It filtered into the minds of all who were on the grounds and it changed them. The barrier acted as a mind control on the students, slowly changing them over the years that they spent in training. The lords and ladies only graduated students when they felt the control on them was complete. They would only need to focus their Will and the student would obey no matter the silent command.

Sarah had told him all this and Kinsami was having trouble believing it to be true. He still didn't trust her yet and didn't want to believe that the castles he had unwaveringly looked up to as a child could have such a dark secret. He didn't believe that they took away free will but Sarah gave him trigger tests. She told him that the first and easiest thing to implant into a student was to never go against the castles, starting with the Lord and Lady towers. In the case of Eckhart, this was Baras's tower where Sarah currently resided. Sarah told him that all he needed to do was try to destroy the tower and he would find that it was almost impossible to even hit it.

Even now he was deciding whether or not he would try the tests. If he did would this mean that he believed Sarah? If he didn't, would he be living a naïve life that was partly not his own anymore? The latter annoyed him more than giving into Sarah. Well, he had already given in to her through fear and submission. And anyway, what's the worst that could happen?

He might blow up the tower with Sarah inside. It wouldn't be that bad with what she had planned.

Kinsami decided to try it and made his way out to the central courtyard. This area was open and gave him a good view of the tower above. In one of the windows, he saw the figure of a person and immediately recognised them as Sarah. She had come to gloat. Kinsami instantly wanted to prove to her he couldn't be controlled and willed a large ball of molten lava straight at her. The coming impact though did not happen as expected. The cliff face forty-five degrees to the right burst open in a shower of rocks and debris as the lava ball hit.

Kinsami slowed himself down. He told himself that it was the heat of the moment and he didn't give himself time to aim properly. He brought his hands in front of himself, fingers curled as if holding a ball. He put his Will to work and a fireball started to grow in the confines of his fingers. It was strong and radiated enough heat to melt straight through the tower. Kinsami directed his aim towards the tower and without moving his hands in anyway willed the fireball forward. It shot off with great speed flying straight at the tower.

"This time I have you," Kinsami proclaimed. He watched the fireball makes its way towards the tower but at twenty metres it started to slow and lose size. Just before it connected with the wall it fizzled out completely. Kinsami started to grow nervous. The first time he rationalised that he misjudged his aim due to impatience. The second was right on the money. Had he not put enough power in the Fireball? This was unlikely but he wasn't completely sure. If this was the case the next question was did he do it subconsciously?

He decided that he would try again not taking any chances this time. Kinsami willed two massive tendrils of hardened magma to rise from the ground. They were lucid enough to twist and turn but kept their form much like two octopus tentacles. He weaved them up into the air almost to the height of the tower itself and then turned them inwards. The sharp, pointed end was facing the building and Kinsami drew his hands together indicating for the tendrils to pierce the building. They didn't come close to touching the tower walls.

As they came inward, they curved around the wall and moved away on the opposite side.

This confirmed it in Kinsami's mind and he grew angry. Time and again he tried to force the tendrils to puncture the side of the tower and time and again they missed. With a massive scream of frustration, Kinsami tried one last time, his sole focus on completing the task. The tendrils connected gouging great marks across the stony surface. He stood there breathing heavily but the small triumph made him happy. He was looking straight at Sarah.

Sarah stood looking out the tower window at Kinsami as he tried desperately to destroy the castle. She could see his belief in the system crumbling with every attack and she knew she had him. A tremor ran up the building as Kinsami connected and this only made her happier. He will be a strong piece in the upcoming battles. She knew he would not harm anyone that did not deserve it but he would still fight on the right side. She returned his glare up until the moment he moved towards the tower.

"Are the preparations ready for the assault," Sarah asked Edward.

"Yes, Five. Everything is in order and we are ready to move out," he replied.

"Good. Kinsami is on his way up. Allow him entry. He needs to be caught up on the mission."

"Are you sure that's wise. He's still technically of the old way. I don't want to see him jeopardize all our work."

"He needs to be there. I have plans for him." At that moment a woman walked in marching straight for Sarah and Edward. She inclined her head to Sarah waiting to be granted permission to talk. Sarah nodded.

"They've returned," she said.

Sarah's eyes widened and she almost hissed in reply. "Where?"

"They have suddenly appeared at Baras's country farm," she looked ill at ease about something.

She was thinking about the moment Malcolm found them.

150

They had been scouring the Earth for days on end seeking signs of Gregory and Dirk when finally Malcolm let out a shout of glee. Everyone looked at him and were instantly envious. Sarah would reward him generously.

Moments later the look of joy left his face leaving him deathly pale. Tahlia looked at his viewing window and saw two yellow eyes looking straight back at them. Fear gripped her heart in cold hard talons and she shouted at Malcolm to shut it down. Tahlia tried to shake the memory of those demonic eyes but they were always there when she closed her own.

"What is it?" Edward asked.

"I haven't seen the likes of it. One moment they were nowhere to be found and the next they were out in the open as if they weren't trying to hide at all."

"They jumped! Gregory is an Empty after all and he did send us into the grey realm," Edward said realising the simplicity of the events surrounding Gregory.

"That would explain why we couldn't find them," Sarah said. "They haven't even been in this realm. We've been looking in the wrong spot."

"So what does that mean for us?"

"There is no change. Either little to no time has passed and he still wouldn't have processed what has happened or he has been trapped in the grey realm as we had and may be sympathetic to our cause," Edward raised an eyebrow at her. A wicked smile crept across Sarah's face and she looked at Tahlia. "Either way, we still kill him. Tahlia, get Vincent out of the dungeons and go kill him... and the boy, Dirk, too," she added as an afterthought.

"Your will, Five."

As she walked out Kinsami walked in. Tahlia shot him a wink and proceeded down to the dungeons. Kinsami paid no heed to the gesture and moved to where Edward and Sarah stood.

"So what have you found Kinsami?" Sarah asked, her expression blank. "Did the tower put up a fight?"

"There is truth in what you say," he admitted after a moment's silence. "But I would like to be one hundred percent sure of the accusations before I commit one way or the other."

"That's reasonable," Sarah said. "It's not like we're at the top of the list of people you trust at the moment."

"No," Kinsami was shaking his head. "You are resting comfortably at the bottom, Sarah."

Sarah laughed long and loud. "See, this is what I like about you, Kinsami. You are always so honest with people. How would you like to join us in a raid on Castle Bodhurst?"

Kinsami baulked at the offer. "I'm not going to join your little gang running around killing everyone," Kinsami said with outright anger crossing his face.

"Heavens forbid no," Sarah said laughing again. "You can join me like you did on our last assault. Like you, I don't like to get my hands dirty either."

"There is nothing that'll clean your hands, Sarah."

"My dear Kinsami," she said moving closer and patting him on the cheek. "Warm soapy water washes everything away."

Kinsami took a step back knocking her hand away. Edward swung his arm out and with the use of Will backhanded Kinsami from three metres away. Kinsami got a surprise but composed himself and ignored Edward.

"Kinsami, you just finished telling me how you wanted to make sure what I told you was fact. What better way than to view firsthand the effects of the mind control."

"And what shall I be viewing?"

"The students, one and all, defending the castle with their lives. Baras is a coward and for whatever reason didn't fight us at Castle Eckhart. Lord Adaman and Lady Sylvia are a different matter entirely."

"Why would the students risk their lives? Surely they would've heard the fate of Eckhart and flee."

"Ah, you see, that is the fun part. They cannot run or cower in a dark corner. The intensity of the mind control is far higher than that of Eckhart. They'll be forced to fight and we'll be forced to defend ourselves."

"Kill, you mean?"

"Kill," Sarah rolled the word over her tongue. "I have always liked the way that word tasted. So direct. So final. No Kinsami,

I do mean defend ourselves, though there will be a lot of death."

"The way I see it you have two choices," Edward said. Sarah glanced at him. "You can either, come and try to stop us or come and find out the truth once and for all. For one your honour would not allow you to stay back and two your pride would want nothing more."

Kinsami glared at the man that read him too well. "When do we leave?" he asked.

"As soon as we step out the door," Sarah said in delight.

The point of the stone shard hovered above her wrist. Small red marks and minor cuts were evidence of failed attempts to end her life. With tears in her eyes, she gathered her courage to try again. Slowly she lowered the blade to touch her skin. Goosebumps ran up her arm at the touch knowing that pain was to follow. She took a deep breath as the edge of the stone blade bit into her skin and she flinched at the pain, bringing forth another failed attempt. She bashed the stone blade into the ground in frustration and burst into tears.

Michelle watched her friend with deep sympathies. She'd tried to talk to Lavi but couldn't get through to her. All she could do was watch as she tried time and again to take her own life, and with great sadness, she could see Lavi was getting closer to the end. Michelle had a splitting headache where the guard Emma struck her. How could she be so stupid? No. If she couldn't show compassion for those that were stuck in the same situation then she was no better than those that had captured her.

She looked at Emma sitting next to a now conscious Vincent. She had the typical blonde hair and blue eyes but her features were harsh. The boys had not seen her as pretty by any means. In fact, she had very little friends at Eckhart. It was a surprise that she ended up in Sarah's circle at all. It wasn't a surprise, however, that the bullying she received for her features in school scarred her deeply and gave her a well of hatred to fuel her mean streak.

The door to the dungeon opened and another girl entered.

Different to Emma, Michelle knew this one to be a bitch. She recognised Tahlia instantly from her class and was in no way surprised that this girl was here. Michelle remembered her to be a strong green and an adequate red user. Skills far beyond her year.

"I'm going to need to borrow Vincent," Tahlia said to Emma. "Gregory and the other one have turned up. Five wants me to take him along for the kill."

"Are you sure you want to take him? The little princess in there," she said pointing at Lavi. "Was able to take him out in her run down condition." Tahlia looked as though she was judging him.

"The girl took me by surprise while I was dealing with another." Vincent said defensively.

"More like flirting with another girl," Emma said. "Unlike us blondies, I know you like the brunettes and Michelle is right up there, isn't she? I've heard you speak her name once or twice in your sleep."

"That's just sick," Michelle's voice exploded from her cell. "He would have better luck with a goat."

"Shut the fuck up," Emma snapped at Michelle, who shut her mouth. "I don't want to hear that screeching, and anyway, the goat would have to have brown fur." Both Emma and Tahlia started laughing. Vincent shot them a deadly look.

"You spoke of Gregory and Dirk?" Lavi's attention was brought to the conversation at the mention of Dirk's name.

"The little rats have resurfaced at Baras's house," Tahlia told Vincent while ignoring Lavi. "We're going to take a trip out to the farm and kill them while everyone else is raiding Bodhurst."

"What! Everyone is going to Bodhurst today? I'm not coming with you," Vincent objected

"Vincent, you can take that up with Five. If two little girls can take you down, Sarah will kill you." Vincent mumbled under his breath. "Incoherent little squeaks won't help. Now get up and follow me."

Tahlia didn't wait for him and left the room. Vincent sat defiantly for a moment longer before better judgement made him move. He moved with speed after Tahlia.

Lavi sat contemplating what she should do. She looked down at the sharp stone in her hand. A trickle of blood was drying on the edge. "Damn you, Dirk," she said throwing the blade aside. Michelle caught the movement and slide over to the bars between them.

"So what's the plan," Michelle whispered to the red head. "She didn't want Emma to hear the conversation.

"Just be ready," was the reply. Michelle wasn't sure what she was to be ready for. There was nothing that they could do behind these bars. Emma would still block any attempt to use Will. What was she planning?

"What are you two whispering about? Emma asked.

"I didn't realise you wanted to hear our screeching voices. Which is it?" Emma glared at Michelle.

"Just keep to yourselves," Emma said. "Or I'll make sure the pain you have felt up until now will be felt again fivefold."

"What does your coin look like Emma?" Both Michelle and Emma turned to look at Lavi.

"Far better than yours," she replied. What's it to you?"

"I just thought if you spent all that time in the other realm it may have affected your coin like it has affected your soul."

Emma extended her arm, fist clenched. She opened it before the girls. In the palm of her hand was a vibrant purple coin with little espers floating from it. She looked pleased with herself and from the amazed look on Michelle's face, she had reason to. The strong colour showed she was tuned into the colour of her soul at a high level. Lavi made sure to keep how impressed she was from showing in anyway, feigning indifference.

"Nothing special," Lavi said, superiority dripping from her voice. Michelle couldn't comprehend what Lavi hoped to gain from this.

"If you think this is *nothing special* show me yours then," Emma said. Her annoyance with Lavi and her disrespect was rising.

"I don't think so. It is for lesser people to go around flaunting their coins. You really don't want to see mine anyway."

"I demand you show me your coin," Emma said walking up to the cage and reaching in with an open palm.

Lavi concealed a smile of triumph. "Are you sure you're *ready*?"

Emma just shook her outstretched hand in impatience. Michelle caught Lavi's signal. Lavi focused for her coin to materialise in her closed fist. As she stretched out her arm to place the coin in Emma's hand, Michelle noticed that Lavi's knuckles were bone white, as if she was fighting to keep the coin in her hand. Michelle didn't know what was going to be revealed, but she knew this was the moment she had to be ready for.

Lavi opened her hand and the coin dropped into Emma's. It looked as though Emma was about to say something but didn't get the chance. The room exploded with a burst of air. Michelle was a couple of metres away but the force this coin produced was unbelievable. Her mind screaming it was the production of Will, Michelle knew that couldn't be the case as Emma would have felt it and stopped it instantly.

Standing at the epicentre of the force, Emma was hit hard. She was sent flying across the room. Bouncing off the roof, she landed awkwardly on a chair made of solid rock. Lavi stood calmly and drew her coin back into herself. The gale force winds died instantly. Emma tried to rise but Michelle leapt into action destroying her cage door and running over to boot the wounded girl in the head. Emma slumped to the floor.

Lavi willed her own door to blow outwards and she walked over to Michelle who was squatting down next to Emma. Michelle had a hand placed on Emma's temple. Moments later Emma's eyes opened with intense pain. She started screaming and flailing about holding her head.

"What'd you do?" Lavi asked raising her voice over the screams.

"I placed a small fire in her brain. It won't burn her flesh but she'll feel the heat from it for the rest of her miserable life."

"Take it out!"

"What? She's done far worse to us and others. She deserves

what she gets."

"A harsh life made her this way and it's not up to us to torment her further. Either kill her or leave her unconscious. Regardless, take that thing out or I'll put her down myself." Michelle just stared defiantly at Lavi not making a move. Lavi waved her hand setting her Will in motion. A sickening crack came from Emma as her skull imploded through the manipulation of pressure. Her screams stopped instantly.

"We will not torture anyone. We are better than that," Lavi told her. She turned to the other inmates. "Anyone who wishes to leave now is the time." Looking down, Lavi saw the rags that covered her body. She pictured a weave of wind in her mind that would form baggy pants and a long sleeve shirt two sizes too big. The colours were a mixture of whites, greens and blues. She willed the clothes to cling to her body only to be released on her command or her death. With that Lavi left the room. Michelle glanced back at Emma's body before following.

The girls started moving through the castle halls, glancing around, and clinging to, the walls. They didn't want to run into anyone, but as they moved further through the castle they realised there was no one within the grounds.

"Where do you think everyone is?" Lavi asked Michelle. "This is creeping me out and putting me on edge."

"They were talking about raiding Castle Bodhurst down in the dungeon. Maybe they've already left."

"Could we be so lucky?"

"Probably not. What should we do now? I don't want to be here when they return and we are in no condition to travel."

"I have a place we can go," Lavi said. "But it's a private, special place for myself."

"Lavi, if it can help us I would be very grateful if you would share this place with me."

"I don't know if I should," she said in two minds. Dirk had found this place and only showed her. She did not want to sully the memories they had created by inviting someone else to their special place.

"What's holding you back?"

'...Dirk."

Michelle knew instantly what she meant. "He took you there, didn't he? It's both yours and his special place?" Lavi nodded. "You know that no matter what I could never steal what you had with him. It may feel that way now but you'll see the memories and feelings that belong to that place will stay with you always."

"Well, okay," Lavi gave in. She didn't say anymore but started moving to the main entrance. Michelle wondered where this place could be that they had visited outside the walls. Lavi lead them around the outer wall and right to where the cave entrance was. Realising no one had been around to close the cave, Lavi found the dark tunnel open before her.

"Has this always been here?" Michelle asked.

"Usually, the cave is closed but Dirk found it and opened it," Lavi looked up at the sun. "Still plenty of night time left."

"Girl you've been locked up to long."

"Just follow me." Lavi led the way into the cave. She didn't expect the phosphorescent glow to still be bright but as she walked through the tunnel the images and words of love Dirk put around the cave started to come to life as if reacting to her presence. Emotions running high, Lavi allowed but a single tear to roll down her face before locking away her feelings. She marched on through at pace. Michelle kept up with Lavi but took the time to take in all the designs and artworks across the cave walls.

"You truly are lucky," Michelle whispered if only to herself. The girls continued along the tunnel and out onto the cliff face. Michelle was in wonder at the moon sitting in the night sky above the ocean. Mystified by this oddity she completely missed that Lavi had stopped, and bumped into her. She looked forward as to the reason for this sudden halt and noticed an old man standing before them wearing a deep blue robe.

"Lord Baras!"

"Welcome, Lavi, Michelle," he said inclining his head towards the girls. "We have a lot to talk about."

A shiver ran up Gregory's spine as he stepped out of the rift into the attic. He had the feeling he was being watched. Looking around he could see no one.

"Allen! Grandpa!" Gregory called and waited. Nothing stirred. "It's me, Gregory." Still nothing. It was strange to him that this feeling was still present from when they had stepped across the portal so he decided to put his Will to use. He didn't know the mechanics of it and nor did he need to. He focused on following the feeling back to the point of origin with his eyes. Upon releasing his Will, his vision speed across a great distance in a matter of moments. When the haze left him he was looking into a room with four, maybe five, people. The closest one was looking straight back at him with a ghostly complexion. Good, they can see me. With this in mind, Gregory gave them one of the meanest looks he could think of.

"They know we've returned, Dirk," Gregory told the other boy. Dirk looked disappointed.

"I had expected at least a couple of hours before they realised where we were. That could have helped us come up with a plan and possibly implement it."

"Nothing we can do now except jump out again?" Dirk just shot him a nasty look. "At least I know how to work it now."

"So what do you think?" Dirk asked changing the subject. He didn't want to be off this Earth again just as much as he wanted Gregory to face his demons.

"You want to save Lavi and we have the castle to take back. There are bound to be other survivors as well. Eckhart needs to be our goal."

"That's all well and good but how do we get there from here? I wouldn't know where to look," Dirk admitted.

"If the doorway in Mandaloo Museum is still functional then we could get through there."

"Again, I wouldn't know where to look. Some old guy in a red pickup drove me from my home straight to the castle gates. The geography was impossible on the course we took though, so that won't work."

"That sounds like my Grandpa," Gregory said with a chuckle. "He is the Lord of Castle Eckhart."

"I don't believe I have ever actually heard that about you,

Gregory."

"Don't start saying *that must be why you're strong Gregory*. Everyone seems to think that's the case. That's why I don't talk about it much."

"Don't worry, I wasn't," Dirk assured him. "There would've been plenty of Lords and Ladies with less than adequate children. You are only what life gives you and the way you use these gifts."

Gregory nodded. A movement caught his eye behind some boxes. A tuft of brown hair was bobbing around just within vision. Gregory looked to Dirk and put a finger to his lips. *Allen,* he mouthed and Dirk smiled.

"These gifts that life has given to me. What do you think they coul...' Gregory was walking as he talked. When he was opposite Allen at the boxes he pounced and dragged him into the open. Allen was kicking and screaming and making such a big fuss about it.

"Allen, calm down," Gregory said to his younger brother. "It's me. Gregory."

"You're not Gregory!" Allen almost shouted. "Gregory has blue eyes. Not yellow." Gregory was shocked. He'd forgotten his eye change was even happening.

"The shift has been gradual since you told us about your eyes changing in the library," Dirk said. "I didn't think twice about it and now I'm used to seeing these yellow eyes."

"Allen it is me. I just got my eyes changed while I was gone. Like a tattoo," he was still trying to struggle out of Gregory's grip. "Do you remember when we ventured into the attic last time? You were so scared you ran off not even halfway in."

"I was not," Allen protested.

"That was just before we went down to Mandaloo and into the Museum. In the same museum, we stepped through a painting and yelled at candles. After the museum I left home for a while," Allen turned and looked up at him. "And look at you now. A whole foot taller and fearless when entering the attic. Even when there are two men you don't know inside," Gregory knelt down by his little brother and looked him in the eyes. "I am Gregory. I am your brother."

160

Gregory saw Allen's walls crumble along with his face. Allen hugged his brother and sobbed.

"I've missed you, Gregory," he said. Gregory patted him on the back consoling him.

At that moment a noise came from the front door. The door was being opened slowly, trying to keep the noise down but the squeak was there no matter what you did. Gregory, Allen and their Grandpa always opened it fast. Not Grandpa then.

"That's no one we know," Gregory said. Dirk was on the defensive instantly. Gregory pulled Allen back from him. "There are some bad people after us, Allen," he told his brother. Allen became worried. "It'll be ok but they may have turned up at the house. Stay up here, me and Dirk will take care of them okay?" Allen nodded his acknowledgement. Gregory turned and made for the opening in the attic floor. Dirk stepped in behind allowing Gregory to lead the way.

"When it happens it'll be quick," Dirk said at the entrance. "Either we find them and take them down or they do so to us." Gregory thought for a moment.

"How do you feel about playing decoy?" Gregory asked.

"I have played bait enough over the last few days. One more time won't hurt." Gregory explained the layout of the house and the area he should find them. Dirk nodded and started walking while Gregory went off in a different direction. Dirk didn't take the time to look at the photos in the hallway or peer into the rooms as he passed. He had a destination and a time limit and he was sticking to it.

Time passed and Dirk was coming to the stairs. If he got down the stairs he would be safe. He started to tread gently on each step, placing his foot as close to the wall as possible. Having read a number of crime novels, Dirk learned the quietest way to walk on stairs was using the outer edges. Half way down he thought he heard movement in a room beyond but nothing eventuated.

Moving faster, Dirk made the base step and almost instantly his body became constricted. He started to twist into a compressed form and found he couldn't breathe. Vincent stepped out from behind a wall and looked like he was manipulating Dirk with his hands through Will.

Gregory was waiting for this moment and from the corner of the upper balcony, he willed an invisible yet infinitely heavy object on top of Vincent. Nothing could be seen apart from a wafer thin blood stain spread out on the ground where he once stood. Dirk fell to his hands and knees gasping for air. His body was aching but otherwise was unharmed.

"Next time you get to be the bait," Dirk said over his shoulder.

"I'm not that stupid," Gregory said with a laugh before he grew serious again. "Keep your voice down. There may be more."

"Let's hope they underestimated us," Dirk said finally able to get to his feet. He saw a flash of movement down the hall in the kitchen. They heard the door creak open and slam shut as someone ran outside. The boys gave chase.

Outside they saw a blonde figure running away, though as they were about to give chase she jumped into the air and started to fly. She had such great speed on her that Dirk expected any moment she would break through the sound barrier. He didn't have the skill to catch her.

Gregory reached out with his Will, like a massive arm, and grabbed the girl by the ankle, slamming her into the ground.

"Or you could just do that," Dirk commented.

"As opposed to?"

"Doesn't matter."

The boys ran over to the girl and Gregory recognised her as Tahlia. She stood out in the all-in brawls he was introduced to the night before Castle Eckhart was attacked. If she was so strong then why was she running? She started to come back to hazy consciousness, and as she recognised the boys her eyes opened wide and she backed away.

"Please I don't want to die," she said. Gregory and Dirk were shocked and appalled.

"You say you don't want to die but you are happy to take the lives of so many students at the castle," Dirk said.

"It's not like that. I had no choice with the castle."

"You mean with Sarah?" Gregory asked. "You would blame

162

that terrible night on your leader?"

"Sarah is a completely different matter and if I wasn't already forced to do such atrocities she may well have forced us. No, Gregory, the reason that I had no choice was because of what I witnessed as a child of your age."

"What do you mean?" Dirk asked. "You are our age."

"Don't forget she was forced to live hundreds of years in the grey realm. That's the reason I was freeing them in the first place."

"A place you put us, Gregory!" She said with such malice. Gregory looked at her questioning her meaning. Dirk realised straight away.

"Those students you saved on the night we fled. You opened a portal to get them away from the fighting at the same time you opened another for us. With your lack of understanding how the portals worked and the fact we ended up in that grey, lifeless world, isn't it safe to say so did they?"

Gregory's face went white at the implications. Not only did he free the group that caused such terror and ended so many lives, it was he who sent them there in the first place.

"I... I never meant to. I mean, I was trying to save you," Gregory didn't know what he could say to Tahlia.

"Forget it," she said. "I'm all the more stronger for it." Gregory had lost his voice.

"You were explaining why you were forced to attack Eckhart," Dirk said seeing his friend's dilemma. He wanted the conversation to flow and Gregory and Tahlia had issues.

"Do you know what a time paradox is?" Both boys nodded. "Good, I landed in the grey realm because of an attack on Castle Eckhart and Gregory's choice to *save* us. In time those that I was with determined that we were the ones who had attacked that night. We were faced with a simple yet terrible choice. Attack Castle Eckhart knowing our fate or try to save our younger selves by foregoing the attack. The downside being this would create a paradox, the result of which could not be determined. Possibly time itself would cease to exist. You know the choice we made."

"Great, you saved time," Gregory said sarcastically. "You're still following Sarah and she hasn't got any grand plans. She sent you out to kill us, did she not?"

"Don't get me wrong, Gregory," Tahlia replied. "She is working towards freeing Will users from the grips of the castles but everyone that was trapped wants you dead. We are happy to take time out of what we are doing to achieve this."

"So you do want me dead," Gregory said. Tahlia suddenly realised her predicament. "So what should we do with you then?"

"I have information you want. Let me live and you can have it."

"What kind of information?"

"Sarah," Tahlia said after a moment. "She uses the Lords tower as her base of operations."

"We could guess that much," Gregory replied shaking his head. "Not good enough."

"There is going to be a raid today on Castle Bodhurst," Tahlia said starting to get worried.

"You have already told us that was Sarah's plan though not in as many words," Dirk told her. He thought to push her a little to get something good. "I don't know, Gregory. Maybe we should just kill her now."

"Lavi!" She suddenly blurted out desperate to give them what they wanted. Dirk turned to look her in the eyes. She noted her desperation bore fruit. "I knew she would be something you'd want to know about."

"Tell me," Dirk said getting up close. Gregory felt her Will building. He instantly brought forward ice spears that floated before her face. Gregory was glad at the effect it had as the build-up of Will disappeared instantly. Dirk was none the wiser to why Gregory had acted.

"Threaten my friend again and I really will kill you," Gregory said. "Now, do you know anything about Lavi or are you just buying time?"

"Promise me that you won't kill me as soon as I tell you," she said.

"Of course. You tell me what you know and you have my word you won't be killed," Dirk reassured her. He didn't care what Gregory thought about this small selfish act but he needed to know about Lavi.

"Lavi is alive," Tahlia told him. This was a big relief for Dirk and he found he had been holding his breath waiting for the answer. He wasn't prepared for what he heard next. "She has been mistreated by some in the group, as many of the captives had and she is feeling sore and sorry for herself. Last I saw she had marks on her wrists suggesting she was trying to kill herself."

"Now you die," Gregory said. He started spinning the ice spears around Tahlia who now had tears in her eyes.

"Please no," she cried. "You promised, Dirk."

"I didn't," Gregory tensed to strike but a hand rested on his shoulder.

"I did, Gregory," Dirk told him. He had snapped out of his shock just in time. "Even if I have to fight you, she has done me a service and deserves that at least."

"She came here to kill me," Gregory said. "I can't just let that go."

"We were ordered to kill both of you," Tahlia wasn't thinking. She had the idea that if Gregory thought it wasn't just him, he may be more sympathetic. She realised too late she may turn Dirk against her also and looked at him.

"She is my responsibility now, Gregory. She won't die by our hand today," Dirk said. He could tell Gregory was more than just a little annoyed.

"That brings us back full circle. What do we do with her then?"

"Can you put her to sleep for a month?" Dirk asked. "That would give us enough time to take down Sarah, her crew, and right all the wrongs that have happened."

"Wait! That's not something..." Tahlia started but Gregory clicked his fingers mid-sentence. She fell asleep instantly.

"Must be a purple ability to put people to sleep," Gregory said.

"Okay, we've sorted out the invaders and have the start of a plan. Go to some museum and get to Castle Eckhart."

"You better take her inside and lay her on my bed, Dirk. She

165

is your responsibility after all."

Dirk nodded and picked Tahlia up in his arms. She was lighter than her figure hinted. Dirk liked the feel of her in his arms and immediately thought of Lavi. This was the first thing he wanted to do when he saw her. He would hold her forever if the world allowed. Carrying Tahlia through the house, Dirk found Gregory's room after a false start in Allen's. He placed her on the white flannelette sheet and covered her with a baby blue blanket. Dirk walked back out and found Gregory. He was talking to Allen about what was to happen and Allen looked worried.

"You'll need to stay behind to look after the girl," Gregory told his brother. "She'll need to be bathed from time to time, fed and protected from harm."

"What!" Allen jumped. "I don't want to see her... Outside her clothes." He wasn't worried about looking after someone or being left on his own, but put a naked girl in front of him and he freaks out.

Gregory was laughing. "Don't worry," he assured his little brother. "I was joking. The girl will remain asleep but she will continue to eat and clean herself throughout her stay as if sleepwalking. You won't even know she is here."

"Okay," Allen finally said.

Gregory embraced his brother before turning and walking away. He waved at Dirk to follow. "Ready, Dirk? We're going to need to fly."

"Ready when you are," Dirk replied. The boys ran outside and took off into the air. Gregory in the lead keeping them in the direction of Mandaloo.

As he looked into the mirror he noted the large pimple forming on his chin. His parents had told him to stay away from the sweet foods but now that he was away from home he was having a hard time following their rules. The pimple was his punishment. He studied the rest of his face. Not the greatest looking or strongest boy around, he wasn't the worst either and he was happy with that. He kept his blonde hair long and shaggy and hadn't started to shave evident by a small growth of whiskers leaving his face untidy. He didn't mind. The glacial blue eyes were what attracted the girls and he used them every chance he got.

Castle Bodhurst had been a God send to him. Life at home was getting him down with the constant rules and curfews. He was expected to keep himself clean and tidy. He had chores to do and his parents even threatened him with getting a job and paying board. He didn't believe it would eventuate with the exams coming up but it was possible. When he passed the exams and was allowed entrance to Castle Bodhurst he was ecstatic. He wished that his parents had stayed home but they didn't. They even cheered. When the exams were over he gave them one last hug and promised to be good before almost running across the portal leading to the castle.

Now he was here, his life was moving from good to great to everything he could've dreamed of. He counted himself lucky that he wasn't part of the terror that befell Castle Eckhart, but he didn't give them a second thought either. He was becoming extremely efficient in the use of yellow and though he had yet to produce any form of green Will, he felt he was close to a breakthrough.

Beverly crossed his mind. Dark hair, dark skin and dark eyed beauty with legs that went forever. He looked at the spot where she still lay naked in his bed cuddling up to one of the pillows. Not the first girl that had graced his sheets and definitely not the last to mess them so. Suddenly her eyes clicked open and she sat up.

"Good afternoon, kitten," he greeted.

Usually, he would be far gone when they woke and he cursed his luck that he was mere moments from leaving. She didn't reply and just stood up looking at the door.

"Are you okay?" Still, he got no answer.

Beverly walked out the door bumping him as she went. That was all well and good for him but the boy was still about to reach out and stop her as she was completely naked. Something in his mind clicked. He lost control over his body and couldn't stop himself when his body decided to walk out the door behind Beverly. He loved the view with the sway of her hips but couldn't fully appreciate it. He was trying to wrestle control back over his body. He tested the use of Will but could not form any colour. His body had become completely automated outside of his control

From the corner of his eyes, he saw more figures leaving their dorm rooms and mindlessly walking towards an unknown goal. They were in different stages of their daily routine with one even sporting a toothbrush still wedged in his mouth, toothpaste on his lips. Out of the slowly building group he could not find a single person that was aware and moving on their own accord. He glanced out a window and saw that the sky had darkened outside as if night descended early. Could it be the same thing that happened to Eckhart?

On cue, explosions rang out in the school grounds. Fuck, fuck, it is Eckhart all over again, was all the boy could think. He struggled in his mind to get even the slightest control for him to build upon, but he could find not even an inch of flesh that would move for him. He helplessly listened as the sounds of fighting got ever closer.

The room exploded in front of him. Beverly was engulfed in flame and melted to the bone within moments. He was screaming in his head as the shock wave from the explosion sent him out the window of the second-storey building. Glass rained down around him as he bounced off a shed roof before coming to rest on the cemented ground.

The animated body got up again. It was too much to hope he was free now. As if it had conscious thought, the body looked at his limp, wobbly left arm dangling at his side. His mind reeled from the damage he saw. Granules of sand started to float into the air and enveloped the length of his arm. The sand slowly sank under the skin and somehow his arm was becoming solid and usable again. He noted with deep dread that the animated body was also in control of his Will.

Against the boy's defiant thoughts he took off at a run around the outside of the buildings, looking to reconnect with the main group. He rode within his mind like a prisoner in a cell, screaming and thrashing at the edges of his consciousness. It was no use however and the body came across someone that he would not have walked up to at the best of times.

Before him stood a woman with black hair and a man of Asian descent. The man was what had his attention as he was cloaked in armour made entirely of flames. The armour had the look of something a samurai would wear and the boy became scared. Around the armoured man were the bodies of a number of students all carved to pieces.

"This one is yours, Kinsami," Sarah said.

Before Kinsami could react, however, the boy, under the control of the castle, acted in defence of his home, creating a wave using the ground to try and engulf the two intruders. He knew it was a mistake but had no control over his actions.

As the wave enclosed over them Kinsami created a massive pressure bomb with heat and blew apart the earth wave. The body made another movement but was cut short by Kinsami as he melted away an arm.

"No! I'm going to die! Mum. Dad. Aaarrggghhh," was the last silent thought of the boy as Kinsami stepped in and destroyed the body completely.

Chapter 9

High above the ground, the wind rushed by his face. It was the greatest feeling Dirk had ever experienced. The world from this height was so insignificant. The land was patch worked with tilled fields and crisscrossed with roads and highways. Clouds passed by underneath casting shadows over the land below. This was the freest he had ever been and he would be forever thankful to Lavi for showing him how to use this gift.

Dirk glanced below and saw Gregory staying close to the ground. He must have a small fear of heights. Either that or he had no care for the beauty and wonder Dirk was experiencing right now. Dirk thought about Gregory's journey until now. He started as an empty slate. He didn't influence anyone and in return had no influences. He gained a rival in Kinsami and friends in Lavi and himself.

Sarah and her group of friends had pulled him into a world of playing pranks and bullying. This changed Gregory but through this, he learnt what it was to be a bully. He learnt about the pain he caused others and the issues that could cause trouble in his life. He learnt the many reasons a bully did what they did. Now, Gregory was trying to get past the person he was and the things he did. For the size of Gregory's sins, that took a lot of guts and determination.

Gregory rolled onto his back as he flew and motioned for Dirk to come down. Dirk flew down to glide alongside his friend.

"The town of Mandaloo is not too far ahead," Gregory said. "I didn't want you getting a glimpse of it before we really got close. The town is a sight to behold regardless the situation we are in."

"Sounds good but I was enjoying the flying. I'll be sorry that we have to stop."

"Well, you have about fifteen minutes low-level flying left so make the most of it."

Dirk nodded and took off at pace having become more comfortable with his control. He rolled around trees and swooped livestock. Following a creek, he travelled fast enough that he created small wakes either side of himself upon the water. At one point he flew close to a young girl playing with dolls. The girl with no grasp on the laws of physics smiled and waved at him as he sped past.

Finally, Gregory motioned to land. Dirk pouted but came down alongside Gregory. He looked around but could not see a town anywhere close by.

"Where is it?" Dirk asked confused.

"Just over the small rise ahead," Gregory replied.

"Mustn't be that great a town if I can't even see it over such a small rise."

"Just wait," Gregory jogged ahead and up the hill coming to a stop at the summit. Dirk followed and he was amazed at the sight he saw. Kind of. The crater and the sheer cliff faces were incredible to see but the town was just wrong. He looked at Gregory, about to comment but stopped when he saw Gregory's face. He looked anguished, his skin draining of all colour.

"What's wrong?" Dirk asked worried.

"The town," he stammered. "The whole area for that matter. It's all changed. It was supposed to be beautiful. The town was supposed to be bright and bustling. I don't know what that shit is down there."

Dirk looked closer and saw that what he thought was part of the buildings and landscape was a web type substance. It was dark and grey in colour and moved with the wind. Dirk wondered at what animal could have produced such a web.

"Not anything we can do now, Gregory," Dirk said. "Whatever's been released down in the town we'll correct, but for now we need to get to that museum of yours and across to Castle Eckhart."

"Okay but let's fly in," Gregory suggested. "It'll make things easier and we can hopefully bypass..." A bird was flying over the town at that moment and swooped low. The town looked like it came alive and curled up to pluck the bird from the sky. It all happened so fast the boys almost missed it.

"If it's all the same with you, Gregory, I'm going to foot it," Dirk told him. "We'll just have to take our chances down there."

"Agreed," Gregory said after staring in the direction where the bird had once flown.

The boys walked forward and jumped from the cliff diving straight to the earth floor below. They pulled up at the last moment and floated the last metre to land softly on the ground.

They started walking towards where the webbing lay. It surprised them that the web they believed to be laying on the land around them was actually floating ten metres above the ground. Underneath, little light got through and the boys had to pause for almost twenty minutes for their eyes to adjust.

"I don't like this," Dirk told his friend. "This area gives me the creeps. I would prefer to be back fighting the imps or the gryphon."

"I agree but this is the fight we made for ourselves. Lavi is on the other side."

"And nothing is going to be stopping me. I was just saying this place gives me the creeps."

"Where possible let's use hand signals to communicate. I don't want to be overheard or alert anything that could be on the inside. This is the work of Will and we don't know what awaits us."

Dirk nodded his hand showing agreeance. The boys walked deeper into the dark underworld of what was once Mandaloo. Nothing below the web had been disturbed in any way and Gregory had a shiver run up his spine at the ghost town. In seemingly random places the webbing funnelled down to connect with the ground. Dirk looked closely at where one came down. It was not a web at all, he realised but thousands of intertwining metal strands. Dirk reached out and flicked the strands giving a small metallic ting sound.

The metal web shivered across the whole surface. Gregory looked at Dirk with wild eyes questioning what just happened. A reptilian screech rose up echoing out under the cover. It sounded far off but he couldn't be sure. Another sounded. This was definitely close. The boys looked for somewhere to hide. Gregory rolled under a raised pickup truck. He had a good view out into the streets beyond. He saw Dirk dive into a skip bin. Moments later a beast of hideous deformity came around the corner only metres away.

It was easily ten foot when standing straight. The beast loped along hunched over with an awkward side skip. A tail that was half its body length again swished out the back for balance. Its skin was scaly like a snakes and Gregory noticed a fluid that dripped from random places on the skin. Gregory realised it was a type of poison that the beast could pass along to cuts and abrasions. The skin itself had a greenish brown tinge to it. Each hand had three fingers with wickedly sharp retractable talons. Its head was small and round with a mouth that stretched from the place an ear would normally be to the other side. Gregory saw hundreds of barbed razor teeth through the small slit of its mouth. It had no nose but instead sported two slits in its place. The thing that would be the cause of many nightmares to come, though, were the eyes. They were slitted from top to bottom with red irises. The black pupils had a depth to them you would expect from the nine circles of hell and they saw everything.

The beast skirted around the crossroad for a few moments before it seemed to pick up a scent. It moved straight to where Dirk was hiding in the dumpster and reaching in a long, lanky arm dragged out Dirk in one fluid movement throwing him to the pavement. Dirk rolled as he hit the ground and looked up at the beast. Though there was fear across his face he did not make a noise. He almost looked at Gregory but stopped himself at the last minute not wanting to give the other boys position away. Dirk made to move away but the beast showed incredible speed and was on him in an instant.

Picking Dirk up by the shoulder, the reptilian brought the talons of his other hand together to form a point. Dirk let out a whimper of pain and watched helplessly as the talons grew to six inches before him. The beast pulled back to strike but never hit its mark. Gregory had brought his Will to existence in the form of two blades made of air. Exceptionally sharp and very manoeuvrable, he threw the blades at the beast. One connected, slicing off the hand about to strike Dirk. The other blade lopped off the front half of a car parked close by.

The beast let out a shrill cry that echoed around the town. Other cries were returned from an unknown distance away. Gregory made one last air blade and willed it in the direction he wanted it to go. It carved the beast in half spilling its guts across the pavement. Dirk landed heavily on the ground below holding his shoulder. Gregory ran over and found that where the beast had been holding him there were small wounds with blood seeping out.

"We need to get you off the street," Gregory told his friend. "There'll be more of those things along soon enough."

"How far to the museum?" Dirk asked weekly

"It's still a few blocks away," Gregory replied. "We need to regroup and form a plan of attack. The building across the street will do for now."

Dirk nodded and Gregory helped him to his feet. Lending Dirk a shoulder, the two boys made their way across the street. A screech rose up close by and Gregory hurried his friend along. Throwing Dirk through an open doorway he turned to try and dispose of their tracks. The footprints were currently a map to their location. Gregory decided he would push his ability to the edge. He willed his eyes to change the way they process light and colour. Consequently, his pupils split and created a figure eight shape. Instantly, Gregory saw the footprints and parts of the ground and surrounding objects the boys touched. They glowed softly with a yellow hue.

Gregory raised every scrap of pavement and material that had a trace of their essence and piled them on the far side of the road. That was all Gregory could do with the time he had. As he was about to go inside another creature came bounding around the corner and almost ran into him. It looked around the area sweeping its gaze past Gregory on two occasions. It saw the carcass of the other beast and went to investigate. Gregory couldn't believe the beast didn't attack him.

A thought struck him at that moment. It'd been a while since he drew in colour to use his Will, and decided to pull in the green. The moment he had drawn forth the colour the beast in front of him turned and looked straight at him. With a

174

low, threatening, clicking noise the beast sprung at Gregory but he willed more air blades right in the beast's path. He let the animal carve itself out of existence. The creature slumped to the ground in pieces. Gregory got rid of any last bit of evidence they were there and escaped inside to Dirk, closing the doors.

"They track using the colour we build around us," Gregory told his friend. Gregory realised that Dirk was breathing erratically and sweating. He placed his hand on the boy's forehead and felt a fever running through him. "The poison!" Ripping open Dirk's shirt, Gregory inspected the wound. Pus mixed with blood was seeping from the open tear. Tendrils of purple lines like spiders web fanned out from the wound. "You better not be about to leave Lavi alone Dirk," Gregory told the semiconscious boy.

The first thing he needed to do was draw out the poison. He adjusted his eyes again and they took on another form. The pupils became like dumbbells and the poison started to glow purple under the skin. He decided that it would be wrong to draw it back through the heart and against the flow of blood. Gregory opened a small cut below the further most poison and then started to pull it through as the poison reached the open cut.

It seeped out onto the floor and started to puddle. Halfway into the process and the amount of poison was half a litre. Gregory was surprised that Dirk had lived through the initial injection. If he'd of been stabbed by the talons he would have died in moments. Gregory finished the process and was happy that all the poison had seeped from the body. He willed his eyes back to normal and started to mend the cuts. Knitting muscle and tissue back together Gregory was happy to see some colour come back into Dirk's face.

Gregory heard movement in the street and he moved to a window. Glancing from the edge, he saw that three of the beasts were sniffing around the pavement Gregory had moved earlier. He knew he could get around them but the trick was going to be getting Dirk out. A soft snoring came to his ears and Gregory smiled that his friend was going to be fine.

Throughout the afternoon Gregory kept a watch outside. He learnt nothing more of the beasts and saw them skitter off after an hour. One had climbed the building across the street and Gregory knew it was watching the area. He willed a small fire into existence near Dirk. The fire was special in the fact it cast no light or shadows. It only produced a comfortable heat to a distance of where Gregory sat. In this, no beast would feel them out. Dirk finally stirred as the streets started to get darker.

"How long have I been out?" He asked Gregory. Dirk's head was light and he still felt pain in his shoulder.

"Only a few hours," Gregory replied. "It's getting dark out there."

"Sorry to put you through this, Gregory. I got too curious with the metal webbing."

"Don't worry about it. We all make mistakes," Gregory said with a sad smile. "They're still out there somewhere."

"How many?

"Just the one keeping watch. They see via the build-up of colour. I can walk through them practically invisible when in Empty mode. When I pull in colour they see me instantly."

"Then they have a weakness," Dirk sounded hopeful before thinking a little more. "Let me guess. I'm the bait?"

"The thought hadn't crossed my mind," Gregory said concealing a smile.

"I can see your grin," Dirk said.

Gregory started laughing. "We know what we are up against now. We will proceed with caution and I'll protect you. The museum isn't far away."

"I hope you're fast enough. Do you remember when you made that window when we were with the warriors?"

"Yes?"

"Can you make a window over the world giving me control over the zooming?"

"Why?"

"Can you?"

"I can," Gregory waited but Dirk continued to watch him. Gregory pulled up a window above the planet they resided.

176

Dirk walked over and looked at it. He touched a point over one of the land masses and the vision started to zoom in. Dirk continued until he had the viewfinder in someone's dining room overlooking a roast dinner.

"Gregory, can you physically open the view into that room?"

Gregory didn't answer, he just did it. Immediately the smells of the roast beef, potatoes, pumpkin, carrots, spices, dinner rolls and gravy wafted through to fill the room. The boys' mouths were salivating and Gregory realised he hadn't eaten in a long time. Gregory watched with amusement as Dirk leaned into the room and started taking chunks of meat and sides. He piled them on a plate and pulled them back into the room. Leaning back in to get the gravy, a small scream came from the other side.

"Thank you, mum," Dirk said. "You make a great roast and I couldn't resist regardless of where I am. Say hi to dad for me." Dirk ducked back in with the gravy and Gregory closed the window.

"Your house?" Gregory asked.

"Yeah. If we are going to die I wanted to have a home cooked meal one last time." Dirk put the plate of meat and roast vegetables in between them. He picked a smaller piece of meat and put it in his mouth. The juices and flavours that came from that one small piece were heaven and Dirk just sat chewing it for a few moments savouring the piece. "We got it at the perfect time too. Do you mind if I put the gravy on."

"By all means," Gregory said gesturing with his open palm. Dirk poured the still steaming gravy over the meat and vegetables. Gregory materialised two knives and forks with his Will and passed a set to Dirk. The boys ate silently savouring the meal that had escaped their palette for so long.

"That was amazing," Gregory said as Dirk was scooping up the last of the gravy with a dinner roll.

"She always had a way with food. At least we can push forward on a full stomach. Do you have a plan?"

"You've already said the plan. You are bait, I am muscle. It has worked in the past and seems to be the best form of attack."

"Not my favourite type of plan by a long shot."

"But you're so good at it," Gregory said jabbing him in the side. "We had best get started. What I need you to do is build up yellow within you. See it there and hold it there. This will definitely attract them to you and you're going to have to move fearlessly. Don't pause and don't look back for fear of my safety. Agreed?"

"Done. Now, which way am I supposed to be running if you're behind?"

"Go left when we move out the door. I'll light up each turn from that point onwards."

"Then let's go," with that Dirk moved to the door and Gregory felt the build-up of yellow within him. As a last defence, Gregory put a hidden barrier of razor-sharp spinning air around the boy. A shriek sounded outside causing Dirk to jump.

"The lookout has alarmed the others," Gregory said. "Run!"

The boys sprinted out to the left and started down the road. Instantly, three of the reptilians were giving chase. Gregory spun on his heel and sent wind shuriken to cleave through the beasts sending multiple pieces of flesh falling to the street.

Two blocks down and Dirk saw the first sign post to turn. Gregory had placed a big, blue, glowing arrow with the name Lavi and a big red heart below it.

"Remind me to hit you for that later," Dirk called over his shoulder while angling down the crossroad. Gregory just laughed as another reptilian was running vertically down a building ahead of the boys. It jumped at Dirk from two stories up but was taken mid-air by numerous air shuriken. Gregory had to dodge the excess body parts. The boys saw that a few of the beasts were starting to group at one side of a crossroad and so took a wide arcing run around them to the other side.

Gregory felt something was wrong as they were not moving to attack but realised too late what was happening. Dirk had entered into the crossroad and two reptilians pounced on him from around the closest corner. As Dirk threw his arms up to protect himself the creatures hit Gregory's invisible wind barrier and were shredded into a million pieces. The swirling

178

motion of the wind sending the chunks outwards, away from Dirk.

"As I said, don't stop," Gregory said to Dirk who had started running again.

"You could have told me about the barrier."

"Where's the fun in that?" Gregory said with a wink.

The group of reptilians at the other side of the crossroad pointed at Gregory and let out a spine tingling screech. Realising they could now see him, Gregory knew they considered him a threat.

"Faster Dirk! They know I'm here!" Gregory yelled. "Two more blocks straight ahead and you'll see the big carpark."

The boys were now sprinting as a flood of reptilians poured from every building and street. Gregory was having difficulty keeping them all back and Dirk realised this.

"You take back. I'll take the front," he told Gregory. Without waiting for a reply he started carving parts of the road with the built up yellow he had stored. Dirk was squashing the beasts into piles of rubble and folding them back out of their path so as to keep the way clear.

The museum car park came into view and the boys were breathing heavily as they ran across the vacant lot to the barred doors. Stopping, they looked back to see hundreds of the reptilians coursing into the car park and heading straight for them. A small tingling sensation ran up Gregory's side building into a powerful pressure erupting from Dirk as he brought his Will into existence. A tremor went through the town and buildings started to cave in. The creatures paused unsure of what to do, before the ground itself heaved over and disappeared into the earth dragging the metal netting down with it and leaving a hole falling for miles below the already large crater of Mandaloo. Gregory took two steps forward to stand on the edge and whistled.

"That's one way to deal with them," Gregory said looking over the drop into the darkness. "Didn't think we were going to make it for a minute."

Dirk walked over and punched him hard in the arm almost sending Gregory off balance and over the edge.

179

Gregory rubbed at the sharp pain. "What was that for?" he asked.

"That sign you put up," Dirk replied. Gregory remembered the small jest with his directing and laughed.

"Do you have your coins?" said a voice behind them. The boys turned and Gregory recognised the doorman from his first visit.

"Why are you still here? Can't you see the destruction of the town?"

"The museum is on sacred ground. None enter without a coin. I'll stay at my post until the next comes to relieve me," the doorman said.

"I think you'll be waiting a while," Dirk replied. "You know him, Gregory?"

"He was the doorman the first time I came here. Pull out your coin and place it in the box beside him. He'll grant us access." Gregory pulled his out first and placed his Empty coin into the box. Dirk followed suit dusting off the granules of sand.

"Enjoy your stay," the doorman said opening the doors. The boys walked in and Gregory was glad to see the place hadn't changed. There was still the same dark marble floor with white marble columns, the many balconies and the numerous murals that lined the walls and roof. Dirk was standing in amazement seeing the museum for the first time.

"Do you want a moment longer," Gregory asked.

Dirk took in a long steadying breath then looked to his friend. "Take me to Eckhart," he said.

Gregory turned and walked the same way he had done on his first visit with Allen. They moved through the rooms not paying attention to the artefacts or the visitors still wandering the halls. After the short walk, the boys found themselves in front of the painting to Castle Eckhart. Gregory led Dirk and with confidence, walked straight into the painting with a thud. Falling back holding his aching nose, Gregory started to go red as peals of laughter fell from Dirk.

"Are you okay?" Dirk asked when he had started to calm down. Gregory just grumbled and swore under his breath.

Walking up to the painting, Dirk put his hand through. There was no resistance to be found. "I seem to be able to go through."

Gregory thought for a moment and remembered that he had entered with Allen, their coins combining. The riddle a simple one when carefully deconstructed.

"Being an Empty gives me no colour to register. I think my Grandpa knew that when he brought my brother along last time. He has manipulated a lot of events. I would like to talk to him if I can find him. We need to enter together, Dirk. Hold my hand," Gregory said reaching out.

Dirk just raised an eyebrow. "It's cute when Lavi does it. It's just creepy when you try. You can hold my shoulder." Dirk didn't give him time to argue as he started to walk through the painting. Diving forward Gregory grabbed Dirk by the shoulder and was almost pulled through the painting. There was no exam room this time on the other side. The boys stepped out into the fields beyond Castle Eckhart. The moon hung high above the grounds and the boys looked around to get their bearings.

"Follow me," Dirk said. "I know a place we can hide out for a while to plan our assault." Dirk started walking closer to the castle walls but didn't make for the entrance. He was angling around the outside.

"There's nothing out this way, Dirk," Gregory said. "What are you looking for?"

"Trust me. I have a hideout just around the bend." Gregory was still dubious about believing the boy but followed along. When they got around the bend he was greeted by a cave entrance. Dirk swore.

"What's wrong?" Gregory asked.

"It's open. There could be enemies within."

"Then let's proceed with caution."

Entering the dark cave, the boys followed the path leading to the cliff face. Dirk was happy that he set the phosphorescence to glow at Lavi's presence. He would have been completely embarrassed if Gregory saw it but as they made their way to the other side, the cave walls started to glow.

Pausing for only a moment as the implications of the illumination struck home, Dirk started to run

"Dirk what happened to being cautious?" Gregory called.

Ignoring Gregory, Dirk ran out into the sunlight and saw the three figures on the cliff side. He recognised Lavi instantly. "Lavi!" Dirk called louder than he meant to.

Kinsami watched as Baras strangled the sun. It was not done with clouds or other things of substance. It was done with pure darkness. A rich, black shadow that materialised and built upon itself, swirling from horizon to horizon creating an infinite night. Kinsami considered the Will user that shared the name of the Lord of Eckhart. He was like the Lord in height and stature. He sported the same hair and eye colour also. Kinsami felt a name held power to make a person who they were and this was calling true. Unlike the Lord though this person did not run away from his duties. He did what he needed to do with unwavering dedication.

Castle Bodhurst was before them across a small valley. It was built to the same dimensions and specifications as Castle Eckhart. The difference came from the colour of the stone used. Where Eckhart was made of the grey stone found in abundance around the castle, Bodhurst was a darker mix also local to its own region. The dark walls gave the castle a demonic look as it disappeared into the Will manifested darkness.

"Kinsami, come here a moment," Sarah called.

Kinsami obeyed. "I have not decided one way or another on the matter at hand," he told her defensively. "Don't ask me to fight for you."

"I would do nothing of the sort. I was going to offer you the ability to see in the darkness Baras has created. Living objects will glow and the landscapes will become more pronounced."

"I am of the red. I'll be able to do so myself."

"Not for this darkness," Sarah insisted. "It's made of Will and there is a specific combination of colours that must be used to allow you to see through it. You just don't have that type of skill."

"What of the students and staff inside? How will they see?"

"When the darkness was set, the students' minds had been taken over by Adaman and Sylvia. They have been transformed and will assault us relentlessly until either they are dead or the Lord and Lady are taken care of. We are not weak enough to die here so if you want to stop the carnage and even free some students, take the eyesight and then take out those that rule this castle."

"Fine then," Kinsami relented. "Just do what you need to and be done with it."

Sarah was smiling as she manipulated his eyes. Kinsami was impressed by the dark clarity he was seeing. Everything was portrayed in hues of purple but like a grayscale painting, the shading and depth were perfect. He watched as Sarah moved from person to person giving them the same ability. Looking over at the Castle, his heart skipped a beat. A strong glow was rising from within and Kinsami recognised it to be the students. There were so many and they would all die today if he allowed it.

Flaming balls like from catapults of old arced across the sky to land randomly along the castle walls and in the yards. Small amounts of the glow were starting to fade away as he saw Sarah and a few others start moving towards the castle. Three were left on the hillside to keep up the rain of fire. Kinsami ran after Sarah.

"You can still stop this, Sarah," Kinsami said almost pleading with the girl. She looked across and smiled a chilling smile.

"You know that I will not, my dear boy," she replied. The use of *dear boy* made Kinsami feel like a child in her presence. "The only person that could make any bit of a difference is you Kinsami and to do that you'll have to get your hands dirty."

They passed through the walls of the castle and into the grounds beyond. Sarah moved off in her own direction as the group made for the great halls and Kinsami followed her.

"I won't kill for you, Sarah."

"I would like to see you last. Here they come."

Kinsami looked up and his face went pale. Before him were

mutated beasts staggering and hobbling towards them. They had bulging muscles that disfigured their look and random horns that protruded from joints and other odd, unnatural places on the body. Kinsami instantly ignited his flame armour. This move saved his life as one of the mutants attacked at that moment sending sharp, serrated icicle shards straight at him. They fizzled into steam on his flames before they had the chance to do any damage.

Sarah sprung forward. She did not do any fancy moves with her Will but produced a short sword of exquisite beauty. It was slender, elegant and judging by the way it cut through the beasts, it was extremely sharp. Red braided tassels were tied to the hilt and runes were etched into the blade. When all enemies had been dispatched Sarah discarded the sword to nothingness and faced Kinsami. She truly looked evil with the splatters of blood upon her.

"A word of warning, Kinsami. I won't be killing anyone else today. It is now time to choose what side you want to fight for. You have seen what the Lords and Ladies do to the students. You can stop it. I've brought you to the fastest route that leads to them. From now on, you decide whether you push forward or walk back."

At that moment another mutated student came running from around a corner, pausing as it spotted them.

"This one's yours, Kinsami," Sarah said. Kinsami was about to object but the monster acted first sending a wave of earth at the two intruders. Kinsami glanced at Sarah and saw her standing there calmly not making a move. Cursing inwardly, Kinsami readied himself. As the earth curled over them, he blew it apart with a pressure bomb. The mutant went to attack again but Kinsami stopped it by melting away its arm. No going back now, Kinsami thought as he destroyed the body stubbornly trying to continue its assault. He glared at Sarah.

"Take me to Adaman and Sylvia. Anyone that can turn a student into a monster and make them fight deserves to die," He said with anger.

Sarah smiled her wicked little smile knowing she had finally won with such a simple ruse. On a whim, she made Kinsami's

184

eyes special. Anytime he saw a student, his eyes would register them as a hideous monster. The fact they were being controlled wasn't enough for him and she was glad she added the final touch.

Twice more Kinsami had to dispatch students on the path to Adaman and Sylvia. He apologised each time promising to stop the bloodshed. Finally, he progressed up the tower and stood before his targets.

"You have gotten stronger, Kinsami," Adaman said. "Though, you're standing on the wrong side."

"I'm right where I belong," Kinsami replied evenly. "Anyone who would manipulate the students this way, who would change them so much, does not deserve to be in charge. They come here to learn and put faith in the system. Many could have run and hid from the assault. Many could have survived. You turned them into tools and sent them off to die. I am here to stop the killing."

"You think the killing will stop if we give them back their minds?" Sylvia asked. "They'll run and hide, yes, but they will also be tracked down and slaughtered like the students at Castle Eckhart."

"I have given Kinsami my word that the deaths will stop once you are gone," Sarah interjected. "You two are the last at Castle Bodhurst that need to die."

"Can't you see she is using you, Kinsami," Adaman said ignoring Sarah. "The Otoma family is one of honour and what you are doing disgraces your family name. Are you going to be her puppet?"

"I have chosen my own path. Sarah has done nothing more than show me the truth."

"Than she is a better puppeteer than I first believed. I can see you won't be swayed. Come on, just try and take us down."

Kinsami made the first move. Crafting a flaming katana, he attacked Sylvia. She was dressed in her crimson red robe and Kinsami knew she would be the harder opponent being of the red. He slashed at her left shoulder and the blade seemingly hit its mark carving through her. She stood unscathed. When he looked down at the blade the flames extended just as long as they had before but the metal of the Katana had been melted away leaving a glowing, red hot stump atop the hilt. How could he take down someone stronger than he was in his own colour?

He decided to focus instead on Adaman in his purple robes. Neither made a move to attack him which annoyed Kinsami greatly. They were being too cocky. He reforged the Katana and attacked Adaman with the same move he tried on Sylvia.

Moments later, Kinsami woke up with the hilt of his own sword pointing in on his stomach. The Blade had been melted away. If not for the armour Kinsami had cloaked himself in, he would have run himself through. Adaman of the purple had just taken control of him and done a small display of power to show Kinsami how worthless he really was.

"Is that all you can do?" Adaman asked. "You lack the training and experience required, Kinsami. Go home and leave this behind you." Kinsami looked to Sarah for guidance.

"Nothing much more you can do, Kinsami, just keep swinging. It'll at least distract him while I have a go at that bitch," Sarah spoke to his concerns.

Both Adaman and Sylvia laughed. As Kinsami reforged the blade one last time, sceptical at how it would help.

"Sarah, when Kinsami loses faith in you, I'll deal with you personally," Adaman told her. He waited for the moment Kinsami swung to take control once more and have Kinsami turn the blade in on himself.

Sylvia had been tense, ready to counter any move Sarah threw her way, when something solid hit her in the side of the head. Reaching up, Sylvia felt a fluid upon her face. It was warm and sticky and as she brought her hand back down Sylvia's eyes went wide at the sight of blood. Nudging against her foot was the bald head of Adaman, blood seeping out into a puddle on the floor. There was a shocked expression frozen on his face from the moment he realised he did not have control of Kinsami at all.

"No!" Sylvia screamed. "How? It is impossible to negate Adaman's attacks. They are absolute."

"Absolute bullshit," Sarah agreed. "He was a disgrace to the purples if he couldn't even realise he was being controlled himself."

"You lie," Sylvia said. She attacked Sarah with molten balls of fire and flaming pillars but nothing was hitting even though the girl did not move. "What have you done, Sarah?"

"Not nice is it?" Sarah said. "You have both been under my control since I walked in here. Now you get to feel what it's like to die at someone else's whim. Kinsami, the moment she dies is the moment I call off the attack. You can use my blade as it won't melt."

Sarah's short sword appeared in the air before Kinsami and he reached out taking it by the hilt. The handle had soft leather bands across the centre and metal grips above and below. It was surprisingly comfortable to hold. He walked over to Sylvia and noting the fear in her eyes drew the sword across her throat to watch her life blood start pumping away.

"Now call off your attack," Kinsami demanded.

"No, I don't think so," Sarah replied in a matter-of-fact tone. Sylvia smiled and half cough, half laughed, before falling over dead.

"I knew it! You're a lying little whore!" Kinsami was raging and closing on the girl with the wicked smile.

"Kinsami, calm yourself," she finally said. "I was just playing with that stupid bitch before she died. It's already done. Jeez, you can be such a princess."

Brow furrowing, Kinsami threw the blade down and stalked away.

Lavi's heart sank with Dirk's voice. The one voice in all of this world she had not been ready to hear and it was calling to her from the cave. As she turned, Lavi was greeted with a wave of warmth that washed over her body. He still looked just as hot, if a little more rugged, as when they shared their last moments together on this cliff side. Lavi's attention then fell on herself. She felt broken and ugly after her struggles in the castle. Her mind asked her how he could want someone like her when he heard what had happened. Dirk would throw her away.

Taking strides towards her, Dirk opened his arms causing

Lavi to become overwhelmed and hide away leaving Michelle to step forward. Dirk was confused as Michelle held a hand up to his chest and shook her head. Lavi didn't know what broke her heart more. The way Dirk softly called out to her, the knowledge that soon he would hate her and think her disgusting or that she didn't give him the chance to do so for her own selfish reasons. What could she do? It was all too much. With tears in her eyes she jumped from the cliff and flew away to escape her pain but she couldn't gain the speed required.

Watching her go, Dirk couldn't understand what had happened. He broke passed Michelle and screamed out her name from the cliff face.

"Dirk... Let her have some time," Michelle said sadly. "She isn't ready to face you."

"Why..?" He asked desperately. "Why won't she see me? What's changed? I've travelled across countless worlds and hundreds of miles to find her. I have fought Imps, Gryphon, reptilians and humans all seeking to end me just for a chance to see her. I have journeyed not knowing if she was even alive... Why has she abandoned me? Was it because I couldn't help her on the night the castle was destroyed?" Dirk broke down. Michelle walked over and put a hand on his back.

"It's not my place to say. She will need to find the confidence and strength herself. You speak of the vast struggles you went through. We haven't just been sitting around either. Give her time."

Shaking his head, Dirk walked over to the far corner of the cliff leaving Michelle to hover close by worrying. Gregory felt sorry for his friend but he was now focused on the old man before him. The man that didn't come to their aid when the Castle was under attack. The man that has done nothing since to rectify the nightmare. Now here he was in the relative safety of this cliff side relaxing.

"Gregory. Welcome," Baras said.

"Save the pleasantries," Gregory told him, anger coming to the surface. "Where have you been? How could you let the destruction of your castle and the death of your students happen?"

"I could no more stop it than you could swing from your own noose," Baras said.

A shiver ran through Gregory as the image of a looped rope dangling before a light flashed across his mind. Shaking his head he let the feeling subside.

"You could have tried," Gregory said. "You are powerful and would've made a difference."

"I would've made too much difference to time and space. I could have destroyed more than just this castle."

"I don't understand," Gregory said at a loss of what to say.

"And so you shouldn't. We aren't here to worry about a castle or the so called lives of a few people. Right now, all I am concerned for is your mental state."

"I'm doing okay," Gregory said. There was a tender warmth for the fact his Grandpa was still concerned for him. "I had a rough time after the horrible night at the castle but Dirk helped me through and I'm starting to recover."

"I'm not talking about that," Baras told him. "I've yet to see that you are truly willing to live. You're running away from your worries and your fears."

"I'm not," Gregory said trying to follow the conversation but he felt it was slipping from his grasp. "I've been facing my demons."

"The Veritas Rerum has you, Gregory," Baras said. For a moment Gregory saw a shimmer run through Baras like a glitch in a hologram. "Sarah is your path to freedom. She is the key. You won't grow until you face her and move past her."

"Veritas Rerum? What do you mean?" Gregory asked. He didn't have a clue where the conversation went.

"She wants you dead," Baras shimmered twice more then disappeared completely. Gregory walked to where his Grandpa had stood and waved his arm back and forward. The man was gone. Turning, Gregory looked first at Dirk who was depressed with his own concerns and then at Michelle who glanced back.

"What the actual fuck was that because that was nothing like my Grandpa?"

"That was Lord Baras," Michelle replied simply. "You need

to take what he said to heart. It'll make sense to you one day."

"You know what's going on don't you?"

"I have an idea. He told Lavi and me a lot of why things have been happening but like Lavi's concerns these are his and I won't talk more about them."

"Well fuck!" was all Gregory said in reply.

Chapter 10

Distraught screams could be heard from the courtyard outside. Screams of the injured. Screams of those in shock. Screams of those who had lost the battle. Kinsami felt for each and every one of those in pain and was glad that he had a part in freeing them. He felt sick to his stomach for what the Lords and Ladies were doing to the students. He realised that he was blindly walking down that road until Sarah showed him the truth. He blindly walked this path as it was the path that everyone in society walked. The Castles were the most prestigious schooling systems for the study and use of Will. How could he have been led so easily?

Glancing at Sarah, Kinsami could admit to himself that he was wrong about her. She was looking out for the people screaming below. Her methods were brutal and he still didn't like everything she did but it was for the best. Next time, he will make sure the students are completely protected. There was only Celes and Nodane, Green and yellow. It was going to be a hard battle but if he could get just one the other would fall.

"Are you doing okay, Kinsami?" Sarah asked. She was confident and calculative. She held herself tall and spoke in a way that deserved respect. Kinsami couldn't believe this was the same girl he once knew. He was seeing her in a different light which he not only liked but respected. She had just finished giving commands to the men and women under her when she came to speak with him. Sarah organised food and sleeping quarters, designated a medical team to help any student that needed it, and organised the reconstruction of any damage to the castle. This was now the new base of operations. Eckhart was not required anymore.

"I am recovering. Sorry for my weakness," Kinsami replied. He had not mentally prepared himself for the deaths he would bring upon those within Castle Bodhurst. When he had sent the head of Adaman spiralling across the room, there was a feeling of separation from what was happening. It was only afterwards that he saw the blood upon his hands. Sarah had

191

seen him go pale then double over emptying his stomach into the Lords tower. She bid him rest by the wall and conjured a warm, soothing washer with Will. She placed it upon his forehead and levitated his mess right out the window. He was thankful for her care and had forgiven her for being so heartless while Sylvia's heart still beat.

"Don't be. There is no weakness in being responsible for your actions. It's not something that I would ask for you to get used to either but I would ask for your assistance one last time at Castle Kirkwall," she sounded almost apologetic.

"I would like to talk to you about the way we proceed with taking the final castle," Kinsami said. He was ready to go into his plans but she shook her head.

"This isn't the time for plans, Kinsami," Sarah told him. "Now, I need to address the people of Castle Bodhurst. I need to put their fears at ease and open their eyes to the truth."

This only impressed Kinsami all the more. He wasn't thinking of the students outside or cementing their base at Castle Bodhurst. He was only thinking of pushing forward. She deserved the position she took. She'd always had a strategic mind. Kinsami nodded at her.

Sarah walked over to the wall facing the courtyard below and peered out the window. The medical tents and the food stands were almost set below and the students were starting to filter in filling the yard. They were too tired to fight those that may have been enemies. They didn't want to fight those that gave them food and treatment.

Sarah brought in a combination of her colours and started focusing on a platform she could produce with her Will. She put her Will into effect. The wall where she was standing started to deconstruct itself stone by stone. The stones took on a life of their own rolling onto the outer wall and creating a stairway that led down to a flat surface five metres above the students who were gathering in the courtyard.

Sarah walked down the stairway and as she got to the platform all eyes turned to her. She could see a variance in the looks on people's faces. Some were openly hostile, some were worn down and others looked scared at what was about to happen. True twilight was setting in and there was a chill growing in the air. This did not suit Sarah so she willed a warmer breeze to help comfort those before her. She knew they wouldn't attack. They had seen she had the power to take over the Castle and kill those in charge with simplistic ease. They now waited for her to make a move.

"Today, I am going to open your eyes to the true reality of the Castle system and the network of lies and manipulation you have all fallen into," she stated to the crowd. Her voice was unnaturally high and echoed around the stone walls of the castle grounds. Most people's expressions didn't change towards her but they would. She was confident that they would all react in a manner similar to Kinsami. Scepticism, followed by doubt towards the scepticism and finally a need to know for sure. It would be easier with these students though as they had all just been taken over with mind control to fight a battle they may not have needed to.

"I know you must all hold a burning hatred in your hearts for the events of today and maybe even our part in the events of Eckhart. It is well placed and I am sorry that it had to be done but in your hearts, this hatred must stay."

"You have destroyed everything we've grown to love. Why should we listen to you?" Came an angry voice from the crowd. Some people were nodding and expressing their agreement. Sarah became sympathetic and nodded along.

"There is no reason that you should listen to me," she answered. "I am not here to force you into something you don't want. I only want for you to know the truth and free yourselves from the hold the castles have on your mind." Seeing that another person was about to speak Sarah held her hand up. "Quiet for a moment. If you listen to what I have to say I'll give you the choice whether you wish to include yourself in this righteous fight or whether you would like to place yourselves between us and our goal." Silence from the crowd.

"First thing that you should be aware of by now is that the Castles have the power to control you anytime they want, for whatever task they want. They had no issues in sending all of you out to die so that they could live. Do you disagree?" Some people had small discussions amongst themselves but no one could come up with any arguments against.

"Both Adaman and Sylvia sent you to die. We had come here for them alone but they forced our hand with your attack and we had to defend ourselves against you. If you had free will would you all have chosen to throw yourselves at us or would of you have been smart? Attacked from the shadows or saved yourselves? Adaman and Sylvia took this away from you because they were scared of us. We are not here to hurt you. The moment we freed you from their mind control the deaths stopped. We have provided medics and food for all of you that have been through so much. Our goal is to free all the students from the control of the castles."

"We have freed Castle Eckhart. We have freed Castle Bodhurst. Now only Castle Kirkwall stands in our way. After a small intermission to plan our next move we'll be taking down Castle Kirkwall. From Castle Eckhart, we learnt a lot and in turn, could save the majority of you. From today's attack we have again learnt a lot. Maybe next time we'll be able to save all the students and only deal justice to those responsible."

"I will not lie to you. You will not get rewarded for this venture. You will not gain respect or be called heroes. You may even be shunned if you decided to help us but ask yourselves honestly. What revolutionary tasks ever worth completing were easy or brought prestige to those that took the courage and stepped forward saying *I will change that*? If you do this, you do this because it is right. You do this because you don't want to see any other person's free will taken from them."

"I won't tell you to listen to your hearts for that is where the anger you hold for me shall be. Listen to your minds and do what you believe is right. Do what you know you would choose even if I were not in the picture. Tonight, me and my friends shall leave Castle Bodhurst. This decision should be made without our influence. If you deny our request you can bar us from the castle and we won't return. If you accept you can find us eight hundred metres north of the gates."

A murmur ran through the crowds. They couldn't believe that this woman who had attacked them with such ferocity to take Castle Bodhurst would give it back to them so easily. They were tense and unsure on how to proceed.

"One last thing. I'll leave you one man who has come to join our cause. He is a survivor of Castle Eckhart and has seen great devastation by our hands. He has not forgiven us for these actions but has seen firsthand the cause is a just one. You will know his name as a powerful yet honourable name. He'll be here to answer your questions while I and those of my original group remain clear of the castle. His name is Kinsami Otoma." Sarah turned and walked back up the steps into the castle tower. She could hear the commotion behind her and knew it was at the mention of Kinsami's name. A strong family name and a great weapon to wield against the masses. Should the Otoma family back this venture many students would join on that alone.

Kinsami had been listening from up in the tower. He followed the speech predicting that would be how she would attack them. What he did not predict however was that he would be left within the castle walls alone with a bunch of students who may yet be loyal to the Lord and Lady that he had killed with his own two hands. Would they overpower him and end his life? That fear was the most prominent as Sarah walked back into the tower.

"Why've you left me with a bunch of students that may very well kill me?" Kinsami asked, his eyes wild.

"My dear Kinsami. Your fears are not necessary here. They believe in your name and they may very well believe what I have told them though they do not wish to admit it. I am leaving the choice to them. They will have questions and you must provide the answers. Will you do this for me?" Kinsami thought for only a moment before answering.

"I will... Five," Sarah almost lost her composure at the use of her title. Keeping the feelings from her face a wicked elation grew within. She had him snared completely.

The students of Bodhurst moved to the great hall once they had been fed and their wounds tended to. Everyone felt most at ease in the hall. It was also the best place to discuss what they were going to be doing in the coming days. No staff members survived or remained at the castle after the raid. Those who fled believed that Sarah would kill them for being affiliated with the castle work crew.

Now Sarah was camped outside the castle and major choices needed to be made. Would they defy her and defend the castle with their lives or would they allow her power over them? The castle system had failed them in a massive way and yet this girl outside the gates wanted to take control. Was it better to be manipulated with no knowledge or to give yourself completely to someone at your own choosing? There was little difference. The only other option was to keep their free will and use the power of Will to hold onto it until death.

Kinsami stood in the far back corner ill at ease with his current situation. So far no student had talked to or even acknowledged him. He was fine with this but always kept an eye out for the exits. He didn't know when one student or another may take it upon themselves to exact justice to someone they deemed worthy. Kinsami would give them a hard battle for sure but if everyone got involved he could not defend infinitely.

Sarah was positive about this venture. Kinsami understood her point of view. He was her most valuable pawn to be used against Bodhurst. She planted the seed in the student body that the enemy was truly the Castle Lords and Ladies. His job was to make that seed grow. They will come to him. She knew they would. They would need to hear his story and when he told it they would conform. She was too calculating to lose.

"So what do we do?" A voice rang out in the hall. Kinsami knew it was beginning. He didn't see the person who spoke but they sounded young.

"We should just bar the gates and tell them to fuck off, that's what," another voice said. This one Kinsami did see. He was almost twenty with an unshaven face and long brown hair. He didn't look impressed in the slightest. The biggest obstacle has been marked.

"No," this time a soft voice. Many people turned and parted slightly. This person was in the back and he had short cropped blonde hair. His expression didn't match his voice though. It was hard and stern as he looked at the other man. He walked forward, looking into the faces of those he shared the Castle grounds with. "We gain nothing by openly rebelling against the Eckhart girl. She has not moved against us except to defend herself. We should consider what she asks at least."

"How do we know that she didn't attack us with the intent to kill us all? Why should we believe her when she says that she only fought in defence?" This person stood behind the twenty-year-old. Kinsami recognised him for what he was. Just a lackey to bolster the kingpins view and push them onto people.

"Were you awake when we were made to attack them? I certainly was and let me tell you, I will never have anyone take over my body again. Not only would I have acted completely different to the hell we were thrown into but every time, we were the ones who attacked first. Can anyone in this room say otherwise?" He looked around the room and found that everyone was looking away. Even those that sought to argue and cause controversy were sitting in quiet contemplation remembering the events of the day. "We have all been victims. I for one, think it would be unwise to continue to fight Sarah."

"But how can we trust her. She did come here in force?"

"Why don't we bring the Otoma boy into the conversation? He was left to us should we have any questions. I don't mean to say we should definitely join her ranks and fight alongside her. All I am saying is we should consider it. When Mr Otoma explains to us what is going on we can then make a more informed choice." They all looked at Kinsami. He wasn't prepared and just stared blankly back. "Well?" They asked

"Well what? You have yet to ask me a question," Kinsami said buying himself a moment and giving himself direction in the conversation rather than talking randomly.

"I thought that was obvious," the older boy said. "Why are you following the girl who killed everyone in Castle Eckhart and who came to kill us? Sorry," he corrected himself. "Adaman and Sylvia?"

"Because her cause is just," Kinsami replied simply. He

wasn't going to answer them properly until they asked him properly. He knew they wanted the back story but they had to work for it.

"Yes. She told us that in the courtyard while we were bleeding. While we were lying on the ground writhing in the pain she brought us," so the one with the soft voice had a little bite. "Why did she start down this road? Why did she kill everyone in Eckhart? Why is someone from the Otoma family speaking for her? These three questions are top on my list and I would like them answered."

"Thank you," Kinsami said to him. "Unlike your friend you know how to structure a question. I will answer the last first. I am speaking for her because she thinks I will be able to win you over with my family name alone. That's not what you wanted to know though. I fought against her at Castle Eckhart and because of my strength she drew me behind enemy lines. She treated me as a guest at first but I believe she would have killed me had I gone against her. I know I am not a match in a contest of Will. Soon though I was slowly shown more and more as to why she was doing what she was doing and I agree full heartedly."

"Honest and not without its worries. The other two questions?"

"These two I fear will be hard to believe and very complicated."

"We will listen. We will decide. You need only speak and then we would ask you to leave Castle Bodhurst. This choice is for us to make without one of her lackeys standing over us."

"Fair," Kinsami let the last comment slide. "Where to start? Who here knows what a time paradox is?" A young girl near the centre of the group stuck her hand up. "We aren't in class here girl. If you know then speak."

"A time paradox is a risk of all time travel. Say you went back in time and killed your parent as a baby. You wouldn't be born and thus you would not be able to kill them. This would create a paradox that some believe could destroy the fabric of time itself."

"Good girl," Kinsami praised. She looked very pleased with

herself. "Now everyone remember that. At my trials the candles had issues. The reason was due to a boy who entered Castle Eckhart this year. I had promised the Lord of Eckhart, who also happened to be this boy's grandpa, that I would hold this boy's secret. He is an Empty." The room erupted in chatter. Kinsami understood that an Empty hadn't been seen for a thousand years so this reaction was inevitable. He waited for them to die down.

"Yes, he is an Empty and a powerful one at that. He started to hear voices and was convinced that there were people trapped in another realm. This would turn out to be Sarah and her friends. The very same people we were spending classes with each day."

"How?" a voice exclaimed from behind Kinsami. He didn't bother to look back.

"I'll get to it but it's complicated. The Empty opened a doorway to this other world and out poured Sarah and friends. They killed everyone they came up against except themselves of course. Eventually, Gregory, the Empty, saved a group of students by transporting them through a portal. This group were the younger versions of everyone that spilt out of the lifeless realm on the other side."

"Some of the smarter people here may be getting an idea of what had happened. Gregory sent the students to a realm that didn't age and they could only watch this world through a window created from their Will. The students spent centuries watching our world's history waiting for the time when Gregory would, in turn, free them again. The reason they killed everyone was because they had already watched their older selves killing everyone. They were forced to or risk creating a paradox and destroying time and space."

"You were right about the complicated part. It's going to take half the night to even get my head around that. What about why they are coming after the castles? You haven't explained that," said the student with the soft voice.

"When they were in the other realm watching our history they saw what the castles were doing. They are creating within all Will users the ability to take over their minds whenever they want. It is wrong on many levels. They are here to free all."

"This is bullshit, Ryan," said the older boy. "An Empty, time travel, mind control. He is a lying piece of shit and deserves to die."

"And yet it is so far-fetched that it might just be true. What proof could you give to us, Kinsami Otoma," Kinsami was impressed the boy knew his name.

"I have none. You decide amongst yourselves and should you decide to join Sarah, she can show you what she learnt over the centuries and believe me, it would take centuries to learn. I shall take my leave."

"No!" said the twenty-year-old. "I won't let you go. You can be our hostage."

Instantly Kinsami cloaked himself in his flame armour and was standing next to the man with a flaming katana to his throat. The man visibly paled.

"You cannot hold me. Do I have your leave to go?" The man just nodded and watched Kinsami walk out. He fell to the floor taking in great gulps of air.

Sarah watched as Kinsami made the short walk from the gates to where they made camp. She understood the situation instantly but had predicted this may eventuate. She wasn't worried though, confident in her path. She laughed as Kinsami tripped on a hidden rock. It was a clear night but the moon had already passed over the horizon making it hard to navigate the rough terrain.

"I knew you couldn't stay away from me," Sarah said with a little smile. Kinsami didn't return it.

"I would have been happier without being stuck with that lot," Kinsami said.

"That lot as you say will be our allies soon enough."

"I am not as confident as you. They are just bickering amongst themselves at the moment. I can see one who has a good head on his shoulders and one who is holding a grudge against us. Both are influential in their own way."

"I suspect you tipped the balance in our favour?"

"What I said was the truth," Kinsami replied evenly. "I told them everything from your entrapment, Gregory's lack of colour and the reasons for the attack on Castle Eckhart. Nothing was influential for better or worse. I did, however, leave on a positive note." Kinsami said with a smile. Sarah didn't ask but trusted in his actions.

"Morning is but a few hours away," Baras said close by reading the stars. "We'll have our answer then."

Kinsami looked at the man. "How did you get your name, Baras?"

"From my parents," the man replied.

"Yes, but was there any influence in your naming?"

"My mother went to Castle Eckhart when the Lord was much younger. She was inspired by him and my name is the result."

"You remind me of him," Kinsami added. Baras just grunted and moved to a fire further away. The rest of the night was uneventful and Kinsami even managed to get a couple hours sleep on the rough ground. He woke with a kinked neck and feeling cold. There was a mist around the castle vicinity this morning and in the east, a lighter grey filtered through.

Kinsami heard the gates of Castle Bodhurst open but couldn't see what was coming. He readied himself for the worst before someone of the green cleared the mist between themselves and the castle. Kinsami saw a single figure walking over to their camp and recognised the man with the soft voice.

"At least the whole of Bodhurst isn't charging down on us," Sarah said coming up beside him.

"He's the man that spoke well of us," Kinsami told her.

"Even better," Sarah said with a smile. "I told you we had nothing to worry about." The man continued to within ten metres of the camp. "Go greet our guest, Kinsami."

"Greetings, Ryan wasn't it?" Kinsami said as he approached the man. "How fared the night?"

"You spoke of final proof to what you said in the hall. I would like to see that before I give our answer."

"Straight to the point," Kinsami said. "It's a good trait not often found in people. Come meet Sarah." Kinsami turned and started walking back to where Sarah was standing. He did not look to see if Ryan was following or not. Humans were always like sheep when it came to things like this. If you start walking and they want something from you they will follow. Stopping before Sarah he smiled as Ryan came alongside him. "Sarah, I would like you to meet Ryan. He's come seeking proof you are everything I have told him you are."

"Oh?" Sarah said raising an eyebrow. "And how shall I prove I am everything you have told them. I cannot possibly know everything you told them,"

"Kinsami told me that you are centuries old and that you have learnt things in that time that you couldn't learn in a regular lifetime. This I would like proof on. If you can show this we are your allies in your fight." Sarah looked at Kinsami

"You are commenting on a woman's age I see. I feel I should be insulted."

"I know you well enough to know you don't care in the slightest. Just show him your ability and we can start moving forward with our plans."

"What plans would they be?" Ryan asked.

"You haven't even pledged yourself to the cause and you are trying to get information. That's rather presumptuous of you," Stuart said nearby. "The plan is to take Castle Kirkwall. Everything else has yet to be discussed."

"You want proof of just how insignificant you are?" Sarah asked. "You have been mind controlled by those you would seek to serve. They threw you away to protect themselves. They speak volumes of your insignificance. Now I will show you how insignificant everything you have learnt up until now with Will is. You'll accomplish nothing in your life more than any other." Sarah brought her Will into existence all around her. Like with Kinsami it was not aggressive but it showed her power and proved her story. Ryan stared in astonishment and disbelief at what he saw. He had no doubt anymore. This girl was the real deal. Ryan dropped to one knee before her. Sarah let her Will fade.

"On behalf of all those left in Castle Bodhurst, I pledge our loyalty. We'll help you accomplish your goals."

"Stand up, Ryan," Sarah told him and he got to his feet. "You may be insignificant in ability and worth but your choices today show you are doing something very significant for this world. Your life and those of the students inside will have meaning. Your worth begins today. Thank you."

Kinsami knew the smile Sarah gave was fake. He had seen her smile so many times and they always had a dark superiority behind them. That was her smile and Kinsami thought it suited her. This fake smile looked pure and full of joy. She wielded it well for Ryan. He was sucked in completely by it.

"Sarah, it is with great pleasure that I invite you, Kinsami and all those who follow your lead into Castle Bodhurst," Ryan said.

"Well that's lucky. I don't have to kill you all now," Sarah said walking past him with a laugh. Ryan became stunned into silence, a worried look on his face.

"Don't worry," Kinsami said slapping him on the back. "She's joking. She has a very dark humour."

Ryan was unsure but let out an uncomfortable laugh before following Sarah back to the castle.

Chapter 11

As the clouds rolled in, a misty haze was evident on the horizon. Gregory had seen this many times before and concluded it was raining heavily over the ocean. The waves had picked up and now crashed against the cliff face far below with a great roar. Gregory would hate to be stuck in the water at this time. He was never the greatest swimmer to begin with. The weather was changing as the winds picked up. It wouldn't be long before the rain made it to the cliff face where he now sat. They could always hide away in the caves if they had to but he was comfortable watching the ocean for the moment.

Michelle sat close by but so far they had conversed little. He didn't quite remember her from the castle and he was surprised. A girl that looked as cute as Michelle would be recognised instantly. With little background, Gregory was having trouble finding words to say to her. He didn't know what to say to Dirk either but that was a completely different situation. The blow from Lavi running away was hard on him and he was sitting with legs dangling over the edge staring blankly out over the ocean.

Should he approach him? Should he try to get some information from Michelle first and go in prepared? The latter sounded the better of the two so Gregory shifted closer to Michelle to keep their conversation as quiet as possible. The last thing he wanted was for Michelle to say something triggering and Dirk to overhear it. He needed tact and sensitivity.

"We can't keep going on like this, Michelle," Gregory said. "In the coming days, we are going to need Dirk and Lavi too."

"And what can I do about that? Lavi has run off and Dirk is hurting. I don't know him well enough to even try to help."

"Help me help him."

"And how would you like me to do that?"

"Allow me to know what happened at the castle. I want to know how to approach Dirk and possibly ease his feelings a little. I understand you don't want Dirk to find out from anyone other than Lavi but I would like to be prepared when I do talk to him."

"I don't know, Gregory," Michelle said confused. "It isn't a happy story. Lavi should be the one to judge who should know. Don't take this the wrong way but I don't know you well enough to know if I can even trust you, either. I heard you were responsible for the mess at Castle Eckhart."

"I was responsible in both trapping and releasing the students who caused the chaos. By default, I am responsible for everything that happened that night and afterwards. For what is still happening."

"Dirk and I have been working towards rectifying my mistake and more than this Dirk has been working so hard to free Lavi. He never once gave up on her. Now, he teeters on the edge of giving up on everything."

"He is stronger than that, Gregory," Michelle assured him. "Just give him time. He'll get through this and will continue on the journey. Lavi believed in him also. She almost gave up until she heard he was coming."

"If it was Dirk that kept her going then why was it she couldn't face him?"

"She loves him too much to face him right now. In the dungeons, we were tortured and abused. She attempted to take her own life numerous times but failed on each attempt. Right now she is struggling with what happened to us, how Dirk will react and possibly losing him. Her self-esteem is low and she is hurting."

"You made it through fine."

Michelle slapped Gregory hard across the face. "You know nothing of my struggles and torture is a far sight better than what happened to her."

Holding his cheek, Gregory realised how rude and insensitive he had been but more than this, finally understood what happened in the cells. He looked to Dirk, sorry for the struggle he was going through. Michelle looked to change the subject. "Before, you said that we'll need Lavi and Dirk in the coming days. You talk about rectifying what happened at Castle Eckhart. Why do you assume I'll be helping you in any way?"

"Will you not?" Gregory asked. "Sarah needs to be stopped. She has moved onto the next castle already. She's possibly killed everyone by now. Even those in charge. Next will be Castle Kirkwall. Can you sit by and let it happen?"

"It has nothing to do with me," Michelle said bluntly. "I've fought to get free of them. Why would I waltz back in and risk my life for a cause I would get nothing out of?"

Gregory couldn't believe what she was saying. "To do good in this world, you don't need a reason. You shouldn't expect anything back for it either. If you do this, you do it because it is the right thing to do. Think of what they did to you and Lavi at Eckhart. Do you want to allow others to go through that? Will you be able to happily sleep at night with the screams of others sounding from the distant castles? You can help, Michelle. We can stop this."

"I've realised I don't like you, Gregory," Michelle said with a hard expression. "You can't put the screams of others on my shoulders. The only part I played in this game was trying to escape being kidnapped and tortured. That doesn't make me responsible for what my kidnappers do next. What makes you so sure you can even stop them? They're extremely powerful."

"I don't care if you hate me. Many people do. I'm the only person who could come close to stopping them though. I'm more powerful than they could dream of being."

"What makes you more powerful? You would die the first time you came up against two or three of them. Especially if they have a purple user. They'll block the colour you gather, or worse, send your attacks straight back at you. You are weak, Gregory. Wake up to yourself."

"Michelle, I'm an Empty." He let that sink in watching her trying to comprehend the immensity of his words. "They can't stop me because I don't use colour. They can't send my attacks back because they won't sense I am attacking. I can do anything I want and they can't match me."

Michelle was left mouth gaping wide. She stood this way for almost a minute before her face became set in a hard expression. She didn't say anything more. Turning around Michelle walked to the far edge of the cliff, opposite to the one

Dirk sat. Gregory was over arguing with her anyway. Dirk was more important right now. He looked at his friend sitting in silent anguish. Time to talk.

Wandering over, Gregory sat by his friend. He didn't say anything for a time looking out over the ocean, watching the turmoil in the waves and the harsh beauty of the rain. This place had a peaceful quality to it that only nature, undisturbed by man, could give. Turning, Gregory let his eyes fall onto Dirk's imperfect face. Tears had dampened his cheeks though his eyes weren't as blank and distant as he first thought. There was intelligence and determination in his look as Dirk turned to look Gregory in the eyes. The first movement Gregory had seen since arriving at this cliff.

"When are you going to take on Sarah?" Dirk asked.

"I want to take her on as soon as possible," Gregory replied surprised that Dirk was the one to bring up Sarah.

"Will you give me three days?"

"What do you need the time for?"

"I'm going after Lavi. I should have chased after her straight away but I was at a loss on what to do. I know what I want to do now. In three days I'll be back with her and we can all move on Sarah together."

"Three days is a long time, Dirk," Gregory said shaking his head. "Sarah may progress further ahead than we want her to in that time."

"Look how long she took to go from Eckhart to Bodhurst. Even if she's moving faster, we should still have a few days spare at least. Just know, you wouldn't have come back to face her if it wasn't for me. You owe me this much at least."

"You're right, my friend," Gregory said. "I'll give you the three days you need. On the third day, you can find us at Bodhurst camped a small distance from the castle. Do you remember the arrows I highlighted in Mandaloo directing us to the museum?" Dirk nodded. "I'll place an arrow above us and make it so only you and Lavi can see it."

"I'll make sure to find you."

"You better," Gregory paused. "But if you don't, I won't think less of you. What'll you do if Lavi is too broken to fix?"

"I'll stay by her side always. I'll do what I can for her no matter what. Even if she hates me."

"She doesn't hate you, Dirk. Michelle told me she only made it through this ordeal because of you. Go to her. Bring her back."

Dirk nodded, placed a hand on Gregory's shoulder and pushed down. Gregory almost lost his balance as Dirk levered himself up.

"I'll see you in three days," Dirk said before leaping over the cliff and taking flight. Gregory watched as he disappeared into the sheet of rain only ten minutes away. Catching Michelle watching him, Gregory paid her no notice. Rising to his feet, Gregory made for the cave. The storm was building on itself and the wind had started to pick up. Glancing back, he saw Michelle had yet to move. He couldn't help stubbornness.

The streets were full of pedestrians and cars. Buildings rose on every side trying to conquer the sky. It was a drab, grey world in the city. No one used colour and the cement walkways didn't help. She walked past a small park at one point. A few trees, grass and play equipment. The children of this town were undernourished for nature. Lavi had grown up on a farm with open land all around her. She could swim in the dam or walk under the canopy made by some thousand odd trees. The thing about the city though, even exposed as she was on the streets with everyone around her, was that she was hidden. No one knew who she was. No one cared.

There was a small pub coming up on the right. It looked old with lantern lights out the front giving the weather stained wood of the shop front an orange glow. Lavi thought the two-storey building would make a great rest stop for the night and she entered walking up to the bar. She thought the way they displayed car registration plates from different states around the walls was a funny commodity but she wasn't laughing right now. She doubted she would laugh again.

The typical bar owner in a blue cotton polo shirt with the bar logo on the front served from the counter. He had a dish cloth in his hand wiping the inside of a large glass with practiced perfection. It was all for the atmosphere than actually any real cleaning but Lavi thought it worked. The man behind the counter looked her up and down. He was sceptical of her age but waited for her to talk first.

"I need a room for the night," Lavi said. She wouldn't look the man in the face.

"I have one available," he replied. Lavi didn't recognise the accent the man had or, for that matter, anyone had. "You need to pay first. Fifty dollars." Lavi reached into the pocket of her baggy pants and materialised a fifty dollar note. She tried handing it to the man who looked at her strangely. "I don't know what currency that is but it won't work here."

"Sorry, I have been travelling a bit. What currency are we currently using?"

The man behind the bar cracked the till and gave her a look at the notes and coins. She saw a one hundred dollar note and decided she may as well get some real change. Reaching back into her pocket she made an exact copy of the one hundred and passed it to the man. "Sorry, that's the smallest I have in this currency. Can you break the change down a bit, though?"

The man accepted this note and gave Lavi back some fives, tens, and a twenty. On top of the notes was a key.

"Number eleven just up the stairs."

Thanking the man, Lavi walked up to her room. It was cosy and had all the amenities she needed. She walked to the bed and laid back. Straight away, images ran through her mind. Images of abuse and pain. Images she wanted to run from as far as she could. Lavi started to feel depressed again and she was starting to think dark thoughts about her own life once more. Dirk came to mind on the side of the cliff looking at her with a desperate expression on his face. She heard him calling her name as she flew off. She needed alcohol. Adults always say how alcohol makes you forget.

Jumping to her feet, Lavi walked out the door and back to the counter downstairs. The barman looked over at her and noted the distressed look on her face.

"What's wrong?" he asked. "Room not to your liking?"

"I need a drink," she replied. "Give me something strong."

The barman's face became serious. "Do you have any ID on you to show your age?" Lavi done a quick calculation in her head and worked out 1988 would make her eighteen. She reached in and materialised a license. Passing it to the barman he took one look and passed it back. "That's no good girl. You need to be twenty-one here."

"I'm twenty-three," Lavi said without skipping a beat. She quickly manipulated the eight to a three and handed it back to the barman. He took another look and his eyes widened a little.

"Sorry. I thought it was an eight," he said. "I'll get that drink for you right now."

"It's okay. A lot of people look at me and believe I'm younger than I really am. It's those preconceptions that cause us to make these mistakes."

"You're youthful beyond your years," the barman said while shaking a variety of liquids in a mixer. "I had you pegged to be about fourteen."

"Thank you," Lavi replied. The barman poured the orange liquid from the mixer over ice then topped it with a blue liquid. The blue mixed with the orange in a way that made it look like icicles.

"An Icicle Sunset," the barman said. "This is one of my strongest and most popular." Lavi paid for the drink and walked over to a round table in the corner. She started to sip the drink and the acrid taste that came to her mouth made her question why adults drank the stuff at all. She continued to sip the drink slowly trying to get accustomed to the horrible mix of flavours.

Lavi watched people come and go. Some got food, others drinks. Some just came to waste money gambling, testing their luck against the fates. After a while, she noticed that one guy who had been sitting in the bar with a bunch of others was watching her. She tried to ignore this as much as possible but he was always looking over drinking drink after drink. There must be something big this man was trying to forget, Lavi thought as she finished off her own drink. The Alcohol had started to make her feel light headed and Lavi ordered another; happy she was starting to feel the drink begin to do its job.

Drinking this one faster, Lavi felt the effects of the alcohol taking hold. The room was spinning and her thoughts were more open. With a deep sense of dread, Lavi found the alcohol was actually having the opposite effect than what she desired. Images of her abuse filtered in. They stole from her something she would never get back again. She could never be whole again. Is this how men were? Judging girls on their looks? Giving them worth only in what they could get from them? Was she nothing if she wasn't giving herself to them? Lavi didn't want to be worthless. She had already betrayed Dirk at the castle. Sarah was right. She was a slut. She looked across at the man.

Gently she started to stir his drink. She was playing with him without realising he wouldn't know what was going on. At that moment his friend hit him and started talking. Lavi stopped her attempts to get his attention at this point thinking his friends would steal him when they pushed him up. The man was looking back and forward unsure what to do and Lavi realised his friends were on her side. Or was it his side and she was to be of use? She tried to give the best smile she could and when he saw it he came over.

"Is this seat taken," he asked with a hand on one of the seats before the girl. Lavi noticed he had the same accent that was prominent in this region. She wasn't worthless now. She would do what she had to as a woman, she would be happy.

"Do you think I am pretty?" Lavi asked the man who was acting rather clumsy.

"Well... Yed... Yes," came the response. Lavi knew it. He wanted her.

"Would you like to take me up to my room?" she asked then. "Would you like to do things to me?"

"Just like that?" the man asked. Lavi started to doubt herself. Was there more she had to do? She didn't know. How was it she could be useful? Was she worthless after all? She didn't hear what he said next. "You don't even know me."

"So you don't want me then?" Lavi put on a pout. She didn't realise she was almost in tears for real. The man became flustered and was flailing his arms around. He said no a lot which only made Lavi more upset before he finally changed his mind and said that she was very pretty with some silly excuse. She thought to keep him interested while she had him.

"So then what would you like to do to me?"

"I would like to take you to somewhere more private at least. My friends back there are... I just don't want them to be around."

"Follow me," Lavi told him. She reached over holding to him so he couldn't get away and started to lead him to the stairs however when she was only part way up he told her to wait. Lavi turned with a sad expression on her face.

"What's your name?"

"It's Lilly," she said. Lavi had been taken from her. Lavi was gone and to him, she would be the woman that men wanted. She would have worth. She continued to the room hoping he would just follow her from now.

"I'm Charlie," the man called after her. Lavi heard his friends cheering for him. They acknowledged her existence. She felt wanted. She felt needed. Lavi continued to walk to room eleven and entered without hesitation. She had not bothered to lock any of her doors since Gregory turned her wall invisible. People could invade her space at any time. What was privacy but a simple illusion anyway? She walked over to stand by the bed and heard Charlie follow her in closing the door.

Stretching her hands up to the ceiling, Lavi drew in all the green around her. When she felt the amount was sufficient she willed the clothes she had coddled herself in to become mist, to float away and vanish. When she turned back to look at Charlie though, he wasn't coming forward. He was hesitating. Was she ugly now that he saw her body? Was she worthless after all? Lavi was feeling the value in herself slipping away and she approached Charlie. She needed to get him to the bed. She couldn't lose what she had gained. Her eyes screamed desperation as she placed her hands on his side drawing him back to the bed.

Lavi knew she had him now and sat back on the bed. When

he put a knee up she moved back a little to give him room. He pulled the rags from her chest. His hand came up to touch her. It wasn't harsh like before and he started to push her gently back to lie down. He was moving atop of her. Everything around the room grew dark. Shadows overtook the light and the face of Charlie started to become that of those who had first used her. She couldn't do this. She wasn't a tool for the use and pleasure of men.

Gathering the green she let her Will free in a burst of air sending Charlie from her and across the room. Lavi continued blowing gale force winds around the room toppling furniture and sending anything not nailed down into the air. When Charlie fled the room in terror she finally let her Will die down and dropped to her knees, tears running down her face, Great sobs racking her body. What was wrong with her? She didn't have time to answer it for herself when she heard a noise at the door and a familiar voice she did not want to hear.

"Lavi?" she turned hoping beyond all hope he wasn't there. Standing in the doorway with eyes wide open was Dirk.

"Don't look at me!" Lavi yelled. She turned away from him. "Get out!" She heard the footsteps and though she yelled at him to leave was a little upset that he did. A blanket fell around her shoulders and she looked up to see Dirk was still with her. Lavi hugged the blanket tightly around her tired frame.

"A man ran into me as I was walking by. He was yelling about a witch creating tornadoes in her room," Dirk told her. "I knew it could be no one else."

"Why did you come?" Her voice was barely a whisper. Dirk could see she was so very fragile.

"You left me on our cliff side with nothing to let me know what you were going through. You fled from me like I was a demon. The look in your eyes was sheer terror. I was upset but I can't let you go. I want to talk with you. I want to know what you are feeling and I want to help you through it all. I'm here for you, Lavi." Dirk didn't speak anymore. He wanted Lavi to say the next words. The silence grew but finally, a little squeak came from the small girl.

"Leave me," he heard.

"No, not this time."

"Leave me," a little more strength had found its way into her words.

"Lavi I'm not going anywhere," Dirk replied stubbornly.

"Leave me alone Dirk! I am broken, useless, my life was stolen from me and now I'm just a mess. What you see on the surface, the bruises, the marks, the cuts where I tried to take my life, they are nothing to the darkness that has crept into my soul."

"Lavi, the girl I know could stand up to anything. You're strong and I can help you through whatever happened. There is nothing anyone could do that you couldn't overcome."

"They raped me, Dirk... They raped me... They fucking raped me," her voice broke and she burst into tears. The crying was uncontrollable now as she rested her forehead against Dirk. She hit his chest a number of times while she was crying. "I'm sorry. My innocence is gone. I've been used," she sobbed. Dirk was shocked. He didn't know what he could say that would help Lavi right now but he rested a hand on the blanket over her back for comfort.

"Why are you apologising?" Dirk asked. "You are the victim in all this and haven't done anything wrong."

"I did. I was dressed like a slut. I was too open with everyone and never showed modesty. I brought this upon myself. Do you hate me now? Can you ever forgive me?"

"No!" Dirk said with force. He had tears rolling slowly down his face as he was getting emotional over the situation. "There is nothing to forgive, Lavi. You hear me? There is nothing at all to forgive. The way you act doesn't give them the right to abuse you. I will never hate you. I love you, Lavi and will always be here for you." Lavi looked up into Dirk's eyes and a new, steady stream of tears burst forth.

"I'm sorry. I'm sorry," she kept repeating as she clung close to him. Dirk wrapped her in his arms and held her close, comforting her. Lavi started to see the shadows again, creeping in all around, blocking out the room. She pushed Dirk back.

"I can't be close to anyone. It makes me remember," she cried. "But please, don't leave me."

214

"I'm not going anywhere," Dirk replied unsure what he could do other than letting her know he was nearby.

Gregory was laughing inwardly. He had guessed accurately how long the rain would take to reach the cliff and he was happy, warm inside the cave. Michelle on the other hand stayed on the cliff side for a full half an hour before the wind, rain and cold drove her to abandon her stubbornness and seek shelter with Gregory. She was dripping from head to toe. The dark dress she wore was torn and patchy. Her hair was curly and sticking to her cheeks and she continually tried brushing it away. Excess water made the dress stick to the curves of her body and Gregory couldn't help but like what he saw.

Michelle had walked in and sat on the opposite wall to where Gregory was sitting. A small stream was twisting along the cave floor between them as it ran downhill towards Castle Eckhart. Gregory noticed that Michelle had started to shiver and wondered why she didn't use her Will to warm herself in some way. Maybe she was of the purple, blue or other colour that she just didn't understand what she could do to warm up. Gregory decided that for being rude before he would help her now as an apology.

Something memorable, but what? What could give an impact? The moment he started to think Gregory gave up. He didn't know what Michelle's likes were. He would just have to rely on his imagination. Leaning back against the rock wall of the cave, Gregory closed his eyes. He had a picture in his mind and wanted to concentrate. Beside Michelle, small cracks opened in the ground. Michelle didn't notice at first but as small shoots started to sprout and grow, she shifted quickly flat against the wall watching. The unnatural event causing her to become stressed.

"Are you doing this, Gregory?" she squealed. "Gregory!"

"Shh," Gregory was motioning for her to be quiet. "It's okay. I'm going to give you a gift."

Michelle wasn't completely convinced but settled slightly. She sat awkwardly watching as the saplings started to grow more and more rapidly twisting with each other. They grew to fill the area in which the two sat. Leaves shot out from branches that were spreading out along the roof of the cave. Michelle saw that on the trunk the words *"I hope this warms your soul'* were etched. At the base, the middle of the trunk made an arch over the small stream.

"Sure it's a great gift and all but I don't see why you would give me a tree in a confined space," Michelle said trying not to let Gregory down too hard over the thoughtlessness. The leaves suddenly started to go brown and fall away, the aged leaves piling upon the ground. At least now she had something to sit and sleep on. Some more floated away on the stream. Michelle saw the branches and then the trunk start to wither and die.

"Gregory, please, you don't need to kill it off," Michelle didn't realise he was such a sook. Would she have to walk on eggshells around him from now on? "I do like it."

"I'm trying to concentrate, Michelle," Gregory said then. "Just wait until it's finished."

With a pout, Michelle looked back at the tree. The trunk was starting to split down the middle ever so slowly. Both sides were leaning at angles that looked as though either one would give way any moment. It was that very moment that they both gave way. They fell in on themselves in a way that couldn't happen naturally. The wood rolled down its own trunk decreasing in size as it approached the floor. When it finally connected it bounced into the air in hundreds of pieces the size of split logs that would go in a fire. One-half landed in the form of a small bonfire. The other neatly stacked itself ready to feed dying flames.

Michelle ducked as flames came to life on the ceiling. She had forgotten her fears from before, fears born from her time in the cage where she was unable to freely use her Will and watched in wonder. The flames spiralled around the roof before running down the wall and finding their home in the small bonfire. The flames licked the dry, aged wood and crackled as they grew larger. Higher and higher they grew until the flames touched the cave ceiling, filling the room with warmth and light.

Michelle's numb body reminded her with a shiver just how

cold she really was as the warmth touched her skin. She moved closer to the flames, hands extended. Before long she was warm and dry and feeling comfortable upon the leaf-filled floor. She found the leaves did not leave an itch upon her skin like a natural leaf might. She looked at Gregory who was comfortable where he sat smiling back at her. Back at her? She found that she herself was smiling. Probably for the first time since the horrible night at Castle Eckhart where her nightmares started.

You have warmed me right to my soul, Gregory," Michelle told him with a tear rolling down her cheek. "Thank you."

"I couldn't let you go cold, Michelle. Not after my rather poor first impression outside. I'm sorry that I was such a jerk."

"Don't be," Michelle said softening. She gathered up a large armful of leaves and walked over to where Gregory was. Dumping them close by on the already large layer, she sat down next to him. "I was being stubborn. It is a trait heightened in reds."

"Red?" Gregory was surprised. "Not wanting to sound like a jerk again but why couldn't you warm yourself? You should have been well equipped." Michelle thought for a moment and then laughed.

"I am free aren't I?" Michelle said. "When I was locked away in the dungeons of Eckhart, I couldn't use my Will. The guard would twist it and force it back at me. I grew accustomed to not using it that I didn't even try."

"First, they stripped you of your free will. Then they forced you to give up your inner Will. I'll take them down, Michelle. You can count on that."

"And I'll be beside you," Michelle told him.

Gregory was moved by this statement. "You don't need to, Michelle. You have your freedom back now. You shouldn't risk it in a venture I have a chance at pulling off myself."

"No, I am free but I still don't have my freedom. Not while they're still on the loose. I'll face them, Gregory, I will win back my freedom from their clutches and with me, you have an even greater chance."

"Thank you, Michelle."

Michelle smiled at him with warmth as soothing as the flames.

Chapter 12

"Yes," Sarah said happily. She was feeling really good about herself as she lay on her bed. She had taken care of Gregory, Castle Eckhart and now Castle Bodhurst. Everything was going her way and she saw little that could pose a threat to her. She'd come a long way from the conniving teen she had once been. Sarah always planned to find a strong husband to live off his wealth and prestige. Kinsami was one she was drawn too and Gregory was the other. She understood now why Gregory pulled her away from Kinsami. Being an Empty he would be the strongest Will user of her time.

Now she was strong herself. Centuries of training gave her more than any person could have in a natural lifespan. She didn't need to live off anyone. Sarah had what she thought of as an army of servants. The world could be hers if she would just extend her hand and take it. That would eventuate but now wasn't the time. She had the rest of her life to achieve this. Kinsami rose to her mind once more. He was still very much an option as a suitor. Though she had spent so much time with her original group, no one stood out as much as Kinsami. No one she trusted to accomplish her goals more. Yes, he would be hers one day. A knock at the door brought her out of her daydream.

"What is it?" she called. "It better be good." Stuart ducked his head into the room.

"Five, sorry for the interruptions but you need to come and see the monitors," he sounded worried.

Be it for disturbing her or for some other reason, Sarah didn't know. "I've left Tahlia in charge of everything to do with the monitors," Sarah said. "Have her look at whatever it is and decide on the best course of action."

"What if she is on one of the monitors in question?" Sarah sat upright. She looked at Stuart and saw that he was indeed worried for other reasons. A sense of dread came over her as premonitions of what she may see came to mind. "We need your decision on this matter."

Sarah rolled out of bed and shimmered for a moment.

Stuart watched as the dressing gown morphed into tight black jeans and a blue blouse. He turned and walked towards the monitoring room knowing Sarah would get annoyed should he wait for her lead.

The monitoring room was located in Castle Bodhurst where the food halls previously were and they were always left in the dark. The windows were tinted and lights left off. This allowed the clarity of the monitors to be heightened ten-fold. Sarah saw Stuart standing near one of the images and she walked over. Each picture was like a simple window created by Will to view places that were far away. They were similar to what Gregory could accomplish only there was no physical movement between the two areas.

"So what am I supposed to be looking at?" Sarah asked. Before Stuart had the chance to answer she saw Tahlia sleeping in a bed with a younger child in a chair beside her, watching over her. Sarah's temper rippled across her darkening face. "That lazy bitch. Why does she think she can sleep on my time? Where is she right now?"

"She happens to be asleep in a bed at Gregory's family home," Stuart told her. "She has not woken for a considerable amount of time. Something Gregory did to her."

"And the boy?"

"Gregory's brother, Allen," Stuart saw Sarah's eyes change. They were now like a lion's locked onto their prey, her wicked smile upon her lips. "You would've seen him when we viewed Gregory going to the museum for the first time."

"Where is Gregory now?" Sarah asked not taking her eyes from Allen.

"He is in a cave behind Castle Eckhart," this got her attention. Stuart nodded over to another monitor and she looked into it. True enough, Gregory was in a cave, lying on a huge pile of leaves. Close by, a fire burnt brightly creating shadows that danced around the walls. Sarah recognised the girl, Michelle, resting her head on Gregory's shoulder. Both looked to be dozing. A small pang of jealousy pricked at Sarah's chest but she dismissed it quickly.

"Was Michelle not in the dungeons below Castle Eckhart?

How is she now there with him?"

"Lavi and Michelle broke free a second time. This time they killed Emma and fled to the cave. Gregory and Dirk were not far behind. They have destroyed more than a quarter of Mandaloo and two-thirds of our reptilian manifestations," Sarah seemed annoyed at this but they could always repair the defences and make more warriors. "There is more...'

"Well spit it out," Sarah said growing impatient. She didn't think it could get worse.

"Lord Baras met with all four of them on a cliff at the end of the cave. He instructed Gregory to kill you and gave information to the others. We had a hard time hearing what he was trying to say. Soon after, Lavi and Dirk flew out over the sea and Gregory and Michelle remained, awaiting their return. The only real words we got from the old man were Veritas Rerum." Sarah smiled at this. "You know what it is?

"No," she admitted. "It was something my father used to speak of. Loosely translated, it means *True Reality*. I don't know to what it refers."

"How shall we proceed?"

"Do nothing for now," Sarah said. "Gregory will come to us in his own time," she thought about it for a moment. "Make sure you let me know when he is on our doorstep. I don't want any surprises. Meanwhile, I think I'll go get a little leverage."

"Your Will, Five."

Sarah walked from the room and down into the courtyard of Castle Bodhurst. She drew in purple in large amounts and then with her Will, crafted an atmosphere within the castle grounds to locate Kinsami's essence. No matter where he was this would draw her to him. She let her conscious thought go and started walking on what seemed a random route. The route unsurprisingly ended at the new quarters of Kinsami.

He was always in his room. She wondered why she even used her Will at all to find him. She walked in without announcing herself hoping to startle him or catch him out at something he may be ashamed of. Kinsami was meditating in the centre of his room. He did not look up or acknowledge anyone entered.

"Oh, you're no fun," she remarked. Finally, he drew in a deep breath and got up turning to face her.

"What were you hoping for?" Kinsami asked.

"Nothing important. Gregory's still alive," she said matter-of-factly. "My assassins failed me and he's gotten to Castle Eckhart."

"I hadn't known an assassination attempt was in the works." If he was surprised in any way by Sarah's comment he didn't show it. Kinsami knew all too well the hatred Sarah held for Gregory and wasn't going to interfere. "Apart from that, I had assumed as much. Will he be coming to Bodhurst?"

"Momentarily, he is awaiting his comrades to return from some unknown mission of Baras's. After that, it is a good bet. Information from the monitor room says he has been instructed to kill me."

"When he comes, I'll be the one to take him down," Kinsami stated. He had a look in his eyes like he had something he needed to prove to himself.

"No, not this time, Kinsami. I'll need you in the days to come. I don't need you going off to die because of some huge ego. I have another mission for you," Sarah said. Kinsami was intrigued if a little let down. "I would have you go to Gregory's family home and retrieve his little brother, Allen. You know him?"

"Yes," he replied. He had not expected a simple kidnapping to be his mission. "I met him at the entrance exams. He had a strong blue coin for a kid."

"Good. I'll use him to fuck with Gregory's head," Sarah chuckled. "Make him on edge and easy to make mistakes. You may get your chance with him after we take Castle Kirkwall. If he lasts that long."

"Let's hope he does," Kinsami said.

Sarah just laughed at this comment. "I have one other task for you. When you arrive at Gregory's, you'll find Tahlia asleep in one of the bedrooms. Make sure the lazy bitch doesn't wake up."

"Your Will, Sarah," Kinsami said.

Sarah had heard Kinsami use her title very little. The use of her name was Kinsami rebelling against her command. This pleased her all the more as she could slowly strip that from him.

The sky was on fire. Crimson reds and vibrant oranges danced amongst the clouds. Today was an unforgettable sunset. A sunset you hoped to find when you camp on a headland overlooking the ocean to be let down by pale yellows and a fast descent of the sun. Today, though, the sun seemed to hang on the horizon casting a large array of fiery colours onto the earth.

From their vantage point on the side of a tall building, Lavi and Dirk could see the sun perfectly through the city. The buildings closest to the sun being painted the same colour as the sky. As the light fell deeper into the city, smaller and smaller amounts hit the buildings, blocked by those in front. Lavi and Dirks building, however, was at the end of a major road and was lit up in a beautiful, crimson red.

Dirk knew tomorrow was the day he would meet with Gregory and Michelle again. Lavi made every indication that, even though she was scarred physically and mentally, she would be fighting. Dirk wished he had more time with Lavi as he felt that he was making progress with her.

When Dirk found Lavi at the inn, they had sat for hours in silence, neither moving, neither speaking. It was Lavi who finally broke the silence asking for some food which Dirk gladly fetched for her with haste. He found that the bar only sold pizzas and he ordered a large meat pizza of some sort with a few lemonades.

Lavi ate like she hadn't eaten in days. Dirk too, on his first bite, realised he hadn't eaten since his mum's roast. The pizza was finished in no time at all and Dirk downed the lemonade in one go. It was hard with all the fizz biting at his throat but he wanted to try and make Lavi laugh. Belching loudly he looked over at Lavi acting proudly. She was shocked at first, not expecting that Dirk would act this way around her then her face changed. Something of a challenge showed in her eyes. With a little push from her green Will, Lavi matched and then tripled the sound Dirk made. A smile crossed her face and for a moment she had forgotten the pain that was inflicted on her. If you thought Lavi was shocked, Dirk almost fell off his chair.

Reaching over, he finished off the last of Lavi's lemonade to her loud objections. Dirk set himself ready to give the next burp his all causing Lavi to grow quiet in anticipation. As Dirk opened his mouth the softest burp came from his throat. Pulling a face, Lavi started laughing at his efforts, seeing him start to blush. Soon, Dirk had joined in and they were both giggling like they didn't have a care in the world.

"I thought I had that," Dirk said wiping a tear from his eye. "I was sure I could trump your talent."

"You are years away from reaching my level," Lavi replied.

Dirk saw the light in Lavi's eyes that had just been kindled, suddenly vanish once more. It saddened him to watch her suffer silently.

They talked about insignificant things, always treading around the topic of Castle Eckhart. Dirk paid for a different room to sleep in. They spent the next few days the same way, talking about random topics. Slowly it became more personal. They talked about their families and how they grew up. They discussed things they liked and disliked and talked about where they saw themselves in years to come. When Dirk answered the last topic, Lavi sunk back into her cocoon. She didn't want to talk about relationships just yet though Dirk's answer involving her sounded nice.

When Dirk suggested they get out of the room, Lavi was more than happy to and decided with the afternoon sun going down they would find the best place to watch it set. Dirk didn't know what people might have thought if they saw them flying to the top of the building but he didn't care right now. All he cared about was that Lavi was beside him and she was starting to function normally. He knew he would have to broach the subject of tomorrow. The day they would go back to war with Sarah. He just couldn't think of what to say.

When the sun was finally tucked away over the horizon the first stars started to come out. Sporadic at first, Dirk started to point out each new one to Lavi as he saw them. He even named some of the constellations as they came into view. The moon was yet to rise into the sky, though with a new moon, it didn't matter much.

"It's always a letdown to see stars in a city," Lavi said. "There's too much light for their beauty to flourish."

"I know. A city never truly sleeps. Even when everyone is safely holed up in their homes, there will always be street lights on the roads and safety lights in the tall buildings. It's sad to think we have to give up such natural beauty to advance in life."

"Are we even advancing?" Lavi asked. "Farmers spend their days labouring in the hot sun and harsh climates and they don't believe it to be a wasted life. All anyone in a city does is make their life easier and themselves lazier. They buy more than enough food only to waste half because they missed the dates to eat it by. They purchase entertainment systems to allow their yards to be neglected. If they have a yard at all."

"I know what you're saying," Dirk nodded. "I won't live in a large city when I'm older. I want the freedom and flexibility of a small town. Somewhere where the stars shine like a million diamonds across a dark velvet sky. Would you like that?"

"I haven't decided what I want to do or where I would like to live," Lavi said as a safety screen from her emotions. She wanted to scream out yes, that would be perfect but all her defences were up and working, even on Dirk. Dirk gave a weak smile and nodded.

"Tomorrow, we go back," he suddenly said. The thought hadn't even come to the front of his mind but he found himself saying it. Lavi was silent a moment.

"Tomorrow we put an end to Sarah," she said in reply. "I would like nothing more than to end her life."

"Have you seen someone die before? Have you watched their life fade away knowing they will never love again or laugh again?" Dirk remembered all those he had seen perish on his journey. "You can't take something so serious so lightly."

Lavi started to laugh. She laughed long and loud, almost hysterically. "I shouldn't take it lightly?" she said. "Dirk, I haven't just watched someone's life drain away, I have taken it myself. You don't know the evils of this world. You talk about never loving again, never laughing again. A person could have their love, laughter and happiness stripped from them while they yet live. That is the harsh reality of life. You're a small boy playing at war. You know too little. You're too clean, Dirk." Lavi kicked herself off the side of the building and started to float to the road below. "Wake me when you're leaving to join Gregory."

Dirk sat there watching Lavi float away trying to work out what happened. What did he say? What did he miss? He could not determine exactly what triggered Lavi but was deeply upset that he had destroyed the progress he was making to get close again. He stayed on the ledge for another hour thinking about what he could do.

When did she sneak in to lie beside him? Without waking him, Michelle had managed to slip down in front of Gregory with her back facing him and put one of Gregory's arms over her waist, his hand resting on Michelle's stomach. He traced the lay of his other arm to find that it was supporting her head and bent around in front of her. His fingers were curled up in her own. Though, she was wearing long pyjama pants and a singlet top Gregory could feel the warmth from her skin mixing with his growing heat. The feeling overwhelmed him though he dare not move in case he woke her.

Michelle was softly snoring which instantly made her all the more cute to Gregory. She felt delicate in his arms and her curves matched him to a comfortable perfection. Two days ago, she stated that she hated him on the cliff outside the cave. Gregory had apologised for any wrong doings and crafted a tree and fire to enhance his apology. She warmed to him at that point and sat closer, casually talking about how the tree had reminded her of one in her hometown. When she grew tired, Michelle even rested her head on his shoulder. That was as close as they had gotten though. Gregory lifted Michelle noting how light she was and placed her on the bedding leaves nearby already asleep. The fire was still burning and Gregory added two more logs to see the night out. Warmth bounced off all the walls giving no need for blankets.

The next day they played in the ocean close by and moved the bedding leaves out to the cliff. A warm breeze was blowing and the night sky was rich and beautiful. The stars were bright and the two counted the number of shooting stars that crossed the Heavens. Michelle just tipped Gregory by one.

To think now she was in his arms after sneaking into his bed. Gregory noted the cave entrance and then ever so slightly glanced back.

He was in her bed! He started to panic thinking how Michelle was going to react when she woke. He didn't have to wait long as his fidgeting got to her. Hearing Michelle moan as she started to wake, Gregory felt her body contort and stretch against his own.

"Good morning," she said softly lifting her head slightly towards Gregory. Gregory lifted his hand quickly from her belly. "No leave it," she told him. She was still snoozing. "It feels nice."

Gregory placed his hand on her hip at first. He slowly moved it further around to her belly as he grew in confidence.

"Stop it. You're giving me goosebumps," Michelle said. With her free hand, she held to Gregory's and drew him up just under her breasts. Gregory stayed like this for half an hour longer. His lower arm was cramping but he endured it so that he didn't break the moment. Finally, Michelle was fully awake and she sat up resting on one arm.

"You were rather confident sneaking into my bed last night, Gregory," Michelle teased. "No hesitation what-so-ever."

"We didn't..?" Gregory's eyes were wide. He couldn't remember and Michelle saw this.

"Oh, how you made me scream. I'll never forget last night," Michelle told him with a shy smile. Gregory's face instantly became red as thoughts crossed his mind. He was trying to say something but nothing came out. Michelle laughed with delight and jumped into a hug. Smiling, Michelle tapped his nose with her finger. "Don't worry, Gregory. My maiden honour is still intact."

"Why would you say that?" he asked still blushing as she got off him.

"Because you looked so innocent a moment ago. I knew you didn't remember what happened. I wanted to play," Michelle said. "You were sleep walking or at least just awake. After relieving yourself over the cliff you walked straight to my bed and wrapped me in your arms. I can tell you it was soft and romantic."

"I pissed in front of you?" Gregory said horrified.

"Don't worry, Gregory. I had a hand over my eyes," Michelle assured him. "I only opened my fingers a little bit."

"I'm sorry," Gregory said.

"Don't be. I'm a big girl. I have brothers."

Gregory wanted very much to change the subject now. "We need to head to Bodhurst today."

Michelle smiled at his tactful sentence but let him move away from his embarrassment. "Do you know how to reach the castle?" she asked. "You know the whole plan rests on getting there."

Gregory's face drained of blood. "I don't know where it is," he admitted. "I only made it back to Eckhart because of the Museum portal."

"Well, you're lucky that I know the way. I have been to every castle and can take you there easily. Lavi and Dirk will be a worry." If there was anyone who looked more relieved than Gregory, Michelle hadn't seen them.

"Leave that to me. I'll leave markers along the way that only they can follow. If they come here first which would seem likely then they are sure to find us."

"When did you want to leave?" Michelle asked. "If we leave now we would get there just after lunch. If we wait too much longer we'll need to set up in the dark."

"We'll leave sooner then. I want to get a lay of the land before choosing our camping spot. It could make a difference before we infiltrate the castle."

"So are you prepared to leave now? I'm ready when you are," Michelle said.

Gregory got a mischievous look in his eyes. "Not just yet," he said.

228

Michelle saw the look and mistook it to be something to do with her. Would she need to fight him off? She would put up a show but knew in the end she would let Gregory win. He suddenly opened a window in front of him and she could see that he stuck his arm through. From her vantage point on the other side, she could only see a circle of mist. A loud scream came from within the window and she rushed over to Gregory's side. He was holding a large plate stacked with pancakes. There were mixed berries upon them and the stack was drizzled with maple syrup.

"Sorry, Mrs McDougal," Gregory called as the window started to close. Michelle stood trying to make sense of what happened. "Dirk's mum," Gregory told her. "I just borrowed some breakfast. From her side, she would have only seen a floating arm stealing her pancakes."

"You really are a kid," Michelle said ruffling his hair. Gregory thought she sounded disappointed but was happy when she sat in front of the plate and started eating. She picked a pancake up whole and folded it in half eating it like a taco. Gregory followed suit.

"These are good," Michelle said as she started on her second one. Gregory could only mumble an agreeance through mouthfuls. When they had eaten the last one and the plate had been cleaned by Will, Gregory used his Will to produce a letter. Placing it on the plate he returned it to its owner.

"What did the letter say," Michelle asked.

"It said "Thank you for the food, mum. Sorry my friend gave you a fright. Love Dirk'. Thought it would make her happy." Michelle smiled at this but said nothing. "Ready?"

"Ready," Michelle confirmed. "We'll need to go back to Castle Eckhart and make our way from there. You should start putting your markers down here."

Gregory set the marker in the middle of the cliff. It stood up and pointed straight into the cave mouth. Impossible to miss if they came back this way. He followed Michelle into the cave and through to the other side then stood waiting at the end for a new direction to aim the next marker.

"The next part, I'm not too good with," Michelle said. "I

have an odd fear of heights produced from when I am flying. I believe the fear is more to do with losing control and plummeting to the earth. It'll be slow going from here."

"That's fine," Gregory told her. "You should believe in yourself more though, Michelle. You've made it this far."

Michelle smiled at Gregory then floated up the side of the cliff face. Placing another arrow at the cave mouth pointing up, Gregory followed keeping to Michelle's pace.

"If you fall I'll catch you so be more confident," Gregory called. "I won't let you fall."

Michelle didn't reply but Gregory thought he saw her speed pick up. They flew to the top of the cliff and straight over. Gregory left an angled arrow showing their flight path. At intervals, he left more arrows and different coloured ones every time they made a course correction.

As they flew up into the flipped night sky, Gregory believed he would see the ocean over the top of the cliff. They were flying directly above the tunnel but when they topped the highest point there was only a desert beyond. He was having trouble comprehending this but he had seen far stranger things and just accepted it. Following Michelle closely, Gregory noticed they were staying at a very low altitude.

"The timing of everything is going to be put off a lot by that cave," Gregory said. "We may need to wait an extra half a day for Dirk and Lavi to find us."

"Agreed. No one thought of the time difference at each end of the cave when the timeframe was given."

"How are you fairing?"

"I'm getting by. I know you're looking out for me, Gregory, but I'm still having trouble."

Gregory flew directly under her and moved to within a few centimetres. "Lower yourself onto my back and put your arms around my neck," Gregory instructed her.

"What do you mean?"

"Just wrap your arms around my neck and let me do the flying. You just tell me at each way point where I should be turning."

Michelle followed his instructions and when Gregory knew

she was secure, increased his speed significantly. He heard a small squeal come from Michelle and slowed back down.

"What are you doing?" Michelle asked. "That was so much fun feeling the wind in my hair and speed of your flight."

"Sorry," Gregory said. "I thought I was scaring you."

"No, that's only when I'm in control. I can't seem to trust myself with flying because of how technical it is for me. I have to keep a number of things in mind when I levitate myself. I have complete trust in you though." That made Gregory happy. If speed was fun, he thought to give Michelle an even bigger thrill.

"Let's take this to a much higher level then," he said. "I'm going to take you sailing on the clouds."

He didn't wait for Michelle to answer but took off faster than the first time. Michelle could hear the wind whistling past her ears and tussling her hair. The land fell away very fast from her as she gripped Gregory tighter. It wasn't from fear that she did this though. It was because if she didn't she would be ripped away from Gregory regardless. As they came up to the clouds she braced for some kind of impact and closed her eyes. When she didn't feel anything, however, she opened her eyes again and all around her was mist.

She didn't expect what happened next. She would never forget it as long as she lived. They breached the top of the clouds and Gregory stopped climbing allowing his body to arc naturally with the momentum they had gained. Their bodies became weightless and Michelle started to float away from Gregory. Time stopped at that precise moment for her. The stars decorated the velvet sky above. The clouds glowed in a dim white below. Gregory was in her arms and all her worries were far away.

As the weightlessness subsided and Gregory took flight again skimming slowly along the cloud tops, Michelle leaned down and kissed him on the cheek. She was caught up in the moment and couldn't stop herself.

"What was that for?" Gregory asked blushing.

"It's so beautiful up here. I would never have come this far myself. You have given me such a wonderful gift and I will never forget this moment no matter where my path leads me. Thank you."

"You're welcome," was all Gregory said in reply as he sailed gently over the clouds.

Michelle let her arm hang down tracing over the cloud surface and dipping inside. "I read somewhere that the atmosphere, temperature and oxygen levels change at higher altitudes. I thought it would be different to this," Michelle said. She got her information after watching a documentary about scaling the tallest mountain in the world and the dangers it brought.

"You are currently within a bubble of atmosphere I brought up from the ground," Gregory replied. "We would most likely die at this height without it."

"Good to know."

Gregory stayed up in the clouds for a while longer before ducking below to leave another marker.

"Not long to go now," Michelle said. "I hadn't planned on your speed. We need to head about thirty degrees right and the castle will come into view after twenty minutes."

Gregory dropped a coloured arrow indicating the course change and this time added a number to show the amount of time left before they reached the castle. Flying on for twenty minutes, Gregory saw that anyone from the castle could have easily seen their approach in the daytime and counted himself lucky that they didn't arrive in the day as planned. He decided to use an eye trick again and changed his eyes to mimic cat's eyes, yellow and slitted. Suddenly everything became misty and blurred. Colours drained away and only a select few remained. The scenery though, stood out far greater than his regular vision allowed for. He could see a group of trees with a rocky outcrop at the centre and a high vantage point close by and decided it would make a great camp.

Placing the last of the arrows above them pointing down Gregory started to Will the area to move in a way that would protect them from any outside view and also allow them to be comfortable. Michelle walked around to watch Gregory and as she waited for him to finish she produced a small fire to see by, give warmth and cook the food they wanted. That's if Dirk's mum didn't cook for them again. Gregory walked over and sat next to her. Michelle suddenly screamed as she saw the large yellow, feline eyes staring back at her.

"What?" Gregory asked.

"Your eyes."

"Oh, sorry," Gregory said changing them back to a more natural look. "I forgot they were still active. They let me see better in the dark when finding a suitable campsite."

"I hate cats," Michelle replied. She then changed the subject to a more serious one. "Tomorrow's day is going to be Dirk and Lavi's last night. They will most likely start to head to us early in their next day so for us that would be tomorrow night. Depending on how far they need to travel we should be expecting them the morning of our next day."

"That sounds like a good assumption. It makes things complicated with the time flip in the cave. I wish it was just simple for once," Gregory said.

"It is simple for us. We only need to wait from this point. Tomorrow we can get a look at the castle and see if there are any easy access points around the walls. After that, we have one last night before the battle with Sarah."

"Are you worried?" Gregory asked.

"I am," Michelle admitted. "She has some strength behind her if she could take down two castles. You're an Empty though and even her strength couldn't match that."

"My lack of experience worries me," Gregory said. "She has been training far longer than I. She will kill on sight and it wouldn't even worry her."

"When it comes down to it, you'll come out on top, Gregory. Enough about that now. Most of our night has been stolen from us. Come hold me like you did last night and let me feel safe in your arms as I fall asleep." Gregory became bashful but walked over to where Michelle had just laid down. Sliding in behind her he wrapped her in his arms and the two drifted off into a deep sleep.

They awoke to a crisp, fresh morning. The fires were burning low and little heat was reaching them now. The only real warmth was in the shared body heat and Gregory started to fidget. He slowly twisted out, away from Michelle, recovering his arms and walked over to the fire. She barely stirred at all. Gregory threw a couple more logs on the dying blaze and sped up the flames with Will, too impatient to wait for the natural warmth

Gregory walked over to the edge of their camp to survey their surroundings. The area beyond the rocky barricade was a lot like that of Castle Eckhart's surroundings. There were hills, valleys and flat grasslands. The cliff faces around this castle were different heights, shape and colour but the area as a whole was similar. Looking at the castle he could have sworn that they were back at Eckhart. The only difference he could see was the colour of the stone blocks. The castle was a dark twin to Castle Eckhart. If the layout was the same Gregory thought it would make things much easier. It would have the same entrances and exits so they could plan more accurately.

Gregory suddenly jumped. Two hands had started to creep around his waist and Michelle's chin popped up on his shoulder. She giggled at his reaction.

"You're rather jumpy this morning. Aren't you used to being touched yet?"

"I have little experience with the advancements of women. Some but nothing substantial. You seem to be very comfortable."

"What are you implying," Michelle said with a dangerous tone in her voice.

"No... Nothing. I wasn't implying anything at all," Gregory said hastily.

"Good," Michelle stopped for a moment. "Gregory..?"

"Yes?"

"What do you think of me?" Gregory started to blush. "Honestly."

He thought about his answer more in-depth when she added the last part. He was going to say she was cute and he liked her but that wasn't everything.

"I'm floating in limbo at the moment," Gregory said. It didn't quite seem to be what Michelle wanted to hear. "As I said, my experiences with women is very limited. In fact, it was right before the catastrophe I brought upon Castle Eckhart that I was starting to get close to a girl. She was giving me attention and I liked it. I wasn't drawn to her but I thought I was starting to like her. I now know my mistake."

"I'm sorry, Gregory," Michelle said. Her emotions were confused and withdrawn. She wanted to be truly sorry for Gregory but she had fallen for him over these last few days and she was jealous that he had someone else that still affected him. "Did she die that night?"

"No, she didn't actually," Michelle's heart skipped a beat. "She started a killing spree."

"Sarah!" Michelle's hands came to her mouth as Gregory nodded. "How could you have feelings for someone like that?" Gregory saw that she was close to tears.

"Don't feel sad for me, Michelle. I said I only thought that I liked her. She gave me attention, gave my ego attention and I reacted by staying close to her."

"And that's what you're doing with me," It was more a statement than a question. Michelle's tears started to roll down her face and she fled the enclosure into the woods. Gregory started to follow but decided to give her some space. Let her process some feelings first before he continued his honest thoughts. She would come back when she was ready.

The afternoon was growing long as Gregory walked back to the campsite from watching the castle. He saw Michelle sitting by the fire with her back to him and he decided he would sneak up on her. He used his Will to muffle any sound from his approach and he sat in behind her, his arms around her waist.

"You didn't come to find me," Michelle said sadly.

"I thought you may have wanted to process your thoughts. I wanted to come but you needed time. I have awaited your return."

"Why?"

"To finish off what I think about you."

"I don't want to know, Gregory. I am happy just with your arms around me. I don't want to lose that."

"You won't be losing anything. Just listen to me, Michelle."

235

She stayed staring at the fire. No emotion showing on her face. "There is a difference between Sarah and yourself. Sarah gave me the attention any male would crave. I started to like her once she made herself known to me. Once she made her intentions clear with what she wanted from me. That was when I started to believe I liked her. With you though, I knew you were beautiful when I saw you on the cliff side. I was drawn to you before you even said anything to me. I know what it is to like someone now because I like you, Michelle. Everything before was just a silly fantasy. I have had other things on my mind since I met you though and haven't expressed myself properly."

"This is how you feel?" Michelle said in a soft voice.

"You asked for honesty."

Michelle seemed to melt into him more as he spoke. They stayed this way in silence while the sky turned from blue to flame to dark again. Michelle then moved forward to sit up.

"My maiden honour," she said softly removing her shirt. "I don't need it on the eve of battle."

Chapter 13

Dust was blown into the air from the dry fields of Gregory's farm. Whatever grass that did grow there was kept low by a large number of cattle roaming the fields. A creek snaked its way across the property allowing for water to be accessed from almost anywhere. The house itself was a two story wood home with an attic on top and a veranda around the outside. It was a creamy white colour and sported a red tin roof.

Kinsami's mood was foul when he finally tracked it down. He had little experience with flying and hit two trees on the journey. He hadn't meant to run into them and was fully aware they were coming, but when he made to change his flight path, his control over the heating and cooling involved in red flight let him down and he flew full speed into both trees.

The flight aside, Kinsami got lost a number of times and swallowed more bugs than he wished to. He was not looking forward to the trip home especially while carrying someone because he knew that Allen wouldn't come along quietly. He would most likely need to be knocked out.

Landing awkwardly on some thistles, Kinsami hopped his way up the stairs to the veranda. He saw that paint had started to peel in places and the wood looked as though it was starting to rot. The place needed renovations especially if Baras was spending more of his time at the castles and neglecting the home. Kinsami was told that Lord Baras wouldn't be home but he was on guard regardless. Not wanting to announce himself to early, Kinsami drew in the red. He used a type of heat distortion to muffle the noises of the floor boards as he stepped along the veranda.

As he got to the old door made half of wood and half of holey fly screen he used the same technique to distort sound. He knew the hinges of this door would be so old they would probably screech from even slight movements. As he was willing any noise into nonexistence, he was able to enter the house silently. Kinsami walked through the rooms looking around corners and up the stairs like someone could pop out at any moment. He moved quietly to the second floor, sticking to the outer wall and saw a door open to what looked like a bedroom. If the door was open someone would definitely be in there. Glancing into the room, Kinsami's theories were proved correct as he spied two figures within. A girl was in bed and a boy on the chair next to her, watching. He recognised the figures instantly.

"Have you fallen for the girl, Allen?" Kinsami asked stepping into the room. He saw Allen jump and it alleviated some of his own annoyances.

"Who are you?" Allen had settled down from the initial shock and focused on the intruder. "Kinsami, is that you?"

Kinsami was impressed the kid even remembered him let alone his name. This would make things easier if he was going to be friendly. "You were watching over the girl rather closely, Allen. I think you may have a little crush on her."

"No!" Allen denied, as all boys his age did. "Gregory asked me to take care of her. That's what I'm doing."

"I don't think he meant for you to take care of her that way," Kinsami thought this may cause a problem when the time came to kill Tahlia. "You're going to have to come with me. We're going to the castles."

"Is it something Gregory wanted you to do?" Allen asked

"No, it isn't but you will get to see him." Allen thought for a moment before he started nodding his head.

"Yeah, that'll be fine. I'll come along," Allen said to Kinsami's surprise and joy. This boy was way too trusting.

"Do you know how to use your Will, Allen?" Kinsami asked the boy then. "Can you fly?"

"I don't know what you mean," Allen said, his brow furrowed. Well, not everything could go Kinsami's way. He drew in the red and produced a floating ball of fire sitting just above his open palm.

"It's something everyone can do though not many people know about it let alone know how to wield it properly. I could show you a little of what I know. Would you like that? It'll help you get to the castle."

"Well, if you think I could do it."

Kinsami highly doubted the boy could pull off the use of

Will after only just hearing about it now. It took Kinsami a week of hard training before he could even utilise the smallest of his Will. "It all comes down to how strong your mind is. Don't be disappointed if you don't get it the first time. Do you remember your coin from the museum?"

"You mean the blue one grandpa kept sneaking into my pocket?"

"Yes, that's the one but he didn't sneak it into your pocket, Allen,"

"Yes he did. He told me."

"No. That coin is a droplet of your soul. It tells you the colour you can work with the best. In your case this is blue. In my case it is red. How about we go out the front?" Kinsami wanted to use this time to draw Allen away from Tahlia. He didn't want to kill the girl in front of him if he didn't have to. Allen agreed and the two walked out the front of the house and into the yard.

"The main thing to remember with this is that you need to fill yourself with the colour you want to use. At the moment you should use blue. You aren't going to achieve anything with another colour. Do you understand?"

Allen nodded. "Fill myself with colour," he repeated.

"That's correct. Picture the colour all around you. Make it the same colour as your coin. See it in the grass, the house, the trees, the stones. Everything you can see, imagine the blue inside it. Can you see it?

"I can see it, Kinsami," Allen confirmed.

"Good. Now draw the colour into yourself. Watch it move out of all the things around you and join with your body. Draw it all into your soul until you glow with the blue. Let me know when you are ready."

Allen concentrated for a moment picturing all the colour around him moving into himself. Part of his mind was telling him that this was a child's game and it wasn't going to work. It was the part of the mind that everyone needed to overcome to do things that were believed impossible.

"I'm ready, Kinsami. I have the blue within me and nowhere else. What do I need to do now?"

"This is the hard part," Kinsami warned. "You are going to use your Will power to make the colour do what you want. Focus as hard as you can. You need to really want this. I want you to make the colour seek water in the air and craft it into a large ball of water similar to the ball of fire I produced. Think only on that and nothing else."

Allen put his mind to work and tried to do as Kinsami said. He couldn't get anything to happen. There were no balls of water or any other miraculous event. Allen became upset.

"Don't allow yourself to give up because you failed, Allen. This is your defining moment. If you allow yourself to believe that it is all nonsense you will never be able to overcome it. Even I didn't get it the first time. You can do it but you need to be stubborn more than anything. You have to keep pushing forward and it will happen in time. Keep practising for a little longer. We'll be on our way soon. I'm going to go make sure Tahlia is comfortable and there is nothing she needs. I'll be back in a moment."

It was all working Kinsami's way. If Allen got any gifts from his family heritage then maybe he would be able to fly back himself. Kinsami doubted it but stranger things have happened. He watched Allen try and fail a couple more times before he walked back into the house and to the room Tahlia was sleeping in. Walking over to the bed, Kinsami shook the girl. Nothing. He produced a small flame and put it close to her right arm. It ate into the skin, burning and flaying it. The acrid smell of burning flesh started to fill the room and a horrible mark was left when Kinsami extinguished the flame but the girl did not stir. Whatever Gregory had done was powerful.

Kinsami decided that the girl would die by his flaming Katana. It would be an honourable death for her. She was powerful as a Will user but was beaten by her better. The girl still deserved to die honourably. He extended his arm out and gripped the air. As his fingers curled over, the hilt of a katana manifested in Kinsami's grip and the blade slowly materialised. Flames roared into life and danced upon the blade with a brilliant heat. Kinsami raised the blade above his head and prepared to strike.

240

"You could have been a great warrior, Tahlia, but by your weakness, you have been sentenced to death. Sleep well, sister."

"No!"

Kinsami turned to see Allen run in and swore. Recovering quickly he swung his sword as Tahlia was engulfed in a massive swirling ball of water. The blade was turned away harshly with the flames extinguished.

"What've you done?" Kinsami demanded.

"Gregory told me to protect her. You won't lay a hand on her while I'm here," Allen said, determined.

"Take it down, Allen," Kinsami said. He was surprised the kid even used Will at all but it must have been due to the heightened emotions brought about by the imminent danger. "If you don't, you will get what she was about to."

"No I won't," Allen replied. He became a little worried but the determination returned quickly. "I will protect her." Kinsami walked over to Allen and used the hilt of the sword to knock him out. He knew one way or another it was going to come to this. Why did he let himself think his fortune was changing?

Allen slumped to the ground and Kinsami turned back to see that, even with the kid knocked out, the churning ball of water was still protecting Tahlia. He walked over and touched the ball softly with his hand. The moment he made contact, however, he pulled his hand back in pain, cursing loudly. The ball was giving off large amounts of power. Allen really did have the talent his family showed.

Kinsami produced another floating ball of fire. This time the flame was so hot that it was burning white. He tried to push this through the water barrier which sizzled, squealed and flexed slightly inwards. The flame though was the one that lost the battle as it was slowly eaten away until there was nothing of it left. The water barrier was as strong as if it was only just conjured.

As Kinsami left the farm with Allen on his back, he was cursing under his breath, his mood darker than when he arrived. Not only could Kinsami not complete his full mission, the reason was due to a child that had no concept of Will. Sarah was going to be angry. He would have to come back at a later date to finish the job for her. For now, his main objective was in for a harsh ride to the castle. Allen would be sure to wake up sore tomorrow.

Dirk and Lavi had followed the arrows left by Gregory. They had been worried about the timing having neglected to factor in the half a day's difference from one side of the cave to the other. Flying with great speed they covered the distance quickly through the night and as the sun was just starting to peak over the horizon, Dirk and Lavi saw the final arrow to the camp. Hoping they weren't too late to help, the pair slowly floated into the clearing weary of the view from the castle.

In the camp, however, their fears were replaced with a kind of amusement. On a conjured pile of pillows and cushions, silks and other colourful and soft fabrics were Michelle and Gregory, naked from the waist up. There were no blankets on this bed and Dirk could see they were asleep in each other's arms, completely unaware that they now had guests. Lavi walked over and shoved Dirk telling him to give them some privacy. This caused Dirk to lose his footing and he crashed into a pile of wood waking Michelle and Gregory.

Gregory took a moment to take in the scene and jumped out of bed as Michelle put an arm across her breasts trying to be modest. Reaching for his shirt, Gregory threw it back to Michelle and looked sheepishly at his friends.

"Looks like you two have had no trouble keeping yourselves occupied," Lavi said. She wore a sad smile trying to be happy for her friends while reliving her dark experiences.

"No, I... we didn't," Gregory started to fumble his words.

"Leave it, Gregory!" Michelle said sharply putting Gregory's blue shirt on. Gregory stopped immediately. "They don't need to hear all the details."

Michelle got out of bed and walked over to Lavi hugging her tenderly. She had been worried for her and couldn't predict whether Lavi would return or not.

"I'm glad Dirk found you," she said. Michelle saw the pain

242

in her friend's eyes.

"Me too," Lavi said softly. "But I'm still struggling."

"It's natural. It may never leave you but with Dirk's help there may come a day it is a little easier to bear at least." Michelle hugged her friend again.

"I'm glad we didn't miss anything," Dirk said, finally getting back to his feet. He gave Gregory a wink getting the response he was hoping for as Gregory looked away embarrassed. "I would have hated to have missed the fight."

"We realised that you may be behind in time when we left the cave ourselves. We decided to wait an extra day."

"I bet you were glad for the delay then," Dirk said. Lavi shot him a dangerous look.

"If you keep it up, you'll be feeling rather sorry for yourself come the fight," Lavi said. Dirk shut his mouth. Lavi then turned to Gregory and Michelle. "So what's the plan?"

"We protect Gregory all the way to Sarah. He'll be the one to fight her as he has the greatest strength and ability. The layout of the castle is identical to that of Castle Eckhart so we'll have Dirk use the yellow and burrow through the walls as close as we can to the tower. A number of students from Castle Bodhurst have been seen on the grounds presumably now allied with Sarah. They may not know the whole truth so, Lavi, we want you to use the green to blow them away with the least amount of damage. Once we enter the tower I'll block each entrance and exit with walls of magma. This will allow Gregory the best shot he can to take out the bitch."

"And if it all goes to shit?" Dirk asked.

"We make it up on the fly or get out of there and try again later," Gregory told them. "We'll have lost the element of surprise but will have our lives at least."

"Okay, I'm in," Dirk said.

"Me too," said Lavi. "When will we attack?"

"As soon as we're ready," Michelle told them. "Would you care for some food first?" She indicated to the table near one of the rocky outcrops surrounding the camp. There were meats, both hot and cold, exotic fruits, salads, sticky buns and pastries, soups and rice dishes. Dirk's eyes grew wide as he saw

243

the table for the first time. He raced over and stood staring at the food. Lavi joined him and picked up a plate.

"Where did you get all this?" Dirk asked. He got his own plate and started piling things on.

"We got the food from all over," Michelle said. "Gregory's very handy that way. Though it may not be as good as your mum's pancakes, Dirk."

Dirk paused and looked at Gregory for a moment. Gregory was grinning. "With the berries and the maple syrup?" Dirk asked.

"The very same," Gregory told him.

"You bastard! That would have been a breakfast to eat."

"You have such a selection of food in front of you and you still say that," Lavi said. "Are they really that good?"

"Oh Lavi, you have no idea," Michelle told her. "It was heaven on a plate."

"Maybe one day, I'll take you to meet her and you can try them for yourself," Dirk told her.

"I would like that," she replied with a coy smile.

Michelle was happy for her friend. Dirk may just get her through her troubles yet. They all sat down with piles of food and started eating. They jested and teased, told stories from when they were younger and for the duration of the meal, acted like it was an ordinary day. When it was done and the leftovers were covered in conjured containers Gregory and Michelle changed their clothes. Michelle only changed from her pyjama bottoms into some dark jeans opting to keep Gregory's shirt before they moved to look out over the castle.

"There she is," Dirk said taking a deep breath. The castle was quiet below as the four looked on.

"We'll go in from that wall there," Gregory said, pointing. He gestured to each point corresponding to their plan and when he finished he asked if they all agreed. Everyone nodded and they took off through the woods, using the cover to get as close as they could to the castle walls. At the edge of the tree line, they were almost directly under the walls and for someone to see them they would need to lean right out. Walking ten metres along the wall, Gregory tapped the dark stone.

"Right here, Dirk. Keep it quiet and move in a straight line. We should come out fifty metres from one of the tower entrances. We don't know what we'll be walking into so when we break through, we move fast."

"Got it," Dirk said and started to draw in the yellow.

"Everyone, start drawing in your colour now so that you have ample amounts when we get inside," Gregory said.

The girls drew in reserves of their own colour and Dirk started to move into the wall. He was making the stones turn to sand creating a tunnel two metres high and curved like an archway, wide enough to fit two people side by side. The sand made the ground awkward to walk on but it was silent and manageable.

After eight metres, Dirk knew he was about to break through. He paused for a moment and gathered more yellow. He had slowly been drawing it in as he went but decided it was time to restock completely. He indicated their position to the others. When he started again it was a matter of seconds before the sun was filling the tunnel.

They peered out and saw that there was no one within the courtyard beyond. This was the shortest distance they would need to cross and, therefore, the most dangerous. The space before them was taken up by a building that had fallen across the path. Gregory surmised that it had been knocked down when Sarah and her gang took the castle. He shuddered thinking that another event like the one at Castle Eckhart had occurred. This played on his conscience also.

"We'll need to get through the building too, Dirk," Gregory instructed. "Will you be up to making another tunnel?"

"Of course," Dirk said. "You don't even have to ask." Dirk set to the task straight away. They were already behind enemy lines so any hesitation meant extra time the enemy had to find them. Dirk attacked this tunnel differently to the first. He thought that the structure may be unstable and tunnelling through might make the building collapse in on itself. This time he constructed the tunnel by rearranging the building as he went and reinforcing the structure of the new space. They made it through in no time and again peered out the end. There was no one outside and they were now much closer to the entrance of the tower than they originally planned to be.

"Let's go," Lavi said nudging her way past Dirk. The others followed and as they walked out into the open, students who were originally of Castle Bodhurst came running in from around every corner. Gregory thought for a moment that the students had won the battle with Sarah until a fireball flew past his head. More and more students started to attack and Lavi stepped in willing strong gusts of wind to rake the lines of students sending most flying across the courtyard and those that didn't were knocked to the ground. Gregory, Dirk and Michelle ran for the tower and Michelle destroyed the door with a massive blast. As they ducked inside Dirk called out for Lavi to follow. He saw that she had a dangerous look on her face and each wave her hand was creating more and more ferocious attacks. Dirk ran back and grabbed her by the arm. This drew her out of the trance and her eyes focused.

"What?" she said.

"We have to go. There will be plenty more fighting on our way out," Dirk replied pulling gently at her arm. Lavi followed him to the tower entrance and Michelle blocked the doorways with a waterfall of magma. It manifested from the edge of the doorframe to fall, perfectly covering every gap. As the magma river hit the ground it flowed out into the courtyard. No one would be able to get through that. Michelle stayed at the base of the tower to keep the doors secure as the others ran up the spiralling steps. They were surprised that there was no one else inside the tower and the door to the Lord's room was open.

"Sarah knew we were coming," Gregory stated, slowing down as he approached the final door. "The assault below the tower was too well executed to be just a reaction. They knew exactly where we were going to enter from and have provided a path for us to the top of the tower."

"We can't go back now," Lavi said.

"I know, just be cautious when we enter the room. We don't know what we're going to find."

Slowly, they moved into the tower room looking for signs of

a trap. There was nothing out of the ordinary. In fact, the room was bare except for a single figure standing at its centre. Recognising Sarah instantly, Lavi let out an angry scream as she jumped into an attack.

"Lavi," Dirk called but she couldn't hear him.

She was racing at Sarah while crafting a lance of wind sharpened to a wicked edge. Thrusting it at Sarah, the attack was turned away easily and Lavi was knocked back across the floor. Her muscles were protesting as Lavi pushed herself up and attacked once more.

"Stop this Lavi. Let Gregory take her down," Dirk said again trying to break through Lavi's berserker rage.

Lavi's rampage made her blind to the short sword that Sarah produced. Thrusting her lance at Sarah, Lavi came up against a wall of flesh. The shock of hitting it made her step back and found that Dirk had stepped in front of her, his shirt stained crimson. Before Lavi could register what had happened, Dirk fell back into her, dragging Lavi to the ground.

Seeing Sarah's concealed attack from his vantage point, Dirk had thrown himself before Lavi. Pain lanced into his side by his heart and as Sarah pulled the sword away a great dizziness swept over him. Hot blood was pumping from his chest as the world spun and he fell backwards into unconsciousness.

"Lavi... LAVI!" Gregory yelled. She turned to look up at him, her mouth agape. "Move Dirk off to the side and look after him...' There was no movement from her. "Nod if you understand. Move Dirk over to the side."

Lavi nodded and finally started to move. She dragged Dirk to the wall closest to the door, ripped open his shirt, and looked at the wound. The sword had gone straight through and Dirk was bleeding badly. Lavi tore Dirk's shirt into strips, biting to start each rip before trying to plug the holes with great wads of cloth. The rest of the strips, Lavi used to tie them in place. She willed a pocket of air pressure to sit front and back, giving strength to the bandaging as well as to help stop the bleeding. Dirk was pale but had gained consciousness once more and winced each time Lavi touched his wound. With nothing more to do Lavi looked back to Gregory who was walking a circle around Sarah. She realised it was to divert her attention from Dirk and herself.

"I've been waiting for you, Gregory," Sarah said smiling. There was a murderous intent in her eyes.

"How did you know I was coming?" Gregory asked.

"I was watching you through the use of Will. I know that you've come to kill me. I know that you've been meeting with your Grandpa. I know you're having a little love affair with Michelle," Sarah thought for a moment. "Where is Michelle by the way? You didn't leave her alone by any chance," she said with her wicked smile. Gregory became worried for Michelle but trusted she could take care of herself. "What? Not going to save her?"

"You're my only concern, Sarah," Gregory said between clenched teeth. He was trying to stay in control and not be blinded like Lavi was.

"How nice that you'd be concerned about me, but Gregory, you're nothing to me. You're about to die."

"Just come and try," Gregory said.

Sarah sprang into action crafting a pillar of fire where Gregory stood moments before. He had seen the ground start to glow and predicted the attack. Gregory tried the same type of move with ice spikes, the sharp points thrusting into the air with a split seconds warning. As Sarah rolled away one of the spikes sliced into her clothing just missing the skin.

A heavy weight fell upon Gregory's mind as he felt Sarah trying to take control. With a thought, he created a defensive wall in his mind that was impenetrable. Sarah let out a grunt showing her annoyance. A sudden burst of wind knocked Gregory from his feet. It hadn't been conjured by Sarah and Gregory looked back at Lavi. Sensing Sarah's mind control on his friend. Gregory crafted a bubble around Lavi and Dirk to stop any more commands.

Sarah tried to crush him, bringing part of the roof down with the yellow but he managed to dive out of the way at the last moment. As he dove, ice spears appeared in his path and Gregory had to project immense heat from himself to melt

248

them down the moment before he was impaled.

A terrible thought came to Gregory as he started to analyse Sarah's attacks. Purple, red, yellow and now blue. Sarah was using more colours than should be possible.

Sarah could see Gregory was starting to understand her ability and, as she had done for Kinsami and Ryan to prove her ability, conjured five elemental balls to circle around her. A red ball burning like the sun. A green ball swirling like a mini tornado. A blue ball that churned like an angry sea. A yellow ball crafted with the strength of the earth. A purple ball that screamed like a thousand haunted souls. This was the first moment Gregory thought he may die. She could use any colour like an Empty and Sarah had spent hundreds of years training and honing her skills for one purpose - to kill him. Gregory saw his death before him and he panicked.

"I need to get out of here," he said. His voice was shaking and shrill. Crafting a barrier that cut the room in half, Gregory trapped Sarah on the far side. Sarah tried to use her Will but couldn't bring anything into existence where Gregory and the others were. She became angry and started yelling abuse at Gregory, banging against the barrier but Gregory ignored her and ran towards the door.

"Run!" he yelled at Dirk and Lavi. Lavi struggled to get Dirk up but he managed to stumble along with her help. Down the tower, they went, Gregory getting further and further ahead. As he got to the bottom he found Michelle waiting for them in good health.

"Gregory, what's going on? Where are Lavi and Dirk?" As Michelle spoke Dirk came hobbling down the steps leaning heavily on Lavi, fresh blood staining a large area of his shirt.

"We have to retreat. She's too strong. I can't beat her," there was a wild fear in Gregory's eyes and he removed the magma barrier Michelle had produced. Without waiting, Gregory was the first out of the door and willed a burst of energy to knock back the students who had been waiting for them. Michelle helped Lavi carry Dirk as they made their way across the empty ground into the first tunnel. When they were halfway in, the students started to follow, almost reaching them by the end of the first tunnel. Michelle saw Gregory was already fleeing through the second tunnel and would be no help to them.

Dirk knew he was dying. He could feel himself getting weaker by the moment. Though there was no blood coming from the bandaged wound, he noticed that the skin around it had started to go dark and realised he was bleeding internally. He was happy though, and would take the blade again and again if it meant he could save Lavi. In the tower he acted without a second thought and knew she was alive because of him. Drawing in yellow from all around, Dirk concentrated on the task he now gave himself.

"Lavi," Dirk said weakly. She turned to look at him while still helping him along. "I may not know how harsh life can be but I believe in doing good for everyone, especially those you love. I love you the most." Dirk freed himself from Lavi and Michelle and took two steps backwards.

"Dirk?" Lavi questioned as he stretched his arms out wide. The pursuing students were about to run him down. Dirk smiled at Lavi as he let his Will free. His skin started to turn pale yellow and harden as his body turned to stone. His clothes stopped moving as they got caught in the transformation, hardening. Stone spires sprung out from Dirk in all directions blocking the tunnel.

"Dirk, no!" Lavi cried as she reached out to him. The students tried to get through but Dirks blockade was solid. Michelle heard them say they were going around to the Castle entrance.

"Lavi, come on," Michelle said pulling her back. "Dirk's doing this for us, so we can escape. Don't let his sacrifice be for nothing."

Lavi was hard to move and there were tears in her eyes. She finally gave in to Michelle's constant pulling and the two girls ran down the second tunnel after Gregory.

They found him at the camp barricading the surroundings with rock walls enclosing the space. They were only just able to get in before he had the place completely fortified. Gregory looked at the girls.

"Where's Dirk?" he asked. Lavi looked him in the eyes for a

250

moment before walking over and punching him in the face.

"What're you doing?" Michelle said.

Lavi ignored her. "It's your fault Dirk is now dead!" She screamed tears rolling freely down her face. "You're fear drove you to abandon your friends. Dirk gave his life so that Michelle and I could get free. You wouldn't know though, would you? You were already back at camp hiding behind a rock. You're an Empty! We needed you!"

"Dirk died?" Gregory's face went pale. "What happened?"

"Fuck you, Gregory! Fuck all of you!" Lavi stormed off to the distant corner of the camp and burst into tears. Michelle left her to her pain and walked to Gregory.

"Dirk sacrificed himself in the tunnel," Michelle said softly to Gregory. "The students of Bodhurst were gaining on us and he turned himself into stone to block the pathway giving us a chance to run. What happened in the tower? How did it come to this?"

"Sarah was too strong for me," Gregory said with tears starting to form. "She has mastery over the five colours."

Michelle was shocked by the statement. "Tell me everything," she said. "I want to know."

Gregory took a deep breath getting his mind straight. Mourning would come soon enough. "When we entered the room at the top of the tower, Sarah alone, waited for us. Lavi went on a rampage trying to kill her and didn't see when Sarah produced a sword. Dirk got his wound when he jumped in front of Lavi. The sword ran through his chest and Lavi tended to him while I took on Sarah. She attacked with flames, tried to flatten me with the rocks of the tower, she tried to impale me with ice spikes and even controlled Lavi to attack me. She tried to control me but I blocked it and put a protection around Lavi and Dirk. At one point she even insinuated that you were in trouble being left alone."

"I had a weird experience," Michelle admitted. "I lost control of my body and ran to the top of the tower. I only regained control when I heard you yelling to run. I just made it back to the bottom moments before you got down."

"She was going to use you to attack me," Gregory realised as a cold shiver ran up his spine. "The moment you got control was when I put up a barrier between us and Sarah."

"Why did you put up a barrier?"

"I...' Gregory hesitated. "I was scared."

"Tell me, Gregory," Michelle said calmly, kissing him on the forehead. "Let me in."

Gregory hesitated for a moment longer then his barriers broke away. "She brought forth balls of every colour to emphasise her strength. At that moment I knew if I continued the fight I would die. I have the same abilities as her but she has been practising for centuries, working out the best ways to kill me. I have only just come into my strengths. I don't have the skill to beat her. At that point, I panicked and you can see the outcome. Dirk died cleaning up my mess."

"No, Gregory," Michelle said bringing him into an embrace. "Lavi was venting when she said those words. You are her scapegoat."

"What do you mean?"

"Dirk's wound was more serious than it looked. He was bleeding internally. I could see it from where I was carrying him. I think he knew this too. Deep down, she knows that her actions were what brought about the end of Dirk's life. She just doesn't want to face it right now along with everything else."

"I was the one who pushed everyone to fight Sarah."

"We all agreed. Each of us individually accepted that we were going into a fight where our lives were on the line. We all knew what we were fighting for and the good we could achieve."

"And now it's over," Gregory said hanging his head in grief. "I've fucked everything up."

Michelle decided to slap him. Maybe it would help. At least it would let him know she was having none of it. He looked shocked. "It's far from over, Gregory. We're going in again. We'll make a plan. We'll face Sarah again together and this time we'll win."

"I don't know if I can," Michelle raised her hand and Gregory winced. "Okay, okay, we can make a plan."

"Not just now though," Michelle said softly. "Now we

remember our friend, Dirk."

Lavi's world came crashing down around her. She was in perpetual darkness never to see the light of life again. Her emotions were raw and she couldn't stop the tears falling. She had been ready to give up on her life when she had been abused in the dungeons of Castle Eckhart. She tried and tried but deep down one thing held her to this world. One shining star in a maelstrom of darkness. That star was Dirk. When she heard that he was alive and coming to Castle Eckhart she could not even hold the sharp stone that was to be her end.

Now that star had burnt out. The beautiful and warm light that filled her with a brighter future was extinguished. The events of the day ran through her mind over and over. She remembered the rushed flight with Dirk unable to enjoy the scenery. She thought to herself how wonderful it was that Dirk was flying with greater precision than she had seen the first time at the cliffs. When he made the comment about meeting his parents she was elated. It was a step forward in the right direction for her. It kindled a fire in her soul that had a chance to dim the darkness taking hold.

The next image that crossed her mind was Dirk in front of her with the tip of a sword protruding from his back. She didn't see the blade or even the moment when Dirk had jumped in front of her. She was in a rage and was blinded to almost everything. She remembered his face as she tried to stop the bleeding. He was pale and she could see he was in pain.

"I love you the most," these words echoed in Lavi's mind and she saw Dirk smiling as he gave his life for hers, turning to stone. Darkness pounded down on her. The images repeated over and over in her mind. The light breaking through with a happy start to the day was only extinguished all the more by the darkness at Dirk's death. When she couldn't take it anymore she screamed. She would not live in this world anymore. She knew it would be easy to take her own life now but she would not do so here. Gregory and Michelle definitely wouldn't allow it, for one. If she was to die, she would be with

Dirk.

Lavi flew to the top of the enclosure and found a small gap just large enough to squeeze through. Michelle had awoken to the scream and saw her pain but didn't move towards her. She didn't know how to comfort her friend. As Lavi made to escape however she started to call her. Ignoring the calls, Lavi was able to wiggle free before flying towards the Castle. She didn't care anymore. If there was someone in front of her, they would feel her pain too.

She landed in front of the gates drawing in large amounts of green. It was a short distance to where Dirk would be but after today she knew it would be well guarded. Lavi willed into existence a small tornado that spun and battered at the gates for a time. Lavi was about to increase its strength when she heard the hinges start to whine. The whole gate, hinges and all, ripped away from the walls and was sent out across the landscape to land five hundred metres away.

Everywhere in the castle came alive with shouts of alarm and fires being lit. People raced out of their dorm rooms to see what caused the destruction and everyone found a single red head storming across the yard. They went on the defensive but Lavi was faster. She sent wind gusts, sharpened like razors, at all who ran out, carving into them at every point of contact. The courtyard was being painted red as blood splattered in every direction. Lavi walked through the blood storm without a droplet touching her.

The students started to become smart and cautious. Some attacked with flames and others ice spikes. One even created quicksand below Lavi. She just swished them aside with her Will and floated across the quicksand. One blue user timed his attack to just after her block. He sent thin shards of ice, sharpened to a wicked point. They were the size of knitting needles so as to try and hide their approach. The desired outcome was gained as they pierced Lavi's back in a number of places. She stumbled for a moment before finding her feet once more and turned. With the extreme force of air pressure, she brought the buildings down on those attacking her.

Turning back, Lavi continued to Dirk. She could see him

now. The statue made from his flesh turned stone. As she reached him, Lavi forced the last of the ice spikes from her back. She was dizzy, teetering on blacking out but she had made it. Tears came to her eyes again as she saw the smile on his hard face.

"Why?" Lavi whimpered. "We were going to grow old together. I was going to meet your parents and try your mum's food. I need you, Dirk," she said banging on his stone chest. She almost fell but levered herself back up using Dirk's outstretched arms. "I love you, Dirk."

There was a movement in the stone and Lavi almost thought she was seeing things due to lack of blood. With tears in her eyes, she wrapped her arms tightly around him hugging into his chest.

"Damn you, Dirk," Lavi said. The stone statue that was Dirk wrapped Lavi in his arms returning the embrace. Slowly Lavi's body shifted to stone to forever be with Dirk.

Gregory and Michelle had watched the whole scene through a one-way mirror. Michelle was about to go after her friend when she saw Lavi leave but Gregory had grabbed her ankle in mid-air. He brought her back to the ground shaking his head.

"But Lavi is out there alone," Michelle said, a worried look on her face.

"We don't know what she is hoping to achieve, Michelle. She may be going to be alone or she may be going to Dirk. Either way, we can't follow. We can't force our wants upon her no matter her choices."

"I need to know," Michelle's tone was no less distressed. Gregory produced the one-way mirror set to follow Lavi where ever she went. They had watched the scene at the gate and guessed her direction. She had gone to be with Dirk. Michelle's hands came to her mouth as she saw the ice needles lance into Lavi. When they saw Dirk move, however, neither pair of eyes were dry. He lived in a stony form in the courtyard of Castle Bodhurst. They watched as Lavi was given the form of stone in Dirk's embrace and thought that it was the saddest yet somehow happiest ending for the couple.

"Gregory, don't let me go tonight," Michelle said. "I don't

want to be alone." Gregory did not reply but kissed her forehead tears rolling from his eyes.

Kinsami didn't bother to report in to Sarah when he arrived back at the castle. He went straight to his quarters and fell on his bed exhausted having given everything he had to keep Allen from harm. Kinsami sported two new bruises on his back that he received while guarding Allen against the oncoming trees. These bruises were so big they almost looked like one single bruise. He wasn't going out of his way right now for anyone else. It took only moments before he was snoring into his pillow.

It took what felt like moments more to be woken up by Sarah sitting on the side of his bed. The room was still dark and therefore, the hour until dawn had not yet past. Sarah didn't look happy and Kinsami immediately assumed she knew about Tahlia. He rested his head back on the pillow.

"The boy stopped me," Kinsami said alluding to Allen. "It was my fault for training him."

"What are you talking about?" Sarah asked, her eyes narrowing.

"Tahlia. Allen stopped me from killing her," Kinsami waited for the reply but nothing came. He looked up again and the anger written on Sarah's face was tremendous. Kinsami realised too late that she hadn't heard. When she finally spoke her words were calm but edged in danger.

"I had come to you to rage about Gregory, happy in the knowledge that you would accomplish your task," she leant over him, putting force across his chest from her arms. She noticed his pain and got a little satisfaction. "Now you tell me that you couldn't achieve what I had instructed you to do because of some little five year old."

"He's older than that," Kinsami said.

Sarah placed a finger on his lips. "Don't interrupt me again," she said seriously. Kinsami knew not to mess with her in this mood. "A little kid who had never even used Will before, stopped you. Did you even manage to kidnap the boy?"

"He is in the dungeons as we speak. Stuart is currently

256

watching him," Kinsami told her.

"At least you accomplished the main goal. Do you foresee any trouble with the boy?"

"No. He was happy to come with me at first. I made the mistake of trying to teach him to use Will so that he might fly back with me. He failed miserably but while he practised I snuck away to kill the girl. He must have followed and his emotions sparked his Will for that one moment. Allen is harmless."

"Looks like you're going to have to make it up to me now, Kinsami. This time I expect one hundred percent success," Sarah knew he wouldn't turn her down. He would never turn her down.

"No, Sarah," Kinsami said. "I've just returned from a mission and am battered and bruised all over. I'm in no state to help you." Sarah placed her hand up under his top, tracing her fingers across his muscles.

"You forget who I am, Kinsami," Sarah whispered in his ear. Warmth started to flow through his body. It was strength and youth rolled into one. "To have control over the five colours means to have control over every component of life. With the right mixture of colour...' She let the sentence fall. Kinsami's body was growing stronger. All the pain he had felt moments before was subsiding.

So Sarah wasn't just death and destruction, Kinsami thought. She was healing him. "What will you have me do, Sarah?" Kinsami asked.

"No," she said harshly. "You will call me, Five. You don't have the privilege of using my true name."

"Your Will, Five," Kinsami said almost sarcastically.

Sarah was happy in the fact her point was made and Kinsami knew she was displeased with him. "Good. What you're going to be doing for me isn't big. I want you to go for a little flight with Baras to Castle Kirkwall, kill the Lord and Lady of the tower and then hold it ready for my arrival."

"Not a big thing?" Kinsami spat. "We've taken two of the castles already. They are going to be waiting for us and you're forgetting, Baras senior is still floating around somewhere making plans with Gregory. I would think, Castle Kirkwall would be where they make their stand."

"Don't worry about Gregory. He and his little friends came for a visit earlier. When Gregory realised he was losing he fled in terror like a little school girl. No, at least Lavi had the guts to return. Gregory is a coward."

"I could have told you that. Is Lavi still here then?" A pang of jealousy passed through Sarah.

"When you leave, Kinsami, and oh yes, you are going to be leaving on this mission, walk through the courtyard and admire our new statue. You may like to use it to give a prayer to Lavi and Dirk's souls."

Kinsami was saddened by the news. Dirk was an idiot. He didn't care for him but Lavi had shown great potential. He had always hoped she would join them someday.

"When do you want me to leave?" Kinsami asked.

"An hour after first light," Sarah said with a glum look of triumph on her face.

"Your Will, Five. Now get off my blanket and let me sleep." Kinsami didn't care to use Sarah's name at this moment and felt the term Five was now a hollow title.

Sarah was about to retaliate but bit her tongue. The reds will always be a stubborn bunch. She would not be drawn into an argument with him. Sarah left the room to the sound of Kinsami snoring. As an afterthought, she willed into existence a fake Echidna on the bed beside Kinsami. She couldn't for the life of her, work out why he was so afraid of them.

Chapter 14

"All our plans have fallen apart. What're we going to do?" The grey light of predawn gave the mist an eerie glow. A slight breeze sent forth a chill that ate down to the bone. Gregory had made sure the fire was well stocked and gave ample heat to stay comfortable. Sitting in quiet contemplation, he'd asked the question of Michelle, having lost his path forward.

"You used to speak of going into the castle alone and defeating Sarah," Michelle told him. She wasn't ready to give up on the fight because she had lost two dear friends. It was because they went all in that Michelle wanted to continue. "We can still do this, Gregory. Two people are still better than the one you had originally planned to be."

"The battle dynamics are different now. Sarah isn't playing by the universal laws we were taught for the use of Will. I thought I had an edge over her. I thought we could beat her easily," Gregory admitted.

"You thought you could just waltz in there like your life wasn't in any danger at all and take her down?" Gregory nodded and Michelle had a look of disgust. "I didn't see you much when we attended Castle Eckhart. I did hear some things about you though. Some I have dismissed because I have gotten to know the true person you are. Others, I can see had some truth to them. You had a following in school did you not? Because of that, you grew to think you were better than others. You are following the same line of thinking here. You completely underestimated the capabilities of Sarah all because you built yourself up on the idea that your Empty status made you invincible. You'll always fail thinking like that. Even the smallest mouse could defeat the hungriest of lions."

"Are you saying I'm a hungry lion?"

"You're hungry for the outcome and prone to make mistakes. This time we're going to be smart about what we do. Let's scan the grounds and work out their weaknesses. That way we can move in and systematically take them out in the order and fashion we want."

"Where do we start?" Gregory asked still unsure of himself.

"Have you fallen so far, Gregory?" Michelle asked. "Or have you always been this lost and hid this fact behind a mask?" Gregory thought about what Michelle just said. He thought about all he had done and the road he had walked leading him to this moment. Something about it felt significant but like the moments at Eckhart, he couldn't put his finger on them.

Gregory bullied people. He'd never had tendencies like this before but with a small amount of coaxing and a lot of praise for his ability, he grew to believe he was greater than other students. His reasons for being a bastard to others were insignificant and stupid.

Gregory would learn from this. He'll know that when others try to bully him it isn't always about himself. Mr Sir was a good target but that's all he'd been. Teasing the large teacher made others praise him more. This evolved to a point where, in his mind, he hated Mr Sir. He knew now this was on him also. No outside factors produced the line of thought.

Gregory wondered if he changed for the better from the night of the castle raid. He became depressed and Dirk helped him through that time of his life, giving him motivation and purpose. Was that why he moved forward with his life? On the motivation and purpose of someone else? Gregory became emotional and tears started to roll down his face.

"What's wrong?" Michelle asked getting worried and bringing him into her arms.

"I haven't been living my own life," he said seeing for the first time the depth of his faults. "I've been living through the motivation and purpose of others."

"That's not a bad thing, Gregory," Michelle told him. "We can borrow another person's purpose or be motivated by someone. We can craft it into our own or in the process of moving forward find a purpose that is more suited to our life." This seemed to calm Gregory a little. "What is it you want?"

"I still want to stop Sarah from causing any more pain. She is my responsibility and I have the best chance at stopping her."

"That's a good start," Michelle agreed. "Is that for you or is it for what you perceive people want from you?"

260

"A little of both, I guess. I don't think I can completely break free from the events running my life until she's gone. The cryptic words my Grandpa said are true. Sarah is the key to getting my life back on track."

"Good. Now, you asked me this question but it better suits you. What do you want to do next?"

Gregory had done this so many times before it was becoming second nature. He opened a window onto Castle Bodhurst. "Let's scout around and see what we can find. There's only one person close to me that I could lose and I want to be as cautious as possible so that I don't."

"I'd like that a lot also," Michelle said with a smile. "Let's scout around the lower levels. See if there's somewhere that we could possibly gain access from the underside."

Gregory nodded. He shifted the way the window viewed the world and moved it above the castle. From this vantage point, the window could see everything. Instead of the ground, great cavities showed where underground rooms could be found.

Gregory zoomed the window in on one of the open cavities. It looked to be a janitor's closet. Inside could be found cleaning chemicals, brooms, mops and buckets. The walls were solid and this room didn't lead anywhere useful. The next room he zoomed in on seemed more promising. It was connected to the central hall and with the right tunnel, they could bypass the whole Castle ground. He started panning around the room and was about to tell Michelle about it when he saw something that chilled his blood. In a cell at the far end of the room was Allen. He looked distressed walking backwards and forwards shaking at the bars.

"That's my little Brother," Gregory whispered.

"What?"

"That's my little Brother!" Gregory shouted this time taking off towards the opening Lavi found. It was a tight squeeze for him. Michelle looked into the window seeing the young boy then flew off after Gregory. She just missed catching him at the opening but got through a lot easier. Michelle gave no thought to falling or hurting herself as she flew. All she thought about was flying as fast as she could. It wasn't long before she caught and tackled Gregory. Both landed heavily on the ground a short distance below.

"What're you doing, Michelle?" Gregory said, angry at being stopped. "I need to rescue my brother."

"I could ask you the same thing," Michelle said with a tone to rival Gregory's. "We were just talking about how we need to be cautious the next time we enter Castle Bodhurst. Now you're running in guns blazing. You have a good chance of walking the same road that Dirk and Lavi took." The harshness in her tone cleared Gregory's head and he became worried.

"I won't leave Allen under their guard for a moment longer," Gregory told Michelle.

"So you have a plan then?"

"The dungeons are close to the outer wall. I'll tunnel underneath and inside. We can smuggle Allen out through the same tunnel before they even notice."

"Then that's what we'll do," Michelle agreed. "And with all this fog around, we shouldn't be seen from the walls either."

Gregory and Michelle flew slowly, keeping low to the ground. They didn't want to disturb the mist too much after getting so lucky with being granted a cover. Reaching the outer wall without incident, Gregory started burrowing on a course he put to memory. He reinforced the ceiling as he went and made sure to cancel out any noise he produced. Michelle kept busy by hiding the entrance to the hole with some long grass and a fern she had to manually uproot and replant.

Gregory had been burrowing for a fair amount of time when Michelle entered the tunnel. She was impressed by the distance he had made and how structurally sound the tunnel was. There was a small amount of discomfort walking through Dirk's tunnels with light at each end. In this tunnel, though, with darkness all around her, she was completely comfortable.

"You better not be using those cat eyes again, Gregory," Michelle said suddenly. She heard a meow come from Gregory and shook her head. "I hate cats."

She didn't need to wait too much longer when fresh air filtered through from in front. Very gently, Gregory burrowed through the last of the wall and came out in the dungeons of

262

Castle Bodhurst. He jumped out from part way up a wall into one of the cells with Michelle coming in behind him.

"Exactly where Sarah wants us," Michelle said.

Gregory grunted but gave her little attention. He was looking across the room at Allen, sitting in the corner of his cell.

"Allen," Gregory called out. "Allen! Can you hear me?" Allen didn't react to Gregory's voice. Fearing the worst, Gregory forced the lock on his cell and ran over to Allen's. Once he had this lock open, he pushed the door, gaining access to Allen's cell. Gregory was about to run over to his brother when something screamed inside his head for him to stop. His brain was working overtime to determine just what had caught his attention but he couldn't work it out. It was like a tingle that ran up and down his spine making Gregory uncomfortable. The cell door rocked back on its hinges and Gregory stood staring, eyes wide at what could have been his demise.

"What's wrong?" Michelle asked. She saw the sudden change in Gregory but didn't have the same view he did.

"Look at the door," Gregory said. "The bastards set up a trap." Michelle looked to where Gregory indicated and saw the melted bars four centimetres from the hinge, top to bottom. She saw a slight flicker of the space directly behind the cell door. Finding a small rock, Michelle threw it in. The rock disintegrated to nothing instantly.

"How do we get Allen out?" Michelle asked.

"No point in keeping up this ruse," another voice said behind them. Gregory recognised Stuart stepping from the shadows. "He isn't there."

"What're you talking about?" Gregory demanded.

"Allen is currently at Castle Eckhart. We put the windows up to trap you but you saw through the ploy. He's alone but well stocked."

"Why would you leave him like that? Why move him at all if you were just going to leave him alone at Castle Eckhart."

"To be honest, Kinsami got lazy bringing him back. Eckhart was closer so he dumped the kid off there."

"Kinsami? He's still alive?"

Stuart nodded. "He's risen up our ranks and is rather close to Sarah."

"I'm going to kill him for this," Gregory said bashing the cell bars.

"If you can get by me that is," Stuart said calmly. He created pale fighters from his Will like he had the night of the battle royale. There were three including Stuart but Gregory wasn't worried.

"How are you with firestorms?" Gregory asked Michelle. She just looked at him and smiled. Drawing in great amounts of crimson red she willed fire to spring from the floor. The fire sprouted in varying places and with a shift of focus, she made the fire sprouts dance across the stones. They gave Stuart no room to move and he lost the two fighters instantly. He almost lost his life as well but used the blue to keep himself in a bubble of cool water while the fire passed.

Letting the bubble burst, Stuart fell to the floor coughing. "So you can do a few tricks. You won't take me down so eas...'

Gregory got tired of hearing him talk. Using a burst of pure Will he pounded Stuart hard in the stomach. Stuart spat blood from his mouth and gave a gurgling cry. Gregory directed the next attack at Stuart's head and Michelle heard the sickening crunch of his skull caving in.

"Just shut up, Stuart. I never liked your whiney little voice," Gregory said before turning to look at Allen.

"Eckhart is going to be a trek out of our way. Especially when Sarah's right above us," Michelle told him. She braced herself for the backlash of that statement.

"He's safe where he is," Gregory said surprising her. "He need only wait a day or two. We should be finished with our task by then."

"Sounds good to me," Michelle said. "I can't wait to be able to have a real date with you," Gregory blushed but before he had time to reply a number of explosions sounded above ground. "Ours?"

"I don't know," Gregory said. "Let's make our escape and regroup at the camp." Michelle nodded and the two made their way up the tunnel Gregory carved earlier.

264

Three figures passed through the mist surrounding Castle Bodhurst. They were dressed from head to toe in light greys and whites. The clothing had been crafted from Will and designed to change with their surroundings like a chameleon. Their movements spoke of years of training in espionage and infiltration. The goal was to take the commander and chief of this rising enemies' head.

Castle Kirkwall had stood by long enough watching the other castles fall to this new threat. There was no communication as to who the enemy was but Lord Nodane and Lady Celes knew they were currently holed up in Castle Bodhurst. This was their chance to end them. They sent their best agents on a mission to assassinate the Leader of the threat and bring peace back to the castles. Now the three agents were on the doorstep of the enemy.

"I can't see shit with all this fog, Bill," one of the three said. He was slightly taller than the others and was one of two males. The other was much more noticeably female. Other than that they all dressed the same and moved with almost identical fluidity.

"It's better that way, Jack," Bill replied. "Our approach is much easier and should one of you make a noise it'll be harder to pinpoint the location."

"Jack's the only one we have to worry about," the female whispered.

"Fuck off, Sammy," Jack's voice started to rise.

"She's right, Jack," Bill told him. "Shut the fuck up and let's get on with it." A movement ahead got their attention and they went on the defensive. A girl, student by the looks of her, with dark hair and wearing a pale green dress, was running towards them, eyes wild. As the three figures came into view and she finally realised they were there, she screamed. Sammy knocked her to the ground with a hand over her mouth.

"That's gone and done it. Everyone in the castle would've heard that," she said. The girl below Sammy had stopped trying to scream and Sammy lifted her hand.

"Please don't kill me," the girl said over and over again.

Sammy slapped her in the face and the girl stopped talking to stare with frightened eyes.

"We aren't here to kill you," Bill said. "We're here to take down the leader of the enemy. What are you doing out here?"

"It's horrible inside," the girl said. "A large group attacked the castle and killed our Lord and Lady. We didn't have a chance. They've been killing, raping and destroying whatever or whoever they please. I escaped from a window and made it through the gates. I thought you were with them."

"You're safe now," Sammy said getting off the girl. "We're from Castle Kirkwall, here to free you. What's your name?"

"Sarah," she said.

"Well Sarah, I want you to head into the forest. You'll be safe there until we've completed our mission."

A frightened look crossed her face again. "No, please. Let me come with you," Sarah pleaded. "They'll find me. They always find runaways. If you fail at least I'll know and can free myself of this life."

"We shouldn't," Jack said to Bill.

"Please, I know the castle very well."

Bill's brow furrowed as he considered it. "Okay," Bill gave in. "Stay behind us and walk only in my tracks. There'll be no stray branches cracked under foot that way."

"Thank you," Sarah said. She bowed almost double over to show her gratitude. "The gates are just ahead."

The three agents of Kirkwall followed by the girl, Sarah, found the gate only metres away and walked into the courtyard of Castle Bodhurst. The mist was thick even within the castle walls and the three used their extensive knowledge of the castle layout along with Sarah to navigate. Moving around the rubble brought down by Lavi, they got closer to the great hall.

Like a curtain lifting on a stage, the mist dispersed unnaturally fast. The three agents found themselves looking at the entirety of the Castle inhabitants standing around the inner walls, on balconies and in doorways. They were completely circled with the student body aiming ice spires and flaming balls at them ready to attack at any moment.

"What is this?" Bill yelled. "Why have you sided with the

enemy?" He felt a tap on his back and saw Sarah get Sammy and Jack's attention.

"Because I opened their eyes to the lies the castles offer," Sarah said leaning in to talk right next to his ear. The three agents started screaming as terrible throes of pain rippled across their bodies. Their flesh was melting straight off their bones and as the bone came into contact with the air they erupted into flames. Even as most of their bodies were bubbling on the ground they still ran in circles screaming in agony. Sarah clicked her fingers finally letting them die in three large explosions.

"Agents of the Castles sent to kill us all," Sarah said to the massing group. "How long shall we need to cower under the dirty boot of the Lords and Ladies? Gregory and his group attacked only yesterday and killed a number of our friends. They've been working closely with Lord Baras of Castle Eckhart planning the attack days before. A new attack today means they're not going to allow us to rest much longer. When we take down Castle Kirkwall we are going to be free. Who here thinks that we should go today... Now?" Sarah waited for the few people she planted in the crowds to start nodding and agreeing vocally. Like sheep, the large majority of the students at Castle Bodhurst mimicked these actions. It was so easy to lead the masses.

"I've sent two of my own agents. They should've already arrived and with some luck, we'll be freed from a large scale battle. Our goal is to save as many people as we can. If they fail, will you be ready to fight for your freedom?" This time Sarah didn't have to have her plants start the cheer. The students were already shouting their agreeance. "I've come to respect all of you and see you as friends. I hope you see me the same."

"Of course," called someone from the balcony.

"You have been nothing but a friend to us," another said. People started calling out how much they loved her and that they were in this together. Sarah was lapping up the praise and almost didn't want to have to stop them. She raised her hands and everyone started to quiet.

"Please everyone, gather what you believe is vital for the mission and we'll be on our way. We're going to be flying from here. Anyone who doesn't want to risk it can stay. Anyone who wants to join but doesn't know how to fly I can help. We are in this together and a united front will speak a thousand words as we come into the airspace of Castle Kirkwall. We won't lose."

"Not with you leading us, Sarah," someone got in before they disappeared to collect items for the trip. Sarah told herself she would remember the persons face but after a moment didn't care enough to try. People started flowing back into the courtyard after five minutes and they were ready to leave in twelve. Eighteen people stayed behind too scared to fly. The rest took off into the air, some with Sarah's help as stated. More fodder for the front line if Kinsami and Baras fail, she thought. The dark mass moved over the land to disappear on the horizon in the direction of Castle Kirkwall.

Kinsami had been flying all morning and his emotions were exceptionally high. Not only had he not crashed into a non-moving object but he was barely using any effort at all to stay aloft. His twists and turns were flawless and he now knew why so many people found joy in flight. It was a pass time amongst Will users that eighty to ninety percent of people dabbled in. All it took was a quick lesson from Baras and now he flew as if he'd been flying for years. Kinsami understood that Baras, like the rest of those trapped in the grey realm, had centuries of time to perfect their Will usage and find better ways to perform their skills. Also, they had a window into the real world that they could use to learn hidden secrets and techniques from unsuspecting masters. He was a well of knowledge.

Kinsami and Baras had passed three other Will users flying in the direction of Castle Bodhurst three hours prior. Neither group acknowledged the other but Kinsami knew that they were going to be trouble. They had the look of warriors about them. Nothing he could do now though. Sarah would deal with them. For all her faults she was still an excellent leader. She kept on top of everything and always had an answer.

He suddenly remembered the small, spiny, stuffed anteater, Sarah left on his bed. He hated echidnas with a passion and he truly hoped there was no one in the hallway this morning. He wasn't able to tell after his flames burst through the wall eliminating the creature. It took three blue Will users to put out the flames.

"Why do you follow Sarah?" Kinsami suddenly asked Baras.

With the wind whistling past their ears, Baras spoke up. "I aim to inherit one of the castles," Baras admitted. "I have grand plans for Castle Eckhart."

"Are you planning to have your own army? You know Sarah doesn't technically own the Castles, right?"

"I know she doesn't own them. I actually hope to get a majority vote from those that are left for the right to rule."

"What're you hoping to get out of it?" Kinsami asked. "They won't just give the castle over to anyone."

"I'm going to reopen the school and use everything I've learnt to teach the next generation. This has always been my dream since long before coming to Castle Eckhart."

This was completely unexpected and Kinsami became lost for words. Baras didn't talk further and the boys flew in silence for another hour.

When they got close to Castle Kirkwall, Baras peeled off and Kinsami followed, realising too late he didn't ask about landing. Crashing into the grass, Kinsami landed so hard he knocked all the air from his lungs. It took some time before he could breathe properly again. Baras walked over and nudged him with his foot. Pushing himself up to rest on his knees, Kinsami looked up sheepishly.

"Take your landings slowly until you get used to them," Baras said. "You need to get the timing and descent lines right."

Kinsami nodded and dragged himself up to his feet. The two boys walked up the rise and looked out at Castle Kirkwall. A grey stone castle with a strong medieval feel. There was a drawbridge and some turrets, towers that ended in conical spires and even an old moat with green, yellow coloured water. Kinsami couldn't quite tell from here but it looked like the water in the moat was bubbling.

"The castle is built over an old volcano. The water that fills the moat comes from an underground thermal spring. The temperature is three times what you could possibly swim in. Don't fall in if you value your life."

"I don't plan on going near it," Kinsami said.

Baras smiled. "There is a sewer access we'll be entering. It's at the base of the walls and the moat water partially covers it. You're going to have to float inches above the water."

"You've got to be kidding me," Kinsami looked stressed. He was happy enough to be flying in the air away from danger but this was going to test him.

"Dead serious," Baras replied. "The path will widen as soon as we're inside. After that, we can choose any access point we want to come out of. It's going to be a simple task to get into the tower undetected."

"Well, at least there's that."

"If you've recovered from your fall then we should be on our way," Baras said. "It'll be best to walk from here. Less conspicuous." Baras got up and was walking away when Kinsami grabbed his arm. He turned back.

"Your dream," Kinsami said. "About the school and teaching the next generation. I just want you to know that I respect it."

Baras dipped his head at Kinsami and the two walked down to the Castle. They walked calmly like they belonged there. No one made to approach them. One person even waved commenting on the weather.

Walking around the moat, they had to shield their noses from the strong sulphur smell. Kinsami spotted the small hole they would use to infiltrate the castle and doubted he could do it by just floating straight in.

"There's not enough room to get through comfortably, Kinsami commented.

"See how it arches up in the middle," Baras pointed. Kinsami saw that there was slightly more room in the middle and nodded. "If you float across to the rock wall, you will need to keep yourself aloft and crawl down to the tip of the arch.

Here, you simply flip in upside down while holding the stones. Hard, but very much doable."

"Show me."

"No, my friend, take it as a lesson in flight control. You need to do this for yourself."

Kinsami swore but didn't argue. Following the instructions from Baras, he flew over to the wall and clung to it. He moved down closer to the heated water and decided to test it with the tip of his finger. Baras stopped him before he broke the surface.

"Don't touch it. The pain will cause you to lose focus."

Kinsami pulled his finger back and started the awkward motion of wrapping himself under and through the arch. Part way through he felt like he couldn't move anymore. He could see how easy it would be once inside but he couldn't find the correct motion to continue forward.

"Baras, I'm stuck! Help me!" Kinsami called.

"Don't fear my friend. Stretch your legs out straight and pull yourself through. Remember, you're still flying so gravity isn't working the same way. Calm yourself, then free yourself," Baras watched Kinsami follow his instructions as someone walked up behind him.

"Looks like your friend is having a bit of trouble getting through," the newcomer said. "You know he could've just put force down on the surface of the water to create a bigger gap."

"Shhh, don't let him hear that," Baras said, holding a finger to his lips. "We've been ordered to take out a few of the bigger rats in the sewers. He's the reason I got caught up in all this. I thought a little bit of suffering was in store," Baras smiled and the newcomer laughed.

They saw Kinsami rush the last movement and the tip of his heel touched the thermal waters for a split second. Kinsami wailed in pain as he hit solid ground. Someone poked their head over the side of the wall but the newcomer waved them away

"Chasing rats," he called out and the head disappeared again. "I think that one movement will cause him enough pain for a while. Get him to come see me in the fern wing when you finish."

"What's your name?"

"Taine."

Baras offered his hand. "Baras," he said as Taine shook it. "I'll come find you as soon as we finish." Baras watched Taine walk away before he attempted to enter the hole in the wall. Baras didn't bother to fly over but rather protected his body with Will as he swam across. The heat didn't affect him at all. He got out where Kinsami was sitting holding his heel and glaring at him.

"What?" Baras asked. "You could have thought up your own way in."

Kinsami ignored the remark. "Who was that?" He asked.

"His name is Taine. If your heel is still upsetting you when this is done seek him out in the fern wing and he'll heeel you."

"Ha, Ha. Funny," Kinsami said rolling his eyes at the pun. "I'm starting to respect you less and less, Baras." Baras just shrugged and started walking down the tunnel. There was little lighting that filtered in through small holes in the roof but after a short while their eyes had adjusted enough to pass by comfortably.

"So, do you know where we're actually going?" Kinsami asked Baras as they turned down another tunnel. He was getting tired of hobbling along and wanted to get out into the fresh air. He couldn't believe how much his heel was hurting from a quick touch of the water. He couldn't imagine the pain he would be in if he had of misjudged the manoeuvre completely.

"I'm just looking for some rats at the moment," he replied. "It won't be too much longer but if we come up out of the wrong opening the rats will give us credibility."

"We've already passed a few," Kinsami said getting annoyed. "You should've told me what you were looking for."

It was another twenty minutes before Baras moved to a ladder leading up to the surface. He'd given Kinsami the three dead rats to carry by the tail and Kinsami was holding them as far from himself as possible. He found the climb to the surface was the hardest part. Eighteen metres straight up and the rats were bouncing very close to his face each time he reached for a new rung.

Baras came out of the grate at the top first and caught the attention of two senior students. They helped him out but knocked him to the ground.

"Who are you and why are you snooping around in the sewers?" One of the boys asked. Baras gave him an odd look.

"Chasing rats. Punishment for our tardiness in class. I'm Baras by the way. Just transferred from Bodhurst last week. Not a moment too soon either."

"I heard they had some trouble. Where are your rats?" Three rats were suddenly launched over the lip of the hole. Kinsami quickly followed coughing and spluttering.

"One of them hit me in the face," he told Baras not realising they had company. He looked at the other students. "What do they want?"

"Just asking us about our punishment," Baras replied. He looked back to the two seniors. "This is Kinsami. He's been my best friend since we were grasping at our daddies ankles. We always attend the same schools." The two seniors were looking sceptical but started backing away when Kinsami offered them the rats.

"You can keep them, kid," they said. "Go let whoever know you've completed your task and stop playing in the sewers." They felt the need to have the last word and look authoritative to the younger students. Kinsami watched them hurry away.

"You're right, Baras," Kinsami admitted. "These rats were worth the trouble." Baras smiled.

"I do like to think ahead," Baras told him.

They walked across the yard, Kinsami holding the rats, and made their way to the central tower housing Lord Nodane and Lady Celes. Kinsami found this to be far easier than he could have ever imagined. He kept all his weight on the front of his feet to relieve a little of the pain and after only a few moments of climbing the tower, they came to the open door leading into the chambers of Nodane and Celes.

"Welcome Kinsami, Baras," Nodane said as they stepped into the room. "We've been waiting for you since you entered the sewers."

"Sorry to keep you waiting," Kinsami said. "We didn't want to show up without a present for you." He dumped the three dead, bloating rats on a small coffee table in the middle of the room.

"Thank you," Celes said. "It would have been rude of you not to. Now how can we help you?"

"We have come for your lives if you would be so kind," Baras told them easily. "We're all being rather polite at the moment so let's keep it that way. If you hand them over willingly, we'll not disturb you any further."

"And if we don't?" Celes asked.

"We shall take them either way," Kinsami said. Celes looked at the two boys.

"I've watched and assessed you both at Mandaloo museum," Celes told them. "You both have great potential and were such good and honour bound boys. How did you find yourselves on this road?"

"Freedom and equality, my lady," Baras told her. "And you will find that I hit my potential over a century ago." Nodane and Celes looked at him strangely. Baras just laughed. "You haven't been informed well at all. No matter. Soon your lives shall be gone."

"You're rather confident," Nodane said. "You'll find that we aren't easy targets."

"Adaman and Sylvia were difficult opponents yet they still fell to me. A yellow and green dominant will pose little difficulty," Kinsami told them. "Why don't we just let the conversation drop here and get into it."

Celes was the first to react, her whole demeanour becoming deadly. She started to form strong gusts of wind around herself and put her Will to work in crafting a sharpness that would carve through the boys. Kinsami reacted with his personal favourite. He cloaked himself in flame armour like a cocoon against attacks. Baras though had a very calm approach to the fight. He stepped forward and raised a hand, his Will coming into reality. Celes was immediately swallowed by a ball of water. Kinsami recognised it from Gregory's home when Allen had utilised it to protect Tahlia. There was one big difference though. Where the inner area of Allen's ball held air for its occupant, Baras's was completely solid. Celes's wind was absorbed into the water ball and started the water spinning with great intensity. Swirling out of control, Celes reached out in vein.

Nodane stepped in to break Baras's focus and free Celes. He crafted spikes that grew from the air and flew at incredible speed. Kinsami watched helplessly as the figure of Baras was impaled by three of the spikes. His face contorted in pain but the bubble of water held strong. Kinsami conjured his flaming katana and raced at Nodane screaming a battle cry. Bringing his arm up, Nodane easily turned aside the long curving slash. Jumping back, Kinsami noticed Nodane used super hard earthen armour that moved like fluid around his body hardening right at the point of impact. This was going to be a nuisance.

Baras's body started to turn dark and then began to crumble away. Kinsami was horrified by the fate of his friend. He locked his eyes on Nodane but became confused. The look on Nodane's face showed he didn't know what was happening to Baras and therefore, suggested to Kinsami it was not of Nodane's Will. A dark shadow grew directly behind Nodane and as he turned trying to focus on the new presence plaguing his peripheral vision a dark blade slipped up through his ribs and into his heart ending his life.

"Baras!" Kinsami exclaimed as the boy shimmered back into the plane of being, his body becoming solid and full of colour again.

"One of my more favourite tricks," Baras said smiling. "You seemed distressed when I was impaled."

"Don't look too much into things. I just didn't want to take on Nodane and Celes alone. Speaking of which, how shall we end this one?" he asked nodding his head at Celes twisting helplessly within the water bubble.

"Leave her. She will drown soon enough."

At that moment by the entrance to the balcony electricity like lightning started to crackle in the air. The area it affected began to widen and a portal opened into the room. Lord Baras of Castle Eckhart stepped out. Another similar opening started directly behind the younger Baras. The younger was about to move away but Lord Baras used his Will to force the younger man through, closing the portal as he left.

Erupting from the ball of water, Celes sat choking for air. Clutching at her chest, she coughed up great mouthfuls of water from her lungs, forcing it out with her Will and the air pressure she manipulated. The only reason she was still alive was due to her highly advanced use of the green and a minor use of blue as a third colour. She was able to draw the oxygen away from the hydrogen in the water giving her small pockets of breathable air.

"Thank you, Baras," Celes said in a weak voice. "Your help is very much appreciated."

"I haven't come to help you, Celes," Lord Baras told her. "My being here has been predestined. I couldn't fight it if I wanted to. Now, you and Kinsami were in the middle of something. Please excuse me while I return Nodane to the Veritas Rerum. I'll be back for one of you when the fight is settled."

Celes's eyes widened but Kinsami just smiled and walked in sword raised. He expected at least a small defence from the woman drained of her strength and as his first swing was deflected with air, Kinsami spun on his heel and brought the blade down again. Celes had no colour within her now and couldn't block the second attack. Her head came cleanly away with the fiery blade cauterizing the cut and stopping any blood. Lord Baras walked over to stand next to him and Kinsami moved a couple of feet away readying his sword.

"You won't need that, old friend," Baras said. He raised a hand and a silvery light lifted from Celes's dead body, filtering into the small phial Baras held. "It was an easy battle for us, don't you think?"

Kinsami looked closely at the old man. He had thought about it before but now he knew without a doubt. Lord Baras did not just look like the young Baras he attended school with. They were the same person.

276

"How?" Kinsami stammered. "It shouldn't be possible."

"When I was trapped with Sarah we spent centuries in that grey, empty realm. If someone let us free early we would have technically travelled back in time. This is no different. I sent myself through a portal that would open into a time long before any of this happened. Don't worry for me, though. I had a family. Gregory and Allen are my grandchildren. I even got to run my own school at Castle Eckhart," Baras suddenly laughed.

"What's so funny?"

"That move I used on Celes earlier, the ball of water. I only used it because I saw Allen use it through the monitors at the time you went to kidnap him. He never would have inherited it if I didn't see him use it first."

"Please, don't confuse me with your time travel talk. I won't understand." Kinsami became sad for his friend. "I'm sorry, Baras."

"You've no need to be sorry."

"No, I'm sorry that you were never able to run a school that would truly benefit those with the power of Will. History dictated you to run a school that was exactly what you were fighting to put a stop to."

Baras had a distant sad look. "I never utilised the mind control like the other castles did. More than this, it led me to the Veritas Rerum."

"What is the Veritas Rerum?"

An alarm was sounding throughout Castle Kirkwall. The students had spotted a large, dark mass moving towards them and became frightened with what was to come. Stories of Castle Eckhart and the more recent Castle Bodhurst had been filtering in and everyone was on edge. One senior student ran up the tower in which Kinsami and Baras were currently positioned. When he reached the door he saw the horror that was held within. His face became white as he looked over the dead bodies of Lord Nodane and Lady Celes before spying Kinsami.

"What have you done?" he cried. "We're under attack and

you have killed...' It occurred to him that Kinsami wasn't from Kirkwall. "You're with them," he said preparing for a fight.

"What's your name, boy?" Lord Baras asked him. The student saw Baras for the first time and paused unsure how to proceed. Lord Baras could help them in this time of need but he was acting rather friendly with someone who had just killed the Lord and Lady of Kirkwall. "Your name?" Baras repeated.

"Just Phillip," he said. His voice was trembling.

"Well, Just Phillip. We're going to have some guests at the castle soon."

"They've come to kill us!" Phillip almost screamed.

"They haven't come to kill us, you fool," Kinsami said. "Just listen to Lord Baras."

"Thank you, Kinsami. I'll take care of this. Phillip, by now you've heard the stories from Castles Eckhart and Bodhurst about the murders and corruption. Correct?" Phillip nodded. "What you have heard are fabrications created by the very Lords and Ladies you are feeling sorry for."

"How can that be?" Phillip asked. Baras decided a few half-truths were in order to sway this young mind.

"It started in my very castle. One terrible night the students started to go insane. They started killing each other and doing horrible things to one another. Sarah was the first to wake and she managed to wake a number of other students. Unfortunately, the rest were either killed or locked up until a cure could be found.

We traced the destructive Will to the Lords and Ladies of Castles Bodhurst and Kirkwall. Through lack of experience with the situation, we moved on Castle Bodhurst in a group to get answers. Fearing an attack, Adaman and Sylvia took control of the minds of every student at Castle Bodhurst and sent them to either kill or be killed. It was Kinsami here who freed everyone by killing Adaman and Sylvia. We even found that those imprisoned at Eckhart were now free of the mind control.

As for Castle Kirkwall, we didn't want to make the same mistake. Kinsami and I came here alone to plead with Nodane and Celes. We made it to the tower with no incident but they

278

took no heed. Without warning, they tried to dispose of us leaving us no choice but to defend ourselves. The result is what you see before you. Furthermore, you have been freed of a mind control that could be utilised at any time they wanted."

"How can I believe what you're saying?"

"How can you not? A hostile force is approaching. Hostile only if they are met with an attack. Sarah means no harm but if there is an army before her she will believe we've failed and try to save you herself."

"By killing us?" Phillip asked

"By defending themselves until they can remove Nodane and Celes."

Phillip was unsure as his eyes darted from side to side. "What can I do?" he finally asked.

"Go. Spread the word that Sarah comes in peace. Have everyone meet in the courtyard and take a seat with the gates wide open. If you feel she is hostile then attack but you will see she'll be glad you are free," Phillip hesitated a moment longer. "Do as I say, Phillip. I am still a Lord." Phillip ran back out the door. Baras and Kinsami heard him calling for the alarm to be shut off.

"Nice story," Kinsami said. "Shall we head outside to meet Sarah?"

"I can't wait to see the look on her face when she sees me standing there," Baras said smiling widely.

"You've changed. Your emotions were monotone before. Now you have a spark behind your words."

"The joys of growing old and living a full life," Baras said with a wink.

"Makes sense."

The two walked out of the tower and into the courtyard. The whole school had followed instruction and were now either seated or standing between them and the gate. They arrived just in time to see Sarah enter with Ryan at her side. She saw Kinsami standing across the yard and made her way to him. The rest of the students from Castle Bodhurst remained outside the gates.

"Where's Baras," Sarah asked.

"I'm right here, Sarah," the older Baras said. Sarah looked across and her face suddenly went white.

"What's he doing here?" She asked between clenched teeth "And more importantly, why haven't you killed him?"

"The service that I provided for you taking the three castles, the time spent in the grey realm together and even the friendship we had before that. I can't believe you would want me dead," he feigned being hurt. Sarah took a closer look at him and saw something she didn't notice before.

"Baras? All this time, don't tell me that you were Lord Baras also. How could you keep this from me?"

"My younger self believed you didn't know. I am bound by history."

"Such an easy cop-out. Where is your younger self?"

"I already sent him back to my past. Let's talk about this later though. I can see that the students are getting restless and you also have Gregory to plan for. He couldn't be too far away."

"Are you going to be okay? With Gregory I mean," Sarah asked referring to the showdown that was yet to come.

"There is more happening behind the scenes than you know. That can wait until later, though. Go address the students of Castle Kirkwall."

Sarah pursed her lips for a moment before she turned to view the students. She saw that some staff members had also stayed to hear her out. She drew in some yellow and made use of her Will to raise both herself and Ryan two metres into the air on an earthen platform. All eyes were on her.

"People of Kirkwall, You've been lied to...' Sarah started to say.

"We know," someone yelled out from the crowd. Sarah glared across in the direction of the voice but couldn't pinpoint the speaker.

"I've come to free you from the hold the Lords and Ladies have held over you...' she tried again.

"Yeah, Yeah. Lord Baras has already spread the word," another voice spoke up. This time Sarah glared down at the old man standing behind her. Baras just shrugged.

"With me here is Ryan," Sarah tried for the third time. "He is of Castle Bodhurst and will tell you of his experience."

"Woman," came yet another voice. Sarah's eyes became wild at the address. "We don't care what you have to say. Go about your business and let us get back to ours."

"Look, fuck you all!" Sarah finally cracked. Her tone became direct and to the point. "I am taking up residence in the tower room. If a boy named Gregory or a girl named Michelle show up they will seek to kill anyone between them and the tower. Take them out and be rewarded. If you have a problem I'm sure there is a dungeon I can find for you. Other than that, go fuck yourselves." Sarah lowered the platform and stalked off into the castle still fuming. Kinsami, Baras and Ryan followed her in. When she calmed down she turned to Ryan.

"I'm sorry you had to witness that. I have a short fuse at times," she told him.

"It's okay," he replied. "If you didn't, I was about to." Sarah smiled at this.

"Thank you, Ryan. If you like, could you inform our friends outside the gates that they may come and go as they please?"

"Happy too," he said before heading out the door. Sarah turned to Baras and Kinsami.

"Now, we only have Gregory to concern ourselves with and this story of ours shall be through."

"Good," Kinsami said. "In the meantime, I'm going to find the boy, Taine, and sort out my bloody ankle."

Chapter 15

"Damn. They just left the castle," Michelle observed.

Gregory walked over and jumped onto the camp boundary next to Michelle. He shaded his eyes against the sun and watched the large, dark mass fly away. "We had far more time with Castle Eckhart," he said. He wasn't very happy about missing his chance at Castle Bodhurst. "We're going to have to move camp soon if we want to keep up."

"We can give chase anytime. We know where they're going," Michelle stated.

"True but is there something better we could be doing?" Gregory asked. Michelle gave him an odd look. He got the sense she was calling him insensitive.

"If everyone has left Bodhurst, who's around to stop us giving our friends a proper farewell?"

"You're right," Gregory said understanding now. "I'm sorry I didn't think of it myself. I've been focused on one thing for a long time."

"You can make it up to our friends right now by escorting me to see them."

"It'll be my pleasure," Gregory replied.

"In life, we get only a few short moments. Always take the time for those you love."

Gregory took her hand in his own. Drawing it to his lips he kissed it gently. "I love you, Michelle."

Michelle was stunned into silence. She felt her face getting hot all the way to the tips of her ears. Gregory watched her reaction and allowed the silence to linger. He saw the effect those words had on her and was happy. She loved him back even without the words.

"Let's get going," Gregory told her and she wrapped her arms around his neck. Gregory understood she wanted a lift. He crouched down and looking at her as if to say, are you ready, he took off into the air at extreme speeds. She squealed with pure joy as the wind whipped her hair. Gregory reached a point high above the Castle and made a long arcing path giving Michelle a great sense of weightlessness. She loved this feeling.

"I love you too, Gregory," she said kissing his cheek. Gregory smiled and flew straight down to Castle Bodhurst and their friends. He landed softly and let Michelle down. The stone bodies of Dirk and Lavi were before them forever holding each other. Gregory understood the moment that Dirk moved they were not dead. They were alive suspended in statue form. If they were to release this and shift to their own bodies, they would pass from this world due to previous injuries.

"I hope you're finally happy, Lavi," Michelle said with a tear in her eye. She hugged her and Dirk in turn. "Take good care of her, Dirk. If I find out you've mistreated her I'll be back." Michelle laughed at the comment but tears were now flowing freely. She turned and walked a few feet away giving Gregory space.

Crossing to stand before them, Gregory looked at each of his friends. "You were the first two friends I made at the castle," Gregory said. He was holding back tears. "I hold myself partly responsible for the situation you are in but I won't let it be for nothing. I'm going back in and I will end Sarah once and for all. I will draw courage from you both. I will not run away again. Thank you and farewell, my friends." Gregory moved to Michelle and pulled her into his arms as his tears fell freely.

"Farewell, friends," came a pair of stony voices. Michelle and Gregory looked at their friends and then back at each other. They smiled sadly before walking along the side of the fallen building coming out into the main courtyard.

A movement as they passed the corner got their attention. There was a girl about their age cowering near the outer wall. With nowhere to run without being spotted, she hoped they would walk on by but that wasn't to be. Gregory and Michelle stopped and looked straight at her.

"P p p please don't k k kill me," she was stammering heavily.

"We aren't going to harm you," Michelle told her.

"Liar," the girl shouted. "I kn n know wh who you are. Please, I c c can't def f fend myself like th th this."

"We know Sarah has moved on to Castle Kirkwall," Gregory told her. "We came to say goodbye to our friends and nothing more. We aren't going to harm you. We'll leave you now." Gregory turned and started walking away but stopped after a few metres. The girl had started to get her hopes up but a feeling of dread returned to her gut as Gregory turned.

"What're you doing?" Michelle asked. "You're going to scare the poor girl."

Gregory waved her away. "Why can't you defend yourself?" Gregory asked the girl.

She looked confused. "What?"

"Why can't you defend yourself? You said you can't defend yourself like this. I just wanted to know what was holding you back."

"Like m my stammer... I have t t trouble drawing c c c colour. I can't f fight," the girl told him.

Gregory stood rubbing his chin while he thought. "Colour... Yes, colour!" He exclaimed. "What is your name?"

"P P Podi," she said confused.

"Thank you, Podi," Gregory said. "You've really helped me. Now, I would like to help you." He walked over to her and started to reach up. She flinched and closed her eyes tightly.

"Gregory, stop this!" Michelle told him. She could see that he was making Podi incredibly uncomfortable. Gregory didn't stop though. He placed a hand on each side of her head near her jaws. Gregory could feel that she was trembling. He focused on what he wanted and brought it into life with his Will. Podi glowed in a yellow light for a moment and then returned to normal. She was quiet for a few seconds more before she noticed nothing else was happening. Slowly, she opened her eyes and saw Gregory standing before her.

"What did you do to me?" she asked.

"I did nothing to harm you, Podi."

"You did something horrible to me. I just know it. Tell me what...' Podi looked like she was replaying something in her head. "Big yacht. Little yacht. Big yacht. Little yacht. Big yacht. Little yacht," she said her favourite tongue twister without stuttering. Tears started to flow from her eyes and she hung her head. "Thank you."

"No. Thank you, Podi. I also opened your Will power to its

full potential. Try when you have some time." Gregory walked past Michelle who didn't quite catch what had happened.

She ran up to him taking his arm. "I know something significant happened but I'm a bit embarrassed to say I missed it."

"She had trouble speaking. Now she doesn't."

"Not that. That was a beautiful thing you did and no one would miss that. You had a eureka moment back there."

"The colour thing," Gregory said smiling. "Sarah draws in colour."

"Yeah, so? We all do."

"I don't. While she's busy refilling her reserves I can push out unlimited amounts of Will."

Michelle's eyes grew wide. "You have an advantage."

"Not only that. The mixing of colour is the most complicated use of Will there is. You need to get the colours perfect. She may have centuries of practice behind her but if she makes a minor mistake she may heal me rather than kill me."

"Couldn't you do the same?"

"No. Remember I don't draw colour. I just do. I never need to mix."

An ecstatic shout echoed behind them. Turning they saw Podi soaring through the sky back and forwards. She was putting her colour control to good use.

"I think you cheat when using Will," Michelle said tapping Gregory on the nose. "You get it way too easy."

"Just born this way," he replied tapping her on the butt before flying off towards Castle Kirkwall.

"Hey!" she called. "Don't think that won't go unpunished." She took off into the air forgetting her fears as she chased him.

The sun set the sky on fire as it sunk below the horizon. Pinks and oranges created a dazzling display across the puffy clouds. No direct sunlight was getting into the courtyard of Kirkwall as it was blocked by the high walls. Kinsami gritted his teeth against the pain. Taine had applied a balm to the burnt heel and was now bandaging it. As he tied it off Kinsami swore.

"Do you have to make it so tight?" he asked.

Taine was surprised Kinsami had visited his room believing he would have his own healers. "This burn heal works best under pressure," Taine told him. "I concocted it myself and have had much praise."

"Do you use it often?"

"The castle is ringed by a natural thermal spring. The temperatures can get into the extremes as you found out. Each year there are countless students who act recklessly around it. They continually try to impress each other by doing almost impossible feats. This continues until someone burns themselves. That is where I come in. The behaviour dies down for a week or so before the next show off rises."

"I haven't seen anyone with burn scars," Kinsami noted.

"Thank you," Taine replied. "That's a big part of why I get so much praise."

A commotion started outside the walls. Kinsami and Taine walked out of the dorm room. The sun was now set and stars were starting to show in the twilight sky. Above the castle walls near the closed gate could be seen flashes. These came in reds and whites and were always followed by an explosion. A black figure flew over the wall to crash into the building a few feet from Kinsami. The cold, dead eyes of the student staring vacantly.

"I may not get to see the true strength of your burn heal," Kinsami told Taine. He knew what was coming and the risks involved.

"What's happening?" Taine asked mystified by the light and sounds coming from beyond the wall.

"It's Gregory. He's come to put an end to Sarah thinking her some sort of evil doer. It doesn't help that she wants him dead either. I'll meet him here in the courtyard and try to talk him down or put my skills against his own."

"He's that Empty everyone's speaking of," Taine remarked. "Will you be able to beat him?"

"I don't think so," Kinsami admitted. The feeling had been bubbling below the surface for some time. Now the fight was

286

here it had boiled over. A fear within, threatening to take him over. He didn't fight it, however. He allowed the fear to run its course passing through him and not holding him back. "Gregory has great skill and potential. It'll all depend on how much of that potential he has unlocked."

"I'll help you," Taine said

"No, Taine. He isn't going to harm anyone that stays out of the fight. I take him on more for my own pride and self-worth than any silly notion of protecting Sarah. When Gregory comes through, stay inside or at least out of his way. Look after those who're hurt for there'll be many. They'll need you before the end."

A horrific grinding noise came from the closed gates. Kinsami saw the stones around the entrance shudder and the gate contort in on itself. While this was happening, a tornado was growing beyond the wall. This tornado was made of flames and gave the area light to see by. The gate exploded into the courtyard. It came to a sudden halt as an edge dug into the ground. Walking into the castle grounds, Gregory moved cautiously. He didn't know where enemies could be hiding. Michelle ran in after him.

They reached the centre point of the yard and Kinsami willed flames to spring to life around them locking them into a ring. They didn't try to escape but stood back to back looking for the source of the new threat. Kinsami walked over to them, cloaking himself in his flame armour and walking through his wall of fire with no ill effect.

"It's been too long, Gregory," Kinsami said to his rival.

Gregory was stunned by this new development. He hadn't planned to be fighting Kinsami so early but was grateful it would be one on one. Michelle recognised Kinsami as part of the Otoma Clan. He was going to be a strong enemy.

"You've been busy, I hear," Gregory replied "Serving Sarah, killing Lords and Ladies, taking castles, kidnapping young kids."

"I looked after Allen," Kinsami said. "Sarah wanted him to be here for the final battle. I kept him far from the fighting."

"Because you couldn't fly him all the way to Bodhurst."

Kinsami's brow furrowed. "Who've you been talking too?"

"Stuart and I had a talk in the dungeons of Bodhurst."

"Sounds cosy. I won't pretend with niceties then. Sarah wants you dead for your actions at Eckhart. I can't change this. I want the chance to fight you before she has the pleasure."

"For what you did to my brother I have wanted the same."

"Tell your girlfriend not to interfere," Kinsami said pointing at Michelle.

"I'll back Gregory all the way," she said, getting defensive.

Gregory put a hand out in front of her. "Just this once, it's important we fight alone. It's the way this battle was destined to be."

Michelle pouted but accepted Gregory's words. She stepped back as close to the flames as the heat would allow. Kinsami produced his flaming katana drawing it from the air. Gregory produced a sword also. This one was short and easy to handle. The blade was wide and symmetrical coming to a point like a triangle at the top. A thrusting, short sword.

Kinsami laughed. "Your sword, if sword it is, won't help you against my katana," Kinsami said. Gregory didn't reply but gave his best sword fighters stance. Seeing this Kinsami shook his head. "Are you sure this is how you would like to proceed? Okay then."

Kinsami ran in holding the katana low and attacked with a sweeping strike, moving from lower right to upper left. Gregory blocked clumsily almost dropping his conjured sword. Kinsami followed with a cross slash and this time Gregory did lose his grip. The sword spun across the arena to land point first in the dirt.

"I concede. You are the better swordsman. I'm surprised I actually blocked those two swings."

Kinsami nodded and threw his katana high, letting it spin as it travelled upwards. On the way down it disappeared into the air. Drawing in ample amounts of the red to finish this fight, Kinsami started small. He produced fireballs that he threw like baseballs at Gregory. Gregory batted them away with his arm like they were nothing. What Kinsami couldn't see was that Gregory had reinforced his arm with his Will. An almost invisible wall of hyper condensed air.

Kinsami could see that Gregory wasn't going down as easy in the use of Will. No more simple attacks then. Kinsami decided that now was the time to use it. He may never get another chance again and would not die knowing he didn't risk everything. He had been working on this form of Will in the sanctity of his room. It was powerful and he had never completed the release of his Will for this move. Three times he had almost burnt down the castles made of stone.

Gregory felt the extreme collection of colour; Red was flowing into Kinsami at a huge rate. More than this, Gregory sensed large amounts of green also. Kinsami had unlocked his second colour. He knew that whatever was coming was going to be big. If he could overcome it, Kinsami would fall.

A glow started in Kinsami's armour as he became a transparent red. His body shifting like flame itself. The flames changed into a raging inferno held in shape by the armour he was cloaked in. He started to grow taller and more menacing. His fingers became long, sharp talons. His head blew out to be triangular in shape with rippling horns. The eyes were yellow and as he swayed his head from side to side an after image followed creating little trails of yellow light. Gregory was horrified by the sight. He took two steps backwards before he bumped into Michelle.

"Believe in yourself," she said kissing him on the cheek. Regaining his composure, Gregory readied himself. Michelle flew over the wall of flames to land on a nearby roof where she could see everything.

With a blood-curdling roar Kinsami sprang into action. He raced at Gregory and actually tried to bite him with flaming teeth. Gregory jumped away and sent two ice shards to stick into the beast Kinsami had become. They hissed and melted down to steam. This seemed to anger Kinsami who slashed left and right at Gregory. Somehow Gregory slipped by the attack and got behind him. He felt part of his hair was singed.

Gregory knew he couldn't compete with Kinsami as he was. He looked back at Michelle then focused. Best to join him then. Gregory willed water like a waterfall to fall from the sky completely engulfing him. It spread along the ground and sizzled as it hit the outer boundaries of the fighting ring. As the water slowed a great water beast stood where Gregory had been moments before. It was the height of Kinsami's fire form with a smoother, more fluid surface of deep blue. The beast Gregory created had long flexible arms and legs that bent backwards at the knees. This gave it great manoeuvrability and agility.

Kinsami let out a bone chilling roar before charging in. He swung a massive arm at Gregory. Small twists and twirls of flame curling off his body with every movement. Gregory caught the attack in a hand that encompassed the fist of fire. Steam instantly started to rise where they connected and the two forms both let out cries of anguish and pain. Jumping back, they circled and charged. Kinsami dropped to the ground and spun with a sweeping kick. Gregory jumped the attack and as he came down used the momentum to punch Kinsami in the face.

Seemingly unfazed Kinsami followed the assault with an uppercut knocking Gregory from his feet. He landed on the ground losing form with water spreading in every direction before coming back together. As he tried to get up, the flaming menace before him opened his gaping maw wide. A blue light showed deep in its throat growing brighter. Like a flamethrower, a great burst of blue fire poured from his mouth. These flames were hotter than anything Gregory had experienced and he twisted in agony as he was engulfed. His body started to shrink as steam was lost to the air.

When Kinsami stopped the baptism of fire only a small puddle was left upon the earth. This too was slowly shrinking as the residual heat left by the flames was still too much for it. Michelle screamed holding her hands to her mouth. The beast form of Kinsami laughed long and loud into the air. A frightening, guttural laugh that ate at the depths of a person's soul.

He didn't notice the mist that was forming behind him as the steam in the air was coming back together. Too late, he felt more than saw the presence of Gregory. Trying to turn,

Gregory caught him in a choke hold. Kinsami thrashed against Gregory as clouds of steam rose into the air. He clawed at Gregory's arm but the fluidity of the water allowed the claws to easily pass through. As Gregory lost his body to the steam he drew it all back around to re-enter him. Gregory's water form was continually reforming with the use of Gregory's Will. Kinsami, on the other hand, was running out of red faster than he could absorb it.

Kinsami's form started to shudder and shrink as the proximity to the water ate at his figure. Finally, he fell to the ground without armour in his true form. He was weak and couldn't rise. Gregory shimmered back to his own form and fell upon Kinsami. In his hand was the short sword sharpened to a wicked edge. Gregory pressed this up against Kinsami's throat.

"The greater fighter won," Kinsami said, accepting his fate. "Finish me like a true warrior."

Gregory's hand was going white at the knuckles as he gripped the hilt. He was shaking and gritting his teeth. Finally, he drew back the sword. "I won't take your life, Kinsami," Gregory told him. "Without a rival how will I ever get stronger? You have amazing potential. If a life is owed then give me yours. Leave this battle behind you and find your purpose in life. That's all I ask of you." Gregory got up and walked to the edge of the flames. Michelle flew down and straight into Gregory's embrace. She held him tightly fearing he may disappear again. For a moment, her world had fallen apart. The ring of flames died away. Outside students from Bodhurst were waiting.

"You have my word, Gregory," Kinsami said lowering the flames. "I'll give meaning to my life." Gregory nodded and then made a run with Michelle towards the castle tower. They blocked a number of attacks directed at them and cleared their path where needed.

As they made the tower door, Gregory focused on his body becoming hard like rock with high-impact speed. He willed himself into this form and smashed through the door, crashing against an inner wall. He looked up at Michelle and smiled a goofy looking smile. Michelle smiled back at him just as a gaping hole appeared in her chest, a large ice spear filling the hole. Michelle's face contorted into a silent scream. She fell to her knees, eyes wide in fear and anguish.

"Nooo!" Gregory yelled. Michelle couldn't feel half her body but she heard the enemy ranks closing in behind. Looking one last time at Gregory she forced her lips into a smile. Using the last of the red she had stored, she willed her body to explode in every direction but forward. The intensity of the explosion was such that it melted the rock around the entrance into the tower. The molten rocks dripped and shifted before cooling into a solid wall protecting Gregory from those outside.

"Michelle, No!" he yelled again bursting into tears. "I need you now more than ever. I love you. Please come back to me." He cried uncontrollably banging a fist against the stone wall blocking the entrance. He cried as he listened to the enemy trying to break through the wall. They hadn't succeeded after twenty minutes when he started to gain control of himself. Looking up the twisting stairs, a change occurred within Gregory. Anger burned stronger than he had ever felt and he used it to fuel himself. Storming up the stairs, Gregory burst into the room at the top.

"You took your time, Gregory," Sarah said standing in the middle of the room. She was about to say more but Gregory made that impossible. As if he were shadow boxing, Gregory started beating Sarah from across the room, his punches connecting through use of Will. The first blow was to her stomach knocking the wind out of her. With eyes wide, she threw up over the ground. The second blow connected on her chin sending her stumbling backwards. Blow after blow continued to connect across the room until she was being beaten against the far wall.

"Gregory!" Baras said. Gregory didn't hear or see him. Baras walked over and back handed him. Surprised, Gregory took a step back holding his chin. He noticed his Grandpa for the first time.

"Grandpa?" Gregory said stopping the assault. Sarah slide to the floor, blood dribbling from her mouth. "I don't understand. Why're you here?"

"I'm here to see you through your last hurdle," Baras replied. "You've come a long way and now is the time to end it."

"I was doing just that until you interrupted," Gregory stated. A wave of energy was felt from Sarah and Gregory saw that she had recovered and rose to her feet. A purple aura of energy was twisting around her, physically viewable to the naked eye. Gregory looked back at his Grandpa. "You're helping her," he stated. He couldn't believe where his Grandpa's allegiance lied. "You were buying her time to recover."

"You have no knowledge of what I hope to achieve, Gregory," Baras told him. "It lies far outside the petty fight between you and Sarah."

"Just leave me alone. I don't want to talk to you right now," Gregory told his Grandpa. He focused his attention back on Sarah who looked ready to attack. She sped at him with lightning speed and great fury. Gregory brought up his guard as she punched him with a purple infused fist. He underestimated the strength behind the punch as it broke through his barriers and connected with his face. His nose felt like it broke sideways and his eyes started to water. He ignored the pain as Sarah continued the assault. Taking two more hits, one in the stomach and the other on the side of his neck, Gregory finally managed to dodge a blow. He started to grow accustomed to Sarah's attack patterns and could predict her more easily. As Gregory moved to dodge an uppercut, Sarah changed her punches and punched Gregory in the nose again, causing him to stumble backwards.

"You aren't a fighter at all, Gregory," Sarah said. "I'm using simple tactics and you fall for them too easy." Gregory held his nose and willed it to reseat itself correctly on his face. A sickening crack and a burst of pain signalled the repair. He blinked away the tears and stared her down. "So scary, little boy."

"I'm not giving up, Sarah. Not this time," he told her.

"That reminds me," Sarah said. She utilised the last of the swirling purple to craft a barrier around the walls of the room.

"Now you can't run away when you get scared. I want to finish this today."

"It wasn't necessary. I want to finish you also."

Sarah just grunted at him with a smile showing she was not impressed. Gregory saw her pause just for a moment as she drew in more colour. This time a green swirl circled Sarah. Now that Gregory had witnessed Sarah's pause to collect colour, he could recognise and use the next one to take her down.

Gregory started his shadow boxing and king hit Sarah in the face. She took the impact of the blow and from part way across the room jabbed twice with her left hand and sent an uppercut with her right. Nothing happened and Gregory laughed. Moments later he felt the impact of her hits as the wind punches exploded into his face. After this came a boxing match from a five metre distance. Gregory was throwing punches trying to hit Sarah. Some connected and some didn't but the pain was always evident when he got it right. Sarah was throwing punches long in advance. Gregory had trouble remembering any of the punches Sarah threw or where she aimed them. She was hitting with far greater accuracy as Gregory seemed to step into every blow. Sarah felt she was getting low in colour again and crafted her short sword.

"You're going to die today, Gregory. Nothing is going to stop that outcome," she said pointing the sword at him. Gregory was having trouble disbelieving her and it was making him clumsy. "You have been nothing but a burden to everyone. You are the reason your friends are dead. You are the reason people have been miserable. This world would be a far better place without you in it. You should give up and die!" Sarah's tone was harsh but Gregory heard himself in those words. He was back in Castle Eckhart with Mr Sir saving his life. This echoed deep into his soul and something started to wake. Something that had always been there on the edge of his conscious thought. When he said those harsh words to Mr Sir he had been scared. He spoke more out of anger at himself and fear for what he had done than any real feelings of hate. Was this true also for Sarah? Did she also have some deeper feeling that made her lash out at Gregory?

"I won't die today, Sarah," Gregory told her. "Not by your hand or my own. I choose life. Yes, I have caused trouble for others. I have gone out of my way to hurt people. My friends have died following me on this road I have walked. But that is a part of the life we lead. We have equal ability to bring pain or happiness. Even when we try to do good we can cause harm to those we love. We need to journey forward always looking for the light. I won't die today. You hear me? Walk away now and you can live also. I choose life!" The light deep within was growing brighter and stronger. He was changing. He understood the world around him more with each moment. He felt he was becoming whole.

"You're a joke, Gregory, and I'll never forgive you for what you did to me," Sarah told him.

She started drawing more colour to restock her supplies but Gregory wasn't going to fight anymore. He crafted a barrier with his Will and placed it around Sarah. It was a single millimetre off her skin and moved as she did. Immediately, Sarah lost the ability to draw in colour. It was only moments before she realised and her face became deathly pale.

"What'd you do?" Sarah screamed at him. "What'd you do to my Will?"

"Sarah, you're never going to be able to utilise Will again. I've blocked you from all colours."

"No! You can't do that. You trapped me in a world with no feelings, tastes or sensations of any type. I was there for hundreds of years. Now that I finally got out you give me a fate far worse. Why do you hate me so much? Give me my colour back." Sarah was almost in tears.

"No. Through your own actions, I have stripped you of your colour. I won't fight you anymore. Go find your own happiness. I'm going to find mine." Gregory turned and walked to the doorway of the room. He willed the barrier to open where the door was located and it parted.

"You won't get away!" Sarah said. She raised her short sword and charged at Gregory. As Gregory turned there was little time to react. He swung his arm, arcing upwards and a burst of sharpened air cut Sarah cleanly in two. The top half, from right hip to just under her left shoulder, slid from the bottom. Her face had a look of anger, eyes staring at him as they fell to the floor. Her legs stumbled and gave out below her moments later. Gregory had a sad look on his face.

"Why, Sarah?" he asked the girl on the floor. "You had a chance at life but threw it away."

A slow clap started behind him. Baras was standing there applauding.

"Why would you applaud this outcome? No one should have died at all."

"You are free, Gregory," he said.

"But at what cost?" Gregory asked. "Sarah is dead. Lavi and Dirk are dead. Michelle...' He had trouble saying it. "Michelle is dead." Gregory's voice was trembling as he said the last.

"I'm not dead, Gregory," came a familiar voice. A figure stepped through the barrier where only a rock wall lay behind. Gregory was shocked to see Sarah standing before him when her body was still at his feet.

"What is this?" Gregory asked. More figures started to step through the barrier in different places around the wall. Some were clapping, others congratulated him. He knew each and every one of them. In the slowly building crowd, he could see the four Lords and ladies, Kinsami and Stuart. Even Allen, Dirk, and Lavi were there. Gregory couldn't understand what was happening but he looked for one face in particular.

"Why do you still linger?"

Gregory's breath caught in his mouth as he heard the voice he longed for. Turning, he found Michelle standing in the doorway. "Michelle..." Tears were flowing freely as Gregory ran over and embraced the girl he loved. Michelle felt so warm in his arms.

"We have but a moment, Gregory," she told him. "Now is the time to say our goodbyes."

"Goodbye?" Gregory asked confused. "I don't ever wish to leave you."

"Your time in this world has now ended. You can't stay. I am happy you found your will to live. I love you, Gregory."

"I love you, Michelle," he said with force. "I love you, I love you."

Michelle drew him into a kiss. The kiss was soft and passionate and Gregory would never forget how it felt. As he drew away, his eyes started to go blurry. He was having trouble seeing and became dizzy. The floor rushed up to meet him as darkness descended.

Epilogue

'Lol :p,' and send. The girl put her phone away for the umpteenth time this morning. Her boyfriend was sending her cute message after cute message and she was getting annoyed. She wasn't about to show him that though. With a yawn she leaned back in her uncomfortable chair. Hospitals never had great chairs to begin with but she'd gotten used to it in the months prior.

The room was a pale lime colour brought to life by the rays of sunlight through the open window. It was a private room with a single bed for patients. A small guest bed was available in the corner for when family members wanted to stay with loved ones. The TV high on the wall had some sport playing. She wasn't really interested but liked the noise in the background. Maybe her brother could hear it too.

She looked at her younger brother. The constant pips of the heart rate monitor hadn't changed in eight months. He was being fed intravenously through tubes but over time had lost a lot of weight. Still a large boy, he was only just above the average weight now. She felt responsible for him. Of course she knew he was being bullied at school for his weight. She saw how the other kids treated him and she'd done nothing. She even laughed along once or twice. That was the hierarchy of the school yard, she told herself. How was she supposed to know he would try to kill himself because of it?

"Why, Gregory?" She asked her lifeless brother, like she did every visit. She remembered vividly the day she found him, a metre above the floor. His face was going black as his weight dragged down on the rope. His eyes had just rolled into the back of his head. She'd gone in to yell at him for the ruckus he was making. The sound coming from his struggles and the chair being kicked away. As she threw his door open she stood in shock, unable to move or even breathe. If not for their mother walking by with the laundry he would have remained swinging from the ceiling.

Now he was hooked up to an experimental, medical, virtual reality unit. Veritas Rerum the doctor had called it. He tried to

298

explain it to her but most of it went over her head. The VR system would interact with the patient on a subconscious level. It would build worlds for the patient using sub conscious thought and lead the patient on a journey to sort through their issues from the real world. They would remain in a coma until the machine determined the patient was ready to move back to the real world.

Gregory was a special case. He was the first patient who had a brain starved of oxygen for an extended period of time. They couldn't be sure of the type of damage he may have succumbed to and how well this form of treatment would work.

A change in the room started to niggle at her mind. Something was different. She looked at the heart rate monitor noting his heart was beating faster. She ran to the door.

"MUM, DAD!" She yelled down the hallway. "GREGORY IS WAKING UP!" Moving back to his bedside, she was joined by her parents.

"What's happening, Alana?" her dad asked. Her mum was holding to her dad's side.

"The heart rate monitor. It's getting faster."

The doctor came in and asked for room. He assessed the situation and when he saw small movements from Gregory the doctor started removing the VR unit. He lifted his eyelids to look into his eyes and saw action.

Gregory's eyes fluttered open on their own. He felt groggy as he looked around the room. Memories of being at high school came flooding in. He remembered being bullied and punished just for his appearance. He remembered how he felt depressed and what he'd tried to do. The next memories that came to mind were those of his life at his Grandpa's farm and then the castles. He remembered that he played the role of the bully, doing and saying things that had been said to Gregory in the real world. Gregory had dealt with his issues by learning about them from the opposing perspective. He understood now that bullying was more about the insecurities and darkness found in the bully. It was not his fault as the one being picked on. He could live knowing that. He could act with that in mind. He would not be weak anymore. Sarah, he understood now, was his final test. She was the bully and Gregory needed to stand up to her. He needed to accept her feelings, her words, her abuse and choose to live regardless.

Alana pushed the doctor aside and put her face in front of Gregory's. Her mum apologised to the doctor as he waved at her saying he understood. He allowed Alana to get close as he continued to assess Gregory. Gregory saw the tears in his sister's eyes.

"Hey, Allen," he said. She gave him an odd look before he realised his mistake. He smiled. "Alana."

"Please, don't do that again," she said hugging him tightly. Gregory coughed and Alana loosened her hold.

"Don't worry. I'm not going anywhere, sis. I'm going to live."

The Beginning

Thank you and I hope to see you again soon.

Books currently in the Aether

Veritas Rerum novels
Pyre of Souls
Veritas Rerum

Hail Atlantis

The Birth of Magic

The Elven King Trilogy

Mage Killer Trilogy

Sword of the Immortal Trilogy
Summoner Mage
Child of Darkness
The Immortal Knight

Novels of the Wandering Swordsman Kiyoshi
A Stolen Sword
Split Personality Swordsman

The Future Past

The Earth Beneath Us

The Boatman – A book of short stories